WARM • AMBER • RESONANCE SEARCHED FROM ONE ISLAND TO ANOTHER

A sour scent led it to the elder, a large blue rock lying just under the surface of the ocean. The amber cloud surrounded the blue rock and shouted: •Open up! There's a hard screaming monster in the ocean!•

Warm • Amber • Resonance had been hesitant to distract the elder, but with an age exceeding a thousand seasons, surely the old one would know if such a strange monster had been seen before. Finally a soft voice murmured from behind the protective shell: ★A hard screaming monster? Let me taste.★

Warm • Amber • Resonance formed a tiny tendril of an appendage and extended it to the elder. Memory juices were exchanged. #I never saw or learned of any such monster. It is your problem. I return to mine.# The blue elder returned to the matter of the fifth cardinal infinity.

George held the *Magic Dragonfly* over the spot where the scanner had seen the colored blobs. "I see the blue thing. It's a big, deep-blue colored boulder, but the amber blob is gone," said Richard.

ROBERT L. FORWARD

THE FLIGHT OF THE DRAGONFLY

A BAEN BOOK

THE FLIGHT OF THE DRAGONFLY

Copyright © 1984 by Robert L. Forward

A Baen Book

Baen Enterprises
8-10 W. 36th Street
New York, N.Y. 10018

First Baen printing, February 1985

ISBN: 0-671-55937-0

Cover art by Bob Eggleton

Printed in the United States of America

Distributed by
SIMON & SCHUSTER
MASS MERCHANDISE SALES COMPANY
1230 Avenue of the Americas
New York, N.Y. 10020

FOR EVE
*Who thought it would be fun
to ride on a flouwen*

Beginning

The torn shred of aluminum lightsail rippled lightly down through the thin atmosphere and settled onto the calm ocean. The robot probe the sail had once carried was now on its way back into the interstellar blackness, its flyby study of the Barnard's Star planetary system completed. The messages of its discoveries would reach earth six years later. The microthin film of aluminum was no match for the ammonia-water ocean covering this egg of a planet. The sail dissolved into a bitter taste of aluminum hydroxide.

Clear ◊ White ◊ Whistle was warming on the ocean surface in the red glare from Hot. Hot became less. The lessness was not like the darkness that comes from a storm shadow, but much sharper. It was almost as if Sky⊗Rock had suddenly moved in front of Hot. Then there was a thin sharp taste of bitterness in the ocean.

Clear ◊ White ◊ Whistle dove under the ocean to escape the bitterness, then came to the surface. The taste was still there. A sounding dive a long distance away, the taste was weaker and the sheet of darkness was being eaten by the ocean. Hot peered through the holes.

For a long time Clear ◊ White ◊ Whistle tasted the bitterness and thought about the strange thing that had come from nothing but was something. Thoughts came to it about exploring the nothing above, but that was impossible. . . .

But only carefully contrived mathematical propositions are truly impossible, mused Clear◊White◊Whistle. I can look into nothing, although poorly. I know Hot and Warm are sources of heat and light, but though I have tried hard, I cannot see them. If only my looking portions could be focused like my seeing portions. . . .

A thought came to the alien, and the large amorphous body of white jelly started to condense. Clear◊White◊Whistle turned into a dense white rock and sank to the bottom of the ocean. The concentrated whiteness of the tissues that constituted its "brain" now thought at a higher rate. Equations for a focusing detector based on time differences went through a sophisticated mathematical transformation to become the equations for a focusing detector using distance differences. This detector would "look" using light instead of "seeing" using sound. The mathematical solution suddenly obvious, Clear◊White◊Whistle, the toolless engineer, dissolved and swam up to the surface as an undulating white cloud. Hot was gone. It had moved behind Sky⊗ Rock, a large object that hovered motionless in the sky above this region of the ocean. The shadow line on Sky⊗ Rock no longer gave off its rocklike, reddish-gray light. The sky was not completely dark, however, for Warm had risen and was now a weak flare overhead.

Using the mathematical equations as a guide, Clear◊White◊Whistle formed a small portion of its body into a sphere and removed the white thought substance to leave a clear gel. Water poured from the gel to produce a dense clear ball. Through the sphere streamed the rays of light from the heavens. They came to a crude focus in the opposite side of the sphere. The white flesh next to the clear sphere looked at the tiny spots of light impinging on its surface. The light patterns showed Warm as a tiny disk of mottled red. Around Warm were smaller bright lights with sharp cusps and fuzzy edges.

A slight adjustment of the sphere into a crude lens and the distorted spots turned into smaller disks. As the lens focused on the moons of the giant red planet, Gargantua, the blackness of the night sky blossomed with thousands of tiny pinpoints of light. Clear◇ White◇Whistle stared with its newly invented "eye" at the myriad multicolored stars in the sky and wondered.

Gathering

Boredom is a Space Marine's worst enemy, but *these* Marines were not bored.

"Close in! You squinty-eyed offspring of a BASIC program. So what if you've lost your outside video! You've still got radar and groundplots! Close in!"

The words came from deep inside a short, chunky, round-faced woman with dark-black skin, a close-cropped head of curly black hair, and a crisp Marine officer's uniform seemingly tattooed on her muscular body.

Major General Virginia Jones punched her supervisory keyboard as her parade-ground voice echoed off the naked beams and taut pressurized walls of the crowded cubicle. Crammed into the compact control room of a Space Marine Lightsail Interceptor, the programmers were short-circuiting the software in the ship's computer to optimize an "unwilling capture" trajectory between their twenty-five-kilometer-diameter sailcraft and the radar image of a lumbering cargo hauler. The huge heavy-lift vehicle was rising slowly from its launch pad deep in Soviet Russia on its way to resupply one of the Russian bases in geosynchronous orbit. Under the rules of the UN Space Treaty, if they could intercept it, they could board and search for illegal weapons.

"Boarding party!" General Jones roared to the deck below. "You've got ten minutes to do the fifteen-minute suiting drill! Move it!"

There was a bustle as hammocks were stowed to give a little more room in the tiny communal barracks. Suits were lifted from lockers and donned—rapidly, but carefully. General Jones looked sternly around at the organized pandemonium and took a bite of her energy stick. She looked at it in distaste, thought blissfully of the excellent mess back at the Space Marine Orbital Base, then stoically took another bite of the energy bar. If it was good enough for her Marines, it was good enough for her.

Like the PT boats in World War II almost a century ago, the interceptors had to be fast. With only light pressure to push them, that meant keeping weight down. It was battle rations every meal when the Space Marines were on interceptor duty.

General Jones carefully watched the captain of the interceptor as he swung his ungainly craft smoothly around. Captain Jesús Méndez was short and handsome, with dark flashing eyes and a youthful wave of hair over his forehead that had Jinjur's mind wandering slightly. Captain Méndez was the best lightsail pilot in space (with the possible exception of Jinjur herself).

The lightsail scooped, dumping its cross-orbit excess speed in the upper atmosphere by using its huge expanse of sail like a sea anchor. It then tilted to maximize the solar photon pressure and rose again in a pursuit trajectory of the bogie. Captain Méndez called on one of the orbiting space forts above him for more power. A powerful laser beam struck the sail with a flood of light five times brighter than the sun. The acceleration rose to one-tenth gee, and they skimmed rapidly above the earth's atmosphere, gaining speed by the minute. Ten minutes later General Jones called a halt to the hunt of the phantom fox.

"Freeze program," she said, then turned and tapped a code word into her command console. The computer memory of the practice pursuit was locked until she released it. The primary purpose of this exercise had been to test the reconfiguration skills of the human element of her computer-assisted spaceship—the programmers. By reconfiguring the software in the computer to take into account its loss of components and capabilities, the programmers could hopefully tune the program to obtain its optimum response time. She wished the interceptors could have the latest in self-reprogramming computers, or at least the touch-screen input terminals, but that was many fiscal-budget cycles away.

General Jones started her critique. The crew wasn't looking forward to it, for General "Jinjur" had not gotten her nickname by being soft on her troops. Fortunately there was an interruption.

"Excuse me, General Jones," said Captain Méndez. "You have a message from the Marine commandant. It is encrypted and marked PERSONAL."

"I'll take it at my console," said Jinjur. She floated over to her console, punched in her password, and read the message.

"I'm commander of *Prometheus*, the interstellar sailcraft going to Barnard!!" she cried.

"Congratulations!" said Méndez. "Could you use a good pilot?"

"I'm already stuck with some Air Force flyboy for my second-in-command, a Lieutenant Colonel George G. Gudunov. Do you know him?"

"George Gudunov? Is not he the one who first came up with the idea of laser sailcraft to go to the stars?" said Captain Méndez.

"Right. It's been so long ago, I'd forgotten," said Jinjur. "I was in high school when the first interstellar robots were sent out. I remember wishing that I were sailing out on them. Now, I'm going to get my wish."

A large, slightly overweight, middle-aged man in a well-worn Air Force officer's uniform walked slowly into the cavernous Pentagon office of the Air Force chief of staff. His round, smiling, ruddy-complexioned face was topped by a thick mane of white hair. George wasn't surprised that he'd been summoned, for the pressure had been building up ever since the robot probe data had started coming in from the Barnard system. His only concern now was his age. At forty-nine he was getting awfully old. It had been decades since he had been in the Pentagon. Being stuck as a flight instructor in the hottest corner of Texas for the past twenty-five years sort of kept you out of things.

George skirted the huge oak conference table, and headed for the large desk flanked by two flags. One flag had a field of blue carrying the Air Force emblem. The other flag was the Stars and Stripes of the Greater United States of America with its fifty-nine stars in four rows of eight alternating with three rows of nine. Next year there would be sixty stars as the Northwest Territories finally became populous enough to become a state of the GUSA. That only left the Yukon to go (and of course, Quebec, if it ever came to its senses). He came to attention in front of General Beauregard Darlington Winthrop III, and saluted, his eyes straight ahead.

General Winthrop glanced up from the papers in front of him, the glitter of four silver stars broadening his shoulders.

"Good afternoon, George," he said. "Sit down."

Colonel Gudunov perched on a nearby straight chair and listened.

"Saw you and Senator Maxwell on the Jimmy Collins show last night," Winthrop started. "Quite some company you keep there."

"They wanted someone that could explain what there

was in the Barnard system that justified the interstellar expedition, and Senator Maxwell suggested me."

"I've got to admit you did an excellent job of explaining the laser drive in terms even my secretary could understand. She talked about nothing else for the entire coffee break this morning." He shuffled some papers, and then drew one out.

"Your friends in Congress have been good to you again, Gudunov." His tone chilled a little. "By all rights, no forty-nine-year-old should be allowed on the Barnard expedition, especially since you're not a Regular, but ROT-C." Winthrop didn't even have the courtesy to spell out the initials of the Reserve Officer Training Corps, but gave it the slang pronunciation he had learned at the academy.

Winthrop straightened and became more formal. "Lieutenant Colonel Gudunov: You have been selected to participate in the Barnard expedition to take place in two years. You are hereby promoted to colonel and will be second-in-command, reporting to Major General Virginia Jones, Space Marine Corps."

George winced and grinned internally at the same time. He had never met Jinjur, but had heard a great deal about her. He had wistfully hoped that he would be chosen to lead the expedition, but that was politically impossible. His many friends in Congress could protect him from the vengeful types in the military, but they didn't have enough clout to go over their heads, especially at his age. He didn't care, he'd got what he wanted—a chance to go to the stars. He only half-listened as General Winthrop dropped his formal tone and verbally lashed out at him.

". . . and I'm goddamned glad you're going. You've been a goddamn thorn in the flesh of every goddamned Air Force chief of staff since you were twenty-three. I don't know why you stayed in the goddamned Air Force anyway after that stupid goddamned trick you pulled in 1998 when you were a goddamned captain.

" 'Why don't we test out the laser forts by using them to push a sail probe to the nearby stars?' you said. Unfortunately the chief of staff agreed with you and approved the test. You made a fool of him when ten percent of the nation's defense capability failed in the first goddamned minute . . ."

". . . As it would have if it'd been a real attack instead of a test," George reminded him, uncowed.

"ALL RIGHT!!!" shouted the general. "Since then you've been protected by your goddamn friends in the goddamn Congress. We can't touch you, but we don't have to promote you any GODDAMN faster than necessary."

He subsided and sat back in his chair. He smiled grimly. "You realize that if you accept this appointment, Colonel Gudunov, you'll never get another promotion. There will be life-extending drugs available, but at your age there is no chance of you ever coming back."

George looked at General Winthrop with a slight air of bewilderment. He then realized that even though the general had been briefed on the interstellar mission, he apparently had not allowed himself to recognize the full truth.

"Sir . . ." said George, hesitantly, "as planned—the mission will take over sixty years. Forty years to get there and twenty years of exploration. Even with life-extending drugs, most of the crew will be old and well into retirement age before the work there is done. Besides, there is no provision for a return flight. This first expedition is a one-way mission."

Colonel Gudunov waited in the VIP lounge while the flight from Cape Kennedy landed at the Washington National Airport. He fished a thirteen-sided two-dollar coin from his pocket, bought a plastican of Coke, pulled up the sip-tab, and wandered over to the window to inhale his morning dose of caffeine and phosphoric acid. He heard the clamor of an approaching group of press reporters and photographers outside the door of the lounge. Underneath the yapping of reporters and the whir and snap of cameras there was a firm tenor voice.

"No comment."

"Excuse me, please."

"No comment."

The door to the suite opened. A pair of huge Marine guards seemed to fill the opening. Then they were gone, herding the press away in front of them. George lowered his eyes to see a slightly disheveled female Marine officer slapping the dust off her uniform with her overseas cap. Suddenly she noticed him and stopped.

"Are you Gudunov . . . ?" she asked.

"I hope so," said George, with a broad smile, taking the unfair advantage that his name sometimes gave him against the fair sex.

"I'm pleased to meet you," said Virginia, extending a pudgy black hand to cancel the sexual overtones of the previous exchange. "Heard a lot about you in my briefings. Glad you got to go on the mission. After all, if it hadn't been for you there wouldn't be a mission. What's next?"

"Choosing the rest of the crew," said George. "You and I were picked by the president and Congress. The choice of the fourteen others is up to us. Actually, the Space Administration doctors and evaluators have prepared a list of those qualified for each specialty needed. Mostly it will just be a matter of following their guidelines."

"Good," said Jinjur. She walked to the door of the VIP suite and looked through the peephole.

"The reporters are gone," she said. "Let's take the Metro to the Space Administration headquarters. It'll be faster than waiting for a VIP limo."

Jinjur tossed the thick stack of résumés onto the table. "The evaluators did a pretty good job," she said. "They chose Jesús Méndez as the chief pilot for *Prometheus*. He's got to be the best lightsail pilot in space. Now for the rock hounds. I really feel at a loss here. These types love to muck around in the mud, while the last thing I want to do is pound dirt again. Whom do the Space Administration people recommend?"

"We have a real dilemma here, Virginia," said George. "The one most qualified has a number of significant problems. He doesn't have an advanced degree, he's too tall for the beds on *Prometheus*, and worst of all, he's forty-three years old."

"You should talk, grayhair," said Jinjur. "Who is he?"

"The head of the Galilean satellite mapping expedition, Sam Houston."

"If he's good, then it doesn't matter how old or how tall he is," said Jinjur. "Sam it is. But we need two of them. Who has the next best recommendation?"

"He's a brave young man," said George. "He has a generally good background, but there's a reservation in it."

"I'm beginning to catch onto your twings, Granddad," said Jinjur. "It must be Richard the Red."

Richard Redwing leaned his hundred-plus kilograms on the ice core drill and lifted himself up on tiptoe. He could feel the motor whining through the gloves of his space suit, but there was no downward motion of the drill. He wished he had some purchase so he could use his muscles to drive the drill bit through the rounded pebble that was blocking its path, but on Callisto there was never any purchase, no topography whatsoever. . . .

". . . and no gravity to speak of," complained the planetary geo-scientist. He finally gave up and pulled the incomplete core from the hole, breaking it into segments as he did so, and throwing the striated columns of ice to the crust in disgust. He moved over a meter and started in again, cursing under his breath in resignation.

He was three meters down when his suit speaker relayed a message.

"I've got good news!" boomed Sam's voice through the speaker. "Can you come in?"

"I'll be there as soon as I finish this core, Sam," he replied. "What's the news?"

"I'd rather wait and see your face when I tell you," said Sam. "See you soon."

Richard loped into the office of the head geologist of the Galilean mapping expedition. He was relieved that he didn't have to duck as he came through the door. Sam was not only big enough in status to obtain special treatment for his living and working quarters, he was big enough in size to need them. At a full two meters, Sam Houston's spare frame had to bend to get through any doors but his own specially constructed ones. Richard's hairline, nearly five centimeters less, went through without ruffling the invisible feather that he subconsciously wore on his head like some people wear a chip on their shoulder.

"Good news!" Sam boomed again, this time in person. He didn't waste time.

"You've been chosen to be one of the crew of *Prometheus*," he said.

Richard was elated.

"Wow!" he said, his normal reserve dissolving into a smiling, exuberant caricature of himself that was more appropriate for a college freshman than a professional.

Richard had stoically resigned himself to the fact that there were hundreds of applications for each position on the crew. When he had lost two toes to frostbite during a mountain rescue in his twenties, he had figured that the minor physical handicap would be enough to keep him off the expedition. It wasn't much of a handicap, but when you have a dozen young, intelligent, fully qualified applicants, why pick one that was stupid enough to lose two toes?

"Gee, Sam," Richard said, "I hate leaving you in the lurch like this, with us five ice-cores behind schedule."

"Found another round-rock layer, have you?" grinned Sam, his smile getting broader as he talked. "But that is neither your problem nor mine," he said. "You aren't leaving me in the lurch."

"But all those cores . . ." protested Richard.

"All those cores are the next director's problem," said Sam. "You weren't the only one chosen for the expedition! We're *both* going to the stars!"

"We need two heavy-lift pilots," said Jinjur. "This handsome young astronaut with the stuttering name, Thomas St. Thomas, is an obvious first choice. What bothers me is the rich bitch, Elizabeth Vengeance," said Jinjur. "Why did the evaluators pick her over hundreds of other candidates for lift pilot? And why would she want to give up all her billions to spend the rest of her life cooped up in tin cans? I think she's on a publicity kick."

"Red was the first of the asteroid belt miners and has more experience landing on small moons than anyone else," said George. "As for her billions, it all came in a lucky find of a ten-kilometer asteroid of nearly pure nickel-iron. I think she is getting tired of being a rich ground-pounder. Did you read her résumé thoroughly?"

"No, I didn't," said Jinjur. "I know her type only too well."

"Read it again," said George. "Especially the hand-written part after the signature."

General Jones pawed her way through the voluminous file, ignoring the numbers in the financial section that seemed to exceed those found in the Space Marine budget. She finally came to a hand-printed line below the scrawly signature. It looked like the scratchings of a grade-school dropout.

"I want to go to the stars," it said.

A tall, aristocratic woman with a lean, high-boned freckled face walked across the exoplush carpet toward the wall communicator. She touched a tiny circle on the control plate and stared at the face that appeared in full color on the screen. She frowned slightly, her green eyes flitting over the image. In a smooth motion her right hand reached down to pick up a hairbrush on a table in front of the viewer as her left index finger touched another circle on the control plate. The image on the screen reversed as if she were looking in a mirror. A few quick brushes of her short cap of red hair and she was satisfied. She blanked the screen and set up a call to her financial adviser. It didn't take long—her calls had priority at Holmes and Baker, Pty.

The face of a young business executive flashed into view.

"Good afternoon, Mycroft," she greeted him.

"The same to you, Ms. Vengeance," he replied. "Although it's still early morning here. What can I do for you?"

"What's my net worth today?" she asked.

"Hummm . . ." he replied. "That will take a few seconds." As he talked, his hands flickered over the control plate in front of him and the numbers appeared at the top of both their screens.

"Well, your stocks are worth about 22,475 million, and you have about five million in your various checking and credit accounts, but that is offset by about a million in short-term debts . . ."

"No—not just my accounts," she protested, "I mean my total net worth—businesses, asteroid mining rights, real estate, homes, cars, everything right down to the clothes on my back."

His hands continued to move across the control plate and they both watched the figure at the top of the screen grow in size, then finally stabilize, fluctuating slightly in the last five or six places as the stock and commodity markets around the world continued with their buy and sell transactions.

"It looks like 61,824 million American dollars, plus or minus a million," he said.

"Damn!" she exclaimed. "I thought I'd be over a hundred billion by now. But it's still pretty good for a slum kid from Phoenix." Her eyes dropped from the numbers and stared straight into his eyes.

"Liquidate it," she ordered. "You have six weeks."

"Yes, Ms. Vengeance," he said with a noticeable gulp. Then, showing an avid curiosity he asked, "What are your reinvestment plans? Mining on the moons of Jupiter?"

Her face took on a pixielike grin as she replied, "No, I'm not going to reinvest it, I want you to turn it into cash. I want ten million in gold coins, one billion in hundred-thousand-dollar bills, and the rest in thousands and hundreds. Then I want you to rent a warehouse to hold it all so I can come and say good-bye to it."

"Good-bye?" he said in bewilderment.

"Yes," she said. "I'm going to give it all to the University of Arizona. Where I'm going I won't have any use for money. I'm taking a tour, Mycroft."

"A tour?"

"The grandest tour the human race can devise. I'm going to the stars!"

"The next batch is really a rubber-stamp choice as far as I am concerned," said George. "We need at least two computer types that understand the computer systems built into *Prometheus*, the planetary landers, and the atmospheric aircraft. The top choice for the hardware side is the astronaut and aerospace engineer Karin Krupp.

For the software side we have David Greystoke. He wrote most of the programs for the computers."

"Don't know him," said Jinjur. "A typical computer-nurd, I suppose. Yet the name sounds familiar."

"*Visions Through Space,*" said George, trying to help.

"THAT David Greystoke?" said Jinjur. "But he's a sonovideo composer."

The computer console screen was alive with writhing, brightly colored abstract forms that roiled and curled in deep blues and lavenders, while scintillating spheres of orange and white rolled over and under the billowing waves of color. The display stopped suddenly, then started over again with the lavender shades just a bit less red in color.

Watching the screen critically was a tiny, thin, quiet young man with orange-red hair—a computer leprechaun. The long fingers on his neat hands played over a special-ized input board as they controlled the computer-generated images on the screen. He finished the sequence, saved it in a computer file, then combined it with sev-eral others. He pushed his glasses back up on his long thin nose, sat back in his console chair, and watched the performance as the computer played the whole sequence back from its memory.

As the artistic computer-animated show was reaching its conclusion, some white letters appeared in the upper portion of the screen.

MAIL FOR DAVID GREYSTOKE

David noticed the words, but waited for the end of the file before saying, "Read mail."

The screen blanked and a short letter scrolled its way rapidly up the screen and hung there. David's eyes wid-ened as he read the message. He gave a quiet smile of satisfaction and reached for his sonovideo panel. As the realization of the meaning of the message sunk into his body, his soul was reaching out through his fingers to create a new optical masterpiece, a moving view of the splendor of the heavens as seen from the bridge of a starship leaving the solar system and stretching for the stars. As the starship approached a distant deep-red point of light, the spaceship grew wings—long, thin gossamer wings. The winged spaceship-turned-dragonfly circled the star, then swooped in to land on a small planet with a tenuous breath of atmosphere. It was all imagination, but the magic of the motion through the imaginary air gave a reality to the golden dragonfly as it settled slowly to the surface of the indigo planet.

"At least three of the planets in the Barnard system have an atmosphere," said George, "including the strange double-one. We're going to need some good pilots."

"I've got one," said Jinjur. "You. Unless you've lost your flight instructor's rating?"

"But I'll have to sleep sometime," said George.

"There's no question about the other pilot," said Jinjur. "Arielle Trudeau wins it hands down. Y'know, after that exploit where she single-handedly landed a crippled shuttle with two dead pilots, I always thought she was the best aerospace pilot in the world. As for the rest of the crew, I don't see why we don't just go along with the choices of the Space Administration experts. Let's call a meeting."

"We'll be missing a few people," said George. "Sam Houston and Richard Redwing are both busy on Callisto. Rather than coming all the way back in, they'll go on out past Uranus and meet us on *Prometheus*. The hydroponics expert, Nels Larson, and the computer expert, David Greystoke, are already on *Prometheus* checking out the systems they designed. The solar astrophysicist, Linda Regan, is stationed on Mercury. We'll pick her up there when we visit the Mercury laser transmitter base. The rest should make it to the meeting. The three astronauts should be on their way back soon if they aren't already on earth."

Two women sat side by side in the Super-Shuttle cockpit. The one in the pilot seat was thin and fair, almost delicate in appearance. She sat quietly, her hands folded in her lap. The flickering deep-brown eyes scanned the board and flight display, missing nothing in their vigilant watch over the nerve center of the multiton spacecraft.

The woman in the copilot seat was working the controls, her strong capable hands making tiny adjustments as her eyes alternated views of the flight display and the curved arc of the horizon outside the windshield. She was a very tall, superbly built young woman with blue eyes and heavy yellow hair that she wore in a single large braid over one shoulder. While she nervously handled the controls, the smaller woman's calm test-pilot voice quietly guided her through the reentry procedure.

". . . Keep nose at right attitude, Karin. Also watch those nose and wing thermometers. If nose goes down, we dive in too fast. If nose goes up, we skip out, miss the landing field, and have to dump our nice shuttle in the ocean."

There was a dull thud. The view outside the windshield started to roll.

"What's happened, Arielle?" said Karin, her voice tight with panic. "I can't seem to get any roll response!"

Arielle didn't move, but her eyes were studying a distant corner of the status board where a light had come on.

"Attitude-control propellant tank is busted," she said. "Shut him down and bring up auxiliary system."

Karin searched over the board, flicked the proper switches, and used the jets to bring the heavy spacecraft around.

"You let nose get low," Arielle remarked calmly. Karin looked out the window at the wings. The white-hot incandescence left green-yellow streaks in her vision.

"Take over!" pleaded Karin. "I'm going to lose it."

"You doing just fine," Arielle replied in a soothing tone. "Besides, we may have computer glitch if consoles be switched now."

The air was getting thicker. The temperature indicators were dangerously high, but as the massive craft shed its orbital energy to the air outside, the temperatures started to drop. They were nearly through the critical reentry phase.

"You start switch to aerodynamic controls?" Arielle reminded, and was pleased to see that Karin had anticipated her.

There was a warning Klaxon and the spacecraft started to roll again. A red message light flashed, indicating that the main hydraulic system was failing. Karin reached to switch on the backup system. Arielle started to warn her to deactivate the malfunctioning system first when the high-pressure oil hit the inactive actuators and jerked them wildly about. The nose dipped and the view outside started to whirl violently. The windshield turned red, glaring white, then black. . . .

A cool Arielle popped the top of the Super-Shuttle trainer and stood up. She stared over the head of the shaken Karin at a grinning brown face peering over the top of the simulator console.

"Thomas St. Thomas!" she said severely. "She's third time on a reentry and you dump two breakdowns at her. You be shamed! Look at her!"

Karin quickly recovered, gave them both a weak grin, and extracted her 190-centimeter frame from the copilot seat.

"The trouble with that pass wasn't Thomas' fault, it was the simulator. It's so realistic I was fooled into thinking it was the real thing and panicked. Shall we try it again?"

Arielle was about to protest when the door to the simulator room opened and the director of the Johnson Space Center strode in, followed by a few minicamers.

"Don't you three ever take a break from training?" he said. He looked at the three envelopes that he held and passed them one at a time to the three astronauts.

"Captain Thomas St. Thomas, Arielle Trudeau, and Karin Krupp."

Thomas got his open first.

"YAHOO!" he hollered. "I'm going to Barnard!"

He looked at the expression on the faces of the two women as they looked at their letters, then he hollered again, YAHOO! we're ALL going to Barnard!"

He leaped over the console, picked up Arielle, whirled her around once, and deposited her on the top of the simulator. He started to pick up Karin, but she just stared him down with her two-centimeter height advantage. He passed her by and proceeded to pump the hand of the director vigorously as the minicamers stored it all on chip.

The Houston TV stations that night ended their news program with a shot of the three astronauts, Thomas with one arm around Karin's shoulder and talking, while Arielle stood in front of the other two. She looked out of place. One would have thought she was a beauty queen, with her pretty face and short, curly blond hair, rather than what she was, one of the best aerospace pilots in the world. As usual, it was Thomas who had the last word as their pictures faded from the screen.

"We're going to the STARS!"

It was another drizzly day in DC, so George stood in the narrow portico at the front of the headquarters building and waited for the crew to arrive while Jinjur was upstairs checking out the meeting room with the Space

Administration staff. The first to arrive were Caroline Tanaka, fiber-optics engineer and astronomer, Carmen Cortez, radar and communications engineer, and John Kennedy, mechanical engineer and nurse, who bore a striking resemblance to his distant relative. They had all flown in yesterday and had spent the morning across the street at the National Air and Space Museum. During a lull in the rain they ran down the short block on Sixth Street to where George was waiting. He greeted them and sent them upstairs to the briefing room.

It was five minutes later when he saw a small figure come up from underground on the Metro escalator on Maryland Avenue, then trot quickly through the rain toward him. It was Dr. Susan Wong. She had Ph.D.'s in levibiology and organic chemistry, and an M.D. in aerospace medicine. She would not only take care of the crew, but would help Nels Larson keep the hydroponics tanks and tissue cultures healthy. George was helping her off with her coat when a Space Administration station wagon pulled up with the three astronauts. They had flown into Andrews Air Force Base in their trainer aircraft.

"Dr. Wong," said George, shaking the water off her coat, "I'd like you to meet three of your future patients, Arielle Trudeau, Karin Krupp, and Captain Thomas St. Thomas."

"Hi, Doc," said Thomas, sticking out a hand.

"Susan, if you please," said Dr. Wong with a shy smile, placing her tiny pale yellow hand with the long surgeon's fingers in the strong brown grip.

"Sure. Susan it is, Doc," said Thomas.

Susan shook hands with Karin, then Arielle. She held onto Arielle's hand and looked quizzically at her face.

"Such a pretty woman you are," she said. "Weren't you Miss Quebec in '02, just before Quebec separated from Canada?"

Arielle blushed. "Yes," she admitted, "but the Quebecois always want to live in past. I want to live in future, so like rest of Canada, I leave Quebec and become citizen of Greater U.S."

A humming sound that had been hovering on the horizon of their consciousness burst into a burbling roar. A high-powered sports car appeared, working its way down Independence Avenue through the Washington traffic. They all turned to watch as the fiery-red Liberian Sword came to an expertly controlled stop in a reserved parking space in front of the building. A security guard took a look at a list and went down to put a special card under the windshield-wiper blades. A tall, redheaded woman dressed in a green satin jump suit that matched her green eyes unfolded herself from the front seat and strode up the short flight of steps toward them. Her long thin legs glistened in their shiny, green, high-heeled alligator boots.

George stared in fascination at the legs. Probably the new mutation-green stock from the hide farms, he thought. He started forward to greet her, but Thomas beat him to it.

"I bet you're the famous Red Vengeance," said Thomas, holding onto her hand. "Few people can afford a Sword, much less drive it so well. Y'know, you're the dream girl of the heavy-lift pilots. We'd all like to take a prospecting trip with you."

Red shook his hand politely with a faint smile on her face. "Not all at one time, I hope," she said. "I'm Elizabeth, and you? ..."

"Thomas," he said. "Thomas St. Thomas, and this is Arielle Trudeau, Karin Krupp, and over there is Colonel Gudunov and Dr. Wong ... ah ... Susan."

Red nodded to each one and stared for a long moment at George as she slowly extracted her hand from Thomas' grip.

George tried to return the look but finally had to

glance away from the deep green eyes. He coughed nervously.

"We're all here," he said. "Let's go up to the briefing room."

Jinjur was waiting at the podium in the front of the briefing room when they entered.

"Get yourself a hot cup of coffee to ward off the chill and have a seat," said Jinjur. "Thomas? You'll be talking right after me, so get your viewgraphs out."

After introductions around, Jinjur returned to the podium. "Welcome, ladies and gentlemen. I don't know all of you well now, but since I am going to be spending the rest of my life with you, I hope that soon you'll all be my friends." She paused, and took a sip out of a coffee cup that had the laser and lightsail emblem of the Space Marines on one side and black letters spelling THE BOSS on the other.

"This is not a military mission, but we will be lightyears away from earth authority. So like the old-time sea captains, I will have final authority on everything. I will allow discussion and even straw votes, but this mission will not be run by popular vote. I know you all understood that when you volunteered, but if you don't agree, then now is the time to say so. There are plenty of others willing to take your place." She waited for a few seconds, then relaxed.

"Enough of that," she said. "We're off on an adventure to visit some exciting worlds. We only got a long-distance look at them as the robotic interstellar probe flew through at one-third light speed, but Thomas and Caroline have put together a picture of the Barnard system. Thomas?" She stepped down and Thomas took her place.

"First let me give some details about the star," said Thomas. "Here is a dull table that summarizes what we know about it." He put a viewgraph on the machine. "Barnard is a small, red dwarf star about six lightyears away. The only star system closer is the alpha Centauri system with three stars. Barnard was called +4 deg 3561 until an astronomer named Barnard measured its proper motion and found it was tearing through the sky at the terrific clip of 10.3 seconds of arc per year, or more than half the diameter of the moon in a century. It is an M5 red dwarf with a temperature of 3330 degrees Kelvin compared to the G0 yellow-white 5770 degrees Kelvin of the sun. Probably the thing we will find hardest to get used to is the dull red illumination. It will be sort of like living by the light of a charcoal fire. Not only is the temperature low, but the diameter of the star is only twelve percent of the sun's diameter. It is going to be cold there except very close to Barnard.

"Now comes the interesting part," said Thomas. "The planetary system around Barnard. The robotic probe only got a glimpse as it went through the system, but it looks as though there are only two planets. However, one of the planets is so large and has so many moons that it is practically a planetary system by itself." He replaced the Barnard data table with an orbital diagram, then walked up to the screen with a pointer.

"The main planet is a gigantic one, called Gargantua. It is a huge gas giant like Jupiter, but four times more massive. If Gargantua had been slightly more massive, it would have turned into a star and the Barnard system would be a binary star system. Gargantua seems to have swept up all the material for making planets, since there are no other large planets in the system. Gargantua has four satellites that would be planets in our solar system, plus a multitude of smaller moons. We plan on visiting as many of them as possible after we have taken a look at the most interesting planet—Rocheworld.

"Rocheworld is a corotating double planet whose two halves are so close to each other that the planets are not spherical, but are drawn into egg shapes. This shape was first calculated by an ancient French mathematician called Roche, hence the name. Rocheworld is in a highly elliptical orbit about Barnard. Caroline, using her three-hundred meter, ten-thousand-element optical multiferometer, was able to resolve the planets and track the orbits for the last two years. According to her, Rocheworld has a period that seems to be exactly one-third the period of Gargantua. We know that such orbital 'resonances' are usually unstable. Whether this nearly three-to-one ratio is real or a coincidence is one of the things we hope to figure out when we get there."

"What are the sizes of the orbits?" asked Karin.

"Small," said Caroline. "The radius of Gargantua's orbit is thirty-eight gigameters, while the semimajor axis of Rocheworld's elliptical orbit is a little over eighteen gigameters. The whole thing would fit inside the orbit of Mercury."

"What are the conditions on Rocheworld and the moons?" asked John.

"We know that Rocheworld and the larger moons have atmospheres," said Thomas. "And that one of the two parts of Rocheworld seems to have a liquid on its surface. But the probe couldn't get very much detail during the flyby. That's one of the other things we're going to have to study when we get there."

There were other briefings for the crew. Some by Space Administration experts and some by members of the crew.

"Now we come to one of the more sobering aspects of our journey," said Jinjur. "Dr. Wong, could you please give us a short medical briefing?"

"Certainly," said Dr. Wong as she rose and took Jinjur's place at the podium. "This expedition is a long one. Longer than the normal life-span of the human body, even with all the medical advances we have made. Therefore, after the initial launch phases of the mission, we will all be treated with the life-extending drug, No-Die. When it has thoroughly saturated our tissues, it will slow our aging processes to one-fourth of normal rate. Thus, the forty years that it will take for us to travel to Barnard will only produce ten years of aging in our bodies.

"Unfortunately, our intelligence will also be lowered by roughly the same factor. That is why No-Die is not used more on earth. Fortunately, you all have been picked as persons with higher than normal intelligence, so that the No-Die will merely reduce your functional level to that of a small child. We will have a semi-intelligent computer on board to keep us out of trouble during the trip out. It will stop administering the No-Die as we approach Barnard so that we will be back to normal intelligence when we arrive.

"As for sexual matters. The engineers cannot make *Prometheus* go any faster. So even if they designed the system for a round-trip journey, No-Die couldn't stave off death long enough to bring us back alive. Thus, this trip is a one-way journey for all of us. The planets there are not habitable without using highly technical life-support systems to protect us against the poisonous atmospheres, so this cannot be a colonization mission. There must be no children born during the mission, and since we cannot count on your intelligent cooperation during the No-Die phase, all of you will have to undergo surgical operations to ensure that your reproductive organs are blocked."

George leaned over and whispered into Jinjur's ear. "I'm already fixed so that I only shoot blanks."

Jinjur didn't blink an eye. "Bang, bang," she muttered.

Dr. Wong continued: "Although this procedure should have no physical side effects, there are occasionally psychological reactions to the loss of your reproductive capability that produce physical effects, including loss of sexual appetite and impotency. If this happens to you, please don't hesitate to consult me." A twinkle came to her eye. "If the normal medical procedures are ineffective, my grandmother told me of some ancient Oriental procedures that are guaranteed to produce spectacular results." She sat down amidst whispered conversations.

"Thanks, Susan," said Jinjur. "Well, that's enough for today. I assume you all have your personal affairs taken care of. After your final physicals and briefings, we'll head down to Mercury to visit the laser propulsion center, then out to Titan for some practice sessions using the lander rockets and the Dragonfly aerospace plane, then board *Prometheus* on the other side of Uranus for the trip out. Good day."

Training

The training of the first true astronauts took them throughout the solar system to learn about the disparate portions of the solar-system-wide machine that would toss them to the stars on a beam of light. First they dropped inward to the orbit of Mercury to see the "engine room" of their star-spanning spacecraft.

They approached Mercury from shadowside, heading for the thin, bright man-made halo behind the planet. This was the "sunhook," a ring-shaped structure of gossamer that hovered halfway down Mercury's shadow cone. The intense light from the sun on the reflective surface was enough to keep the sunhook levitated against the pull of the planet below. As Mercury rotated about the sun, the play of the solar photons on the ring kept it centered about the shadow cone. Hanging below the sunhook, at the point of a cone of tethers, was MERLAP-4C, the Mercury Laser Propulsion Construction, Command, and Control Center, safely suspended in the deep shadow of the planet.

As they docked, the crew could see through the portholes the bright dress uniforms of the small contingent of Space Marines at Mercury Center waiting to welcome

their General Jinjur. Jinjur led the way through the air
lock to the piping of a bosun's whistle. There were portholes in the short metal docking tube, and she looked up
to see that portions of the sail were tilting, turning from
a dull gray to brilliant white as the ring control computer added sail to compensate for the weight of the
docked spacecraft.

They were greeted by Linda Regan, a short, bouncy,
young woman with long bouncy curls. Karin looked
down in envy at the naturally curly hair, then her expression changed to that of puzzlement.

"Haven't I seen you somewhere before?" she asked.

"I wondered if you would remember me," said Linda.
"I was a sophomore cheerleader at USC when you were
a second-string forward on the men's basketball team."

Linda led them to a large central room used as a
combination dining room and meeting hall. They were
met there by the director of the center.

"I want to welcome our distinguished group of astronauts to the Mercury Laser Propulsion Construction,
Command, and Control Center," he said. "It is here that
we will generate the propulsion energy to send you off
to Barnard's Star. When the mission starts next year,
we want you to know that we will be behind you, pushing all the way."

There were a few chuckles. He smiled and continued.
"There is one very important fact you must always remember while you are here on Mercury Center, especially when you're off looking around on your own after
the planned tours." He paused for effect, "You're NOT in
free fall."

With those words he pulled himself over to a table
fixed in the center of the dining hall. Using it for purchase,
he crouched and jumped upward to the center of the
domed ceiling, where he held onto a light fixture. He
damped out his motion and hung there some ten meters
overhead.

"Mercury Center is not in orbit, but is floating at a point some eight thousand kilometers above the surface of the planet. The pull of Mercury is counteracted by the large ring sail that you all saw as you arrived.

"The gravity pull from Mercury at this distance is weak, only one part in three thousand of earth's gravity, but it's enough to kill you." He paused to let the last words echo off the walls of the large room. His voice took on a stern tone as he continued. "And the more free fall time you've had, the more likely you'll forget, so I want you space veterans to pay close attention.

"Suppose you're outside being shown something and you let go of your handhold for a second," he said. He let go of the light fixture for a few seconds. As far as the group could tell, he just hung there as if he were in free fall. He regained his hold on the light fixture and said, "For the first few seconds, you will only fall a few millimeters, and you can easily regain a handhold. If you let yourself get distracted for ten or twenty seconds, however . . ." He released his handhold and started counting. After ten seconds he had dropped noticeably. When he reached the count of twenty he desperately attempted to regain his handhold on the light fixture, but he had dropped over half a meter and it was out of reach. He stopped trying, then turned to look down at them.

"You will continue to accelerate," he said very solemnly as he slowly fell toward them. "If we don't see you within two or three minutes and launch a rescue vehicle—you are *dead*." His feet punctuated the last words as they hit the tabletop with a dull thud.

"Now," said the director. "Let me turn you over to my chief engineer, who will explain the things you will be seeing during your visit here."

Their first tour took them out to one of the laser generators. There were a thousand of them, spaced in a sun-synchronous orbit about Mercury—a sparkling diadem for the innermost planet. Each generator consisted of a large, lightweight reflector thirty kilometers across that collected the sunlight and concentrated it on a light-pumped laser placed at its focus. The astronauts visited the sites in small flitters and did all their observing from behind the heavily tinted portholes of the tiny spacecraft, for it was too hot outside for ordinary space suits.

Red Vengeance, who had gazed down at many a planetoid from orbit, suddenly broke her contemplative silence.

"How come the terminator is curved?" she asked. "I thought the lasers were supposed to be in a sun-facing orbit. In that case, we should be right over the terminator and Mercury should be cut in half by its shadow."

"For the same reason that the lasers and their collectors are here flying around Mercury instead of in their own orbits around the sun," said the engineer conducting the tour. "Light pressure may not be much, but the solar photons would blow those lightweight collectors away if they were not anchored by gravity to the mass of the planet. In fact, the light pressure is so strong that the orbit plane is actually pushed a few hundred kilometers toward the dark side."

"Things have sure progressed since the first space-fort days," said George as he gazed at the huge expanse of collector that seemed to go on and on to some distant horizon like the surface of a small sea. He paused, then queried in a perplexed voice, "The collector has a funny color to it."

"That's the special coatings," said the engineer. "The solar flux here at the orbit of Mercury is almost ten kilowatts per square meter, but not all of it can be used by the laser. The coating on the collector only reflects those portions of the sunlight that are at the right wavelength to be converted into laser power."

"*Prometheus* needs 1300 terawatts of power for propulsion, and there are 1000 lasers, so each one has to produce 1.3 terawatts," said George. "That's a lot of power. What's the efficiency?"

"The overall efficiency of solar power to laser power is only 20 percent, but the important thing is to get rid of the 80 percent that you don't use," said the engineer. "The total solar flux incident on the 30-kilometer collector is 6.5 terawatts, but only about 1.5 terawatts is reflected to the laser itself; the rest just passes on into space."

"So the actual efficiency of the laser is quite high," said John. "Still, even two-tenths of a terawatt is a lot of heat to get rid of."

"Not if you have a high enough temperature and a big enough surface area," said the engineer. The flitter moved closer to the laser itself. "They're about to do a test," he said.

Control jets flashed on the side of a hundred-meter mirror. The mirror turned and deflected the focused sunlight from the collector sail into the end of a block-long, office-building-sized laser with four jet-black wings spread out into the darkness of space. After a few minutes the central portion started to glow a deep red, then turned yellow as the base of the radiating fins took up the deep red color.

"Is the laser on?" asked George. "You can't tell, I guess; nothing to scatter light from the beam."

"The laser radiation is in the short infrared, so you couldn't see it anyhow," said the engineer. "But you can tell it's on by looking at the color of the beam-deflector mirror."

They looked at the deflector mirror at the output end of the laser and saw a deep red glow near the center, where a small fraction of the 1.3 terawatt laser beam had been absorbed in the mirror instead of being deflected off to the distant laser beam combiner.

"The tests are coming along fine," said the engineer.

"All the lasers should be operational long before launch time. Let's go look at the beam-combiner."

A few hours later the small group had moved from the orbiting ring of lasers to the combiner at the outer Lagrange point.

The collector lens of the beam-combiner system looked like a fine lace doily sprinkled with dew. It was sitting in space a number of kilometers away from a long cylinder that was the main portion of the combiner. The lens was an open net structure that faced the distant planet with its sparkling crown of laser generators. In the openings were transparent sheets of plastic a hundred meters across. They flashed the colors of the rainbow as the flitter moved by.

"Those are hologram lenses impressed in thin plastic," the engineer explained. "There are one thousand of them in a close-packed array some three-and-a-half kilometers in diameter. The light from each orbiting laser is captured by one of these lenses, which collect the beams and send them on to the smaller lenses in the beam-combining cylinder. There, the one thousand separate beams are combined into a single coherent beam of thirteen hundred terawatts of power and sent on to the final transmitter lens."

They flew behind the cylinder and stared back at the Gatling-gun appearance of the output of the beam-combiner. They could see right through.

"It seems to be empty," remarked Jesús.

The engineer laughed. "No, all the internal lenses are there, all right. The reason that you can't see them is that they are made of ultrapure plastic so they don't absorb the laser light. Also note that the top and bottom mirrors are not aligned with each other. That's because the beam-combiner not only combines the various laser beams into one beam, but also transfers from solar system coordinates to Barnard coordinates," said the engineer. "Barnard is 4.3 degrees above the ecliptic, so the top mirror has to be tilted slightly. As Mercury orbits around the sun, the top mirror rotates to keep the beam pointed at Barnard."

It was a long journey out to the transmitter lens. This was the other major portion of their spacecraft that would remain in the solar system while the rest of the ship made the journey to Barnard. The transmitter lens was situated halfway between the orbits of Saturn and Uranus where the sun was weak and space seemed cold. The lens was under construction and was already ten kilometers in diameter. The gossamer structure of threads and plastic sheet was invisible until they went around to the far side and looked back at the sun. The light scattering from the threads lit up the spiderweb structure and they could see the evidence of the alternating rings of plastic and emptiness. The construction was progressing slowly, since only a small crew of robots were assigned to the repetitive task of adding threads and thin sheeting. There was plenty of time to work on the lens, however, for the first hundred kilometers would suffice for initial test and for propulsion of the interstellar craft during the first five years of the mission. More diameter would be added, as needed, during the forty-year duration of the mission, until it reached its maximum size of a thousand kilometers.

The training drew to a close. From all over the solar system the crew came in small groups to board the interstellar spacecraft, hanging below a silvery sail as big as a small moon. *Prometheus* was a cylinder some sixty-six meters long and twenty meters in diameter, an insignificant seed hanging by shrouds from the thousand-kilometer diameter lightsail. They flew in from the backside of the sail, where they could see the hexagonal truss work that held the large, ultrathin triangular sheets of aluminum sail, and docked at the air lock, coming out of the top deck. The top two decks would take the brunt of the cosmic radiation during their subrelativistic journey, so they contained the storage areas and the work area for the computer's motile.

Running completely through the length of *Prometheus* was the lift shaft. It was four meters in diameter and ran from the starside science dome on the back side of the sail to the earthside science dome in the center of the bottom control deck. A lift elevator was available for heavy cargo, but the crew mostly ottered their way up and down the shaft using the handholds built into the walls.

After the top two decks, the next forty-four meters were taken up by four Surface Lander and Ascent Modules arranged in a circle around the lift shaft. They were upside down, with their landing rockets pointing upward and their docking ports attached to four access ports in the hydroponics deck. Below the hydroponics deck, which supplied another layer of protection from cosmic rays, came the two crew decks. Each crew member had a luxurious hotel suite with a private bathroom, sitting area, work area, and a separate bedroom. The wall that separated the bedroom from the sitting area was a floor-to-ceiling view-wall that could be seen from either side. In addition, there was another view screen in the ceiling above the bed.

Below the crew quarters was the living area deck, with a dining area, lounge, exercise room, and two small video theaters. Separating the lounge from the dining area was a large sofa facing a three-by-four-meter oval view-window that was the focal point of social life on the ship.

The control deck at the bottom of the checker stack was all business. Here was another air lock, all the electronics, and the consoles to operate the sail and the science instruments in the two science domes. In the center of the control deck was the earthside science dome, a three-meter-diameter hemisphere in the floor surrounded by a thick, circular, waist-high wall containing racks of scientific instruments that took turns looking out the dome or through holes in the deck directly into the vacuum.

Prometheus was already on its way out of the solar system, flying slowly on the rapidly diminishing photons from the sun, when the exploration crew boarded. It was skippered by a busy checkout crew. As each load of astronauts boarded, their ship was taken back by some members of the checkout team.

The first three to board *Prometheus* were General Jones, Colonel Gudunov, and Karin Krupp. They were met at the air lock by David Greystoke, who with Karin had designed and "trained" the semi-intelligent computer that operated the sailcraft. David introduced himself while Karin found the suit locker, and after fussing over each suit, started to hang them up neatly in their racks.

George noticed a fuzzy metallic object in the corner. It was about as tall as he was and looked like a six-armed chimney-sweep brush. From the tips of each of the fibers in the brush there flickered bursts of pure-color laser light. George noticed that the blue beams scanned over the bodies of the crew as they moved around, while the red and yellow beams monitored the rest of the room. The green beams, however, seemed to be for illuminating various portions of the brush itself, giving the brightly reflecting metallic surface of the multi-branched structure a deep green internal glow.

"That must be the 'Christmas Bush,'" said George to David.

"Yes," said David. "It is the hands and eyes of the central computer. Let me show you what it can do." David took George's helmet and tossed it at the bush in the corner. "Put this away for me, James," he said.

The helmet sailed at the Christmas Bush in a nearly straight trajectory in the low gravity. Crouching like a

miniature stick figure with three "legs," the Christmas
Bush jumped into the air. The smaller twigs on the
bottom side of the hexfurcated structure whirled, propelling the bush through the air. The top portion of the
bush opened up into three furry paws that grasped the
helmet gently with fuzzy fingers. The bush shifted
position, swam over to the suit locker, and put the
helmet in its proper place in the suit rack. As it performed, it uttered a series of happy barks and came
bounding back to pause in midair in front of David, one
of its rear twigs wagging in the air and the tiny cilia
near its front portion emitting a series of breathy pants.

Jinjur listened in amazement, then broke into laughter at the performance. "Maybe 'Fido' would be a better
name than " 'James,' " she said, still laughing.

David smiled. "No, that's not its normal response
pattern. I deliberately programmed that 'eager dog' response into James's repertoire as a method of chiding a
crew member whenever they got lazy and misused one
of James's motiles. That's one of the reasons that the
main computer program has the name James."

"It sounds like an English butler," said George.

"Exactly. James and its motile is here to serve us just
as a good butler would, but the computer will be respon-
sible for running the ship and taking care of the legiti-
mate needs of sixteen crew members. Note that James
did what I asked it to do, but at the same time it gently
reminded me that I should have taken care of that
particular job myself. Now, let me show you some of its
other tricks." He reached into his shirt pocket and pulled
out a pressurized ball-point pen. He unbuttoned his
shirt front and used the pen to push out a bit of lint
from behind a buttonhole. He kicked over to a nearby
wall and deliberately made an ink mark on the wall. As
he kicked back, he dropped the bit of lint into the air. As
he came to a halt back with the group, they watched as

two tiny segments of the bush detached from one of the arms of the Christmas Bush.

The larger submotile jumped from the main bush to the wall, and like a spider, used its fine cilia to cling to the wall and walk over to the ink smudge. The cilia scraped the ink out of the wall pores and formed it into a drying ball. The wall now clean, a subsection of the spider detached and swam off through the low gravity, while the remainder of the spider jumped back to the main bush where it resumed its normal place. The smaller one, a minuscule cluster of cilia not much bigger than the bit of lint, flew rapidly through the air with a humming sound like that of a mosquito, captured the floating ball, and flew out the door to another part of the ship, zigzagging as it went.

"It's picking up other bits of dust on its way to the dustbin," explained David. "They're too small for us to see, but its little laser radars picked them up from their backscatter.

"The Christmas Bush will normally stay in its assembled shape," said David. "It's easier for James to control that way, since each portion has a significant amount of computer power built into it. Each segment, down to the tiniest hexad of cilia, is practically identical in shape. There is a hexagonal central body that is the point of attachment to the next larger level of the structure. From six 'shoulder joints' on the central body radiate 'arms,' each with an 'elbow' joint. At the ends of the arms are attached the next smaller hexad, one-third the size. That smaller central body acts as the 'wrist' and its six 'fingers' form a 'hand.' But unlike a human hand, each 'finger' has a smaller 'hand' and so forth for ten levels. The smallest 'fingers' are cilia only twenty microns long. Each has its own tiny rechargeable perma-battery in the central section, 'muscle' portions near the ends, and logic and control circuitry. Each also has diodes that can both emit and receive laser light at many different frequencies. The various levels of structure are only connected mechanially, not electrically. The logic and power connections are through the laser diodes."

"Because it's laser light, the efficiency of power transfer is nearly ninety-five percent," said Karin. "James feeds power from lasers in the corners of the room to the main trunk to keep that battery charged, and the bush trickles the energy down to the various sticks, twigs, and cilia with the green lasers that you see. The power beams are modulated to send information back and forth between the logic circuits in each twig and branch until you have a fairly sophisticated computer. All James has to do is tell the bush where to go, and the bush generates all of the subcommands needed to trifurcate its 'feet' and walk or swim there. If a smaller portion is detached, however, then James has to use some of its own brainpower to run it, so that's why the motiles are usually kept in clumps. Yet housekeeping is a continual chore, so don't be surprised if you see a spider walking across the ceiling above your bed. It will just be collecting all the dirt and dust you've made that day."

"I'm not so sure I'm going to like living with mosquitoes and spiders," said Jinjur. "That's one of the things I really liked least about being a ground-pounder."

"Once you've gotten used to your imp, Jinjur," said David, "I'm sure you'll get used to James's other minimotiles."

"Hummm. The 'imps.' I guess they're necessary, but when Karin was talking about them in the briefings, I really didn't look forward to the experience."

"They're not so bad once you get used to them," said David. "And there's no time like now."

He turned to face the Christmas Bush. "Could I please have two personal imps, James? One for me and one for Jinjur?" He held out his hand and two portions of the bush detached and flew through the air to David's finger, where they perched like two skinny sparrows.

"These personal imps are to stay nearby at all times so James has a way of communicating with you. It doesn't really matter much where you keep them, but I like to have mine riding my shoulder." David put one of the imps on his shoulder. It scrambled for a second and soon was perched on his collar, looking like a tarantula with six hairy legs. Jinjur noticed that one leg was resting gently on the side of David's neck.

"They not only serve as a means of communication," said David, "they also allow James to keep track of the state of each crew member's health." He turned his head slightly and talked to the imp.

"How'm I feeling today, James?" he asked.

The cilia on the legs of the tarantula vibrated into a blur as it spoke. "Pulse 75, Temperature 37 C, blood pressure 140/80, blood constituents all fine except your triglycerides are a little high. Probably need to get that weight down. Calcium levels are slightly up and bone density is down, but that is normal for free fall."

David continued his briefing. "The personal imps have special illuminators and sensors that can monitor the small blood vessels in the skin and practically carry out a complete blood analysis. James doesn't know my weight yet, but after a few hours of monitoring the frequency response of the various portions of my body as I push myself around the ship, it'll be able to tell from the changes in frequency whether I've gained or lost weight, and even which portion of the body contains the new fat."

"Pretty nosey," said Jinjur. "But I guess it's better than being wired with thermocouples and pressure sensors. I don't particularly care to have a spider sitting on my shoulder. Can I put it somewhere else, like in my pocket?"

"You could," said Karin. "But James would sound

kind of muffled unless you left your pocket unbuttoned. Here, let me show you how I wear mine." She turned to look at the Christmas Bush. "James?"

Another imp-sized motile detached from the bush and flew over to Karin where it landed in her hair. The imp flattened into a crescent moon on the side of her head opposite to her braid. Karin turned her head to show them the shiny barrette in her hair with its twinkling, multicolored lights. "Pretty, isn't it?"

Jinjur grudgingly admitted that it was, and reached to take the other imp from David's finger. She held it in her hand, looking at it closely. She jumped when it spoke. "Hello, General Jones. May I be of service?"

She scowled, a little annoyed with herself for being startled, then forced a determined grin.

"Well, to start with," she said, "you can cut the General Jones business and call me Jinjur like everyone else. I may be boss of this outfit, but it's not a military mission and titles often get in the way."

"Certainly, Jinjur," replied the imp. "Have you decided where you would like to have me?" Jinjur looked at the imp, bemused at herself for talking seriously to such a tiny, fragile bundle of fibers and twigs.

"Do you know what a hair comb looks like?" she asked.

"Like this?" the imp asked. Quickly the six-legged star reconfigured itself into a six-pronged comb with most of its mass and lights clustered into an ornate comb-back. Tiny cilia clutching gently at her skin kept the comb balanced in the light gravity.

"Yes," said Jinjur, her face expanding into a pleased smile at the sight of the bejeweled comb. "I used to wear them when I was a teenager in high school, so I guess I could get used to you in that form."

She picked up the comb in her other hand and started to place it into her hair. She hesitated, then brought the comb down to talk to it.

"You look pretty fragile, Imp. Are you strong enough for me to use you as a comb?"

"My motiles are quite strong. They are made of the hardest dura-steel. You will find them as hard to break as a needle." There was a pause, then James continued as Jinjur lifted the comb to her head and stuck it in. "You must learn to realize that the imps are only sensors and transducers. You must not think of them as individuals. Someday, in some emergency situation, you might be tempted to try to save them."

Jinjur wasn't really listening. She had turned to face the glass port that looked into the darkened air-lock. She noticed a flat space where her short Afro had been squashed by the helmet in her space suit. She reached for the imp comb to fluff it out.

"Allow me," said the imp in James's most butlerish voice. Jinjur's hand hesitated. The imp splayed out into its normal star shape, moved rapidly through Jinjur's hairdo, and within one second every hair on her head was in its proper place. Jinjur's eyes widened as the star reconfigured into a comb shape and resettled into its place behind Jinjur's ear.

"Thank you, Imp," she said.

Karin laughed. "Isn't it nice having your own personal hairdresser at your beck and call?" she said.

"I thought we weren't supposed to have the imp do personal things for us," said Jinjur.

"The personal imps are with you all the time. Their job is keeping you healthy, happy, and informed. You can have them help you in any way that they can," said David. "Misusing the main motile is discouraged, however, since it is essential to the proper operation of the entire spacecraft."

"Let's see the rest of the ship," said Karin. "Lead the way, James." She followed the Christmas Bush out the door with David, Jinjur, and George following. George noticed that the bush had left a motile behind. It buzzed up to hover in front of him.

"Colonel Gudunov?" it queried.

"Hop aboard, James," he said. "And please call me George."

"Certainly, George," said the imp as it settled on his shoulder. Within five minutes George's peripheral vision had stopped seeing the softly blinking cluster of lights that flickered in the low-right-hand corner of his eye. The imp would be his constant companion for the rest of his life.

The rest of the crew boarded and they started the shakedown phase that tested out the crew, computer, ship, and distant lasers as they sailed away from the solar system driven by a combination of solar light and laser light.

Traveling

The day finally came. Deep down in the gravity well of the sun, concentrated sunlight from square kilometers of collector were injected into a block-long laser in orbit about the innermost planet. Glowing warmly, the laser burst into bloom under the sunlight, followed by another and another until a thousand lamps were lit. The beams of invisible radiance converged on a glistening spiderweb lens that gingerly arranged the thousand wasp-hot beams until they met side by side in a crystal-clear cavern of variable index of refraction to emerge as a single, calm, coherent beam of unfluctuating light. Glancing off a tilted mirror, the light sped outward from the sun, channeling the terawatts of sunpower out into the cold of deep space. The beam traveled for two hours before it reached the first of its targets—the transmitter lens—drifting out in space between Saturn and Uranus.

A thermal sensor on the topside of a mechanical spider noticed an increase in the temperature of the sun-facing portion of the mechanism it was monitoring. The change in temperature was duly noted and passed on to the control center at the next engineering check period.

Although the temperature increase was significant, it was still well within the design limits for the mechanism. The spider continued laying down the thin layer of plastic sheeting between the spoke threads that stretched out ahead of it for hundreds of kilometers. The huge spiderweb was only partially completed, but the finished central portion was adequate for the purpose, and its alternating rings of plastic and emptiness sufficed to capture the powerful laser beam and send it out of the solar system toward the distant speck of aluminum reflectance.

Two days later most of the crew were down on the control deck, watching the screen that showed the output of an infrared telescope focused on the inner solar system. A bright light from a point near the sun grew stronger as the lasers there were turned on one by one. They drifted to the floor as the sail billowed under the light pressure. There were cheers over the communication link with Mercury Center, but the crew on *Prometheus* was strangely silent.

"We're on our way," said Jinjur. "I guess it's time."

Everyone looked uncomfortable.

"I wonder if we'll notice it?" asked George.

"According to most clinical studies of No-Die," said Dr. Wong, "the effects come on so gradually that most users have no idea they're mentally impaired—unless they're asked to do some difficult task. Even then, there's a tendency to believe it's only because they're 'tired' or 'sick,' not because the No-Die has slowed their mental processes."

"I'd be just as happy being fooled," said Jinjur. "I don't think I could stand knowing I was a drooling idiot."

"It won't be that bad," said George. "We'll probably be able to button our own clothing and clean up our own messes."

David noticed some disgusted expressions and tried to cheer them up.

"Besides, even if we forget how to tell our right shoe from our left, we still have James and the Christmas Bush to take care of us. It can button our shirts, tie our shoes, and wipe our noses."

Jinjur spoke to her imp. "Put the No-Die in the water, James."

"It is done," replied a low whisper.

Sam Houston, who had been quiet most of the way out, spoke up. "I'm going to my room and open my last bottle of Scotch. Anyone for a drink—straight?" He ambled over under the hole in the ceiling, and crouching his two-meter-long body low, leaped up the lift shaft. He was followed by five others.

Meanwhile Jinjur made her way to the galley. George was there, filling his monogramed drink flask from the water spout.

"I thought I'd get a head start," said George. "At fifty-one I need to slow down fast if I'm going to make it to Barnard."

"You're not so old, George," Jinjur said softly. "At least you still have all your hair, and it's beautiful." She brushed her stubby black fingers through the gray waves on George's head and grabbing a handful, gave his head a friendly shake. She lifted her drink ball with its monogram THE BOSS from its place in the rack and filled it from the coffee spout.

"I don't think I could stomach drinking just water, knowing what's in it. At least this way I can blame the taste on the ersatz coffee flavor." She took a deep draft, held the hot liquid in her mouth for a moment, hesitating, then deliberately swallowed. She looked up at George, who was slowly sipping away at his flask of water.

"I hear the No-Die slows everything down. Even your sex drive."

"That's right," said George. "It's one of the first things to go."

"Rowrbazzle!" Jinjur said softly.

"What?" asked George.

"Just swearing," said Jinjur. "Like a good general I've been keeping myself under control. It doesn't do to have the boss sleeping around with the troops. Now that we're under way and there's nothing to do but coast, I'll soon forget that there's any difference between boys and girls."

"I can still tell the difference," said George. He reached over to her well-stuffed shirt and grabbed the button under the most strain. "Girls button their shirts the wrong way." His fingers slowly and deliberately undid the button, releasing the tension.

She grinned at him. Reaching up to her chest she took his hand in hers. "I'm sure there are other differences," she said. "Let's go up to my room and see if we can find them."

"Let's do a scientific experiment," said David. "Why don't we have a chess tournament. That way we can monitor our mental level. James can keep track. It has the Chess 9.6 grand-master program stored in it."

"Count me out," said Richard Redwing. "I'm not at that level."

"James can adjust the program," said David.

"Oh, what the hell," acquiesced Richard. "Not much else to do anyway."

"We can't be playing chess all the time," said Karin. "We do have some things we're supposed to do, even if most of them are make-work."

"One session each day with James should be enough for a scientifically valid sample," said Dr. Wong. "If you plan a 'chess hour' right after you've had your sleep shift, you should be at your best. The exact time is not important, however, just that it be the same time every ship day."

"I'll think I'll start right now," said David. He pulled himself up to a console. As he was wiggling in the seat to firmly attach the Velcro sticky patch on the back of his jump suit to the console chair, the screen flashed and there was a full color display of a chess set in perspective.

"White or black?" asked James. "And what level of play?"

"I'm brave enough to take you at full grand-master level, James," said David. "But I'll take white just to be on the safe side."

The board rotated in space and David reached out a finger to a pawn on the screen and gave it a push. It was immediately countered by another pawn. A few more pushes, a move of a knight and a bishop, and the game was under way.

"I wonder why we play these silly games every day," said George. "I'm bored with this board game." He gave a delighted chuckle at his joke. "Get it, James? As a board game it's boring."

"Yes. A real pun, George," said James. "Your last move, however, has a slight problem. When you castle on the queen's side, you are supposed to move the rook three spaces and the king two spaces, not three spaces for the king."

George looked at the board on the screen and frowned. The king and rook were blinking, indicating an erroneous move. He shook his head, then said in an annoyed voice. "Well—*fix* them!" The pieces were put in their proper place and James made his move. Still angry with himself, George jabbed a finger at a piece on the screen and moved it forward.

James muttered a polite machine cough. "Are you sure you want to make that move?"

George looked carefully at the screen, bewildered. He couldn't see anything wrong. The piece he moved was certainly not in any danger. "Yes. I'm sure," he said, and was relieved to see James move his queen somewhere else on the board, leaving his piece untouched. He moved again. Then it was James's turn. A rook slid across the screen into his back row.

"Checkmate," said James.

"What'cha doin', Jinny?" asked George. He gazed vacantly at the black smudges that Jinjur was marking on the floor, wall, and ceiling of the exercise room with a black crayon. They were big squares—big enough to stand in.

"Making a chess game," said Jinjur, marking up another square, and staying inside the lines most of the time.

"On the ceiling?" asked George.

"Sure, Georgie," she said. "This is going to be the neatest chess game ever. Three-dibenshenal."

"Three-dibensinal?" asked George.

"You know. Three-D. Up and down and sideways," she replied. "See. I'll show you." She stood in one of the crayoned squares. "Each one of us will be a chess piece, and we can jump anyway we want." She jumped to the mat hanging on one wall. Her feet, clad in corridor boots with sticky bottoms, slammed into the wall and she stuck there. She then slowly pulled herself to the wall by bending her knees, then jumped to the ceiling, where she stuck again. She hung downward in the light gravity.

"Tell the rest of the gang to come here," she said. "Then we can all play."

"OK, Jinny," he said, and started out the door.

"And tell them they'd better come," she hollered after him, "or I'll tell James to turn off their cartoons. After all, I'm the boss."

Soon twelve of the crew were bouncing around the exercise room, playing 3-D "chess."

"I jumped you, Richie," screamed Jinjur. "I'm the boss and I say I jumped you first."

"No, you didn't!" hollered Richard. "I jumped you first. Didn't I, Georgie?"

"I'm jumping you *both* now," said George. "So you're both out and I win."

"No, you didn't. You're a cheater!" screamed Jinjur. She was so mad she was jumping back and forth from the ceiling to the floor, making a half-somersault each time.

"I am not a cheater," replied George, getting angry. "You're the cheater."

"Cheater! Cheater! Georgie is a cheater!" sang Jinjur as she backed away and pushed herself out the door.

"I'll get you, Jinny," said George, moving after her as fast as he could go in the low gravity. "I'll get you yet."

The game broke up with everyone following along as George, his face livid with anger at the insult, chased after Jinjur. The chase took them all the way up the lift shaft, around the hydroponics tanks, and back down the shaft again. By the time everyone had reached the living area deck again, they were all tired. Their imps buzzed in their ears.

"Time for a rest, everyone," said James. "I've got a nice movie for you to watch. It's an old Roadrunner cartoon that you haven't seen before."

"Oh, boy! A Roadrunner cartoon," exclaimed Karin. She led the way to the theater. The crew settled down in a heap on the long bench seats as the music started and the video wall flickered into life. George was exhausted and lay back to rest. Somebody lying on him moved to a new position and his view was blocked. It was Jinjur. Her shirt had come unbuttoned while she was racing through the ship, and James had not made sure that she had put on all her underclothing before letting her out of her room. George stared at the large black mound blocking his vision. Grunting, he pulled it down with one hand and rested his cheek on it. He could see the cartoon good now, and the soft part of Jinjur made a good pillow. He fell asleep.

Senator Beauregard Darlington Winthrop III was in his third term as senator of South Carolina, an office he easily won after finishing his term as Air Force chief of staff. Now, as chairman of the Senate Appropriations Committee, he wielded an influence only slightly less potent than the Senate majority leader. Space Administration officials winced when they heard that budget-hearing time was coming around again.

"Ah'm sure," said Winthrop, putting on his Southern senator voice. "You honorable gentlemen realize that this nation, as rich and as glorious as it is, cannot afford *every* space boondoggle. Ah trust that you've come up with a budget that realizes that there are people here on the ground that desperately need money to keep their family businesses alive. . . ."

He probably means subsidies for the tobacco farmers, thought the Honorable Leroy Fresh, as he prepared to defend his budget before the committee.

"There is one item that the chairman noticed in the preliminary reports that he would like to question the Honorable Dr. Fresh about, if he may." Without waiting for a reply, Winthrop continued. "I notice this line-item number hundred and eight, for four hundred million dollars to expand the transmitter lens for the Barnard laser propulsion system. I didn't notice that item in the previous year's budget, and since the mission is not slated to reach Barnard for another twenty years or so, surely this could be deferred a year or two to release a few funds to succor the poor people of this nation?"

Leroy was ready for this one. "May I remind the chairman that the reason the item was not in last year's budget was that it was removed by the Senate Appropriations Committee, as it has each year for nearly the past decade. The transmitter lens doesn't have to be full size at the start of the mission. It can be built slowly as time passes and the Barnard expedition moves farther and farther away, but the lens must be made ready for the deceleration phase, which requires it to be at maximum diameter. The amount of money in the budget is that needed to bring us back on schedule."

"But the lasers are to be turned off soon," said Senator Winthrop. "And the Barnard lightsail will be merely coasting on its way to its destination. Surely we can defer work on the lens expansion since it's not being used. Especially since I notice in line-item hundred and nine the fifty million dollars for the construction of the tau Ceti lens. The increase in diameter planned for each lens is fifty kilometers. Surely that indicates that they should have equal budgets. Perhaps we should just make those two lens-construction items both equal in size at fifty million?" Senator Winthrop looked around at his committee and smiled.

"Is that agreeable, gentlemen? ... Oh, yes. Excuse me, Madam Ledbetter. Is that agreeable, gentlemen and lady?" He raised a blue pencil and scratched away at his copy of the budget.

"But Senator Winthrop, sir," Fresh protested, "the Ceti lens is going from a diameter of twenty kilometers to seventy kilometers, while the Barnard lens is going from three hundred twenty to three hundred seventy kilometers. Even though both have the same increase in diameter, the increase in area of the Barnard lens is eight times larger than that of the Ceti lens. The cost goes as the square of the diameter."

"Well. Ah must admit Ah'm a little 'square' when it comes to that scientific math, Dr. Fresh, but Ah'm pretty good at figures when they have a dollar sign in front of them." There was a polite laugh at the chairman's joke from the committee and staff. Fresh was silent, knowing that he had lost another skirmish. "After all," said Senator Winthrop with a smile that seemed entirely sincere over the TV cameras, "that's what we have you scientific types for, to take care of all that 'square-root' and 'cube-root'-type math stuff. And Ah must say," he said, with only a trace of sarcasm, "you've been doing an excellent job on an austere budget—like the true Greater American patriots that you are. Now, let's go on to line-item one thirty-three, the billion-channel receiver to search for signals from aliens. Surely a single channel is all that you need. It's obvious. One receiving antenna, one receiving channel . . ."

Leroy Fresh was getting old. He had been on the job for fifteen years now, through one change of administration after another. It didn't seem to matter which party was in charge, the results always seemed to be the same. "The future can wait till tomorrow."

Yet tomorrow was none too soon for the Barnard expedition. Even light would not hasten its slow crawl over the void of space to accommodate the whims of the Congress of the Greater United States of America.

"Dr. Fresh?" said a distant voice.

The administrator revived from his daydreaming stare across Maryland Avenue at the steamy scene of tourists moving in lines through the wet summer heat to enter the air-conditioned comfort of the Air and Space Museum. He swiveled in his chair and stared at an angular face draped in waves of crisp red hair.

"Yes, Anita?" he said.

"The Barnard Lens Construction Committee is here with its recommendation," she said. Leroy knew from the tone of her voice that there was a problem.

The committee burst into his room. Leroy's attention was soon fixed on the committee head. He was Dr. Fred German, a quiet, methodical engineer whom Anita had brought to his attention. Dr. German's anachronistic crew-cut surrounded him in an aura of competency.

"If we are to get the Barnard lens finished in time," said Dr. German, "we will have to move a lot more thread and plastic, but at less cost. The recommendation of the committee is that we use the prototype antimatter-energized rockets as space tugs as soon as the propulsion engineers have finished their studies. They can carry ten times the cargo of a laser-energized spacecraft and get there and back in half the time."

"I object!" said another individual. Leroy recognized her as Nicole Heppelzik, the perennial pessimist of the Advanced Programs Section. Anita had recommended that she be on the committee, for if there was anything wrong to be found, Nicole would ferret it out.

"Let's listen to what Nicole has to say," said Leroy. He nodded at her.

"The cost of the antimatter fuel is exorbitant," said Nicole.

"The Space Command says they will supply the fuel," said Fred German. "They want to get some data on multiple start and restart of the superconducting magnetic nozzles."

"But suppose the magnetic bottle for the antimatter fails?" said Nicole. "You'd have spacecraft and cargo spread all over the solar system."

When the administrator heard this, he knew what decision to make. If all Nicole could do was question the permanence of a passive system like a superconducting magnetic bottle, there was no real concern.

"So you recommend replacing the Barnard lens cargo tugs with antimatter-powered versions," he said.

"Yes," said Dr. German.

"But . . ." said Nicole.

Dr. Fresh waited for a second, then said, "Proceed, Dr. German. That lens must be up to its full thousand-kilometer size in three years. If you can do that *and* keep within the congressional budget constraints at the same time, perhaps we can even bring Senator Winthrop over to our side."

He swiveled in his chair and looked back out his window at the scene outside. Anita was already in the office and shepherding the committee out the door.

The door shut, and then he felt Anita near him as she checked the settings on the autoskeleton that powered his left side.

"Did I handle that right?" he asked.

"Just right," said Anita, and he could tell from the twinkle in the blue-green eyes that he had—this time.

"Any news from the president on a successor?" he asked hopefully.

"None," Anita replied. "She's having great difficulty finding someone qualified who is willing to accept the post."

"Then I stay," said Dr. Fresh. "I'm not good for much, but I can at least make a decision."

He detected a tiny hint of a tear in the corner of one of Anita's eyes.

"Somewhere," he grumphed, "there must be a naive, opportunistic young whelp with a masochistic streak who would like to run the most up-and-down bureaucracy in the history of mankind." Anita was annoyed that he should be saying such things. She strode out of his office, her long red hair curling up at the edges in the breeze, leaving him to his picture window and the mysterious aches and pains in his left side.

I hope that antimatter tug does the job, he said to himself.

When the priority call to the administrator came in from the relay station at Saturn, there was no one there to take it. Anita recorded it for the next appointee and passed a copy on to the acting administrator.

"One-third of the Barnard transmitter lens was destroyed when the debris from the explosion hit the web," said the agonized voice. "We'll never be able to get it finished in time now."

It was six months before the elections, and the thought of leaving sixteen brave people stranded in deep space brought the nation up short. Suddenly, to be prospace was fashionable.

Senator Winthrop's sixth term in office was marred by a change in power. A Republican-Libertarian coalition took over the majority party representation in the Senate, and Winthrop was relegated to the minority seat on the Appropriations Committee. The first action of the new chairman was to call for testimony from the newly appointed administrator of the Greater National Aeronautics and Space Administration, the Honorable Perry Hopkins.

"I'm pleased to have you with us today as the new head of GNASA, Dr. Hopkins," said Senator Rockwell. "I know we're all concerned about our brave crew of astronauts who are approaching Barnard, ready to stop. Now, in the past, this committee, under the leadership of our distinguished minority head"—here Senator Rockwell turned to nod at Senator Winthrop down near the end of the table—"found it expedient for the sake of the small farmers of this nation to defer certain items of expenditure for the space program. We realize that this may have caused you some problems in the past and we want you to know that the time has come for the space program to receive all the resources that it needs to carry out its mission.

"Tell us—what do you need to rectify the tragic consequences of that unfortunate accident so as to bring this great nation's crew of astronauts to a successful conclusion of their epic space voyage?"

Perry had been expecting something like this, and he appreciated the excessive verbiage that Senator Rockwell was spouting. He needed the time to keep his proverbial temper under control. It was just three weeks since his confirmation by the Senate and now his doctor was telling him that those pains in his stomach were ulcers. Gahd! What a job! He finished chewing a Gelusil tablet, took a sip of water from the glass sitting in front of him, and started to answer.

"I wish I could tell you, Senator Rockwell," he stated, "but I'm afraid I can't. And I can't because there *is* no answer. The previous GNASA administrators have reported to this committee an *infinite* number of times that more work needed to be done on the Barnard transmitter lens to keep it on schedule. But *that* . . . [careful now, Perry, calm down] . . . *the* previous chairman always felt that only the minimum needed to be done each year and the rest could be postponed until some future date. Well, gentlemen, as a result of losing a big chunk of the transmitter lens, that date was a year ago."

"Do you mean to tell me that there is no way to allow our brave astronauts to come to a safe landing at their destination?" said Senator Rockwell.

"I don't mean to be melodramatic, Mr. Chairman. And I have exercised my staff for alternatives, but unless someone comes up with a miracle, that crew is as good as *dead*."

"But surely with a crash effort . . ."

"There are only so many robots in space, and due to the low demand for space robots, there is only one space robot factory," said Perry. "Even if we could speed up the production line by five times, and even if we had some magical way to transport those robots instantly over the millions of kilometers to the transmitter lens and put them all to work, there isn't enough web and plastic in the solar system to make up for twenty years of neglect. At best, we could get the tear in the lens repaired and get the diameter up to sixty percent of that needed. Even if the lasers were up to power, that would only suffice to strand the crew some two lightyears beyond Barnard, with no hope of getting back. I'm sorry to bring you such bad news, gentlemen, but it's the best I have!"

Anita heard Perry coming down the hall. Above the chirping and harping of the minicamers she could hear the clump of his boot heels sinking deep into the aging vinyl tile that floored the dingy halls of GNASA headquarters.

Anita got up to rescue Perry from the reporters. She stood in the doorway to Perry's office, glared the reporters back, then slipped through the door and locked it behind her. Perry was stomping up and down behind his desk, cursing under his breath and popping Gelusil tablets into his mouth one after the other. "Gahd!! Why'd I ever take this fucking job!" He paced some more. "There must be some way to save that crew!!"

Anita knew that Perry was the person to revitalize the moribund GNASA organization. If she could only get him away from his Washington office.

"Perhaps if you went out to the various centers and talked to the engineers you would pick up some ideas," she said. "They may sound far out to the engineer who thought of them since they're conditioned to the usual starvation GNASA budget, but *you* know you've got a blank check from Congress; it's just that you can't predate it a year."

Perry stopped pacing. He was no dummy. He had been Anita's boss for all of three weeks.

"When do you have my plane leaving?" he asked.

She smiled and gave him a wink—he was going to be a good boss. "Your jet is at National Airport, ready to go." She reached into his In box and pulled out a sheet of paper.

"You have an appointment tomorrow morning at GNASA/Lewis in Cincinnati, then you go down to Huntsville on Friday. Saturday it's back to Dulles for a week-end with Mary. Don't forget it's your wedding anniversary on Saturday. Then Sunday evening you're back in the jet for the West Coast. JPL, GNASA/Ames, and the High Power Laser Center in Chino. You're to spend two days there since this is primarily a laser problem . . ."

"I'll be . . ." said Perry. He took the list, stuffed it into his briefcase, put on his overcoat and scarf, then stomped down the long corridor to the elevator and the soggy cold February Washington weather outside.

It was the first visit of the new administrator of GNASA to the centers. Instead of spending his time with the brass, Perry insisted that he be allowed to talk to the engineers. In some of the larger centers that took two shifts in the main auditorium. When he delivered his message that the space program was on the move again, morale soared. There was still some hesitancy to suggest new ideas, however, and Perry found himself dragging them out during his walk-around tours. There were many good ideas around that had been festering in the innovative brains of these stifled engineers.

One amazing one was an idea for building a tower into space using a rapid-firing gun at the bottom of the tower, shooting superconducting pellets to a turnaround magnet at the top. It seemed ridiculous, but the numbers said it would work. What they needed right now, however, was a tower to the stars.

Perry picked up some ideas for increasing the speed of construction of the large lens structure, but they still couldn't overcome the lack of materials. He was stuck. The power available from the lasers at the Mercury Center was fixed. The laser wavelength was fixed. The distance to Barnard was fixed. The time for turn-on of the lasers was fixed. The only thing he could control was the size of the transmitter lens and he didn't have the time or materials to make it big enough.

Perry was visiting one of the little side-labs in GNASA/ Chino in his walk-around with the director, Dr. Cheryl

Billingate. The young man in charge of the lab was Dr. Mike Handler. Dr. Handler's face had a trim brown beard and an evangelical look as he expounded on the esoteric subject of his research. Perry was impressed with the demonstration. Handler used a medium-power laser in a complex mirror arrangement to levitate a cloud of clear crystal microscopic beads inside a vacuum chamber. Once he had the beads levitated, he took away the mirrors and the beads shifted slightly in position, but stayed levitated.

"It's a new way of making large optical structures," said Dr. Handler with fervor. "The interaction of the light with the beads organizes the array of beads, which in turn structures the beam of light that forms them. Kilogram for kilogram, these are the lightest-mass optical structures ever constructed."

Perry began to feel that perhaps this trip was not in vain. One of his problems was that there wasn't enough material to make the transmitter lens.

"What's the material," he asked. "Is there lots of it?"

"Just glass, with the proper chemical dopants to produce the desired absorption lines."

"How big can you make a lens?" asked Perry.

"If you're thinking of replacing the Barnard transmitter lens I'm afraid it won't work. There's not enough laser power to keep the lens organized, even in free fall."

"Fart!" exploded Perry, his hopes dashed. There was a shocked silence, which Perry didn't seem to notice.

"Why don't you show him the tripling experiment, Mike," said Cheryl, trying to cover the awkward moment.

"Sure," said Dr. Handler nervously. He flicked an asbestos screen in front of the high-power laser beam for a moment. With its support gone, the bead lens dissolved into a pile of sand at the bottom of the vacuum chamber. He took another vial of beads from a rack, poured them into a hole in the top of the vacuum chamber, and sealed the hole. He readjusted his "priming" mirrors, then pressed a button. A stream of tiny beads shot out into the invisible beam of high-intensity infrared radiation and quickly formed into a thick, lens-shaped structure. As the density of the lens increased, Perry noticed a green tinge forming. Cheryl reached over and turned off the room lights. In the vacuum chamber was a greenly glowing lens of beads. The back side of the lens was almost invisible, but by the time the light had passed through the lens it had changed from an invisible infrared color into a brilliant blue-green. The scattered light from the intense beam illuminated the room with its weird laser-light that gave everyone a green-speckled appearance like ghosts captured on a piece of grainy film.

"The material in those beads is nonlinear," said Dr. Handler. "At the intensities that we're running, the non-linearity is driven so hard that nearly all the incoming infrared light is turned into green light. Of course we must conserve energy and momentum. For each three infrared photons going in, we only get one green photon coming out. But since the energy of the green photon is three times that of the infrared photon, the energy per photon is tripled."

"Do you mean that cloud of beads is cutting the wavelength of the laser light by one-third?" asked Perry.

"Exactly one-third," said Dr. Handler. He was slightly puzzled by the administrator's enthusiasm over what he considered a side-show trick. He wouldn't have done the demonstration if Cheryl hadn't asked for it.

Like a good administrator, Perry waited to see if one of the scientists would pick up on the significance of his question. They didn't.

"If a laser beam has its wavelength cut by one third, then a lens of a given size can sent it three times as far," said Perry. He waited. Nothing.

Hell. He would take the credit. He turned to Cheryl

and spoke at the black-lipped, green-powdered mask surrounded by green-blond hair.

"I want your people to do a systems study for me, Dr. Billingate. Please tell me the cost and time to deliver of a frequency-tripling bead array to place in the output of the laser-beam combiner at Mercury Center. If you people can repackage those infrared photons into shorter-wavelength bundles, then the Barnard transmitter lens is big enough as it is."

As he was talking, Cheryl was thinking. "Your idea should work, Dr. Hopkins. My initial estimate is six months plus travel time to Mercury, but it will probably cost over two hundred million dollars. Not counting the transportation costs," she added hastily.

"My dear Cheryl," said Perry, feeling expansive and free again from tummy pains. "You've been an administrator in GNASA much too long. I'm sure you can boost that two hundred million dollars higher if you really try. Believe me. We have a blank check. Let's not write too small a number on it."

Sand is cheap, even when re-formed into microscopic perfect spheres lightly loaded with an expensive chemical. The few tons needed were shipped within five months, and even with transportation costs Perry had a hard time getting the bill up over five hundred million. He made a lot of friends in Congress for that one.

Meanwhile, Dr. Handler had worked out a lens "growing" technique. Once at Mercury, he set up his lens-forming mirrors and used them to construct a lens only ten centimeters in diameter. He had the Mercury Center engineers then slowly widen their infrared beam while he controlled the electrostatic jet that added beads to the lens. It was slow, painstaking work, but within three days they had a sheet of beads a meter thick and 3500 meters across. Into one side poured 1500 terawatts of 1.5 micron infrared light, and from the other side emerged

1499.9 terawatts of half-micron blue-green light. The beads grew warm as each radiated away its minute fraction of the 100 megawatts of power lost as heat in the tripling process.

For two years the Mercury Center laser system captured sunlight as it streamed by Mercury and turned it into a blue-green column of power that flashed across the solar system. On the way to the transmitter lens it focused down to a ten-meter waist of raw energy. Any stray asteroid that attempted to cross that invisible maw of power would have been vaporized. The blue-green photons sped on, marching together in perfect step. Their ranks relaxed as the kilometers passed, but they were still in perfect formation a half hour later when they hit the partially tattered, partially repaired inner portions of the Barnard transmitter lens.

Half of the photons went through the empty portions of the spiderweb unimpeded. The others had to fight their way through three crest-lengths of clinging, cloying atoms of pliant plastic, that willingly absorbed, fervently held, then reluctantly released the disciplined blue-green troops. The emerging horde took up step again with their brethren that had not been to the R and R camp, and many a tale was passed back and forth during the next six years as they marched steadily outward to the stars, their column straight and true as that of a Roman Legion's.

Stopping

"Laser beam contact!" James announced to General Jones, its normally soothing baritone taking an imperative edge.

"Wha?" murmured Jinjur, her eyes glued to a video screen displaying an old John Wayne battle movie. Deep within her mind she sensed a martinet screaming at her, "Wake up, you dummy! You're in charge!" She shook her head. . . . This was no way for a mission commander to act. She floated clumsily across the control deck to pull herself into the central command seat.

"Report ship status, James!" she rasped in a weak imitation of her parade voice.

James spoke through her hair imp. "I detect low-energy laser beams from earth. It is time to stop. I quit putting No-Die in your water a month ago. It is now time for the rest of the crew to be taken off." There was a slight pause as the friendly voice of the computer took on a formal note. "As commander, you have the authority to countermand this prearranged plan, but you will have to elucidate your objections in detail."

Jinjur blinked at the confusing words as James dropped

back into his normal voice, "But you *do* want me to stop the drug, don't you, Jinjur?"

"Yes! Yes! Do it! Flush out the tanks, get rid of that stuff! I want to be me again!"

"Take it easy, Jinjur," said James. "I'll do it right away. It will take a few months, however, before everyone recovers completely. I'll be looking forward to it. It sure has been dull playing nursemaid to a bunch of ageless imbeciles."

Jinjur, knowing that the computer had everything under control, let her stupefied brain relax and floated slowly back to watch the Marines on the screen storm up the beach for the thousandth time.

Three months later the crew was back to normal. The precursor laser beam from earth had been getting stronger as Mercury Center tuned up the transmitter system. Full power would come in about ten days and they needed to be ready. A few strayed from their work stations to peer down the earthside science dome in fascination at the orange speck of light glowing like a bright jewel in the belt of Orion.

"I'm almost glad there was trouble with the transmitter lens," said David, trying to absorb every nuance of the scene with his artist's eye. "It always bothered me that we could never see the laser beam that was pushing us because it was in the infrared."

"Don't you wish we weren't moving so fast, so the jewel would look like an emerald instead of a topaz?" said Karin, her arm resting against his shoulder as they both looked down through the dome. The precursor beam was not very strong, but it did give a perceptible acceleration to the sail and the crew started to readjust from decades of living in free fall.

"It'll change," said David. "We're moving at twenty percent of light now, so the blue-green laser frequency is red-shifted by eighteen percent to orange, but as we come to a stop at Barnard, it'll move back to green."

"Like modern alchemists," mused Karin. "Transmuting topazes to emeralds."

"Just a wave of the magic relativity wand."

They heard noises at the air lock and turned to look. The Christmas Bush was getting ready to go out. James opened the inner airlock door, and the bush seemed to drop all its needles as it came apart. The major trunk and limbs stayed in one piece, but 1080 of the 1296 twig-sized clusters on the bush detached themselves and swarmed into the lock, each one about two centimeters across. James pumped the lock down, then opened the outer door. The twigs swarmed out across the hull to the shrouds that stretched out to connect the central payload with the sail that stretched its silvery sheen past any horizon the human eye could see. Like mechanical mice climbing a ship's hawser, the twigs marched in single file, splitting their forces each time they came to a branching in the shroud pattern. The twigs moved rapidly, but they had three hundred kilometers to go and would not reach their posts for nearly a day.

Jinjur was at her console on the command deck, monitoring the loading of a copy of James's memory into a computer stationed out on the outer rim of the sail. It was one of three redundant units spaced around the rim that had stayed dormant during the trip out. The computers were not as powerful as James, but were complex enough to be semi-intelligent and had been given names.

It was the job of Snip, Snap, and Snurr to run the deceleration stage of the interstellar sailship. They were now only a quarter of a lightyear from Barnard and it was time to stop. To do that, the sail would be divided into two pieces, a circular inner portion three hundred kilometers in diameter that supported the main spacecraft and the crew, and an outer, ring-shaped portion that was a silvery doughnut one thousand kilometers in diameter with a three-hundred-kilometer hole.

On the way out, the whole thousand-kilometer sail worked as a single unit and was driven by the light pressure from the launching laser. The deceleration phase was trickier, however, and would require all the brain-power of Snip, Snap, and Snurr if the humans were to be brought safely to a stop at Barnard. The outer ring sail had to be reconfigured to be a concave mirror. Its purpose was to reflect the beam of laser light coming from Mercury Center back the other way and focus it on the payload sail to slow it down.

One-third the way out on the sail, 1080 mechanical tarantulas waited for their light-beam orders. A pulse of laser light from the remains of the Christmas Bush standing up in the starside science dome sent a coded signal out to each one of them, and the tarantulas started walking, snipping the weak links between the inner and outer sail. The spiders had to travel almost two kilometers, snipping as they went, while always making sure they stayed on the inner portion of the sail. It was about an hour before they finished. The spider imps then started their day-long journey back across the three-hundred-kilometer sail and down the shrouds to re-attach themselves once again onto the Christmas Bush.

The orange precursor beam became stronger. The outer ring sail accelerated under the light pressure, while the inner sail, with its heavy payload section, accelerated more slowly. As soon as the two portions of sail had drifted a few thousand kilometers apart, Jinjur took command and started to turn the central sail around. She was accustomed to the lightweight Marine intercep-tors, however, and soon got bored with the slow response of the huge sail with its ponderous payload. After six hours she turned the ship over to James.

James waited patiently as the hours passed and the sail continued to turn. As soon as there was some optical leverage, James sent a command to the triplets and a multitude of actuators twisted the distant ring sail into a curved lens that captured the square kilometers of laser light coming from the solar system and focused it down on the leading edge of the central sail. The concentrated light poured onto one side of the sail and accelerated its ponderous rotation. As the angle of the sail increased, Snip, Snap, and Snurr readjusted their mirror and spread the light more uniformly, still keeping up the rotation. As the central sail was almost halfway around, the ring sail readjusted again, and started to bring the rotation to a halt. The teamwork of the four computers was perfect. The rotation stopped at the same instant the central sail was exactly 180 degrees around. The central sail now had its back to the light coming from the solar system while it faced the focused energy coming from the ring sail. Since the ring had ten times the surface area of the central sail, there was ten times more light pressure coming from the ring sail than from the solar system. The acceleration on the humans built up again, stronger than before, but now it was a deceleration that would ultimately bring them to a stop at Barnard.

"This is terrible," said Richard as he stomped heavily about the lounge. He almost dropped his squeezer as he collapsed into a chair and stuck there. He looked with annoyance at Sam, who had found some old Scotch bottles in his room and was now practicing pouring water from one to the other.

"The deceleration is only ten percent of earth gravity, Richard," said Sam. "It is what we expect on the moons about Gargantua. Think of it as practice."

"You can have it," said Richard. "I'll stay here on *Prometheus* and let you do down."

As the days passed, the tenth-gee acceleration built up an appreciable velocity difference between the slowly decelerating central sail with its heavy payload and the ring sail shrinking in the distance. After a few months even the human eye started to notice the difference in colors impinging on the lightship. Toward Barnard, the brilliant beam from the tiny doughnut of a ring sail slowly changed from orange to red, while from the other side, the direct beam from the earth began to take on a definite yellow tinge. After a year the beam from earth had shifted color from topaz through amber to emerald, while the ring-sail beam had darkened to a red so deep that only some of the crew could see it. They were now within lightmonths of Barnard and the crew took out telescopes, particle counters, and other sensors and began collecting the scientific data that was the primary reason they had been sent on the long journey. They soon were all busy looking out the rechristened Barnard-side science dome.

The astrophysicists, Linda and Caroline, formed a team to study the small deep red sun they were approaching. The aerodynamicists, George and Arielle, concentrated on the supergiant planet Gargantua, while the planet-ologists, Sam, Richard, and Elizabeth scanned its retinue of moons. With the help of Carmen's radar, Thomas tried to pin down the orbital dynamics of all the bodies in the system, especially the motions of that strange double-planet, Rocheworld.

As they were passing through the outer asteroid belt beyond Gargantua, the science activities took more and more of their time. It was only David who occasionally made himself travel to the starside science dome to look in awe at the brilliant aquamarine jewel studding Orion's belt.

After twenty months of work, most of the long-range science had been done, and the precious information sent on its long journey back to earth. The crew relaxed and spent a lot more time in leisure activities.

Since they were no longer on shifts, they took to gathering together at dinnertime. One evening, David waited for a pause in the conversation and made a quiet announcement.

"Arielle and I have been working on a surprise for you," he said. "We felt that our joy over our arrival at a new world needed some outlet different than producing another batch of scientific data. So we came up with a little show," he said. "Our problem is that we need some practice time. Could we prevail on all of you to stay inside your rooms after dinner for the next three sleep periods and not peek out?"

Red leaned over to George and whispered, "Is eight hours too long to stay trapped in my room?"

"Not long enough," George answered. Red and George handed their trays to the galley imp and joined the rest of the crew on the lift platform that would take them to their rooms.

The next morning George noticed that the large private sonovideo console and screen that had been in David's room was now installed against the theater walls on the living area deck. Since the console was there anyway, that evening after dinner David played them one of his newest creations. George watched Arielle out of the corner of his eye. Her body was swaying slowly to and fro as the sound and sight possessed her. George knew how she was feeling, for the music and video brought back memories of the first time *he* had soloed, the exhilarating feel of being high in the sky, soaring like a bird. The music glided softly to an end.

"That one is titled *Dragonfly*," said David. "Now if you please? Arielle and I have a lot of practicing to do tonight."

Two days later, David announced that he and Arielle were ready and the show would begin right after dinner.

David had joined them at dinner and ate sparingly, while Arielle stayed in her room. George noticed that the galley imp didn't clean their trays after dinner, but stacked them up and scampered off. He looked at the ceilings and walls—not a housekeeping spider in sight. James and the entire Christmas Bush must be involved in the show. The lift platform came quietly down through the ceiling and stopped at floor level.

"I'd like all of you to come and arrange yourself in a circle on the lift platform," said David. "You'll want to sit so that you can see into the lounge and exercise room, and up into the lift shaft."

David turned to his console and checked all the settings. There was a touch screen and special keyboard for the music and another set for the color video display. In addition, there was a third touch screen that was obviously a recent addition to David's normal console.

"Our offering tonight is called *Flight*," said David simply. He turned to the console, flexed his long fingers, and nodded. The lights throughout the spacecraft went out. George looked down through the hole in the platform and noticed that even the Barnardside dome had been darkened. The only light in the room came from the soft twinkling of the personal imps. The men were all wearing their imps on their shoulders and couldn't be told apart, but he could recognize the women, like Jinjur with her comb imp and Karin with the crescent moon on the left side of her head. There was a scurrying in the darkness and down the lift shaft came a number of minibushes, each about the size of a personal imp. Two went to each person, climbed up on their shoulders and formed cups about each ear, making a nearly perfect set of stereo earphones.

The prelude started. Light and airy at first, it moved on to other themes, one of which George recognized as being the theme from *Dragonfly*. He wanted to close his eyes and listen to the music, but David's colorful magic on the video display hypnotized him.

The visual hold of the screen faded as the prelude came to an end. There was a slight noise from the top of the lift shaft and George looked up. At the far end of the sixty-meter tube was a faint white light. The music started, soft and tinkling. The white light came down the shaft . . . and finally George recognized what it was. It was Tinker Bell, the fairy from *Peter Pan*.

Arielle was almost nude. The only covering for her body was a tiny, glowing-white triangular patch of Christmas Bush over her pubic area and two tiny five-pointed white stars riding on top of her small conical breasts. Her hair was ablaze with a cap of a thousand white lights that framed her sparkling dark eyes. Attached to her shoulders were a pair of fairy wings with ribs made of Christmas Bush that held between them a gossamer membrane of clear plastic. On her feet were glowing-white slippers with Mercury wings.

She circled slowly down the shaft, her wings a blur as they supported her in the weak gravity. She held a wand in her right hand, and from the glowing three-dimensional star in the tip there fell sparks, tiny mosquito imps that trailed behind, then sputtered out. George was entranced by the motions of the supple naked body. It was the most beautiful thing that he had ever seen, sexy but not sensuous.

Tinker Bell visited each person in turn, tapping each on the head with her magic wand. Then she did a little dance in the lounge and ended by landing on the top of David's console just as the music stopped.

The lights on the pieces of bush covering Arielle went out. David's video screen went black. Even their personal imps dimmed.

Suddenly in place of the fairy was a snowy-white dove. Arielle was now completely covered with a feathery net of glittering white. Her arms were covered with branches that turned the arms into wings and her lower legs and feet were turned into a tail. The dove flew around the room to the swooping music. Then, fluttering over their heads, it flew up the lift shaft, doing midair tumbles and acrobatics.

Like the tumbler pigeons I used to have when I was a kid, thought George. The white bird climbed higher and higher in the shaft while the soft music drew out to its soft climax.

The lights went out again, and the music shifted to a slow majestic theme. The lower science dome became transparent and Barnard sent a red beam of light up the center of the lift shaft. George looked up to see that the four-meter-diameter shaft was now filled with a slowly rotating parasol carrying a long cylindrical body covered with tiny lights. It was *Prometheus* coming to a stop at Barnard. Slowly the twirling sail dropped downward in the beam of light, the air trapped in the shaft playing the part of the photon pressure that the real sail used.

As the miniature *Prometheus* cleared the ceiling of the living area deck, Arielle pulled her arms down from over her head and spread them out to her sides, pulling the bush sail apart as she did so. Before their eyes the bush rearranged itself about her body and turned her into a miniature version of the *Dragonfly* aerospace plane, complete with lift fans that kept her levitated and a ducted fan behind her feet that pushed her forward. To the strains of the *Dragonfly* theme, she soared through the close confines of the lounge and exercise room, her long wings nearly touching the floor and ceiling during her banking turns. The miniature airplane flew back over their heads, then spiraled slowly up the lift shaft.

No wonder she's such a great pilot, thought George. She doesn't 'fly' a plane, she 'is' the plane.

The slow ascending spiral of the music faded and the lights came on. There was a long silence, then the room burst into applause. David stood up at the console, bowed once, then waited patiently for the applause to cease. There were cries of "Encore" and "Arielle! Arielle!" but David waved them to silence.

"We decided before the show that there would be no curtain calls and no encores," said David. "It would destroy the magic of the moment. Besides, even with the Christmas Bush helping, flying is hard work and she couldn't do an encore. Arielle is up in her room changing, but I'm sure she'll be down soon for something to eat."

There was a clatter from the dining room. The galley imp had returned and was setting out three large trays of food. There was a hiss of a room door opening and a voice echoed down the lift shaft.

"Mm! Smell good!!"

Arielle, wearing an oversized shapeless sweat suit, dove down the lift shaft ladder and made her way to the dining room, waving aside the compliments in her eagerness to get to the food.

First she swallowed a large glass of water—she liked hers carbonated—then asked for another.

"Flying make me thirsty," she said as she picked up a finger chunk of Chicken Little, dunked it into James's secret sauce, and popped it in her mouth.

"That was marvelous, Arielle!" exclaimed Karin. "Do you think I could learn to fly like that?"

"Sorry," said Arielle, starting on a dish of French fried zucchini sticks and reaching for the next glass of water. "You too big." She munched another zucchini and swallowed loudly. "You'd be like airplane with too many cargoes and not big enough wings."

She looked over the remains of the three trays, found a cold zucchini stick in back of a plate and finished it off. She turned to her still-admiring audience, stretched unselfconsciously, and yawned.

"I am tired. The show is hard work. You like?" she asked. There was a chorus of approval from the rest of the crew as she beamed with pleasure. "I go to bed now," she said. She walked across the room to where David was closing down his console.

"You work hard, David," she said. She took his glasses off his nose and started stroking his forehead.

"Maybe it time for you to go to bed too?" she asked, looking at him. She took his hand and he let her lead him to the lift-shaft platform. Together they rode it up through the ceiling. Every man left in the lounge was conscious that the sound they heard was that of *one* room door opening and closing.

A few months later, the time came to turn off the laser beam. The central sail had been slowed until it was firmly in the gravitational grasp of the dull red star, while the ring sail carrying the abandoned semi-intelligent orphans, Snip, Snap, and Snurr, faded into invisibility among the sprinkle of stars in the heavens. The whole crew was watching out the starside science dome as the time came. The blue-green aquamarine flickered, then guttered slowly into oblivion, leaving a faint yellow-white star in its place. They had arrived at Barnard's Star, their home for the rest of their lives.

With the laser power off, *Prometheus* had to make do with the weak red photons from Barnard. Although not powerful enough to have slowed the lightsail in its headlong relativistic flight, the light pressure was enough to swing the sail into a looping orbit that took *Prometheus* on a journey past the planets in the system. By using the light from Barnard to add to their orbital speed, Jinjur and James could travel away from the star to the outer portions of the system, while tilting the sail the other way would slow their speed in orbit and allow *Prometheus* to drop in closer to the sun.

Tacking carefully, *Prometheus* rendezvoused with Gargantua and allowed itself to be captured in a trajectory that would take them past all of the moons in this miniature solar system. The eight larger moons of Gargantua had been detected by the flyby probe some fifty-three years ago and had been given proper names beginning with Z. In order of size they were Zapotec, Zouave, Zulu, Zuni, Zion, Zen, Zodiac, and Zeus.

After the crew of *Prometheus* arrived, they found many smaller moonlets. According to the prearranged plan, these were to be treated in the same manner as the smaller asteroids in the solar system and given a Z number in order of discovery as soon as the complete orbital parameters of the moonlet had been calculated. The crew couldn't resist giving some of the more interesting ones Z names, however, and soon there were moons named Zinc, Zygot, and even Zipcode.

"What's our first stop, Sam?" asked Jinjur, as she started her work shift and sat down in the central command post that Jesús had just vacated.

"That would be Zapotec," said Sam. "Except for the smaller moons like Zeus, it is the farthest out and we will reach it first in the inward portion of our flyby orbit. Zapotec is the largest of the moons of Gargantua. It is bigger than Mercury and has a thin atmosphere like that of Mars. I have some recommendations for the initial exploration probes for Zapotec."

"None for Zeus?" asked Jinjur.

"Later," said Sam. "On our first pass we should only expend a few orbiters and landers on each of the larger moons to complement our remote sensing survey. Later, after visiting the rest of the planetary system, we will return with probes educated to extract the maximum amount of scientific information out of each moon."

"What gets dropped off here?" she asked.

"Since Zapotec is like Mars, we know what to expect in the way of dangers. I recommend using three probes on this one. Richard is ecstatic over the volcanic chain ringing the south pole, and the equatorial rift valley that goes two hundred degrees around the planet. The rift valley is fifteen kilometers deep. We should be able to examine an excellent cross-section of the crust using a tether-connected dual crawler."

"I didn't know a creepy-crawler could climb cliffs," she said.

"It can't," said Sam. "But for this moon we will replace the standard one-kilometer tether between the two crawlers with a fifteen-kilometer one. Then instead of just rescuing each other from craters, cliffs, and oceans, one crawler can lower the other over the cliff to take samples as it descends."

"Sounds fine," said Jinjur. "What else besides the obligatory orbiter?"

"An airplane," said Sam.

"Zapotec has no atmosphere," protested Jinjur. "You can't fly an airplane in a vacuum."

"I admit the air on Zapotec is thin by earth standards, but it is ten percent thicker than the atmosphere of Mars. We will send an unmanned probe that's a modified version of the Dragonfly airplane. It has a huge wingspan and a light payload. With its VTOL jets it can land vertically, take up samples, then take off and fly a thousand kilometers to a new spot."

Sam went to the bottom of the lift shaft. Instead of pushing himself upward in the low gravity, he asked his imp to call for the elevator. The doughnut-shaped platform swooped down from its parking spot in the starside science dome. Jinjur and Sam waited until the elevator came to a halt. They were joined by Richard and Karin and the four stepped on the carpeted upper surface to be lifted back upshaft until they came to a painted number 42 on the shaft wall.

"An orbiter with two aeroshells," said Sam to Karin.

Karin scanned around the wall at the four doors and palmed one open. Tucked in a triangle-shaped room between the cylindrical shaft and the cylindrical bodies of the huge surface-lander rockets was a spacecraft. A portion of the Christmas Bush was crawling over its surface, checking it out. Karin reached in and slowly extracted the half-ton spacecraft. Its inertia was evident from the strain in her muscles. Richard stepped across the doughnut to help.

"I've got it just fine, big boy," said Karin. "Thanks anyway."

"Is the orbiter ready to go, James?" Jinjur asked her imp.

"I'm in perfect condition and ready for my mission to Zapotec," replied Jinjur's imp in a strange computer voice with a sibilant overtone. It was the orbiter speaking.

"I didn't realize you could hear us," said Jinjur, apologizing to the orbiter, "I'm sorry . . . ahhh . . ."

"*Carl*," said the orbiter. "I have no mechanisms for hearing, or speaking for that matter, but James has me hooked up through your imps. Any last instructions?"

The lift headed starside as Sam talked to *Carl*.

". . . start in an equatorial orbit, drop the airplane and creepy-crawler near the big equatorial rift valley, and stay with them until they are finished. Then switch to a polar orbit while they head south and explore the volcanoes. We'll be back in a few years to take up where you left off."

"Don't rush," said *Carl*. "The more time my processor has to correlate images, the better will be the final batch of processed information."

They reached the top deck, and Karin and Richard pushed the orbiter into the middle of the Christmas Bush's workroom. The bush was busy weaving cloth using a bright green artificial thread that it had reconstituted from the lint fibers it had collected over the past four decades.

"Do you need any help?" asked the bush.

"No thanks, James," said Karin. "As long as you send a few imps down to unlatch the fasteners on a thin-atmosphere airplane and a creepy-crawler, we can do just fine. Besides, it's important you finish that shirt for

Red. Her old one is getting kind of threadbare, and our eagle-eyed friend here is getting a bad case of googly-eyes."

Richard snorted and headed back to the central shaft. The lift took them down to get the airplane at level 33. Wrapped up in its protective aeroshell, the airplane looked like a clam. The aeroshell was three meters in diameter, but quite light for its size. They had to stand it on edge as they took it up to the workshop.

"It's hard to believe that has an airplane inside," said Jinjur.

"Let me open it up and give you a peek," said Karin. "I was involved in the design of the folding wings. We use the same principles in the wings of the Dragonfly planes." She popped a few fasteners and lifted the top of the clamshell.

"Hi, *Wilbur*," she said, peering down to look at the video scanner in the stubby nose of the airplane buried under fold after fold of wing. "Do I look different than you thought I would?"

"I had access to pictures of you taken through James's video cameras," said *Wilbur* through her imp, the computer voice deep and matter-of-fact. "But since my scanner is designed to work in Barnard's infrared illumination, you do indeed look different than I had expected. There seems to be a glow about you, especially in the chest section."

Karin slammed the lid shut while Richard roared.

"Let's go get the creepy-crawler," said Karin, heading for the lift. Soon they returned with *Pushmi-Pullyu*. The two crawlers were identical except that one had a reel on the front, while the other had a reel on the back. Between them ran a short length of high-strength line. When they entered the workshop area, the Christmas Bush detached two of its arms and left the arms to continue the weaving task. It disappeared into a storage

room and soon came back with a reel containing a
much longer length of thinner line.

"Will it hold?" queried Sam.

"It has a safety factor of only three instead of ten,"
said the bush.

Sam thought for a second, then nodded approval.

With the help of the bush and Richard, Karin assembled the orbiter and its two probes, then she and Richard suited up and took the spacecraft through the upper
cargo air lock. They pushed it through a hole in the
still-accelerating lightsail and watched it drop toward
the distant cousin of Mars.

"Good-bye, *Carl*," said Karin. "Take good care of *Wilbur*
and the *Pushmi-Pullyu*."

"I will, Dr. Krupp," said *Carl*. Karin could almost
hear a sibilant toothiness in the happy smile of *Carl's*
voice as the orbiter gave a short burn of its rocket and
headed off to carry out the job that it had been designed
and trained to do.

Now that they were in the gravitational pull of
Gargantua, Jinjur tilted her sail for maximum deceleration. *Prometheus* dropped inward at a faster rate in an
elliptical orbit that would take them past the other
planets in the system. They passed by Zen and Zion,
two tiny planetoids with orbits inside Zapotec, then
dived in farther to catch the innermost of the larger
moons, Zulu.

As *Prometheus* approached Zulu in its elliptical dive
into the gravity well of Gargantua, the resolution from
their telescopes rapidly became better than the quick
snapshots that had been made by the Barnard probe
when it had sped through the system. Jinjur got up from
her command console at the center of the control deck
and wandered over to stand in back of Sam to look over
his shoulder at the science screen. There were two pictures of Zulu on the screen, an old one from the probe

and a new one fresh from the optical telescope in the science dome on starside. Jinjur stood up on tiptoes in her corridor boots, the weak acceleration making it easy to stay on point, and peered past Sam's imp at the screen. The imp, noticing her presence, scurried around to the other shoulder. Sam, feeling the motion of his imp, glanced around into curious brown eyes peering over his bony shoulder. He nodded, then turned back to the screen.

"There have been few changes in the past fifty years," said Sam. "Zulu is like Ganymede. Its surface is a thick layer of striated ice over a deep ocean. Unlike Ganymede, however, Zulu is as active as Io."

"Volcanoes on a water planet?" said Jinjur.

"Not lava volcanoes, but water geysers," said Sam. "There are hot spots all over the planet where streams of steam and hot water shoot tens of kilometers up into the atmosphere. Here, let me superimpose an infrared map."

A false-color infrared image appeared on the screen, showing a sphere of deep blue with red, yellow, and white spots on it.

"The yellow and white regions are the hottest points. They indicate the peaks of underwater volcanoes. Let's watch this spot, it was yellow a few minutes ago. Now it's white." Sam's finger pointed to the screen and his other hand turned off the infrared overlay to leave the optical image on the screen. Slowly, at a point just above his finger there grew a small circle. It became larger and fatter until it was a brilliant white doughnut.

"Wow!" said Jinjur. "That was a big one."

Sam read off the numbers on the side of the screen as a computer-generated cursor ring tracked the outer edge of the doughnut.

"Fifty kilometers in diameter and still growing," said Sam. "They go out to two hundred kilometers. The fly-by probe caught one of these eruptions when it went by, so they have been going on for at least fifty years."

"Where does all the heat come from?" asked Jinjur.

"Zulu has a thick rocky core. The core supplies heat from the decay of radioactive elements, like in the earth's core. In addition, there is tidal heating from Zouave and Zuni rocking the core about its normal, tidally locked orientation toward Gargantua. The core is very likely molten iron at the center and there is convection going on, because we have already started to pick up evidence of a magnetic field one hundred times stronger than the magnetic field of earth."

"Have you decided on the probes?" she asked.

"Yes," said Sam. "An orbiter and two amphibious landers with chemical analyzers. But instead of sending the orbiter directly to Zulu, I want to have it spiral inward slowly."

Sam got up from the console and walked to the lift shaft. Karin saw him call the elevator and joined Sam and Jinjur as the elevator took them up the shaft to level 34. Karin popped the panel and together they pulled an orbiter from the wall. The orbiter had two aeroshells, and as Sam talked to the robot, Karin jumped up a few more levels and handed down two identical landers that looked like miniature amphibious tanks, with a boatlike enclosed hull and a tread system that would act as tracks on ice and as paddle wheels in water. The landers had numbers, but someone had painted names in bright blue script on their sides: SPLISH and SPLASH.

"Now, *Jacques*," said Sam. "I want you to take your time orbiting in. Zulu is losing water at a high rate because of the steam it's making and its low gravity. I suspect that the water molecules that escape from the gravity of Zulu don't have the energy to escape from the gravity of Gargantua. They will stay in a torus centered at Zulu's orbit. If that is the case, Zulu will pick up the molecules again in another orbit. I would like a profile of the water density of that torus before you settle down to explore Zulu."

The imp on Sam's shoulder spoke in a strange nasal accent as James transmitted the orbiter's response.

"I will establish an orbit tilted to the orbit of Zulu. After some cycles I will have explored it not only radially, but out-of-plane," said *Jacques*.

After launching *Jacques*, they left Zulu behind and closed in on Zouave. It was bigger than Zulu, but the optical and infrared telescopes showed a featureless disk.

Richard was sitting at the science console, but instead of telescope images he had a copy of Carmen's radar console on his screen. Carmen had activated the X-band detectors spaced around the three-hundred-kilometer periphery of the sail, and she was sending burst after burst of high-power chirped radar pulses out the X-band transmitter on the main body of *Prometheus*. The short radio waves penetrated the clouds that obscured the surface of Zouave, then bounced back to the detectors. James took each of the detector responses, calculated the closure phase and amplitude, and synthesized a radar picture of the surface of the planet beneath the cloud layer.

"Looks pretty interesting," said Richard to Carmen through his imp. "In fact it seems to be all up and down, with no flat areas to indicate seas."

"The thermal microwave radiation from the surface indicates a temperature of a hundred and ten degrees absolute," said Carmen. "Looks like it's too balmy there for liquid nitrogen rain like we had back on Titan. Y'know, I never thought I would be saying this, but that orange ball of smog looks so much like Titan I'm beginning to feel homesick."

"It may be too hot for liquid nitrogen, but it sure's cold enough for regular ice and dry ice," said Richard. "Where's all the snow?"

"They're dielectrics at that temperature," said Carmen. "The radar goes right through them until it hits the rock underneath. Here, let me adjust the threshold level so we can pick up the weak reflection at the surface of the snow layer."

Richard watched his screen as the computer shifted bits of information. Suddenly the rugged terrain turned into a smoothly rolling landscape. "What's the pressure?" he asked.

"I estimate nearly three atmospheres," said James.

"Gee, we'll be able to work down there with just heat suits," said Richard.

"Over my dead body," said Jinjur. "Nobody is going no place under that pall of smog until we get a favorable report from a lander."

"I know that," said Richard. "I was just musing. I'm getting cramped living in this checker stack. I want to get out and stretch my legs."

"That'll come soon enough," said Jinjur. "What landers and orbiters shall we use?"

"No orbiter at all," said Richard. "Nothing to see but smog. And no lander in the usual sense. They'd probably get buried in snowdrifts."

"What then?" asked Jinjur.

"A couple of balloons. At that pressure level, they'll be able to carry a big payload." He and Karin took the elevator up the lift shaft and soon a rocket tug was on its way, hauling the aeroshells that would be released in the upper atmosphere of Zouave. Inside each aeroshell was a deflated high-pressure balloon and a sophisticated semi-intelligent payload. *Tweedledum* and *Tweedledee* would spend the next two years floating between the high cloud layer and the frozen surface below, landing occasionally when the winds were calm enough to take surface samples, then going on their way again when the winds rose. Slowly, the picture they collected in their leisurely motion across the surface of the planet would be built up into a map of Zouave in James's distant memory.

*   *   *

The lightship continued its climb up the elliptical orbit. It began to close in on the multicolored marble of Zuni. A little larger than the earth's moon, it shouldn't have been able to retain an atmosphere. But it did, and quite a spectacular one at that.

"It's like a miniature earth," said Thomas, watching the screen over Richard's shoulder.

"Carmen? What's the radiometric temperature?" Richard asked of his imp. A voice across the control deck echoed the imp's reply.

"A balmy forty degrees centigrade at the surface," said Carmen. "And those clouds down near the surface are water, not ice crystals."

"Must be tidal heating from Zouave," said Richard. "For sure Barnard and Gargantua aren't hot enough to keep it that warm."

"How come it still has air and water when our moon doesn't?" asked Thomas.

"Don't know," said Richard. "We'll ask Sam when he wakes up, but my guess is that like Zulu and Zouave, Zuni is losing air and water constantly, but most of it stays in orbit and is picked up again. In addition, I think Zuni is capturing the leakage of water from Zulu and smog from Zouave. The strange mixture of chemicals and water raining down from the sky is probably what makes the different colors that we see."

"Is there any chance that there's plant life down there?"

"That was my first thought when I saw those colored patches near the edges of the lakes, especially around the big lake in the southern hemisphere. Unfortunately, there's no sign of chlorophyll bands, but then chlorophyll wouldn't work well in the dim red light of Barnard. If there *is* any life, it might use some other mechanism to collect energy than photosynthesis. Lots of work for the landers to do."

"What kind of landers shall we use?" asked Jinjur, coming over.

"There are a lot of shallow lakes and there may be some interesting things to be found if you muck around on the bottom. I definitely want to send some submersible amphibious types, like *Burble* and *Bubble*. I was thinking about balloons too, but the pressure is only a half-atmosphere and they couldn't carry much. Besides, they'd probably get caught in one of those thunderstorms. I think I'll risk a flyer though. *Orville* can move fast enough to keep out of the way of the weather fronts or land in a sheltered valley and fold up its wings if it gets too rough." Richard got up from his console and headed for the lift shaft. "Could you get Karin for me, James?" he asked his imp. "I'm going to need help fitting an extra aeroshell on the orbiter spacecraft *Bruce*."

Thomas hadn't been out in a while, so Richard stayed inside while Karin and Thomas launched *Bruce*, *Bubble*, *Burble*, and *Orville* off on their exploration of Zuni. They could see the varicolored moon in the distance, and they both stood outside for a while after Bruce had shrunk into invisibility. They stared in awe at the shining blue lakes and the curl of a weather front that extended over the terminator to the dark side. Thomas cycled through the lock while Karin stayed outside to watch the lightning flashes on the dark side of the distant moon. Zuni was a prime candidate for a manned lander. They would be back.

Having taken a tour of the moons about Gargantua, Jinjur next set her sail for a close inspecion of the giant planet itself. For a month she and James used the weak light from Barnard to drop the orbit of *Prometheus* closer and closer to the gigantic planet.

Gargantua rotated only once a week, much more slowly than Jupiter. As a result, its weather patterns were not the multiplicity of spotted belts and zones as there were on Jupiter, but instead it had a multiplicity of gigantic cyclones that were spawned near the equator and careened their way into the higher latitudes, where they dissipated into storm fronts. Except for the size, they looked quite similar to the weather patterns on earth.

Gargantua had a larger rock core than Jupiter. The core not only gave Gargantua its high density and magnetic field, but it showed up as permanent spots in the weather pattern. There were certain hot spots near the equator that seemed to be the seed spots for the hurricanes and colder spots that seemed to deplete the strength of any cyclone pattern that wandered near it. The most amazing feature was not near the equator, but at a point near the south pole. The crew didn't notice it at first, for it was summer on Gargantua.

Arielle and George were sitting side-by-side on the control deck. Arielle was at the right science console studying Gargantua's gargantuan weather patterns while George was at the left.

"Look at this, George!" said Arielle. "She is cute!"

George cleared his screen.

"Ready!" he said.

Arielle punched some keys on the console and his screen started a time-compressed video display of a huge weather pattern that had been spawned by the 22 S latitude, 22 E longitude hot spot and had headed south. A few weeks later it passed over the southern terminator heading for the south pole hidden in the darkness. Instead of disappearing, however, the cloud pattern rebounded from the south pole blackness and broke into two smaller storms, both of which eventually made their way over the terminator on either side of the point where the storm had first entered.

"There must be something there," said George.

"Most certainly," said Arielle, turning serious. "I made doppler velocity measurements on clouds there. They all move north."

". . . and that's the only portion of Gargantua that we

can't see," complained George. "What we need is more light."

"I can give you that," said Jinjur's voice through George's imp.

"We have searchlight?" asked Arielle.

"Unless you're a light sailor, you don't think about it," said George. "But if you've ever been in a lightsail race and had to pay a fine for disturbing the darkness in some sleepy burg in Switzerland by flicking the full sun at them during a tight tack, you quickly learn that a lightsail makes a good searchlight, and we have one that is almost big enough for Gargantua."

Some seventy minutes later, they finished their orbit of the northern polar regions of Gargantua and dipped down below the equator. James tilted the sail slightly and a beam of reddish photons from Barnard illuminated Gargantua's south pole.

"It's a *tit!*" said George, whose eyes never missed one.

It did look like one. Not three degrees from the south pole of Gargantua was a large permanent mound half as big as Jupiter, rising 5000 kilometers above the normal Gargantuan surface of 98,000 kilometers' radius. In the center was a central peak—"A nipple!" George insisted. It was as big around as the earth and reached upward another 1000 kilometers.

It was a gigantic atmospheric volcano. A hot spot deep in the core was ejecting metallic hydrogen in a continuous geyser that spurted upward at high pressure to climb for 20,000 kilometers through the thick atmosphere until it burst into outer space. As it rose, the metallic hydrogen, released from the internal pressure, converted back into hydrogen molecules, then atoms, then ionized plasma as the kinetic energy in the stream was converted into heat. The electric-blue "teat" of the atmospheric volcano gave off continuous lightning flashes as the flowing hydrogen ions rose into space, recombined back into hydrogen atoms and molecules, then fell back onto the upper cloud layers. Now a gas, the falling hydrogen built up into a permanent "high-pressure" area that slowly spread out in an atmospheric version of a lava shield and ultimately flowed back into the surrounding countryside.

The scientists had a field day with their instruments each time they passed over the "tit" as it slowly twirled once a week about the south polar axis. Behind them, trying not to get in the way, was Thomas, snapping shot after shot with his 70 mm electrocam. Whereas the scientists were interested in data, Thomas was interested in the rapidly varying light display, especially when they were right over the volcano and staring down into the blazing blue bowels of the gigantic planet. Six years later, it was one of his snapshots, not those of James and the planetary scientists, that made the cover of *National Geographic*.

They were on their twenty-fifth pass over the south pole of Gargantua, and George was analyzing some infrared images when he felt a strong black presence at his back.

"Are you and the beauty queen *quite* finished?" said a deep voice. "I realize that I am *merely* the commander of this mission and my job is to make sure that you wizard types are kept happy and well fed, but I *do* have a *few* more planets to visit."

George looked at Arielle. Arielle looked at her nails. Two were chipped from the constant tapping of screen and pounding of keyboard during the past thirty-six hours. George turned to face Jinjur and gave a weak smile. "I guess we're nearly done. Anytime, General Jones."

Jinjur made her way back to her control seat. George could almost feel the "stomp" in the corridor boots as they contacted the soft carpeting in two percent gravity. He turned back to his console to see if he could extract some more data before they had to leave. Jinjur punched her console and soon a display was on her screen. It came from the radar console that Thomas was using.

"Do you have an orbit for Rocheworld, Thomas?" she asked.

"James and I have the trajectory of Rocheworld pretty solid, but there is something we found that raises some questions," said Thomas off to her right. "Rocheworld is in a highly elliptical orbit with a period that James is sure is *exactly* one-third that of the orbital period of Gargantua. The elliptical orbit brings it within 4.6 gigameters of Barnard at periapsis, then it swings out to 32 gigameters of Barnard at apoapsis. Once every three orbits Rocheworld passes within 6 gigameters of Gargantua."

"That's just outside Gargantua's moon system! That sounds significant," said Jinjur.

"James and I think that one of the two parts of Rocheworld must have once been a moon of Gargantua, with the other one being another moon in an elliptical orbit or an interloper from outer space. The only way we'll find out is to visit there."

"Those eggheads with the mammary gland fixation really bollixed our science schedule," said Jinjur. "Is there some way we can make up the time or will we have to chase the eggbeater?"

"Doesn't look good," said Thomas. "Rocheworld is on its way out and we're still down in Gargantua's gravity well with an undermasted sailboat instead of a diesel cruiser. There's no way we can meet it in time for its next close passage. We'll just have to catch it on the fly somewhere else in this system."

"OK," said Jinjur. She looked across the control deck at George and Arielle. "Had enough sight-seeing, you two?" she said. "Don't forget, we'll be back after we've completed the preliminary survey."

George punched a few more keys on his console. As

James followed those commands to extract a few more pieces of information out of the images coming up from Gargantua, George turned and looked at Arielle. She shrugged her shoulders in resignation.

"All yours, Jinjur," George said. He got wearily up from the science console chair. Stumbling a bit on unused legs, he made his way to the lift shaft and his bed. Arielle went to bed too, but first she stopped off at the sick bay to get patches for her cracked fingernails, then the galley to get a bite to eat. She had a double helping of protocheese with real garlic from Nels's hydroponic gardens, two algae-shakes with energy sticks mixed in for crunch, then still hungry, she finished with a dessert consisting of a half-pound of whitemeat sticks from Chicken Little—her real-meat ration for a week—sliced into thin strips and hot-cooked with James's secret recipe of herbs and spices.

Landing

Their preliminary survey of the Gargantuan Z-system completed, Jinjur started the long trip back into the inner Barnard system to map Rocheworld, the most interesting feature of this strange stellar system. She had just accepted James's spiral-course recommendation when Red said, "Why are you doing it that way? It'll take forever."

Jinjur smiled as she patiently explained. "I sure wish this tub had the instantaneous rocket power that the ion ships do. You're spoiled, Red. Those laser-beam-powered ion rockets that you used in the asteroid belt got you used to 'driving' from one place to another. These lightsails have to 'sail.' It may take longer, but you never run out of fuel."

"Yeah . . ." said Red, still not convinced. "But you light jammers never had to give up half your claim on a billion tons of nickel-iron just to get a fuel stake for your next trip. Out on the belt we learned a lot of tricks to cut down on the light bill." She turned and looked around the control deck.

"Where's a console? I want to do a few orbit calculations." She spotted an empty console, padded over, and fixed herself down.

A half hour later she was back. "We're presently in a low polar orbit about Gargantua and are planning to stay in that orbit while we spiral out. . . ."

"Right," said Jinjur. "We'll stay in the polar orbit, avoiding Gargantua's shadow as much as possible. Then we'll tip over and spiral into an orbit in Barnard's ecliptic plane to match orbits with Rocheworld."

"If instead," persisted Red, "we switched to an equatorial orbit as rapidly as we could, we could get out faster and catch Rocheworld earlier."

"Really?" asked Jinjur. "We'd spend half of our time in shadow."

"If we switch to an equatorial orbit and time things accurately," said Red, "we can be crossing Zulu's orbit just in back of it, and it will toss us out to Zouave. We'll actually want to decelerate a little before we hit that orbit, but if we do that right, I figure we can gravity-whip this parasol out past six of the eight moons and arrive at Rocheworld seven weeks early."

Jinjur pulled up a copy of Red's screen, looked at it for a moment, and then in a semiserious tone spoke at the imp above her right ear. "James? You should've spent more time riding ion ships instead of dandelion seeds."

"Yes, General Jones," said James contritely.

"Do you think you can improve on Red's trajectory?" she said severely.

"With difficulty, General Jones."

"Do it."

"Yes, General Jones."

There was a three-second pause. Even Red knew that most of it was for her benefit. The screen blinked, and there in purple was an alternate trajectory. It followed Red's almost exactly for the first four moons, then drifted off. After the fifth moon it added another before it took off for the last moon and Rocheworld. Jinjur saw Red nod in approval.

"We can save three more hours this way," said James.

When *Prometheus* had first arrived at Gargantua, Rocheworld was on the inbound leg of its highly elliptical trajectory. While they were taking pictures of the giant planet and its moons, the tiny double planet went through its close periapsis passage about Barnard. The point of closest approach was on the same side of the sun that they were. They tried to follow it across the distant red disk with telescopes, but most of the detail was hidden by the deep red glare of the fuzzy globe of light. Rocheworld was now coming out again to meet them, slowing rapidly as it climbed up out of the deep gravity well. They dropped inward, then applied full light-braking to match orbits with the twin planets.

Like a pirouetting pair of gumdrops, the two plane-toids that made up Rocheworld whirled along their orbit. The two lobes were gravitationally distorted into egg shapes that looked like an infinity symbol when seen through Thomas' low-power camera lens. Six years later, the scientifically blurred, but artistically fascinating image was "the" Christmas card of 2075.

Jinjur approached the double planet with caution.

"Don't get too close, James," said Jinjur. "I want you to spiral in slowly and monitor the shape of the sail as you do. The rotating, double-lobed gravity pattern of that eggbeater is something that neither you, nor I, nor the designers of the sail ever had any experience with."

"I am already noticing some tilt-brim flutter of the sail," said James. "It is easily damped out by the actuators."

"Just don't get careless," warned Jinjur. "The last thing I want to do is spend the rest of my life under an umbrella with a tear in it."

Jinjur padded to the science consoles and looked over

the shoulders of Sam and Richard as they busily ordered the various image sensors into operation. There were mechanical sounds from the center of the control deck as different sensors emerged from their storage places, took their turn looking out the Barnardside science dome at the nearby planets, then retracting back again into their niches.

"How does it look?" she asked.

"The visible and infrared images are excellent," said Sam. "But the X-ray and gamma-ray images are blurred by the atmosphere. The radio images show nothing but modest temperature variations. There don't seem to be any radiation belts, which means a low magnetic field."

"Does that mean there's no shielding from cosmic rays?" asked Jinjur, slightly concerned.

"There is nothing to worry about," said Sam. "Although the atmospheric pressure is only twenty percent of earth's, the gravity is lower so the scale height is higher. The blanket of air is adequate to stop the cosmic rays. In fact, it is so thick that the two planets share a common atmosphere."

"I think we'll be able to fly from one lobe to another in the *Dragonfly* without having to switch to rocket propulsion," said Richard.

"That doesn't sound right to me," said Jinjur. "Aren't they a couple of hundred kilometers apart? Increased scale height or no, there isn't going to be much atmosphere left at those altitudes."

"The gap is only eighty kilometers," replied Richard. "And don't forget that the gravity drops to zero between the two planets, so the 'gravitational' altitude there is different than the physical altitude."

"What a weird planet," said Jinjur. "What else have you learned?"

"Show her some of the pictures," said Sam. "I'll keep the science sensors going."

Richard flashed some images across his screen in rapid

succession and stopped at a picture that showed the two lobes fully illuminated.

"This is the best shot that shows the egg-shaped tidal distortion of the two lobes," said Richard. "That particular shape was first calculated by Roche in the 1880s. He was primarily interested in the shapes of two closely spaced binary stars. I'm sure he never thought that there'd be a binary planet named after him."

He switched to a closeup picture of one of the lobes. It showed a mountainous region with deep valleys.

"Sure looks rocky," said Jinjur.

"That's why this lobe of Rocheworld is called the 'Roche' lobe," said Richard. "It just happens that the word 'roche' means 'rock' in French."

"How come the valleys are all going the same way?" asked Jinjur.

"That's the rift valley region," said Richard. "Let me get another version."

The screen flickered some more and finally stopped with a closeup picture of a large conical mountain peak with a rounded top and sixty-degree slopes.

"That's the pointy part of the Roche egg," said Richard. "The mountain peak is a part of the original Roche sphere that was pulled up into this shape as the two planets slowly came toward each other due to tidal friction. Sam and I expect that the rift valleys were formed at that time, with the 'stretch marks' in rings where the material was pulled up.

"What we don't understand are the deep valleys going 'downhill.' They look almost like river valleys, but they're completely dry. That'll be one of the first things we want to look at when we land there."

"What's that fuzzy thing there on the side of the mountain?" she asked.

"That's a volcano," said Richard. "You'd expect a lot of tectonic activity in a region under as much stress as that one. Here, let me get some action in the picture."

He punched a few keys, then the picture was replaced by a twelve-image stop-motion replay of the eruption of two volcanoes on each side of the conical mountain. The plumes blossomed straight out from the sides.

"How come the plumes don't fall downhill?" said Jinjur.

"That's one of the strangest things about the shapes that the Roche mathematics predicts," said Richard. "The surface of that conical mountain with its sixty-degree slopes is all at the same gravitational potential, even though the shape is not a sphere. The same goes for the other lobe, where the mountain is made of water."

Richard switched to another image. There was the same conical shape, but Jinjur could tell from the color and smoothness that it was the surface of an ocean.

"This is the wet lobe," said Richard. "It's named the Eau lobe since 'eau' means 'water' in French. The shape of the Eau lobe is almost identical to that of the Roche lobe, except that its surface is almost completely covered with a water-ammonia ocean. The ocean is shallow on the outer portion of the lobe, because we can see some crater rims and mountain peaks showing through, while on the inner portion the ocean gets much deeper because it is pulled up into a mountain by the gravitational attraction of its twin."

"It looks like it ought to fall down," said Jinjur.

"What's even more remarkable," said Richard, "is that the gravity at the top of the mountain is only a half-percent of an earth gravity, while at the base of the mountain the gravity rises to a tenth of a gee. This is one time when you have to forget your long-taught prejudices about the behavior of water under gravity and believe the mathematics. The surface of that water mountain is all at the same gravitational potential and the water is just seeking its natural level. The mountain doesn't just stand there looking impossible, though.

There's plenty of action. Let me show you the movie that Sam and I pieced together."

As the double planets rotated about each other each six hours, the tides and heat generated by Barnard pushed the ocean and atmosphere around. Each half-rotation, the water mountain would drop twenty kilometers, then rise again, driven by the tides. The atmosphere, meanwhile, driven by a combination of tides and heat, blew back and forth once per revolution. When the water mountain was rising and the atmosphere was going from Roche to Eau, the peak would be strangely calm, with only small breakers showing at its base, for the air was rushing down the slopes. Three hours later, the wind would be blowing up along the rising slopes of water. As the wind moved upward, it drove the water ahead of it. The wind-driven swells moved upward toward the peak where the gravitation was weaker and the surface area was smaller. The swells grew into waves that reached hundreds of meters in height as the gravitation and the available surface area dropped to nearly zero at the same time. The ring waves finally met in a ring geyser that shot a fountain of foamy water up toward the zero-gravity point between the planets. There the geyser dissolved into a spray of water vapor, some of which drifted across the zero-gravity point to spawn tornadoes and thunderheads that dropped rain which dried to salt specks before it reached the rocky surface below.

"A lovely place," remarked Jinjur. "Shall we drop in for a visit?"

"Yes!" said Richard. "Drop us down right on the equator of the rocky one. That's far enough from the tornado belt that the lander won't be disturbed, and Sam can poke around in the rocks while I go fishing on the other lobe."

"This planet is the dream of an astrodynamicist," said Thomas. "I'd like to 'bug' it all over before we go down for a close look, especially the Lagrange points. They're very sensitive to orbital perturbations."

"I thought you only had Lagrange minima when one mass is bigger than the other, like the sun and Jupiter," said Jinjur.

"They're much more stable then," said Thomas. "Especially the co-orbit points. But you get almost the same thing when the two masses are the same size. There's the obvious minimum where the gravity drops to zero between the two planets, then there're the famous L-4 and L-5 points, the only truly stable ones."

"Those I know about," said Jinjur. "They're always sixty degrees ahead or behind the planet in its orbit around the sun."

"In this system it's different," said Thomas. "Since the two planetoids are the same size, the Lagrange points are not at sixty degrees, but ninety degrees. That's where I want to put the communication satellites. The gravity minimum will keep them there with minimum fuel, and any perturbations will give my Rocheworld computer model some exercise. Perhaps we'll learn something."

"Will they be able to communicate well from there?" asked Jinjur.

"Two Comsats at the L-4 and L-5 points will cover most of the two worlds except for the outer poles," said Thomas. "I propose to put another Comsat in counterorbit to their rotation so that we get frequent contact with any point on the two lobes."

"Fine," said Jinjur. "You and Karin go up the shaft, break them out, and transfer them to the lander."

The lift went up through the ceiling to level 21. There, three Comsats, *Clete*, *Walter*, and *Barbara* were activated and lifted to the hydroponics deck. Nels Larson met them and helped push the three high-inertia loads down the humid green world of water-filled walls, the fact that Nels had no legs making no difference in this low-gee world. They stopped at a porthole in the ceiling.

It was open, and Thomas looked up to see the innards of SLAM 1 and the flashing green limbs and short red hair of a busy heavy-lift pilot strapped into a blue acceleration harness checking out a long dormant, sleeping giant of a rocket. Crouching low, he launched himself through the porthole overhead. Securing himself, he reached down to take one of the Comsats from Nels.

The lander soon filled up with its crew, who were busy shifting their personal belongings from their luxurious apartments on *Prometheus* to the crowded vertical beds they would be using while the SLAM was in free fall. A few days passed, the checkout was completed, and it was time to go. Jinjur escorted George to the lock between the SLAM and *Prometheus*.

"Take your time and do it right," said Jinjur. "We have the rest of our lives for exploring, but only four landers."

"I will," said George. He reached for Jinjur's shirt-front and half unfastened the button under the most tension, then fastened it again.

"See you soon," he said, and closed the air-lock door, making sure it was space-sealed.

A strange, yet familiar computer voice spoke to him.

"SLAM 1 ready for departure, sir."

It was Jack, James's alter ego for the computer in the Surface Lander and Ascent Module.

"Let's go," George replied. He heard pumps working and the outer lock door creaked slightly as the air in the small volume between the SLAM and *Prometheus* was pumped out. George's personal imp jumped to the door and searched the seams for any sign of leakage. Finding none, it jumped back to his shoulder.

For the few seconds that the imp was not on his shoulder George felt both naked and bereft. James could afford the luxury of a lock imp on *Prometheus*. Life would be more Spartan for Jack's landing crew, since only a Christmas "Branch," a one-sixth portion of a Christmas Bush, was assigned to the lander computer.

George cycled through. Karin was waiting for him, standing on the ceiling. She and Jack's Christmas Branch double-checked the docking air lock, then Karin turned to help Sam check out the many instruments on the science consoles. Both were apparently able to read the labels and indicators as easily upside down as right side up. George paused at the wedge-shaped passway through to the next deck, and holding onto the ladder rungs welded into the consumables column that ran through the center of the ship, he looked up to see Arielle and Richard busy stuffing equipment and supplies into the storage bins next to the galley.

"Breakaway in five minutes," he warned.

"We'll be ready," answered Richard.

George continued around the central column, walking on the ceiling of the bridge. Carefully avoiding the large glass docking window at his feet, he nodded at Thomas and Red, who were buckled upside down into the blue and red pilot and copilot harnesses in front of their consoles, then continued on to the computer and communication consoles.

"Jack is ready," said David Greystoke up at George. Like the two pilots, David was hanging upside down from the floor overhead in a green zero-gee harness.

"Take her away, Captain St. Thomas," said George.

"*Prometheus* has given us clearance for breakaway," said Karin from the console next to David's.

Thomas grasped the controls and nodded at Red. She flicked a red switch cover and threw the switch that had been protected underneath. There was a loud clunk from the docking port overhead, followed by a series of clattering ripples as the clamps that had held *SLAM 1* to the outside of the lift shaft on *Prometheus* were retracted. Nothing happened, for they were still held to the sailship by its acceleration.

Thomas pushed a control forward and the bridge crew hanging from the overhead floor sagged a little farther in their harnesses as the acceleration increased. Thomas and Red looked out their docking port window as the huge cylinder tilted and swung out from its cradle on the lightship. As soon as the edge of the hydroponics deck had been cleared, Thomas switched to other control jets and slowly flew the ponderous cylinder out through the shrouds and away from the sail.

"The *Eagle* has left its nest," said George to his imp.

"Good hunting, *Eagle*," came Jinjur's voice.

For two days they spiraled in from orbit, letting Jack get used to the strange double-lobed rotating gravitational field and taking detailed closeup pictures of their planned landing place on Roche.

"Looks like Mars," said Sam to Richard.

"With fewer boulders," said Richard as he blew up the picture on the screen until he could see the pixels. "Looks like it's been swept clean. We could land just about anywhere with no trouble."

"I would prefer to land by this mesa," said Sam. "The ten-meter scarp will allow us to examine a large cross-section of the crust."

"Looks like the edge of a stream bed," said Richard.

"So do many features on Mars," said Sam. "But those streams flowed millions of years ago and the waters that flowed have evaporated into space. Here the erosion probably occurred when the Gargantuan moon and the interloper first interacted. Since Eau is twenty kilometers smaller than Roche, the rain clouds formed over the lowlands on Eau rather than up in the Roche mountain plateau, and all the water ended up on Eau. I bet those stream beds are as old, if not older, than the ones on Mars."

"The only way to find out is to go down and count craters," said Richard. "But don't you want to land on the mesa, just in case?"

"Then the excursions that Elizabeth and I will make on the exploration crawler will be limited to the mesa," said Sam. "I plan to take longer trips than that. Please land on the stream bed near the cliff, Jack."

"I will inform Captain St. Thomas," said Jack.

Eagle approached Rocheworld in the ecliptic plane, but going in the opposite direction to the spin on the planetoids. As they moved closer and closer, the orbital track on Red's pilot console took on a wavy appearance as the two lobes pulled the track this way and that.

"It's time to release *Barbara*," said Jack.

"I'll get her," said Karin, who had been floating around the deck with little to do. She pulled herself over to one side of the bridge and opened a storage locker.

"I'd appreciate a hand out of here," said a contralto voice through Karin's imp.

Karin grasped the communications satellite carefully at the base of its antenna and pulled it free from its fasteners. She nudged the heavy spacecraft around the bend to the docking port entrance. Carefully she inserted the Comsat in the exact center of the lock, making sure that its folded antennas would clear the outer door.

"Keep in touch, *Barbara*," she said.

"That's my job," said *Barbara*.

Red watched the orbital track until the wavy track had neared its minimum, then her finger gave a slight nudge to a button on her control stick. Karin felt a slight tug on the sticky patches of her corridor boots.

Nicely done, thought Karin. It's those years in the asteroid belt.

The velocity difference imparted by the tiny flare of control jets was small, but a minute later Karin could see *Barbara* slowly rise up out of the docking port without a single trace of spin or tumble. When the Comsat was about ten meters away Karin sent it a message.

"You may fire jets when ready, *Barbara*."

There was a burst of tiny jets as the spacecraft rotated its orientation, then a larger burst as the Comsat took off to take up its station in an orbit that rotated in an opposite direction to the rotation of the two planetoids. That way it would pass over each outer pole twice each rotation so that no point would be out of sight of a Comsat for more than three hours.

With the Comsat launched in its counterrotating orbit, Red expertly rotated the huge cylinder end over end. As the spacecraft rotated to a halt, Red talked to her imp.

"Announce imminent gees to all hands, Jack," she said.

"Thrust will commence in one minute," boomed Jack's voice throughout the ship.

"Just a second," shouted Richard up through the passway. "Let me get my soap! I haven't had a real shower since we decelerated at Barnard."

There was a slam of some doors, and Karin, monitoring the engineering board, noticed a light go on under the hygiene-water-expenditure sign. She shook her head. Red, serious as ever, checked over the main engine controls and glanced at Thomas, who nodded back. She pushed at the four-levered throttle bar. They went from free fall to a tenth gee and stayed there, Red playing with the relative adjustments on the throttles as she looked at her track and the motion of the two lobes on her screen.

For a while Karin could look out of the corner of the docking window in the ceiling of the bridge and see the outer poles of the two lobes moving majestically across her view, slowing perceptibly as Red decreased their counterrotating orbital speed. As the thrust continued, the rocket tilted upward until the lobes could no longer be seen. Karin climbed heavily down the passway on the ladder and clumped her way around to the viewport lounge. The lounge was full, including a dripping Richard wrapped in a towel, oblivious to the exasperated mosquito-imps attempting to cope with the water dripping from his hair and body in the accelerated environment.

The period of thrust lasted for fifteen minutes. The tilt of the spacecraft came back to horizontal as the rotation of the lobes slowed and stopped until they were stationary. Barnard was in the sky and the two lobes were brilliantly lit with a flat red glow.

"We're at L-4, Karin," said Red's voice through the communication imp. "Time to dump *Clete* off."

Karin left her perch on the video-room partition and floated her way back through the galley and up the passway to the storage locker.

"*Clete*, L-4," said Karin.

"Jack so informed me," said *Clete* through her imp. "If I might trouble you?"

"No trouble at all," said Karin, taking the heavy satellite out of the locker and pushing it through the free-fall air to the docking port. "Just part of the taxi service."

She cycled the lock and went back to watch Red do another of her minimal bursts.

"You're on the up cycle, *Clete*," said Karin. "Keep bouncing so we can see you at the cold poles."

"Let's take a break before we insert the last one," said Thomas to Red.

"Let me move *Eagle* to the inside first," said Red. "With *Clete* bouncing up and down through the L-4 point, we don't want to be in the way when it comes back down." She fired a burst from the attitude jets, then turned the controls over to Jack.

"Give Thomas and me a call in eight hours, Jack. We're going to rack up a few winks."

Eagle's two pilots snaked their way down through the passway and George's gray thatch appeared in the wedge as soon as they left.

"Since it's going to be quiet for a while, Karin, I thought you, Arielle, and I could check out *Dragonfly*."

"I'd like David along too," said Karin as she swam to the passway and ottered through.

For the first entry into the air lock leading to the aerospace plane, Karin, ever cautious, put on a full space suit and cycled through. George peered through the porthole in the door and saw Karin pull a cloth wiper from her thigh pocket and wave it in front of the long seal between the fuselage of the aerospace plane and the V-shaped notch in the side of the rocket lander. After a while he saw her crack her helmet, then take it off. She listened carefully, then put the helmet back on and sealed it again. She then went to the door built into the copilot side of the *Dragonfly*, and lifting panels, she pushed the window inward. She cracked her helmet once again and stuck her head in to look down the long corridor. She floated back out, put her helmet back on and sealed it, then carefully closing and sealing each door she had opened, she made her way back into the *Eagle* through the air lock.

"It's safe to go in without suits," she said. She made her way to the suit locker while Arielle and David cycled through and floated through the narrow copilot hatch into the magical realm of the aerospace plane— *Dragonfly*. Arielle was the first through the hatch and was greeted by Jill, the semi-intelligent program in the aerospace plane computer.

"Hello, Arielle," said Jill's soprano voice. "I'm glad to see you. Is Rocheworld as interesting to fly in as Titan?"

"Ho!" said Arielle. "It is much interesting. We can go very high there. There are lots of thermals and we can *fly* from Roche to l'Eau."

David swam in through the lock, all business.

"Self-check routine zero," he commanded.

Through his imp, a mechanical voice said, "7613FF."

"Check," said Jack.

David consulted a printed checklist and nodded agreement.

"Self-check routine one."

"Surface Excursion Module One going through systems check," reported Jill's voice. There was a long pause. During the wait, Arielle and David were joined by George and Karin.

"Five sensors out of spec, two tanks with measurable level of degradation contaminants, and a missing flask in the galley," Jill finally reported.

"This one?" said Arielle. "I was going to fix me a shake."

"Wait till after checkout!" exploded Karin. "Right now Jill is busy."

"Oh. That's why we no have algae shakes." Arielle put the flask back and swam up the length of the corridor to join George on the flight deck. They took Jill through a few simulated landings, while Karin, back on the engineering console, inserted a few "emergencies" to keep them all in practice.

"That's enough," said George, after he had botched an engine-out landing and Arielle had intervened at the last second with an imaginary blast from the space thrusters to float them to a stop. "Jill looks in good shape, and it's time for Thomas and Red to pull gees to arc over to L-5 and dump Walter. Let's seal up *Dragonfly* and get some dinner."

"I'll be there later," said Karin. "Have to check out those low sensor readings and the impurity reports."

"I be glad to eat your dinner for you," said Arielle as she unbuckled and flew out the hatch.

"You just leave my dinner alone," shouted Karin after her, ". . . you skinny, bottomless pit!!"

After dinner Thomas and Red went upstairs to the bridge, with Karin following to monitor the systems on the engineering console. The rest of the crew gathered in the lounge to watch the scene out the viewport and to settle their meals in the acceleration.

"Shall I take the copilot harness?" asked Red, as they made their way up the passway.

"Nope," said Thomas. "I may be good at up and down, but for the roundy-rounds, you're the pro. You get the blue harness and I'll watch and see how you do it."

Eagle was in a synchronous orbit about Rocheworld. To move from the L-4 point to the L-5 point Red decided to bounce up out of the plane of rotation far enough so that when they came back down, Rocheworld had slipped in an extra half-rotation on them. She tilted the *Eagle* and initiated thrust in the main rockets. The viewers in the lounge sank into their seats as the tilted scene slowly rotated in the viewport. Darkness set on Eau as Roche blocked the sun. They looked down at the northern cold poles as the sun rose again on Eau. Large circular storms could be seen on the cold crescent as a snow of water and ammonia rained down on the mountain of water. They stopped at L-5, where *Walter* was dispatched in a bouncing orbit that alternated with that of *Clete*. Now like the outer poles, neither cold pole was more than three hours away from a Comsat.

Thomas and Red went down to confer with George.

"We've only been up four hours," said Thomas. "And Red did all the work on that last one while I just dozed away in the red harness. We can land it on Roche if you want us to."

"What's your recommendation, Jack?" said George. He noticed that the imps on both Thomas and Red spread their fingers on the necks and jugular veins of their charges, scanning their vital signs.

"I have no objection," said Jack.

George's imp vibrated with a voice that he had not heard in some while. "James sees no problem either," said Jinjur.

"Take her down," said George.

"Stand by for deorbit burn," said Thomas. "This'll be

the most gees you'll have felt for decades, so make sure you're fastened down."

Slowly Thomas pushed forward on the throttle to the main rockets. He and the rest of the bridge crew sank in their harnesses while uncomfortable groans were heard from belowdecks.

"That's only a half-gee," said Thomas with a grin. "We go to three gees just before reentry."

The rocket engines blasted a powerful glare over the darkened planetscape of the Roche highlands below, then they throttled down to a more controlled thrust as the huge cylinder floated down through the miles of atmosphere, letting the friction of the cold thin air do its work in dissipating the energy of the falling eighty tons of matter.

The ponderous, top-heavy bulk of the rocket ship *Eagle* slowly drifted downward on a rippling flame of rocket exhaust. The crew members left back on distant *Prometheus* were gathered at videos and consoles, monitoring the landing on Roche through the quartet of video cameras looking down from the four sides of the lander. The lander was drifting inward as Thomas looked for a good landing site. He peered down at the ground in front of him as he maneuvered the controls, while Red watched all four video scenes on her split-screen display and Jack kept up a running commentary through their imps.

"Two-hundred meters . . . four and a half down . . . kicking up some dust . . . four forward . . . drifting to the right a little . . . contact light . . . engine stop. . . ."

There was a pause, then the lightsail crew burst into cheers as Thomas' exultant voice came through strong and loud.

"*Prometheus!* Rocheworld Base here. The *Eagle* has landed!"

Flying

A quiescent blob of milky white jelly rested in the dark ocean of Eau. Clear◇White◇Whistle was an expert surfer and had ridden the last ring wave all the way up the water mountain. It had stayed poised on the face of the wave, halfway between a forced dive and a forced tumble for nearly an eighth of a rotation, while the others of the pod had fallen off along the way. Roaring☆Hot☆Vermillion, usually the best surfer of the pod, went too far up a wave in an attempt to outdistance the rest of the beginning of the run and had been broken into three parts and foamed out right at the start. Warm•Amber•Resonance and Bitter◯Green◯ Fizz had been with them, but they too finally had to take a forced dive, leaving Clear◇White◇Whistle to navigate the last half of the mountain on the side of a wave that was bigger than many of the rocky ridges on the bottom of the ocean.

It had been thrilling to be surfing at speeds that were so high that the sonic pings returning from the lower scattering layers had shrieked into the upper register. The fun was over and it was time to think. Time to think deeply and clearly. Clear◇White◇Whistle often wondered about the type of thinking it did. Most of the others in the pod, and indeed most of the others in the ocean, were all the same in their thinking. Numbers, mostly. Some about arrays of numbers. Some about all the numbers between oh and one. Some about the numbers that were not numbers but could be.

Clear ◇ White ◇ Whistle felt alone. It knew all about numbers—enough to do that kind of research itself. But it wasn't content with that. The numbers had to mean something. It felt exultant yet perverted as it tried to impale the numbers on the lights in the sky.

Clear ◇ White ◇ Whistle searched the water around it. It could see nothing except the rocky bottom far, far below. Secure in the knowledge that it could not be seen, yet still secretive, it raised an appendage of thick, milky-white jelly. The end floated in the water above the central part of its body. By concentrating, the end of the appendage became thicker and disk-shaped, but it was still milky white like the rest of the appendage. Then, fighting the sexual joy, yet exulting in the perverted self-gratification, Clear ◇ White ◇ Whistle seductively extracted its white from the clear gelatin lens floating on the smooth surface of the calm ocean mountain. The milky body below the surface adjusted its shape until the spots of light on its surface were of minimum size. Like Galileo, gazing on the proscribed heavenly spheres, Clear ◇ White ◇ Whistle returned to its solitary study of the stars.

Clear ◇ White ◇ Whistle had given the bright red glare of Hot the number-name Oh. The bright red light seemingly burned into the white flesh. Oh was flanked this rising by a pattern of smaller dots, numbered 6, 32, and 47, while Warm—number One—was still hidden in back of the ocean. Warm would make an appearance soon and Clear ◇ White ◇ Whistle resolved to wait for it. Meanwhile, the positions of all the rest of the numbers in the sky were measured and compared against its memory. None had changed over the many seasons it had first looked at the sky except perhaps for a slight shift in the yellow point of light at the end of the straight string of low-numbered lights.

Clear ◇ White ◇ Whistle had been studying the points of light whenever it had some time off to itself. In this darkness it again puzzled over the behavior of the light numbers. Most of them were simple. They could be handled by a simple coordinate transformation, since they never changed their relative position. However, the mathematics of One and its higher number lights was nearly impossible. For a long while, One wandered about in the sky like a broken flitter. Then every 480 rotations of the sky, it got brighter and brighter until it looked as though it were going to rival Oh in the sky.

Clear ◇ White ◇ Whistle thought that it knew all the light numbers. This time, however, there was a new light in the sky. It varied rapidly and moved downward toward Sky⊗Rock until it disappeared on the Hot-limned side of the rock. It moved much more slowly than the other specks of transient light that Clear ◇ White ◇ Whistle had occasionally seen at other dark times. Perhaps the brighter the falling specks were, the slower they fell. Yet that thought didn't really satisfy Clear ◇ White ◇ Whistle. It very much wanted to know the logic by which the specks of light in the sky moved, especially the motions of One and its smaller lights, but the form of the mathematical rule eluded its most concentrated thought.

With the landing safely over, George let out his breath. For safety he and the crew members who weren't actively involved in the landing had strapped themselves into their bunks. He hung uncomfortably in his vertical sleeping rack in the 10 percent gravity, his feet not quite touching the deck. As he unfastened the straps he could hear thuds from the cubicles around him as the rest of the crew left their sleeping racks and filed down the narrow corridor to the rest of the ship. Most made their way to the miniature lounge and crowded around the viewport to look out at the alien scenery. George clumped his way up the ladder through the passway and went over to congratulate Thomas.

"A fine landing," he said, helping Thomas with a recalcitrant fastener on his harness.

"Couldn't have done better myself," added Red, who was still busy powering down the landing systems and readying the ascent module for lift-off in case they ran into any trouble.

"Why, thanks, Red," said Thomas, a pleased smile on his face. "Those are high words of praise from an old ion pilot like you."

Red glanced at him with an annoyed expression. "I'd prefer the phrase 'experienced' rather than 'old,' sonny boy," she said. Then she added eagerly, "But I'll forgive you if you let me land the next one."

"It's a deal," agreed Thomas, glad to have gotten out of his gaffe so easily.

"How's the atmosphere, Jack?" asked Karin. "Can we imitate Buck Rogers and throw off our helmets after a precautionary sniff and run through the meadows in bare feet with the wind blowing through our hair?"

"I'm afraid not," said Jack through her imp. "My analyzer only confirms what we measured from orbit. An atmosphere of methane, ammonia, water vapor, and hydrogen is definitely poisonous all by itself, not to mention the trace amounts of hydrogen sulfide and cyanide gas that my analyzer can pick up now that we are here."

"Hydrogen sulfide?" said Karin. "That's going to make for a stinky air lock even after purging."

"You won't notice it," said Sam. "Your nostrils will be anesthetized by the traces of ammonia."

"My locks have been designed with minimal trapped volumes," said Jack. "After pumping down to vacuum, then flushing with air before the final cycle, I should be able to keep the amount of ammonia, hydrogen sulfide, and hydrogen cyanide released into the ship at low level. Unless you have a very sensitive nose, you won't notice it."

"I *have* a sensitive nose," said Karin. "It's an engineer's best tool."

"I would like to go out and examine the local geology," said Sam. "May I suit up?"

"If it's OK with Jack, then it's OK with me," said Karin. "But aren't you forgetting protocol? The commander of the ship gets to be the first one to set foot on the new planet."

"You are correct, of course," said Sam. "If it hadn't been for George we wouldn't be here."

"I'm coming," said George, making his way down the passway ladder.

George went over to the suit locker and started dressing, with Karin and the Christmas Branch helping. Richard joined them.

"Why don't you and Richard get suited up too, Sam?" said George. "The lock should hold three of us with a little crowding and there's no need to make this a dramatic one-man production."

The three men, meticulously checked out by a clucking Karin, cycled through the air lock and opened the outer door to look thirty-six meters down to the surface below.

"Looks like the high-desert regions in California," said Richard. "Dry, dusty, and windy."

"And bare," said George. "At least the high desert has a few cacti and scrub plants." Holding carefully onto the handrail on either side of the outer door, George stepped on the top rung of the Jacob's ladder and started down the ninety rungs to the bottom. Sam waited until George had made his way down a few meters, then followed after, his long joints having an easier time with the widely spaced rungs. Richard unfastened the winch I beam from the ceiling of the air lock and swung the beam out through the door so the end of it hung two meters away from the side of the lander. He rolled the winch out until it reached the end of the beam, then fastened the hook on the end of the winch cable to his suit belt. He grabbed the cable, and using it to hold himself vertical, he stepped off into the air.

"Lower me down," said Richard to his imp, and the winch started to pay out the cable, Richard twirling slowly about at the end. He passed by Sam, who had paused at the place where the ladder left the side of the ship and turned into steps on one of the landing struts. Richard had Jack halt the winch when he was still two meters from the surface. He had brought along a video camera to record George's first step off the landing pad onto the soil of Roche.

As he made his historic step off the landing pad, George looked toward Richard and his camera and started talking.

"This is but the first step on mankind's long journey . . . WATCH IT!!!" He rushed over to catch Richard.

Richard, both hands working the camera, had tried to hold himself upright on the cable by tucking it under one elbow. Top-heavy with the camera, he had lost his balance and toppled over, his helmet narrowly missing a boulder as he swung upside down from the hook. George held Richard by the helmet and had Jack lower him the rest of the way to the ground.

"We almost lost you," said George in a soft voice. "If your helmet had cracked, you wouldn't have lasted a minute in this poisonous atmosphere."

Richard got up, his suit dusty from the dry soil.

"I'm sorry I messed up your speech," said Richard.

"That's all right," said George. "I wasn't really sure what I was going to say next anyway. I was thinking of saying '. . . mankind's long journey into the galaxy,' but that sort of puts a limit on mankind's explorations. I could also have said '... universe,' but by the time mankind has explored just this galaxy it will have evolved into something else and to say that mankind will explore the universe is equivalent to saying that it was a crew of plankton that first landed on the moon."

"No plankton here, anyway," said Sam, taking a sample of the soil and chipping a chunk off the boulder that nearly got Richard.

"Weathered igneous rock with lots of vesicles," he said to Richard.

As the two rock hounds took off, sniffing at rocks, cracks, and scarps, George looked up to see other suited figures making their way down the side of the ship. One was efficiently climbing down the rungs of the Jacob's ladder. That was obviously Karin. The second one was helping a tiny one attach itself to the winch cable. The thin suit poised delicately in midair, then rode down to the surface.

"Like gliding!" said Arielle with an excited voice.

George helped Arielle unfasten the cable and Jack rewound the winch for the next member of the crew.

"It's so desolate," said David as he landed. "Kilometers upon kilometers of nothing but rocks and sand. What a dreary place."

"Sam and Richard seem to find it interesting," said George, pointing out the two figures off in the distance. One had climbed halfway up the nearby scarp leading to the mesa and was obviously trying to chip a sample from a rock imbedded in a yellow-red layer there. The other one crawled into a small cave near the base and came back out, holding something in his gloved hand. He walked back toward them.

"I found something interesting," said Sam. He held out what looked like a piece of molten orange glass.

"What a strange-looking rock," said Red. "I've never seen volcanic glass that color."

"It's not a normal glass," said Sam.

He put the end of the piece of orange glass on a boulder and hit it with his pick. The tip of the rock shattered into tiny bits like a piece of tempered glass. All the bits were identical and very tiny. The bits had two faceted ends connected by a thin waist. They had the size and shape of a tiny ant.

"Let me see," said Karin, taking a few of them and holding them up to her helmet. "They look like orange-colored models of Rocheworld." She took a bag from her tool pouch and placed the bits of glass into it.

"I think I'll take these in and have a look at them under a microscope while Jack does a chemical analysis. Perhaps that will give us a clue. We're too used to rocks that form either in vacuum or in earth air. It could be this strange chemistry can produce material that crystallizes in such an odd form."

Later Karin called the crew together. "It's time to lower the *Dragonfly* to the surface and put its wings on. I want to get through the lowering phase before Barnard sets behind Roche."

"Do be careful!" said Arielle.

"We won't hurt your pet," said Karin. She walked around to the front of the lander and stood at the base of the landing strut that had been modified to act both as a leg for the lander and as a lowering rail for the aerospace plane. Karin watched a point near the tail of the plane.

"Release hold-down lugs, Jack," she said, then nodded in satisfaction as the clawlike devices swung clear. The aerospace plane shivered slightly as the hold on it was loosened, but it was still hanging vertically from its nose hook.

"Lower top winch!" she called, and slowly the nose of the airplane tilted away from the lander, the tail staying in place at the top of the lowering rail. Karin could now see the cockpit windows and the large triangular slash in the side of the lander as the plane pulled away from the side of the ship. The rotation continued until the airplane was leaning away from the lander at an angle of about thirty degrees.

"Now both winches!" said Karin. Jack started the bottom winch, and letting out both the nose cable and the tail cable at the same speed, it lowered the aerospace plane slowly down the lowering rail, still at the thirty-degree angle. As the plane moved down the rail, the tall rudder on the plane finally cleared the side of the lander. About two meters from the end of the rail, the tail winch stopped, while the upper nose winch continued to pay out cable. Slowly the huge plane rotated, and as it approached the horizontal there was a notice-able tilt to the lander.

"Lower landing skids!" said Karin, and slots appeared in the belly of the aerospace plane and three skids came out. They reached to within a half-meter of the surface.

"Lower her down!" said Karin, bending down to watch underneath. Slowly the plane was lowered to the surface.

"Done!" she yelled, then raced to detach the lowering cables from the front and rear of the aerospace plane. The winches retrieved their cables, their job done.

"Just in time, too," said George, as the sky reddened a more deeper red than the normal illumination. "Looks like a beautiful sunset tonight. Let's get everybody back on board before it gets too dark."

"If you please?" said a small voice through his imp. "I like to sleep on *Magic Dragonfly* tonight."

"Oh," said George, "sure, Arielle, if you want to. Won't you be lonely?"

"I'll stay too," said David. "We both have a lot to go over with Jill."

After everyone was back inside, Sam went up the passway to see how Karin was doing with her analysis of the bits of orange glass.

"Hello, Sam," she said as his head appeared above the floor of the bridge and the rest of his long body continued its upward rise. "I've got one of the bits under a microscope. Want to take a look at it?" She moved aside and Sam bent way over to peer through the eyepiece.

"The central waist has four sides," said Sam.

"Yes, there is a central crystal that is four-sided. Strange enough in itself, but the faceted balls at the end seem to be of the same material, as if it decided to switch to a more complex crystal form. The basic material is clear. Jack is still working on the chemistry, but it is a very complex molecule similar to the silica gel crystals that are used to keep things dry. Like silica gel, it's highly hygroscopic. I put one in water and it puffed up to double its size, became soft and gel-like, then fell apart. The orange color comes from a very thin surface layer that doesn't penetrate into the interior and scrapes off quite easily."

"Could it be a life-form?" asked Sam.

"I doubt it," said Karin. "It's not complicated enough for its size. Besides, what would it eat? So far, Jack has found no evidence for smaller life-forms such as bacteria. I'm sure it's just a strange crystal type."

"Hmm," mused Sam, rising up from the microscope. "Tomorrow I'll look for more samples, but now I think I'll go to bed."

It was their first night on the new planet. George and Sam, the "old folks," had gone to bed. The activity on the ship slowed and the remainder of the crew gathered in the lounge, snuggled close together. They looked out from the forty-meter height advantage of the viewport window along the long slopes of the conical inner pole that stretched out toward the distant globe of Eau hanging above them in the sky. The shadow of Roche on Eau had nearly covered the whole globe and there was only a thin red arc of illumination at the top.

"The sunset's almost gone," complained Karin.

"Good," said Red. "Now we'll be able to see the stars and Sol once more."

"Feeling homesick Red?" said Thomas. His arms were around the two women and he gave Red a squeeze.

Red nestled her head on the young man's shoulder.

"Not really," she said. "Earth doesn't have that many good memories for me. My father left us when Mom got too sick to work and I had to drop out of school to raise my three sisters and take care of her. Once I got on my own I was so afraid I might be poor again that I spent all my waking hours in a blind quest for money."

"Don't you ever regret giving up all that money and becoming a space nun, sworn to a vow of poverty?" said Richard. He was sitting on the floor with the back of his head resting on the lounge seat.

"Never," said Red. "For the first time in my life I'm having fun." She squirmed again against Thomas and her left hand tousled Richard's hair.

"Funny kind of fun," said Richard. "A nerve-wracking job landing an eighty-ton spacecraft on a wildly spinning double planet, then tomorrow the real work starts when Karin forms her slave gang to put the wings on the *Magic Dragonfly*. It all sounds like work to me."

"Sure it's work," said Red down at the tousled head. "But it's fun kind of work. I'd do it even if I weren't getting paid."

"Which we aren't," reminded Karin.

"See!" said Red. She turned to Thomas, whose dark face was almost invisible in the fading light.

"Where would Orion be now?" she asked.

"I'm not positive about anything anymore since I landed on this whirligig, but I think it's on the opposite side of the sky from Barnard and should be rising over Eau shortly."

"I see four bright stars in a line just above Eau," said Richard from the floor.

"That is Orion," whispered Jack through Richard's imp. "The yellow star at the right end is Sol." The ship was so quiet they could all hear the whisper of the imp.

The red rim about Eau faded away and the stars bloomed in the sky. Jack turned off the lights and through the thin air they could see the black velvet of the sky sprinkled with multicolored tiny gems.

Below them was the wingless *Magic Dragonfly*. Beams of light were streaming out the cockpit windows and the bulbous, eyelike scanner domes to spread patches of light on the dusty surface. The air was still and cold as the icy stars sucked warmth from the ground. One by one the lights on *Dragonfly* flickered off as David and Arielle closed down their checkout activities, then like the others above them, they spent the evening gazing at the sky through the cockpit windows.

The dawn was breaking over the distant arc of Eau when Karin assembled her press gang. Everyone became common laborers as they helped Karin and the Christmas Branch assemble the outer wing panels of the *Magic Dragonfly*.

The panels were hollow, graphite-fiber composite structures designed without internal bracing so that the wing panels nested inside each other. The nested wing sections fit neatly inside the lower portion of the lander on either side of the rudder of the *Dragonfly*. Using the upper winch, Karin and Jack carefully pulled each segment out one at a time and lowered them to a waiting team of spacesuited humans.

After the wing panels were unloaded and arranged, Karin and Jack lowered a bundle of small struts and two long telescoping poles. Before she came down, Karin unfastened the lower winch and brought it with her to the plane.

"OK, Jack," she puffed as she clambered up to the top

of the aerospace plane with the heavy winch and attached it to a waiting fixture. "Have the branch install the struts in the first section."

She motioned to the suited figures scattered about her below on the ground.

"This will be just like we practiced it on Titan," she said. She tossed down the end of the cable from the winch. "Set up the tripod over the section the branch is working on, then when the branch has installed the inner braces, hook the cable to the central lifting lug and get out of the way." Karin looked up at the sky. They had been working hard since daybreak and Barnard was already overhead. They were behind schedule. Slightly exasperated, she allowed a note of irritation to creep into her voice.

"And hurry up! We've only got an hour and a half of daylight left."

George picked up his pace as he went with Richard to pick up the tripod poles.

"Give a person a little authority and they turn into a Captain Queeg," muttered Richard. Jack was a little slow on interpreting the proper routing of the message from Richard's suit imp, and it was only when Richard had gotten to the word "authority" that Jack realized that the comment was for George's ears only and not the general channel. A chorus of chuckles and giggles rippled through the net.

"I heard that, Richard," said Karin. "If you'd like to come up here and play steeplejack I'll be glad to trade places with you."

"No thanks," said Richard, "steeplejacking is squaw work."

The tripod was assembled and the first section was raised into place, the Christmas Branch riding up on the inside.

"We're about ten centimeters off, Jack," said Karin. The branch extended its body between the hanging section and the wing stub, then contracted to draw the two sections closer together. Karin straddled the narrowing gap, and using a long-pointed pry bar between two aligning lugs, she pulled the wing section forward until the edges were lined up.

"Hold it!" said Jack as the edges were about to meet. A large spider-imp scurried around the narrow gap, removing the thin plastic protective cover from the sealing material. Karin could feel internal fasteners clicking into place beneath her feet, then the pressure on her pry bar lessened as the fasteners were rotated to pull the two wing sections together. Karin got up and glanced below her chin at the array of telltales in the neck of her suit.

"That took us fifteen minutes," she said. "We'll have to do better than that on the rest of the sections if we're going to finish before sunset."

Richard glanced again at George. He didn't use his imp this time, but instead made motions with his hands as though he were playing nervously with some large steel marbles.

The outer wing sections, being much lighter, were on well before dark, and Jill was able to pump them down, check for leaks, then refill them with fuel from the main tanks of the lander while the tired construction crew reboarded the lander for a last dinner together. Tomorrow they would break up into two teams. Sam, Red, and Thomas would stay with the lander. Thomas would remain in the lander as commander of Rocheworld Base, while Sam and Red would explore the region around the lander using a crawler. The other five would take off on the *Magic Dragonfly* to visit the other side of Roche and the distant globe of Eau hanging in the sky on the eastern horizon.

"I won't say that I'm sorry to see you go," said Sam. He popped the last of Nels's cherry tomatoes from

Prometheus' hypdroponic gardens into his mouth. The tomato was good, but getting a little wrinkled from sitting in Jack's refrigerator this long. It was the last of the fresh food. It was basic mush and frozen foods from now on. "After I get your sleeping racks stored away I'll be able to stretch out at night."

"Enjoy it while you can, Sam," said George. "We'll be back in a few weeks. It's only twenty-two days or eighty-eight rotations until Rocheworld reaches periapsis about Barnard. The weather on Eau is likely to get a little rough with the extra heating and I want to have the *Dragonfly* tied down here for those few days."

The next morning the exploration crew suited up early and gathered outside the lock of the aerospace plane.

"Now we'll see what this magic carpet can do," said George.

"*Magic Dragonfly*," reminded Arielle. "It can do everythings."

"Take me to a strange land, where I've never been before," said George.

"All right," said Arielle. "Hop on board."

Pilot and copilot-commander waited as David, Richard, and Karin passed through the air lock of the *Magic Dragonfly*, then the two figures grinned at each other as they followed them inside. The slimmer figure hesitated and let the larger one enter the lock first. During the wait, tiny fingers hidden in sausage-finger gloves stroked softly over the duralloy hull. Then, the "magic" for the *Magic Dragonfly* stepped aboard.

Arielle made her way forward toward the flight deck through the busy humanity inside the plane. She had some trouble getting past the science console area, since David and Richard were busy setting up the next day's schedule. She slid her thin body past this blockade only to confront a long torso stretching horizontally across the aisle from the port science blister to the starboard science blister. The head of the muscular body was buried deep into the port science electronics, and the rest of the body seemed to be ignoring the 10 percent gravity of the planet below. Arielle launched herself in a soaring low-gee dive over the human tollgate. She did a midair flip and straightened out so she was flying through the air feet first. George looked around just as the human bird fluttered to a landing on the raised platform between their seats on the flight deck.

"We are ready?" she asked, buckling herself into the pilot seat.

"Lift-off!" said George.

Arielle glanced at the console and took over the controls. She smoothly increased reactor power and adjusted fan pitch and speed at the same time. The *Magic Dragonfly* floated slowly upward into the ammonia skies on its fans.

Once they had reached adequate elevation, Arielle pushed the VTOL controls forward and they responded by tilting the huge electric fans in the wing of the plane until they were pushing the craft forward as hard as they were lifting it. Automatic servomechanisms took over, and the power of the nuclear reactor was increased to provide more heating to the streams of thin atmosphere that were captured by scoops in the side of the plane.

Arielle added a notch to the throttles, and the heat exchangers between the nuclear reactor and the frigid air turned cherry red. The heated methane, ammonia, and water vapor began to stream out the rear jet at high velocity, impelling the *Magic Dragonfly* forward.

Richard sat at the science console, orchestrating the first portion of their mission.

"I'd like some altitude first, please, Arielle," he said. "And, David, if you and Jill can look through the memory for ground scans taken during the descent of *Eagle*, I'd like one with a shadow angle similar to what we have now."

The aerospace plane banked as Arielle moved the *Magic Dragonfly* into a lazy, spiraling climb above Rocheworld Base.

"Scanners are all active," said Karin from the engineering console.

"I'd like the radar-mapper image," said Richard. His hands flew over the screen as he shrunk the radar image into half the screen, then placed the old image from the Eagle in the other half screen. It was the same region, but they were taken at different angles and distances.

"Rotate and rectify, Jill," he asked. The old image distorted as Jill rearranged the bits in the image. Richard's hands played over the command list and the old image faded into a deep red, while in the center a small white circle indicated the smaller region that was now being scanned by the radar mapper on their magic carpet.

"There's an interesting feature to the north, Arielle." He placed his finger on the fuzzy red blob. Arielle glanced at the small video to one side of her main display. It was a reproduction of Richard's science screen with a blinking, green, fingerprint-sized blob overlaid on a red blob. Arielle continued a half-turn, then straightened out the *Dragonfly* on a northerly climbing course. Soon the region of high-resolution, radar-sounding data grew in size and moved northward until the red blob was revealed as a small crater that looked as though it were perched on a teardrop-shaped mesa, the blunt end of the teardrop facing due west.

"Looks like a Martian crater," said George. "I can see it coming up ahead. There are flow lines that look like the crater was made in the bed of a stream and the stream flowed around it for some time before it dried up."

"It's only a hundred kilometers from Rocheworld Base," said Richard. "I think I'll put that on the visit agenda for Sam and Red."

"I don't think they're going to like you for that," said David. "They'll only be able to travel in daylight. It'll probably mean fifteen hours in suits just for three hours of daylight on site."

"They're dedicated rock hounds," said Richard. "Besides, the crawler will do most of the work."

Arielle took the *Dragonfly* in a slow circle about Rocheworld Base while Richard picked out a few more targets for the base-sticking crew to visit. Arielle then applied more power and headed for the outer pole to start a spiraling survey of the entire globe.

"Lots of craters on this side," said Richard.

"Like the moon, but with air," said George, scanning the horizon out the cockpit window. "I don't see any more signs of erosion."

"We would expect most of the precipitation to take place in the cold crescent that runs from the north pole to the south pole through the inner pole," said Richard. "Those portions receive proportionately less sunlight than the warm crescent that stretches out along the equator from the outer pole."

"I see some white stuff on the ground up ahead," said George. "Especially on the north side of crater rims."

"We getting close to north pole," said Arielle. "She is probably snow."

"Probably a mixture of ammonia and water ice," said Richard. "The temperature there is minus a hundred degrees centigrade."

"And I thought it was cold at Rocheworld Base," said Karin.

"We'll soon find out," said Richard. He put his finger on his screen. "Arielle, could you bring us down here in the middle of this large crater? I want to get some snow and bedrock chunks for my collection."

"We descend!" said Arielle, putting the *Magic Dragonfly* into a dive. Darkness came again as they approached the site. Using radar, Arielle and Jill carefully landed on a flat place not too far from the central peak of the crater, the ammonia snow blowing out from beneath the VTOL fans into the bright beams of the landing lights.

"Three winks, everybody," commanded George. Karin and David had anticipated George and were already in their bunks. It didn't take long for the rest to join them. Daybreak and a full schedule were only three hours' nap away.

The next day George and Richard donned their heated exploration suits and were carefully checked out by a mother-henning Karin. They clambered down from the *Dragonfly*'s air lock and started their half-kilometer trek to the central crater.

George stepped in a small patch of ammonia snow. Snow particles flew everywhere as his heated boot vaporized the ammonia crystals.

"Please try to avoid the snowdrifts," said his suit imp. "I only have a fixed amount of energy for heating and when it is half gone, I must insist you turn back."

"How far can I go with the present charge?" asked George.

"Twenty kilometers," said the suit imp. George humphed and continued toward the peak a half-kilometer away. He did try to avoid the snow, however.

Richard looked carefully at a couple of large rocks on the way out, but didn't use his geologist's hammer until he reached the base of the peak. He looked back to make sure that he was still within sight of *Dragonfly* so that Jill could have direct laser communication with his helmet receiver and the suit imp.

"I'd like the suit imp outside," he said. "I want it to take a rope up to that overhang."

"You aren't going to climb, are you?" asked Jill in a concerned tone through his imp.

"Yes," said Richard. "I want to get some samples from the top."

"I could send the imp to get them," said Jill.

"As smart as you are, Jill," said Richard, "I still want to see what's up there so we don't miss anything. Don't forget we are only under a tenth gee and I have an Alpine guide license."

By the time he had finished arguing with Jill, the suit imp had wiggled its way outside through the valves in the life-support pack. It took the end of Richard's rope and scampered up the cliff, its tiny cilia giving it a grip like a fly. The anchor was embedded firmly in the ledge and Richard walked his way up the steep slope. The maneuver was repeated three times until Richard was at the top of the peak. He disappeared from view, the suit imp staying on the crest in view of *Dragonfly*.

"It looks like a small volcanic crater," came the relayed voice.

Richard appeared again at the top of the peak and rappelled his way down. He went slowly, looking carefully at the surface passing beneath him. Occasionally he would stop and take off a small sample while George stood back to keep out of the way of falling bits of rock. Finally Richard was back on nearly level ground. He handed a small sack to George.

"Here, you carry this," he said. "I've got more to get. Let's backtrack, Jill."

Following the computer's directions, Richard zigzagged back along the path they had come, ignoring some rocks and taking samples from others that he had thought interesting on the way out. As their load of rock samples grew, it finally dawned on George why Richard had never used his hammer on the way out.

At the very last snowdrift before they reached the plane, Richard took out some sample bottles and a long stainless-steel wand with a claw at one end. He placed a bottle in the claw and locked it. Then he placed the tool and bottle in the snowbank until the vaporization stopped. Taking the frigid instrument by the handle, he quickly dipped it deep into the middle of the drift and scooped up a sample of snow. A quick flick of the lid with a gloved finger and the snow was trapped in the bottle before it had time to vaporize. The sample bottle was packed in an insulating case, along with a control sample of air. The case would only be opened by Jill's analytical imp after it had been put in the small freezer in Jill's work wall, where the computer could re-create any environment of Rocheworld from the hot outer pole of Roche to the frigid north pole of Eau. Richard and George cycled through. It was getting dark and it was time for another rest break before taking off again.

George and Richard were still asleep when dawn broke over Eau, and Arielle lifted the *Magic Dragonfly* on a whirlwind of snow particles. She gained altitude, then headed south and inward as they resumed the long spiral survey path that would take them within sensor distance of every point on the egg-shaped surface.

"It sure gets dark in a hurry," said Karin, looking out the cockpit window. Arielle was back in the galley getting something to eat and Karin was flying the airplane from the copilot seat. Since Jill was an excellent autopilot, however, her work consisted of leaving her hands off the controls and looking out the window at the scenery.

"Now that we're entering the inner pole region," said David, "we'll have a lot more dark time than daylight time. When Barnard isn't hiding behind Roche, it's hiding behind Eau. Right now we get about two hours of daylight and four hours of night during the six-hour rotation period. It's worst right at the inner pole, where its ninety minutes of daytime to four and a half hours of night."

Arielle made her way forward and returned to the pilot seat. "Me and Jill find way to get more daytime," she said. "We plan our flight path around inner pole so we always be on the sunshine side." She nodded at

Karin, dismissing her, and her eyes started their vigilant watch on the indicators and the view out the cockpit window.

Karin got down and returned to the engineering console to monitor the performance of Jill's scanners. There was a noise in the back and Richard pulled aside the privacy curtain to the crew quarters and came forward.

"We must be getting nearer the inner pole," he yawned. "I feel lighter already."

"We're down to six percent gravity," said David from his console.

"Any sign of volcanoes yet?" asked Richard as he sat down at the science console. "I'd like to visit a few of them."

"That could be dangerous," said Jill through his imp.

"Not if we're careful and pick one that isn't ripe for an explosion. Where's our history file of the inner pole region from the Comsat cameras?"

"I've got it right here," said Karin. Her fingers flickered over the directory menu at the side of the screen, and soon they were looking at HISTORY, COMSAT, VISUAL, INNER POLE, VOLCANO WATCH. She transferred her screen to his and got up.

"I think I'll get some sleep. We can't all be up at the same time." She went through the privacy curtain.

The sequence of pictures of the inner pole volcanic field flashed rapidly by on Richard's screen. Day and night passed and volcanoes erupted periodically.

"I can't really tell much with the changes in lighting, Jill," he said. "Please feature-extract the craters and the plumes, then run those by."

There was a second's pause as Jill rearranged bits, then a cartoon version of the inner pole region appeared on the screen and ran through the compressed-time history.

"Again!" said Richard, and the sequence repeated.

"Do it again and watch these three here." His finger tapped at the screen where there were three volcanoes in a line that pointed toward the inner pole. Jill expanded the view until the three filled the screen. First one volcano would throw up a plume of hot gas and dust, then the middle one would start, then finally the one nearest the inner pole would join them. They stopped in reverse order.

"Those three must be interconnected by an underground vent," said Richard.

"The periodicity is quite regular," said Jill. "The magnitude of the eruptions vary, but they always occur every three hours when Barnard is either behind Eau or Roche and the tides are strongest."

"If they are that predictable, then we can visit them between eruptions," said Richard. "Set your course so that we arrive just after an eruption."

"But just because we have records of twelve eruption cycles doesn't mean that they sometimes won't have an eruption between their normal cycle time," protested Jill.

"The first thing I'll do when we get there is put down a seismometer and hook you up to it," said Richard. "Then if the volcano starts to get rambunctious, you'll hear the rumbling in time to take us out of there."

"I hope so," said Jill with a worried tone.

"I hope you appreciate that 'concerned mother' tone," said David, who had been watching over Richard's shoulder and heard Richard's imp. "The psychologists thought it would be a good safety feature and asked me to develop it so people like you would go out of their way to avoid dangerous activities in order to keep Jill 'happy.' It turned out to be tough, took me three days playing with my synthesizer before I got the aggrieved tone just right."

"Pretty sneaky," said Richard, returning to the console.

They approached the triplet volcano during darkness. Arielle took the *Magic Dragonfly* to altitude and flew high over the plumes of hot gas and ashes so that they could take pictures. The light from Gargantua gave Jill's electrocameras enough illumination so that excellent photographs of the plumes could be obtained.

"We seem to be awfully high," remarked George.

"Better safe than sorry," said Arielle. "Gravity here is only three percent of earth gravities. Is easy for those monsters to throw a rock at us."

George looked at the display in front of him. He had trouble reading the altimeter. The numbers were not what he was used to. Finally he comprehended. "That says 83,200 meters!" he said. "We're eighty-three kilometers high! Are we on rocket power?"

"I just take her up on the nuclears jet until she won't any more climb," said Arielle. "Jill has good cameras, so we don't have to get close. Don't forget, when you lower the gravity, you higher the scale height. Good view, no?"

"I can see the curvature of the horizon," said George. "Especially at the inner pole."

The eruption subsided and Gargantua set. Arielle spiraled down and zoomed toward the first of the three craters.

"No lava," said George as they hovered over the cinder cone.

"This kind only shoots hot gas and dusty ashes," said Richard. "How's the temperature, Jill?"

"Quite hot inside the vents," said Jill. "But you should be able to get fairly close without exceeding the insulation limits on your suit."

"Can you take her down closer, Arielle?" asked Richard. "I want you to check the consistency by blowing the fans at it."

Arielle slowly lowered the huge airplane on its VTOL fans, then slid it backward to see if the blast from the fans blew a trough in the surface. At first the surface held, then large chunks broke loose and tumbled away.

"It looks like it has the strength and density of Styrofoam insulation," said George.

"I not land on it," said Arielle. "I hover for you, if you wish to go out. Gravity is so low I only need five percent of fan speed. You hardly will feel the breezes."

"OK," said Richard. "Take me over to that vent near the lip of the crater."

Expertly Arielle slid the *Magic Dragonfly* along the rolling ash surface to a twenty-meter-wide vent with a slightly elevated lip.

"I take you to top? Or do you walk up the slope?"

"Just drop me off at the base," he said. "There may be some gas still coming from the vent and it might blow the *Dragonfly* around."

Richard left to get his suit. Karin was waiting for him. She was already suited up and holding onto one end of a strong cable. The other end was fastened to a belt loop on Richard's suit.

"What's that for? I'm not going to need ropes to climb that slope."

"This is for that first step out of the lock," said a muffled voice. "If Arielle is worried that the *Magic Dragonfly* could sink in that stuff, I'm going to worry about you. You may have size eleven feet, but there is so much muscle-bound mass sitting on top of them that you're likely to sink straight to bedrock. As much as I hate to admit it, I want you back."

"Just so you can pick on me," said Richard plaintively. Karin took him carefully through the suit checkout, then as the inner door cycled, she circled around in back of him and picked him up bodily in the light gravity. Arms ineffectually waving in protest, Richard was carried into the air lock.

"At least I pick on somebody my own size," she replied, finally putting him down. He turned and glared at her grinning face through her helmet as the inner door closed, the lock cycled, and the outer door opened. The two looked out from the floating airplane at the dark, ashen crust a few feet below.

"Looks pretty solid," said Karin.

"Ash particles are red-hot and bristly when they come out of the vent," said Richard. "They have a tendency to stick together."

"Shall I lower you down?"

"Nope. Might as well give it a good test." He turned to look at her. "As my seven-greats-aunt on my mother's side used to say when she was looking for my seven-greats-uncle . . . 'Geronimo!' "

Richard jumped from the door and floated down to the surface in the 2 percent gravity. His boots made a depression in the crusty surface, but he didn't sink in.

"Did I detect a note of disappointment before Jill cut our imp link?" he said, looking up at the suited figure in the lock above him.

"Who? Me?" said Karin sweetly. She jumped and landed beside him.

"Lead the way," she said. "We've only got one hour left of this minimal day before it gets dark, and then it will *really* be dark since Gargantua won't rise until three hours later."

The two climbed the ashen slope until they got near the lip of the vent.

"You dig in and hold the rope while I go up to the rim," said Richard. "I doubt that there is an overhang, but funny things can happen with sticky ashes like this stuff when it collects in a low-gee field."

He took his geologist's pick and cut two deep heel-holes in the crust. Karin sat down and put her feet into the holes. She took her pick and slammed its point into the ground behind her. With one hand controlling the line through her belt, the other through the wrist loop of the pick and her feet in the heel holes, she was ready. Richard walked to the edge of the vent, Karin paying out the line as he went. He looked over the edge, then leaned forward to look down. The only thing keeping him from falling was the rope in Karin's frantic grip.

"Richard! Stop that!"

Ignoring the frantic cries, Richard leaned over still farther in the low gravity and swayed from side to side as he slowly looked down into the crater, taking shot after shot with his chest camera. He finally returned to the vertical.

"No overhang," he said. "You can come up here if you want. I'd like to have you lower me to a ledge about five meters down to get a sample from inside."

"Easy enough," said Karin. "In this gravity you only weigh a few kilos. I could lift you with my little finger."

"I'd prefer you use two hands," said Richard.

Karin dug in again and Richard went over the side. The noises coming from inside Richard's suit stopped abruptly as the laser beams that linked their suits were broken. Karin felt bereft without Richard's constant presence through their imp link. There was a movement in the sky as Arielle lifted the *Magic Dragonfly* and positioned it above the vent. Line-of-sight communication was reestablished with the airplane and Karin could hear Richard's voice again.

". . . it's a lava tube. This crater hasn't always been just hot gas and dust. Looks fairly recent too." There was the sound of grunting as Richard's pick pounded the rock to obtain a sample.

"Hold tight! Coming up!" Karin held tight to the throbbing rope and soon Richard's toes appeared over the edge and he lifted himself upright. He handed her a big clear stone.

"I won't be sure until Jill analyzes it, but I think it's a diamond."

Karin rolled the rough stone between her fingers, then looked coyly at him.

"Oh, Richard! How sudden! Now we're engaged."

"You've got it all wrong, beautiful"—he said, starting

down the slope toward the landing *Dragonfly* at a speed that made sure there was plenty of distance between them before he finished the sentence—"it's payment for services rendered!"

Rising slowly on its fans, the *Magic Dragonfly* first gained altitude, then speed as the nuclear jet cut in.

"Where to now?" said Arielle.

"Head for the inner pole," said Richard, "but take us over the big lava volcano. I want to get some infrared pictures."

Arielle headed the *Magic Dragonfly* toward the inner pole in the deep Roche darkness. They hadn't far to go and the gravity dropped even more. Using Jill's radar, they found a flat place and landed to wait for daylight.

Karin came up from the back, bouncing as she came.

"This is ridiculous," she said. "All that dirt out there and it isn't keeping me on the floor."

"You keep forgetting that equally large ball of dirt overhead," said David. "Why don't you put on free-fall boots? The floor has loop carpeting."

"They're back at Rocheworld Base," said Karin embarrassedly. "I was so busy checking everyone else's kits that I didn't check mine. Besides, I didn't expect to run into free fall in an airplane!"

"This is magic airplane!" said Arielle. "It can even abolish gravity. It almost sunrise, we shall go?"

"Yes," said George. "Up, please—and don't stop until up is down."

Arielle started the lift fans at low speed and the *Magic Dragonfly* rocked and lifted rapidly in the half-percent gravity at the inner pole. She switched to the nuclear jet and started a tight spiral climb upward toward Eau.

"Ten kilometers and climbing," she announced as the ball of Barnard rose behind Roche while Gargantua rose from behind Eau. The sunlight from Barnard illuminated the water mountain above them while the ground below was still in darkness.

"Twenty kilometers and climbing," said Arielle. "Gravity now less than one-three hundredths gee." Things started to float around in the cabin in the currents from the air-conditioning system. The room was soon full of busy mosquito-imps cleaning up the air.

"No ring waves," said George, looking up. Barnard now illuminated one-half of the conical ocean with its red glare, while the other half was more softly illuminated with the reflected light from Gargantua.

"Since it's been daytime on Roche, the atmosphere on the Roche lobe has been getting warm, while Eau has been in the dark and getting cold," explained David. "The air flow is from Roche to Eau, or down the water mountain."

"So no waves," said George. "Any that get formed spread out as they go down mountain."

The drone of the lift fan engines slowed.

"Forty kilometers altitude and stopped," said Arielle. "We at midpoint."

Falling

Karin took the diamond from her coverall pocket and suspended the rock in midair. It drifted slightly in the air currents but fell neither toward Roche or Eau.

"Zero gee," she announced.

"With the sun now shining on Eau, the ammonia will start to boil out of the ocean and the wind will start blowing the other way," said George. "If we are going to get any water samples or make any measurements we'd better do it soon."

"We go down?" said Arielle, starting the lift fans. The aerospace plane gathered speed and within a few minutes was hovering over the surface of the rounded tip of ocean at the inner point of Eau. The gravity had risen to a half-percent of gee and things once more took on their normal orientation, except overhead was now a conical mountain of rock instead of a conical mountain of water.

"Three meter above surface," said Arielle. "The wind are drooping down."

"Lower the sonar scanner, Jill," commanded Karin. There was a bumping noise from beneath the ship as the small package of sophisticated sound-generating-and-detecting equipment dropped out of a hatchway on the bottom of the plane and splashed into the water.

There was a blip on the screen as Jill fired the first strong burst of sound down into the depths. There was a pause as the trace made its way slowly across Karin's screen. As the green line approached the right side of the screen, there was a blink, and the scale increased ten times. The blip, now moving only one-tenth as fast continued across the screen, passing one depth marker after another.

"It's really deep," said Karin. "The marker is at fifty kilometers and still going."

"That's five times deeper than the deepest ocean on earth," said George. "I wonder what the pressures are like down there."

"Shouldn't be too bad," said David. "Don't forget the reduced gravity."

"I think the signal must have been attenuated by a muddy bottom or something," said Jill through Karin's imp. "I'll try a longer burst with a chirped frequency and then compress the returns."

"Fine," said Karin, then watched as a ten-second-long, slowly rising whistle of sound wended its way into the depths.

"There it is!" cried Karin as a return showed up on her screen.

"That is a return from the first signal," said Jill. "I will reconfigure the screen." Instantly the engineering screen was rewritten with a time display that contained a new length scale, while below it was a two-dimensional picture of the bottom surface that grew second by second as the acoustic pulse made the round trip to the bottom at fifteen hundred meters per second.

"The bottom is a hundred and fifty kilometers down!" said Karin. "We're on the top of a mountain of water a hundred and fifty kilometers high!"

". . . and it doesn't fall down," added David.

Karin watched the screen as the second and third pulses returned with their information and the details on the map cleared up. Richard looked over at her screen and pulled a copy of the map onto his screen.

"Those circular features are obviously volcanic craters," he said.

"What are those jagged features?" asked Karin. "They look like underwater Alps."

"Perhaps that's what they are," said Richard. "There are certainly enough tidal stresses to cause mountain building."

"There was nothing like that on Roche," said David. "Lots of volcanic craters to match the ones you see there, but nothing like those mountains." David pulled a copy of the display onto his screen and peered closely at it.

"They seem to avoid the craters," he said. "How tall do you estimate them to be?"

"About two kilometers," said Richard. "Not really big for mountains considering the gravity. If they are mountains . . ." he added.

"Pull the sonar in, Jill," said Karin. "Don't forget to get a sample. I want to analyze the water."

"My scanner has a built-in analyzer," said Jill. "The ocean at this point is minus twenty-three degrees centigrade and warming, with a composition of forty-four percent ammonia and fifty-five percent water, with trace amounts of methane, hydrogen sulfide, and hydrogen cyanide dissolved in it."

"Any trace of anything unusual?" asked Karin eagerly. "It would sure be wonderful to find a life-form. Even the tiniest microbe would pay earth back for what it cost to send us here."

"Nothing," said Jill.

George had been looking out the cockpit window at the horizon. "The waves are rising," he said. "If we are going to get any more samples and bottom maps, we'd better be moving."

"We go up!" said Arielle, and the *Magic Dragonfly*

leapt into the air and moved along the flank of the mountain of water, trying to stay as long as possible in the rapidly diminishing patch of sunlight.

"Can't you bring her down a little lower?" asked Karin. "The sonar is breaching the surface in some of the troughs."

"You argue with Jill," said Arielle with a fatalistic shrug of her shoulders. "I could go lower, but she is not allowing me to try."

"Jill!" said Karin. "We're at a hundred meters and the waves are only thirty meters high. Surely we could go down another ten or twenty meters."

"No."

Arielle suddenly reached for the controls and thundered *Dragonfly* upward on its rocket thrusters.

"Arielle!" yelled George. "Rockets!?!"

In reply Arielle swiveled the plane on its lift fans in time for George to see a large tsunami heading off up the mountain.

"Its direction of travel is different than the wind waves," he said. "That must have been caused by an underwater disturbance."

"There was a big underwater noise not too long ago," said Karin. "Must have excited that tsunami. I wonder how tall the wave was?"

"Eighty meters," said Jill.

"Then Arielle didn't really have to use rockets."

"If *Dragonfly* had been where you wanted it," said Jill, "that would have been the only thing that would have saved us." The tone of the computer voice was unusually severe.

"Hoist on your own petard!" laughed David.

"What are you talking about, David?" asked George.

"I'll let Karin tell you," said David, getting up and making his way back to the galley.

"Karin?" asked George.

For a while Karin didn't answer, then she said, "After David had all that trouble developing a 'worried mother' tone for Jill, I volunteered to do the next one. It was the severe 'I told you so' tone that you just heard."

"You did a good job," said George. "After hearing that voice, I certainly wouldn't argue with Jill over a safety matter. Wouldn't want to get on her bad side."

Barnard set behind Eau. They watched it go, then Arielle took the *Magic Dragonfly* around to the other side to await sunrise two hours later. They hovered at altitude, resting and napping until the sun rose again from behind Eau.

"Wow! Look at those waves!" said George.

"Surfer's paradise?" asked Karin.

"Purgatory," said David. "Those waves are so big there's no way you could ride them, even if you didn't need a suit to survive."

"It would still be fun to try," said George. "I learned to handle the big killer waves at Diamond Head, so I ought to be able to take on these, especially in the reduced gravity. Just think, a three-hundred-kilometer ride on a thirty-meter wave."

"Until you reached the top," reminded David.

"Yes ... the top ..." said George, looking out the window at the sunlit side of the mountain of water. Heated by Barnard, the ammonia-water ocean had gotten warmer and the ammonia had boiled off into the atmosphere, raising the pressure on Eau and causing a stream of wind to flow up the mountain to funnel through the narrow gravitational neck onto Roche. As the winds climbed the mountain, they pushed the waves ahead of them. When the waves converged on the low-gravity point at the top of the mountain, they became enormous.

"That was a BIG one," said George, admiring the fountain of water that appeared at the top of Eau mountain. In the light gravity, the spume of water from the implosion of the one-kilometer-high ring wave shot twenty kilometers into the air, where the spray was tossed up still farther by the rush of air from Eau to Roche. Lightning flashed, and clouds formed in the turbulent saturated air. David came forward to look out the cockpit window.

"Look," said David, pointing at the clouds above and below. "The clouds are swirling one way north of the peak and the other way in the south."

"It's the Coriolis force," said George. "Whenever you have mass flow in a rotating system, the Coriolis force makes the flows move in circles. We have the same thing on earth. Counterclockwise hurricanes in the Northern Hemisphere and clockwise ones in the Southern Hemisphere. It's significantly different here, though. On earth, the maximum Coriolis force is at the North and South Poles, but there are no strong air currents, so the maximum storm action is in the midlatitudes. Here the air currents are at a maximum right at the center of rotation."

"They look like giant tornadoes," said Karin. "One stretching north and one going south."

"They are," said Arielle. "But they are lazy ones because of low gravities. Not to be afraid."

The exploration survey turned routine. They would fly a hundred kilometers, hover to dip down the underwater sensor package, measure the distance to the bottom, analyze the water content, then take off again for the next survey point.

"I'm beginning to see a definite pattern in the water composition," said Karin. "It matches the weather and temperature patterns."

"The usual yin-yang pattern?" asked David.

"More like the two halves of the cover on an egg-shaped baseball," said Karin. "Barnard heats up the equatorial and outer pole region to about zero degrees centigrade, and the ammonia boils out of the ocean, leaving it water-rich and heavy. The high-pressure atmosphere then travels to the cold region and the ammonia rains down on the spin poles and the inner pole, making the ocean there ammonia-rich and light."

"That would explain the ocean current patterns I'm getting from the Doppler-radar mapper," said David. "There is a general motion from the cold arc to the warm arc. That would be the lighter, ammonia-rich liquid returning over the surface, while the heavier water-rich liquid closes the circuit along the bottom. Makes for a topsy-turvy ocean, hotter at the bottom than on the top."

"I wouldn't call zero-C hot," remarked Karin. She started the winch that would retrieve the ocean-sensor package from beneath the waves and nodded in turn to Arielle, who smoothly lifted the *Magic Dragonfly* up into the air on its VTOL fans and transitioned into level flight. The nuclear jet kicked in and the *Magic Dragonfly* screamed through the thin air toward the next survey point.

Warm•Amber•Resonance lay spread out on the surface, basking in the red rays of Hot, the heating light. Hot was getting bigger and the heat that it emitted was increasing, while Warm was shrinking again and would soon fade away, not to return for 480 days. The huge body relaxed even more and spread into a thin layer in the shape of a rough circle a hundred meters in diameter, a large amber blotch that rode the waves as they rippled underneath the jellylike flesh.

Then, weakly, there came a high-pitched noise. The acoustic senses in the amber creature went on alert. It sounded like a whistle from an underwater volcanic vent, but it had no direction. It seemed to come from every direction at once! The noise grew louder as if some invisible monster were emitting a hunger cry.

Warm•Amber•Resonance searched the water beneath with burst after burst of sound pulses from its body, but it could see nothing. Then just after the shriek from everywhere had reached its peak, the red glow from Hot flickered into blackness for an instant. Frightened, the vulnerable sheet of amber rapidly contracted into a three-meter ball, its sonar still searching for the source of the danger. It sank to the bottom as the ocean liquids were squeezed from the jellylike flesh to turn it into a tough, plasticlike rock.

"Anomaly found!" said Jill to both Karin and Arielle. A picture appeared on their screens. Jill had outlined the anomaly with a blinking green circle, but the cue was unneeded. In the center of the screen was a ragged circle of amber ocean.

"It also appears in the infrared scanner," said Jill. The same scene in the false colors of the infrared display flashed on in place of the video scene. The blotch was still amber in this scene, indicating it was significantly hotter than the water.

"Must be a plume of ejecta from an underwater volcano," said Karin. Richard looked up from his seat in the galley, put down his bowl of vegetable soup, and came forward, bounding in the low gravity in his eagerness.

"I'd like to see that!" he said, stopping himself by grabbing on Karin's shoulders. "Can Jill find the spot again?"

"We on our way around," said Arielle, putting the *Magic Dragonfly* into a wide turn. "Should be easy to see something that big."

"Are you sure this is the spot?" asked Richard as they hovered a hundred meters above the surface of the ocean.

"I have *Clete* in sight, so my navigation accuracy is better than one meter," replied Jill.

"Go up," said Richard. "Perhaps it floated off from where we saw it." Arielle took the plane rapidly to altitude. They went up a kilometer, the scanners in the eyes of the *Magic Dragonfly* vigilantly searching the rapidly increasing circle of ocean.

"The currents aren't more than a few kilometers an hour in this region and it only took us twenty minutes to return. We would have seen it if it just drifted off," said David, monitoring the IR scanner while Karin and Richard looked at the visible display.

"Let's go back down and take a look underneath the surface," said Richard. "Even if the cloud has dissipated, the underwater volcano should still be there."

Arielle pushed the down button and the magic elevator dropped smoothly to a position ten meters above the top of the waves. Karin lowered the under-ocean sensor package and it splashed into the water. Through the noise of the splashing the sonar sensor on the package heard some high-pitched squeaks, then echoes of those squeaks from distant rocks and underwater hills. They were too few to obtain an accurate direction fix, but they seemed to come from nearly directly below.

Jill hesitated before starting the sonar sender, waiting to see if the strange squeaks would reoccur, but the volcanic vent had fallen dormant. Jill started the sonar pinging, and soon a picture of the bottom built up on Richard's screen.

"There's nothing but mud and a few rocks here," he complained. "I don't see any sign of a vent."

"The water composition is just what it should be," said Karin. "If there were significant volcanic activity you'd expect an excess of impurities like hydrogen sulfide."

"Then the blotch wasn't volcanic," said Richard. "But what caused it? And where did it go?"

"Barnard will set in twenty-five minutes, and we are behind schedule," reminded Jill.

"OK," said Richard. "Why don't we continue the survey and I'll finish my soup. But would you rerun the data on the video in the galley? Maybe I can puzzle it out during dinner.''

Warm•Amber•Resonance stayed quietly on the bottom for a long time with its senses alert, but it could see nothing. The strange noise returned, then its screaming changed to a throbbing. The throbbing grew loud, then faded away, only to return once again. Suddenly something big and hard appeared with a splash at the top of the ocean. The amber rock fell silent while it carefully analyzed the last few sound pulses it had bounced off the strange monster. It was not too big, but it was as hard as a rock. None of the pulses traveled to the inside of the monster. If it was that hard, how did it float? The creature was quiet for a while, then it gave off a blinding burst of sound that repeatedly flooded the bottom with illumination. Warm•Amber•Resonance stayed motionless and waited while the sound that reflected from the bottom reached the top again, self-illuminating the hard visitor from the sky. Then tiny doors opened in the monster and sucked in water. Strange, stiff appendages with inset circles pointed this way and that, while burst after burst of sound throbbed from the underbelly of the creature. Then as suddenly as it began, the being stopped its seeing, and without seeming to move anything, it swam upward and out into the nothing above the ocean. The throbbing noise increased, then faded off, to be replaced by the hideous shriek that thankfully also faded off. The dread creature was gone. The amber rock dissolved into a floating blob of jelly and swam rapidly away.

Warm•Amber•Resonance had lived 374 seasons and was a leader of the pod. This hard-screaming monster was something unknown. There were others that were much older, such as Sour#Sapphire#Coo. Perhaps the elder would know about the strange monster.

Warm•Amber•Resonance was not exactly sure where

the elder was, but since the research problem the elder was working on was a difficult one, it would take many returns of Warm before any solution would be found. For that length of concentrated thinking time, Sour#Sapphire#Coo would have to rock up under a protective shell. The shell required periodic exposure to air to maintain itself, and that meant going to one of the Islands of Thought. Warm•Amber•Resonance traveled at top speed, but it was still two turns of the sky before the chain of islands on the warm pole was reached.

"I give up," said Richard many hours later. "I don't see anything more in those pictures than we did before. The amber blob is definitely there, not drifting much as we pass over it, then as we go over the horizon it looks like it starts to shrink, but the foreshortened perspective makes it difficult to be sure of that. Then when we return twenty minutes later, it's gone!"

"I'll keep working at the analysis," said David. "You'd better get your programmed sleep. You don't want to miss your island vacation trip, do you?"

"Are the 'Hawaiian Islands' coming up?"

"They're only nine hours away on the science schedule," said David. "And I know you want to get out and swing your pick at some of the outcroppings."

"Right! Wake me up as we get near. My pick is getting rusty on this water ball." He headed for the bunks in the rear, grabbing a protoprotein cookie for a belated dessert as he passed the galley.

The "Hawaiian Islands" were six rings of low mountains spread out in a line that crossed over the outer pole of Eau. The ocean was shallowest in this region and was only a few hundred meters deep, allowing modest mountains to stick their peaks above the surface. Each island was named after one of the Hawaiian islands, Hawaii, Maui, Lanai, Molokai, Oahu, and Kauai. Richard was awake and suiting up as George flew a high-altitude survey pass over the chain. Karin made her way back through the crew quarters to check Richard out just in time to see Arielle climbing into her upper bunk dressed in her bunny pajamas.

"Aren't you going to stay up and see the islands?" asked Karin, a little surprised.

"Piloting is hard work," said Arielle. "I would have fun to see them, but I now get my beauty sleep." She closed the Sound-Bar door as Karin continued on her way.

So that's her secret, mused Karin to herself. Must try it myself some day. She closed the privacy curtain behind her, and striding up to the suited figure standing in front of the air lock, she unceremoniously began punching the buttons on the chest console and reading the responses. Richard rocked slightly with each punch. Used to this kind of treatment, he ignored Karin and talked through his suit imp to George.

"Fly back over from the sunlit side and let me watch on my holovisor," he said, reaching up a gloved hand to pull a dark gray lid down over his visor. The inside of the visor lit up with tiny little laser diodes into a hazy image of mostly blue with some reddish splotches. Richard forced his eyes to relax, and as they stopped trying to focus on the nearby points of light from the diodes, the holographic multicolor laser pattern re-formed itself into an image of a rectangular video display at normal console distance, the array of tiny lasers generating at the surface of the visor the same light patterns, complete down to the phase, that would have crossed the surface of the visor from the video display if it had really been there.

"With their ring shape, they look more like atoll islands than the volcanic Hawaiian Islands," said George.

"They were only blobs on the flyby probe pictures," said Richard. "But they're not atolls, either. Those are formed by coral. Although I'd love to find even some low form of life like coral, I don't expect it here."

"What caused those rings, then?" said George. "Volcanoes?"

"My guess is that they're impact craters from a large meteorite," said Richard. "The meteorite came in at a low angle and broke apart in the upper atmosphere."

"I'm going down. Any particular one?"

"Find a flat spot on the inner side of Hawaii; I'm more likely to find some folded-back inner crust there."

"Which one is Hawaii?"

"The big one at this end. They're named in the same order as the Hawaiian Islands back home."

George was silent as distant memories of indolent days at Diamond Head flooded through his mind. He blinked back a tear of homesickness and started the long descent.

Karin patted the broad shoulders of the suit as Richard stepped into the air lock and cycled through.

"You be careful, now, you big lunkhead," she said. "I'll be right out to back you up as soon as I get my suit on."

As the outer door cycled the second time, Karin was surprised to see Richard standing at the door with an armload of rocks.

"I got some real beauties!" he said, his enthusiasm bubbling though the communication link. "Here, take these and put them in the air lock. Then come out and help me get some more." He tried to pile his armload into Karin's hands, but the stack slipped and a half-dozen sharp rocks tumbled to the floor of the air lock, leaving gashes and nicks in the mirror-smooth floor.

"Richard! You lummox! Now you've done it!"

"What did I do? The floor just has a few scratches in it."

"And those few scratches with those rough rocks probably increased the surface area inside the lock by ten times. It'll take forever to pump it down! Haven't you ever wondered why the lock has no extraneous equipment and all surfaces are mirror smooth? It's not so you can admire your handsome face in them. Those floors and walls are made that way so not one duralloy molecule sticks its head up above the rest to add to the surface area."

"I remember the briefings now. And those rock scratches have lots of jagged hills and valleys."

"Just eager to adsorb hydrogen sulfide and hydrogen cyanide and release them again when the lock is refilled with inside air."

"I'm sorry," said Richard, really contrite.

"Well ... it isn't really that bad," admitted Karin, "The Christmas Branch will polish the scratches smooth with a plasma gun while we're gone. Besides, our suits are the major contributor to contamination. The suit imp polishes them up when they're in storage, but they get roughened every time we go outside." She carefully placed the rest of the rocks inside the air lock and joined him outside.

"Well, that's about it for Maui," said Richard, glancing around at the cliffs above them.

"Are you planning on visiting all of them?"

"No, just Hawaii and Maui during this daylight period, and Molokai and Oahu the next day. These three-hour daylight periods sure chop up a work schedule. You just get interested in something and it gets dark."

"Richard," called David over the suit imp. "I've been going over the pictures that the scanners took on the way in. Pull down your holovisor, I want to show you something."

Both Karin and Richard reached up to pull down their holographic viewing screens. Hidden behind gray visors, they watched as David zoomed the view down into the center pond of Maui. The mountain ring was about ten kilometers in diameter, but it was not continuous. There were a number of places where the ocean had broken through passes in the ring and had flooded the interior of the impact crater. Not far from one of those entrances was a small blob of amber and an even smaller blob of blue.

"Jill would swear from the spectrum that the amber blob is the same type of stuff as the large amber blotch that disappeared. She's not sure, though, since this blob is under a meter of water."

"What does the infrared sensor say? Never mind . . . the water would kill that."

"There is a slight increase in the surface water temperature," said David. "But that could be explained just in terms of the difference in reflectance of the blob underneath."

"That's only a half-kilometer from where we are!" said Richard. "I'm going over for a look."

"I'll come over and pick you up," said George. The *Magic Dragonfly* lifted and floated over to them. George landed and waited until the dust had settled before he opened the air lock. Karin and Richard sat at the entrance and held on to the hand bars on either side of the door as George ferried them around the inside of the island arc.

Karin glanced in back of her, then tapped Richard with her free hand.

"Look at the scratches," she said.

Richard looked back. The scratches were still there, but their interiors were now just as mirror smooth as the rest of the floor.

Warm•Amber•Resonance searched from one island to another. A sour scent led it to the elder, a large blue rock lying just under the surface of the ocean. The amber cloud surrounded the blue rock and shouted:

•Open up! There's a hard screaming monster in the ocean! What is it!?!•

There was no immediate reply, but Warm•Amber•

Resonance didn't expect one. Sour#Sapphire#Coo had taken for its research project the derivation of an example of the fifth cardinal infinity. It had been twelve seasons of the visitations of Warm since the massive blue elder had left the pod and traveled to the Islands of Thought. Warm•Amber•Resonance had been hesitant to distract the elder, but with an age exceeding a thousand seasons, surely the old one would know if such a strange monster had been seen before and whether it was dangerous. The wait was necessary to allow the thinker to complete its present train of thought and put all the portions of the unsolved problem in a state where they could be picked up again without error. Hot traveled around to the other side of the world, and the tides rose again. Finally a soft voice murmured from behind the protective shell:

#A hard screaming monster?#

•It is too hard to float, but it does. It swims without moving. It can even swim in the nothing!•

A crack opened in the shell.

#Let me taste.#

Warm•Amber•Resonance formed a tiny tendril of an appendage and stuck it in the crack. Memory juices were exchanged.

#I never saw or learned of any such monster. It is your problem. I return to mine.#The crack closed and the blue elder returned to the problem of the fifth cardinal infinity.

Warm•Amber•Resonance was so busy absorbing the brief taste of the masterful strokes of the thought processes Sour#Sapphire#Coo used in its solution thus far that at first it didn't hear the high-pitched noise. The exchanged memory juices finally absorbed and incorporated into its own, the amber cloud suddenly reacted.

•The monster returns!!!•Like a tuna sensing a shark, the amber blob formed into a slim swimming shape and sped off into the deep ocean.

* * *

Before landing, George hovered the *Magic Dragonfly* over the spot on the ocean where the scanner had seen the colored blobs.

"I see the blue thing. It's a big, deep-blue-colored boulder, but the amber blob is gone," said Richard.

"Again?" said George.

"Yep. But that boulder isn't dissipating," said Richard. "Let me down onshore; I want to wade out and get a chunk."

"Richard!" said Karin, her cry echoing that of Jill through Richard's suit imp.

"When is low tide?" persisted Richard.

"In a half hour," said Jill.

"And how much will the water level drop between now and then?"

"Over a meter."

"Which means I'll be able to walk right out to that rock and chop off a chunk and hardly get my feet wet."

"But your suit . . ." protested Karin when Jill didn't respond.

"If my suit is good enough to keep out this poison we call an atmosphere, it's good enough for the cleaning solution that we call an ocean," said Richard. "And the extra amount of heating power I'll need for the short trip is nothing to worry about. Right, Jill?"

Karin and Jill reluctantly agreed to let Richard have his way. Karin insisted that she tie a safety rope to him before he started out and he let her. His first steps into the retreating ocean were dramatic, as clouds of evaporating ammonia boiled off at each step, but soon the outside of his suit was as cold as the water and he plowed through the thigh-deep ripples to the deep blue boulder. Once there, he looked it over carefully, then raised his pick and broke off a small piece. It was lighter blue inside. Richard put the prize into his collection bag and waded back to shore.

"Maui has too many tourists this season," he said. "Let's take a hop over to Molokai." He and Karin got into the air lock. They closed the door this time as George lifted for the short trip to the next island sixty kilometers away.

"Any more islands?" asked George after Richard and Karin had climbed back through the air lock.

"We've done four—Hawaii, Maui, Molokai, and Oahu," said Richard. "That should be enough for a nine-hour tour. Besides, it's almost sunset again. Let's head back to the inner pole."

"I recommend that course," said Jill. "It's only fifteen days to periapsis, or sixty day-night cycles. The weather at the inner poles is already getting stormier as it gets warmer. I would like us to be back at Rocheworld Base at least ten days before periapsis."

"That gives us five days for survey stops. Is that going to be enough?" asked Richard.

"It should be," said Karin. "We have most of the place mapped, and the data matches the atmospheric and ocean models well. It's just a matter of getting enough samples to keep the statistical errors down. Except for those islands, this place is pretty dull. It would have been different if we'd found any evidence of life, but no such luck."

"Did you get an analysis done on that blue rock?" asked Richard.

"Yes," said Karin. "It was very similar to that silica-gel-type crystalline rock that Sam found over on Roche. It must take a strange chemistry for that to form. Neither Jill nor I have been able to come up with a good process yet."

Two days later, it was George who first spotted Roche from his vantage point at the cockpit window.

"Land ahoy," he shouted throughout the ship as the

edge of the twin world showed its brown over the blue-gray waves. After another half hour, they were within line of sight of Rocheworld Base.

"Welcome back," said Thomas. "Red says from down below that she can see your contrail from the viewport window."

"Pretty good eyes," said George.

"Especially when in back of a thirty-centimeter telescope," broke in Red's voice. "Even though we're nearly always in contact through one Comsat or another, it's still nice to see you directly."

"We'll be home soon," said George. "A few more survey stops to fill in the gaps in the records, then across the neck in time for periapsis."

"Watch that weather," said Red. "There's a nice storm brewing above the water mountain and it's coming your way."

"We'll fly over it," said George. "See you soon, beautiful." George got a weather map from *Clete* and talked it over with Jill.

"It's moving fast, but we should be able to take one more survey sample before dark, then get back to altitude before it arrives." As he spoke, George put the *Magic Dragonfly* into a steep dive and headed for the ocean surface. He brought the plane to a hovering stop in the strong surface winds, and Richard let down the ocean sampler into the rolling seas.

"That's some wind," remarked Richard as he monitored the drop through the bottom video camera. "The cable is trailing thirty meters downwind. Hold it for a minute until I get a return from the bottom. . . . Got it! Take her up!"

George applied power and climbed the *Magic Dragonfly* into the scruffy sky. The sun was setting, but George easily kept track of the clouds by the nearly constant lightning flashes. There was a crash from the galley as the plane dropped a few hundred meters in a vicious downdraft, then they were forced into their seats as an updraft sent them spiraling skyward again. George raced in front of the storm to stay in quieter air while he climbed. They were going around the mountain now and Rocheworld Base dropped below the horizon behind them. The air became smoother as the nuclear jet thundered them upward, then finally George put the plane into a turn and headed back up the mountain. Arielle had been sitting in the copilot seat. Her hands were in her lap and her eyes were busy scanning the instrument panel and the view outside. George looked over at her, put the plane on autopilot, and stepped down into the aisle. Arielle slipped quickly over to the pilot seat and strapped herself in. She left the plane on autopilot. Her hands went back into her lap and her eyes kept busy.

"We've passed over the front, and there's a clear region before the next front," said Richard from the science console. "One of our survey points is there. If you're willing to try a night landing we can get it out of the way and be that much closer to going back."

"Give me good weather maps, good radar, and good altimeter, and I don't need to see," said Arielle. "But just to be on safe side, I turn landing lights on near the waves."

Arielle took the controls and spiraled down into the inky blackness below. The distant orb of Gargantua was now too small to be of much use as a source of light, but she didn't need light, for the radar picture of the clouds and surface were all that she and Jill needed. As they came down below five hundred meters altitude, Arielle turned on the landing lights. Their position was on the high-gravity equator, where the gravitational pull peaked at nearly 12 percent of earth gravity. The waves were smaller but faster moving, and looked somehow harder as they scudded along. Richard dropped the sampler in the ocean and waited for the sonar return from the bottom. It came almost instantly.

"The bottom is only thirty meters down," he said in amazement. "This must be some sort of an underwater plateau."

"The water composition is radically different, too," said Karin from the other console. "There are lots of dissolved gases and strange chemical compounds. The temperature is also anomalously high."

"I think we must be near a volcanic vent field," said Richard as he watched the sonar map build up to show a slope rolling off to one side. "Let's head upslope and drop the sampler in again."

"OK," said Arielle. "Uphill in which way?"

"Toward Roche."

"Toward Roche we go," she said, lifting the plane and moving it a kilometer east, then lowering it again.

"The bottom is getting closer," said Richard.

"And the water is getting warmer," said Karin.

"Another kilometer Rocheward?" asked Arielle.

"Arielle!" Jill interrupted. "Radar. Ten kilometers and moving toward us!"

Arielle glanced at the radar display to see a large, rapidly moving cloud breaking away from the more slowly moving front that was approaching. Beneath the cloud was a swarm of smaller, swirling clouds. She pointed the video cameras in the *Magic Dragonfly*'s eyes in that direction, and the sensitive cameras turned night into day on her screen. The scene was illuminated by nearly continuous flashes of lightning inside towering columns of foam.

"Waterspouts!" she blurted. Cutting the cable on the ocean sounder, she banked the *Magic Dragonfly* into a tight turn and headed south at right angles to the course of the waterspouts. She didn't try for altitude but skimmed the surface of the water. The nuclear jet thundered in as the fans faded and some of their irreplaceable monopropellant fuel was poured into the afterburner as Arielle accelerated the plane to top speed. Like a rocket ship taking off horizontally, the *Magic Dragonfly* shot forward. A column of foam internally illuminated by lightning moved in front of them.

"Damn!" said Arielle and threw the stick over. The left wing tip grazed the foamy tops of the waves below, then swung upward again as the right wing dipped. They missed the first spout, but a second one rose up above them and dumped its load of water in their path. The airplane shuddered as it hit the cloud of huge droplets. There was a loud bang from the engine compartment, then silence.

"The jet heaters shut down!" cried Arielle. "No time to reset!"

The powerless plane started to drop in altitude, perilously close to the tops of the waves. Arielle fired the attitude control jets to decrease their rate of descent. Made for space, they could not levitate the *Magic Dragonfly* in 12 percent gravity. With the rockets fighting off the crash. Arielle brought the VTOL fans up to speed and stabilized the altitude as she turned off the rockets. More precious fuel gone.

She returned her attention to the radar screen just in time to see a tiny twister cross her path. The twister was too close to miss. The right wing of the *Magic Dragonfly* sliced into it and was sucked upward. Arielle almost pulled them out but the dipping left wing dug into the top of a large wave, spinning them around. The *Magic Dragonfly* crashed heavily into the deep trough in back of the wave.

Crashing

Arielle lifted her face. Her right hand still gripped the control stick. It was bloody and had two deep gash marks in it. There was a small stone in her mouth. She spat it out. She watched the bloody hand move the stick in slow motion as her left fluttered over the control board like a dying bird.

Lift! her mind commanded as she applied power to the VTOL fans. There was a low throb from the right wing.

Karin clamped her throat shut and shook off her harness. She ran to the rear and donned her suit, for once without consulting a checklist. The helmet snapped into place and she took her first breath. She pulled herself forward on the sloping deck and pounded on two Sound-Bar doors, while holding them tightly shut with her body.

"David! George! You OK?" she hollered through her suit imp.

"Yes," came the muffled replies.

"We've crashed in the ocean. Don't open your bunk door until I check for air leaks!" She glanced up at Richard. He slowly and cautiously took a deep breath of

163

air and held it. She took his suit out of the locker and helped him with the hard part, then made her way forward on the steeply sloping deck to the front.

Arielle was gunning the controls in time with the lurches of the waves and firing the attitude jets in an attempt to lift the *Magic Dragonfly* into the air. She looked around as Karin approached. Karin was horrified at the sight of the beauty's face. Arielle's upper lip was a torn bloody strip hanging down over a gap in her teeth.

"We'f crathed," she said in a plaintive voice. "And there'th thomfing wrong with Jill."

"I'm OK," came Jill's voice, calm and steadying. "I just can't see anything on my radar. It's the water covering the radome, of course. You might as well stop trying the fans and rockets, Arielle. The left fan is broken. Even if we could lift out of the water, we couldn't build up enough speed to clear the jets."

"How's the hull, Jill?" said Karin.

"There's a minor leak in the left wing fuel tank, but I have a minibranch making sure it gets sealed. No evidence that the life-support hull has been breached."

Richard came forward in his suit. When he saw Arielle he blanched and went back for the first-aid kit. The Christmas Branch took it away from him and led Arielle back to the shower to wash her off and repair her torn lip with a neuskin patch. An imp came scampering out from under the pilot seat carrying a large white tooth with a bloody root.

Karin opened her helmet and sniffed the air. It smelled funny, with an acrid smell of fear. The odor died as the air-conditioning fans continued their work of keeping the electronics cool. She and Richard headed for the back. Karin heard a few mewling sounds from the shower and reached down to pick up the soggy, red-stained jumpsuit from the floor outside the shower and put it in the sonic washer, then knocked on the Sound-Bar doors and told David and George that it was safe to come out.

She was starting to put away her helmet when Richard took it away from her.

"I've got it," he said. "You and Jill have to figure a way to get us out of here."

"Are you sure the left fan is out?" Karin asked Jill.

"Both fans were in the maximum forward position to maintain speed when the left wing struck the top of a wave. Immediately thereafter there was an overload in the acoustic sensor on the fan drive shaft followed by a rapid increase in back reaction from the electric motor, raising the drive current to dangerous levels. I shut the motor down."

"It's jammed then. I'd better go out and take a look at it."

"Although we are afloat, the air-lock exit is underwater. I do not advise exiting."

That stopped Karin for a moment. "Richard showed our suits can handle water," she said.

"My air lock is not designed for liquids," said Jill, using her severe tone.

Karin knew her computer.

"If I can't get out the air lock," she said, "then I can't fix the fan. The crew will have to stay inside until the life-support systems fail and then we will all die."

There was a pause. Not a full second, but a noticeable fraction of one.

"The purging systems of the air lock can be reconfigured to accommodate liquids," said Jill. "Cycle time will double since I will have to purge twice. Once with superheated air to evaporate any residual drops and liquid films, and once again to ensure purity before breaching the inner lock. You must have your suit cooling on full power during the hot-air phase."

"Fine," said Karin, putting her helmet back on her head. "Cycle me through."

There was a moment of panic as a gush of water splashed down from two vents in the ceiling of the air lock. Karin ducked under the thundering jets and peered through a rivuleted visor at the foaming swirl on the floor. Her feet were cold and she felt the warmth of the boot heaters as her suit tried to compensate for the loss of heat. In a minute the sub-zero ocean water of Eau was up to her waist. The buoyancy of her suit in the water began to lift her feet from the floor. She grabbed onto wall rungs to keep from being swept under the crashing foam.

"Let some air out of my suit," she hollered. "I'm floating." She heard a hiss from her backpack and the water pressed hard on the wrinkled glassy-foil covering of her suit. As impermeable as metal, the glassy-foil was as flexible as plastic because of its noncrystalline structure. Nearly a millimeter thick, it could shrug off anything except the point of a knife blade. It did wrinkle under pressure, however, and the cold water pressed through the thermal layer of the suit and chilled her skin. The water burbled in and the air vented out until the door could be opened, letting a giant oscillating ball of air loose to make its way to the surface. Karin followed it out.

"Leave the lock open and the lights on," said Karin. She swam out into the broadening column of light, then reached for the permalight on her belt. The spearing ray of light swung up to illuminate the fan well. There was a black gap where one of the blades was missing. The blade next to it was distorted and torn.

Karin looked at the nightmare of twisted high-strength steel. It reminded her of Arielle's mouth and was just as devastating to the inherent beauty of the *Magic Dragonfly*. She kicked downward and tilted herself back until her chest camera was pointing at the scene, while pulling down her holovisor to monitor the picture as seen through the viewfinder of the electrocamera. It was blurred. The camera lens had been designed to interface between space and air, not water and air.

"Can you compensate?" she asked Jill.

Instantly the blurred image snapped into sharp focus as Jill adjusted bits to compensate for the index of refraction of the water as well as the slowly varying distance to the image.

"Got it," said Jill.

"Now to get a top view," said Karin, kicking up to the surface and grabbing the trailing edge of the wing. She raised her helmet above the water and just before it was engulfed in a breaking wave, she saw the dawn rising over Roche. Silhouetted in the pink light was the Christmas Branch, carrying an electrocam and making its way carefully back over the water-washed wing.

"I have that side," said Jill.

Karin clenched her chattering teeth and let herself drop beneath the waves. A few strokes and she was back in the lock. A water lock this time, as powerful exhaust pumps sucked the water from beneath her boots.

"We'll have to ballast the boots and the backpacks so the suit can stay inflated and prevent contact of the legs and arms with the cold suit," she said.

"Good idea," said Jill. "Now turn around and let me dry off your back."

As Karin turned and rotated her body under the blasts of hot air, she could see steam rising from the shiny metal film of her suit. The suit cooling cut in and she was just beginning to complain that it was getting too hot when the cycle shifted. A few minutes later she was inside the plane. George was standing there with a worried expression.

Karin took off her helmet and reported.

"It doesn't look good. The fan is busted. One blade twisted beyond repair and another one missing."

"Can you clear the twisted one and get the rest rotating?"

"Maybe," said Karin. "But that will leave it unbalanced. I could remove another and turn it from a six-blade to a three-blade propellor, but I don't think that will lift. Perhaps we could jury-rig another blade or two, or perhaps arrange a counterbalance."

"You work on it," said George as Richard helped her out of her suit. Richard's arm brushed hers and he felt the clammy cold.

"You're frozen!" Richard said with concern.

"Not much worse than a deep dive in the Pacific Northwest," said Karin. Still she didn't complain as he moved around behind her and gave her a long hug, his strong arms giving the firm muscular ones beneath them a warm embrace.

"How's Arielle?" she asked as she basked in his warmth.

"George and the Christmas Branch reinserted the tooth, and she now has an imp brace in her mouth holding it in place. The neuskin patch should heal the tear with at worst a hairline scar, but she's going to have a fat lip for a while." Richard, his own arms too cold to be of much good anymore, let her go.

"I think I'll go forward and check out the instruments," he said. "You and Jill had better concentrate on fixing that fan."

He headed up the rocking corridor while Karin returned to the task of hanging up her suit.

◇ Come see what I found! ◇

☆ What!?! ☆

◇ A big animal as hard as a rock, but it floats! ◇

☆ Wow! Where? ☆

◇ This way. ◇ The milky-white cloud streamed off through the ocean, followed close behind by the red one. They approached the floundering winged metallic whale with caution.

☆ You're right! ☆ said the red one, sending pulse after pulse of sonar signals at the distant object. The pulses varied in pitch and complexity as the powerful voice of Roaring☆Hot☆Vermillion attempted to peer into the inner portions of *Dragonfly*.

☆All I can see is the outside! It's too hard!☆

◊There are some portions that are not as hard. Come closer.◊

The two moved closer to the drifting aircraft. They were curious, but still cautious, since the huge plane was as big as they were. As they moved, their sonar pulses continued to scan its length.

◊There are places near one end where you can almost see through. Those are also places where you can 'look.' The beast seems to have small hot suns inside it, and they shine out through those places.

☆LOOK? SUNS!?!☆ The red alien was bewildered. Its body was sensitive to light and when it was spread over the upper surface of the ocean basking in the warmth, it could tell roughly where the sun was in the sky, and whether a cloud had passed in front of it, but it had no eyes, so it didn't know what the heavens looked like. Its visual world was one of sound. Its sound pulses allowed it to see everything in its underwater kingdom, including the insides of its comrades. This was the first time it had met a beast that wasn't completely transparent to its piercing stare. As it approached the hard-shelled creature, the various portions of the red body could feel the diffuse beams of light coming from spots near one end of the long central body. As Roaring☆Hot☆ Vermillion got closer, its body could look better, since some portions were quite close to the light sources.

◊Get real close. Then you can not only see a little better, you can look better too.◊

The red cloud pressed itself onto the hard glass of the cockpit window and tried to see in through the murky glass. Its burst of sonar energy penetrated from the water into the glass quite easily, but on the other side was nothing but air, so most of the sonar signal reflected back and only a small portion entered the cockpit to illuminate the objects there. The acoustic return also suffered the same loss as it moved from the low-density air back into the high-density glass. There was not much left of the sonar signal by the time it flowed back through Roaring☆Hot☆Vermillion.

☆Can see some hard things inside, but there is a nothing in the way and it makes it hard to see.☆

◇Are you looking too?◇

☆Yes. Many little suns. Too far away to look at well. They are all blurred together.☆

Arielle looked out at the reddish-colored haze obscuring her right side window. Must be another one of those strange-colored blobs. Suddenly her head hurt. She stood up and moved around, trying to shake the feeling.

☆Something is moving inside!☆ A blast of high-energy sonar sang through the glass and burst into the low-density air beyond. Arielle winced again, although she didn't know why.

☆It is a long thing with a sphere on one end and straight portions coming out of the sides and bottoms! It's too much work to see. I give up. Let's go surfing?☆

◇Maybe I can see.◇ The white cloud slithered over the red one and flowed onto the next panel of glass in the cockpit window.

Arielle noticed that while the right side window of her cockpit window still had the reddish tinge, the front window on the right now had a milky-white appearance. There didn't seem to be any blending of one into the other. She frowned. She didn't like it. Her eyes shifted to pay attention to the perfect break between the two colors at the cockpit window frame.

Clear◇White◇Whistle tried again. It sent burst after burst of sonar into the strange hard beast, but saw nothing new.

◇ You're right. There's a nothing in the way. It's like trying to see above the top of the ocean. ◇

☆ Let's go surfing! I can feel a big one building up! ☆

◇ Let me try looking. ◇

☆ I already tried! Too blurry! ☆

Clear ◇ White ◇ Whistle didn't answer, but formed a portion of its body into a disk shape. The disk grew thicker in the middle, and the milky-white color of the flesh faded away into clarity as the milky macromolecules containing the genetic essence and nerve tissue flowed out of the disk region, leaving only the clear, basic structural substance of the alien body.

A portion of the red cloud darted about the construct, noting its shape and looking at its clear color.

☆ Strange! What is it made of? ☆

◇ It is me. Or part of me. ◇

☆ Why does the disk bulge in the middle? ☆

◇ So I can 'look' at things from a distance. ◇

☆ Can't! You can only look at things when they are right next to you! ☆

◇ With this fat disk I can. ◇

☆ Really!?! Let me look! ☆

◇ Hold still! ◇ the white one commanded, and holding the disk between the skin of the red one and the cockpit window, it used the crude lens of jelly to focus an image of the interior of the cockpit on the skin of Roaring ☆ Hot ☆ Vermillion.

☆ It looks tiny!!! ☆ came a roar. ☆ What is it? ☆

Clear ◇ White ◇ Whistle took the lens away and put it in front of its own body.

◇ There are lots of little suns. Some square. And there is that moving thing you saw. Looks funny. The sphere has ugly fuzz on it, and a slit that keeps opening and closing. ◇

☆ I can feel that big wave getting closer and closer! ☆

◇ You're right. I can feel it too. ◇

The lens was dissolved. The two huge blobs slithered

to the top of the wing and launched themselves onto a large curling wave that washed over the drifting *Dragonfly*. The two aliens surfed expertly along on the wave, their recent discovery ignored in the excitement of the ride.

Arielle's headache lifted, and as it did, she noticed out of the corner of her eye the lifting of the milky and red haze from the windows of the cockpit. She moved forward, and kneeling on the copilot's seat, she tried to peer out into the murky water.

There was nothing.

Arielle was tempted to ask Jill if the computer had seen anything, but then she realized that Jill's electronic video sensors were just as limited as her electrochemical video sensors were in this frigid ocean. She swung around into the seat and ordered a position update from the console. There was an almost imperceptible delay in the response. Arielle's test-pilot-trained brain noted the anomaly.

The barrage of sonar sounds had taken Jill unaware. It had heard some strange pings and chirps from a distance a few hours ago, but after they had disappeared she had relegated the noises into its permanent memory under "Geology, volcanic, vents, noises from." The noises reappeared, however, and at close range—so close that they were obviously not volcanic in origin.

The science-scan video cameras and the other sensors built into *Dragonfly*'s body helped put together the picture. There was a red blob and a milky blob of water that moved slowly—like unformed clots of seaweed, seemingly moving with the tide. The blobs were completely amorphous, with no structure seen in either the video or infrared sensor. The inside video camera had confirmed the colors when the two blobs washed against the cockpit windows. The shape information went to a portion of Jill that had been programmed to be on the alert for signs of alien life-forms. There was no match to the program, for it had been trained to recognize symmetry and nonrandomness as an indicator of life. The information was bounced back into memory and the alien-finding portion of the program was turned off.

The sonar input, after processing in both frequency space and time space, was also sent to the test-for-alien-life program. Soon urgent messages were running through the master bus, calling back the stored shape information and activating a search through every sensor that had collected the least bit of information at that critical time period.

There was a moment's pause as Jill responded to the bothersome query from the human Arielle concerning a position update. That done, full computer brainpower was applied. Strange scents were extracted from the noisy data in the chemical sensors that monitored the outside conditions. Unfortunately, there was no new sensor data coming in, so the analysis had to make do with the sensor records. But the records were not good enough. Jill was almost sure that it had seen evidence of life—an intelligent life-form. But what it had seen was not what the humans had expected, so the evidence was not conclusive. Jill would not bother the humans until it had done more calculations.

Jill thought.

"I need better sensor data," said Jill finally.

"What's the matter?" asked Karin.

"I'm blind," said Jill. "I have lots of information from the infrared and video cameras on the two scanners in the 'eye' domes, but they are half awash in the ocean. Besides, as an airplane, I'm used to having the long-distance vision of radar. How can I protect you if I can't see things coming from a distance?"

"There's not much I can do," said Karin. "Your radar dome is under the ocean and the water won't pass the microwaves. If you're going to insist on being a boat, you'll have to find some way to have me change your radar into a sonar."

"OK," said Jill. "Please change my radar into a sonar."

"Can't be done," said Karin, slightly perplexed.

"You said that all I had to do was find some way to change my radar into a sonar," said Jill. "So I did."

"You did!!!" exclaimed Karin.

"We have a complete set of spare parts for the under-ocean scanner," said Jill. "The sonar array of the ocean scanner has almost the same design features as the microwave scanner in my radome."

"That would make sense," said Karin. "They both have the same wavelength, even though one uses radio waves, while the other uses acoustic waves."

"The piezoelectric sonar array uses higher voltages and lower currents than my semiconductor-diode radar array," said Jill. "But I have reconfigured the electronic driver to handle that. All I need is someone to replace the microwave diode array with the piezoelectric sonar array."

"Can't the branch do that?" complained Karin. She could still feel the bone-cold waters pressing on her flesh.

"Not by itself," said Jill. "It is out there now, rewiring the connector . . ."

". . . All right! All right! I'll do it."

Karin donned her suit and slowly cycled through the outside lock. It was still dark, so she took her time as she swam under the wing and along the left side of the *Magic Dragonfly*. She got out her trusty Swiss Army Mech-All, and rotating it until she came to the correct slide switch, she pushed the switch, and a strange screwdriver was instantly formed from one of the many triggerable memory structures in the complex metal-alloy head. The blade was shaped like the curved surface of a penny. Karin jammed the blade into one of the curved slots on the radome and twisted. A flat metal screwhead popped out. Karin sank down a little and attacked another slotted inset screwhead.

"Here," said Jill, its Christmas Branch handing her a thick circular plate of metal with crossed slots in it. Karin took the microwave transmitting array and handed the branch a heavier cluster of square ceramic tiles.

The branch took the cable dangling from the back of the sonar array and connected the cable to a jet-black box. There was a pause and Karin hollered.

"Ouch!" said Karin. "It makes my teeth ache."

"Good," said Jill. "That's the tooth-sensitizing frequency. How about this?"

"I feel sick," replied Karin.

"The infrasonic portion is working," said Jill. "Now the ultrahigh band. Do you hear or feel anything?"

"Bowwow," said Karin, her ear tips trying to curl up. She closed the radome, being careful not to leave any trapped air that would impede the sonar signals.

"I can see!" said Jill through her imp. "I have to wait a number of seconds before the distant parts of the image comes in, but I can see again!"

"What can you see?" asked Karin.

"We're on the side of a gradual slope that extends for kilometers," said Jill. "The slope reaches a plateau some ten meters under the surface of the ocean. There are some volcanic vents there."

"Richard was right," said Karin. She began to feel the cold. "I think I'll go inside and tell him."

"I have already informed Richard of our find through his imp," said Jill.

"I think I'll go inside and tell him anyway," said Karin.

George was sitting at the science console monitoring the flow of data from the imager memory banks through the satellite data link to *Prometheus*. Even though they might not be able to get off this world, at least their data would.

There was a buzz and a blinking light indicating that a communication link from Rocheworld Base had been opened. He switched the communication console controls to his science console and answered.

Red's face appeared on the screen. Her hair was tousled and there was a suspicious redness around her eyes.

"I may have a solution to your problem, *Dragonfly*," she said. "I don't know whether it will work or not . . ."

A deep voice broke in from the other side and Thomas' face peeked into the pickup.

"Sure it'll work," said Thomas. "I'd've never thought of it, since all I've ever done is haul cargo from heavy-gravity planets. It took a rock hound like Red to think of this one. I have Jack figuring out the optimum trajectory and the fuel margins we will need for various hovering times, but it should work fine."

"Great!" said George. "But what is it?"

"The ascent module doesn't have enough fuel to take off from Roche, land on Eau, and take off again," said Red. "Even if we lighten it by throwing off everything movable. It does have enough fuel, however, to take off from Roche, travel over to the zero-gravity region between the planets, hover for a minute over the water mountain, pick you up, and still escape out to the L-5 point. *Prometheus* can then sail in and pick us up from there."

Greatly relieved, George's face lit up as he listened to Red.

"That sounds terrific!" he said to the hopeful faces on the screen. "I hope Jack doesn't find anything wrong with it."

"Fortunately, we have lots of time," said Thomas. "How're your consumables holding out?"

"No problem there," said George. "The good food is going fast, but it will last us for a few more weeks. Then we have the emergency rations, and if worse comes to worst, Jill can make us sugar syrup out of the soup we are sitting in. We're probably good until one of the recycling units develops a failure that Karin and Jill can't fix. With that kind of time, we could even paddle the plane the thousand kilometers up the mountain."

Jill's voice broke in. "The distance from our present position to the top of the water mountain is 1243 kilometers."

"Thanks," said George sarcastically, thinking of the sweat each one of those kilometers represented.

Another computer voice interrupted. It was Jack this time. "The proposed mission plan is feasible. Hovering time near the peak of the water mountain varies from twenty minutes at high tide to thirty seconds at low tide. I have left a reserve of fuel for final rendezvous maneuvers with *Prometheus* at the L-5 point. The reserve can be used if it is necessary to extend the hovering time."

"Good!" said Thomas, turning and leaving the screen. "Show me the trajectory on the command console."

"Are you sure you can get there?" asked Red.

"Don't worry, Red," George said. "I was only kidding about swimming or paddling this flying submarine. I'm sure Karin will figure out some way of getting some propulsion for *Dragonfly*. We have plenty of power, it's just that we're used to flying through air, not water. I'll see you later; I'm going to tell the crew the good news that we have at least one way off this smelly egg." He turned off the communications console connection and talked to his imp.

"How does it look to you, Jill?" he asked.

"I have all the mission data from Jack through the data link," it said. "The only problem that was not mentioned is that we have to work out some way to protect you from the ascent module jet exhaust. Jack was planning to turn off the jets and free-fall slowly down while the crew is pulled up with a winch."

"That sounds a little tricky," said George. "I'm sure

we can arrange some sort of blast canopy made up out of some of your wing panels with a pickup ring on top."

"I hadn't thought of that," said Jill. After a second's pause it said, "That will work too; the metal is light, but it will not be in the jet long."

"Good," said George. "Are there any other potential problems in the plan?"

"How you are going to travel those 1242 kilometers?"

"I thought you said 1243?" said George.

"I did," said Jill, "but we are coming to another high tide and the currents in these regions are twenty kilometers an hour. We have moved closer to the peak."

"Well, that's a start," said George. "Too bad we can't anchor somewhere while the tide is going the other way."

"You can," said Jill in its detached voice. "The water is only a few tens of meters deep in this region."

George gave a long laugh, his emotional relief at finding a means to rescue his command finally breaking through to the surface. He pounded a key on his console to link the audio pickup to all the imps and suit imps on the ship.

"Avast there, ye sky lubbers!!" he boomed into the mike. "Hit the deck and come a'running! This is Captain George, and I want every man-jack and -jill to assemble amidships. I have good news, me hearties, we're setting sail for home."

As he said those words, George had another thought, and whispered to his imp. "How much cloth do we have on board?" he asked. The reply was lost in the confused clamor of voices coming over the audio link on the console. There was one voice that he took particular care to answer.

"Yes, Karin," he said. "I want you and your crew too. We'll probably never be able to get *Dragonfly* in the air again, but Red has come up with a plan where we don't have to. Instead of making *Dragonfly* into an airplane again, we're going to make her into a boat, and we'll need you in on the planning session since you're the only one other than Jill who knows *Dragonfly* inside and out. Unfortunately, Jill doesn't have any imagination, and that's what we're going to need a lot of if we are going to get off this world while we're still on decent rations."

Within less than a minute, George heard the first of the air-lock cycles as the outside crew boarded and came forward wearing their suit briefs. Arielle had been sensibly asleep, her calm test-pilot nerves allowing her to keep up her necessary rest schedule. David, unable to get to sleep, had forced his tired body into a suit and had gone out to work with Karin and Richard, wanting to do something, anything, to take his mind off their predicament. Arielle tried to find a decent place to get dressed, but finally gave up and came out in her sleepwear—a pair of warm pajamas with elastic cuffs and booties. Her spare frame had always suffered under the temperatures that the endomorphs around her found comfortable. In her furry-pink suit, surrounded by a smelly crew dressed in sweaty suit-tights, she looked like a small child captured by a pack of space pirates.

David swiveled in the computer console chair (practically his private preserve). His thin face seemed even leaner with its hint of orange-red stubble. He blinked his eyes tiredly a few times and shook his head to keep awake in the unaccustomed warmth of the body-heated room after his hours in the cold seas of Eau.

"Don't keep us in suspense, George," he said, pushing his glasses up on his nose. "How're we going to get home? Are they going to send another SLAM down to pick us up off some mud flat?"

"I'm sure Jinjur would do that if it were necessary," George said. "But Red has come up with another idea so that we don't have to waste two landers on the same planet. If we can get to the low-gee region on the top of the water mountain, she can pick us up there with the ascent module." Karin listened to George's speech, whispered for a while to her imp, then finally broke into the conversation.

"We could use the tidal currents to get there, dropping an anchor when they're in the wrong direction, but that wouldn't work when we start up the water mountain. The ocean becomes tens of kilometers deep. We could think about a sail, but neither Jill nor I have been able to come up with enough mast and sail to make a significant difference. There is another alternative, and that is to use *Dragonfly*'s VTOL fans in a slow-rpm mode as a water propeller instead of an air propellor. Not very efficient, but it would give us a number of knots. The problem is that only one of the VTOL props is working. If we just ran that one, we would go in circles." Karin stopped and her eyes widened for a second. The rest of the crew could almost see the light bulb above her head. She whispered something to her imp. There was a moment's pause, then the crew heard a slow throb coming through the hull from the undamaged right engine. George walked upward to look out the cockpit windows.

"We're moving," he said.

Karin jumped down off the galley counter and strode forward. She sat herself down in the copilot seat and tilted her head to one side to line up the center of the window brace with one side of the rocky globe hanging in the sky ahead of them.

"Have you got the rudder hard over?" she asked Jill.

"Yes," said her imp.

Karin watched, then shook her head slowly as the nose of the craft drifted off to the right. As they started to turn back the way they came, Karin called a halt.

"The fan can move us at a significant speed," she said. "But even with the tail rudder and ailerons doing their best, we still travel in a circle, going essentially nowhere."

"How about a sea anchor on the portside, way out on

the lip," suggested David, trying to dredge up what little he could remember of his distant sailing lessons on earth.

Karin didn't answer. She leaned back in the copilot seat, her mind flipping through page after page of the engineering manual for the *Dragonfly*. Jill was not idle, and Karin would occasionally nod as something was whispered into her ear by her imp. Suddenly she rose from the chair, strode down the length of *Dragonfly*, and entered the narrow corridor at the rear that led to the air-conditioning and renewal banks.

Although Jill had a brain that used as little electrical power as possible, that brain still used a significant number of picowatts per thought. The air conditioning on *Dragonfly* was not meant for the comfort of the crew, but to keep Jill's brain cool enough to eliminate "soft" errors due to thermal excitation. Karin opened a louvered door and peered up. She stopped, went back to the suit locker, obtained a permalight, and returned. She flashed the brilliant white beam up past the cracks between the flutes on the cooling fins of the air-conditioning system to the air fans overhead. She stopped and punched a seldom-used code into the permalight's microcomputer. Her thumb on a two-way variable switch, she sent the beam upward again. A few practiced flicks and she could see in the strobing flashes of light the air fans seemingly slow and come to a stop as the blinks of light from the illuminator in her hand matched the turns of the blades.

"How about those?" she asked her imp. "They're small, but one or two of those run at the proper speed could push enough water as the VTOL fan."

"Those are part of the air supply," Jill remonstrated in her severe tone. "Regulations do not permit any diversion of primary life-support systems to other purposes."

Karin replied in a firm voice, "The purpose for which the fans would be used are essential to the welfare of the crew. Please record my recommendations in your priority memory banks and verify with the commanders of *Dragonfly* and *Prometheus*."

There was a short pause. Karin heard a gruff "She's right" from the front of the aerospace plane. Then she heard Jill speak again through her imp.

"The substitution you suggest will work with proper control of the relative rotation rates of the two fans. There will be a twenty percent degradation of the air flow throughout the *Dragonfly*. That will leave us at only ninety percent of nominal. My motile branch is not capable of removing the fan. The masses and gravity are too much at this location."

"That's all right," said Karin, greatly relieved that the computer had given in so gracefully. That probably meant that the substitution was a piece of cake.

It wasn't.

Jill's branch did all it could by unscrewing bolts that human fingers could never have reached, but the bulky fan was in its bay to stay. There were access plates that allowed the whole air-recycling unit to drop out of the bottom of *Dragonfly* for installation and maintenance, but they could not be used when they were deep under the smelly ocean of Eau. Karin was dripping sweat before she finally had twisted the recycling units aside enough to get the fan through the door. At that, she had had to trim some of the support structure with a laser cutter. The sharp edges of the one-meter-diameter fan and its support seemed to reach out to nick her flesh as she struggled into her suit-all, then into the space suit that proved to be as good in water as it did in space.

Despite her weariness, she carefully went through the checklist with Richard, then checked him out. She sent him through the lock first, then inserted the fan, allowing it the privilege of having the lock all to its razor-tempered self. After Richard had removed the deadly square with its slowly rotating fan from the lock, she cycled through, then followed him as he floated off under the left wing. Karin reached to her tool belt for a large omniwrench and took care of the obvious bolts on the outside, while a large segment of Jill's inside branch snaked its way into the wing and took care of the inside connectors. Karin motioned Richard back while the last of the connections were loosened. The heavy fan with its missing teeth dropped from the wing and settled slowly in the low gravity.

The next chore was to install the small air-conditioning fan in place of the much larger propeller. Richard had no problem positioning the fan in place with most of the blades underwater, but the amount of space left required some sort of bracing. Karin looked over the situation in the dimming light, making length measurements as well as illuminating the scene with her versatile permalight. Dusk settled in on Eau and the two called it a day. They hung the fan in the gaping hole on *Dragonfly*'s wing, swam to the hull, and cycled through.

George and Arielle were relaxing for the first time in many days. They were watching one of David's sonovideo compositions in the large-screen display above the computer console. Each one had an extra section of the Christmas Branch on their ears as stereo headphones. David was improvising some additional audio and visual effects to add to the recorded composition of *Flight* that would thrill billions of others six lightyears away on earth when they heard it a half-dozen years hence. Listening to the music and watching the video, George thought that David was at his peak, tired as he was—or maybe it was because he was so tired. George looked quickly at the console and saw with relief that someone (probably Jill) had turned on the high-fidelity sonovideo recorder. This exultant evening of genius would not be lost.

There were noises from the rear of the aerospace plane. They really didn't interfere with the concert, but George's command responsibility made him pay attention. He finally identified the sounds as that of two large people trying to take a shower in the same small booth. He made a motion with his hand near one ear as though he were turning a knob and the volume on his earphones increased, drowning out the noise from the rear. He relaxed and looked with relief at the beautiful video caressing his eyes.

Twenty minutes later Karin came through the privacy curtains. She picked her way through the relaxed humanity clustered around the computer console and went to one of the cockpit consoles. George saw her pass and got up to follow her.

"Where's Richard?" he asked.

Karin smiled a knowing grin. "He's snoring away in a bunk. Had a lot of exercise today," she explained.

"So have you," said George. "Don't you think you ought to get some sleep before daylight in three hours?"

"We need to make a bracing structure. I thought Jill and I could design it before I go to bed. The branch can be building it while I get a good nine hours sleep. I've been on the go for thirty hours." She patted her tummy. "Hmmm. My stomach thinks my mouth's on strike." She interrupted Jill's computations to order a double dinner of chili, then flipping her braid over her shoulder she turned to George.

"It's going to work, George," she said with a grin. "We should be chugging our way up the mountain in less than a day." Relieved, George returned to David's performance.

The music through the imps grew stronger. David was now improvising, and the effect was like a fairy nimbly scampering up the stairways of the gods. George's eyes had automatically closed as he heard the charismatic sounds, but then he forced them open as he realized that he was in the chamber of a lyrical genius, one who wrote emotions with the colors and tones of light and music rather than the scratches and snarls of writing and speech.

No longer was this place a dingy, crowded corridor filled with aching, sweating bodies, but the vast empty corridors between the starlanes of the galaxy. His eyes, his ears, his soul drank in the new freedom from the fleshy bondage that had been the inheritance of the human race ... for the long-fettered gray mass of the human brain now saw greater things.

The greater things drifted in from the ghostlike shrouds of haziness. Then—with the music adding substance— they grew to take over the vision, still avoiding the direct glance, the firming up, the human desire to make desire a reality.

David, inspired by his own feedback, took off on another improvisation. The scenes repeated, yet were different in a subtle, yet significant way. The music counterpointed from one disparate theme to another, while the images mixed and blended. There were new, more complex interrelationships. The scene and sound came to a dramatic climax. As it did, George knew only that he didn't have enough experience to appreciate it. If he had heard and seen that display on the screen without preparation, he would have hollered for a repair technician. Yet he knew that the sonovision was just as the artist had wanted it, but he, George, was only dimly able to recognize its majestic complexity.

The remains of the music and scenes echoed through the hallways and chambers of his mind. There was a long pause, in which the only sound was that of David taking a few deep breaths, Karin pecking at keys up front, and a long sonorous rumble from a bunk in the crew quarters.

"Oohh!!!" said Arielle, her breath finally released. "Oh!!

Nife!!" she said again, her gaze passing through the blank screen on the bulkhead to the stars beyond. She finally noticed where she was. Blushing slightly, she pulled her long, pink bunny legs up to her chin and grew silent. A shy grin flickered on her lips above her clasped hands.

George, still out of his element, tried to express the gratitude that he felt for witnessing what was obviously a rare moment in artistic creation. He knew only that his faulty sense of appreciation had captured but a small portion of the fountain of genius that had flowed over him.

"That was really, really good, David," he said. "I mean I really, really liked that one. It really made a really great impression . . ."

He had the sense to stop.

Meeting

In the next two day-night periods there was no further sign of the strange blobs and their noises. Jill's program had still not decided what the phenomena were. They were obviously not intelligent life-forms, since an intelligent being would certainly want to explore such a strange artifact as Jill.

Then Jill's sonar, peering ahead through the endless ocean, heard a response to its searching pings. They had the same pitch and structure as the noises that it had heard nearly twelve hours ago, strong, loud, and almost raucous.

☆Hi!!! Hi!!! Hi!!!☆ said Roaring☆Hot☆Vermillion.

◇Who're you talking to?◇ said Clear◇White◇Whistle.

☆It's the big floating rock! It's talking now! I think it wants to play!☆

The red cloud increased the speed of its body ripples and slithered off toward the distant pinging ahead.

Jill's sonar system saw the distant blobs separate. One came directly at it at high speed. Jill increased her interrogation rate and switched to a modified chirp in an attempt to pick up shape information. The blob was about three meters wide, ten meters long, and one meter thick, but it had almost the same density as the ocean and had no discernible internal structure.

◇Careful!◇ came the call from the distant white cloud. ◇It could be a new type of Gray⊗Boom! It might explode and catch you.◇

The thought slowed the advance of Roaring☆Hot☆ Vermillion, but didn't decrease the volume of its voice, which it raised to a shout.

☆Hɪ!!!!! Wᴀɴᴛ ᴛᴏ surf?!?!?!☆

Jill took in the sound, then echoed it back.

"Hi! Want to surf?!" it said, then waited.

Roaring☆Hot☆Vermillion paused a second, nonplussed at hearing its own voice.

☆Hɪ!!☆

"Hi!"

☆Hɪ! Ho! Hɪ!☆

"Hi! Ho! Hi!"

Roaring☆Hot☆Vermillion caught on quickly. This thing obviously didn't know how to communicate, so was limited to repeating what it heard.

Although the thing didn't seem to know anything about talking, it still was smarter than the hunters and flitters, who had their own sounds and could not imitate the spoken voice. This thing could even imitate Roaring☆ Hot☆Vermillion's overtone patterns. The obvious way to see if it could be taught to talk was to take it through some simple mathematical logic. First the numbers, then mathematics, then formal logic, then with a few physical referents such as you, me, water, dirt, sky, and some diagrams on the bottom, and they should be conversing in a light-period.

☆One! Two! Three! Four! Five! Six! Seven!☆

There was a pause as the numbers trilled through the water. Each spoken number was by its multiple tonal and pulse-code pattern a living example of the concept of the number it represented. The word "Three" was a melodic triplet of sounds with each note given its own triple-tongue beat. Each number also had its own set of overtones that were distinctive as bell, violin, and brass. The number "Seven" was a manifold wonder that Jill stored in memory in its pristine acoustic beauty to present to David when he was in the mood to compose.

☆One plus one equals two.☆

☆One plus two equals three.☆

"One plus three equals four," interjected Jill.

The red cloud turned itself inside out.

☆HEY!!! VERY GOOD! Won't take long for you to learn!☆ There was an outpouring of sound beamed off into the distance.

☆Come here, Clear◇White◇Whistle! This strange hard floater is as smart as a new-found one!☆

☆One plus one plus one equals ...☆ said the red cloud, waiting for the answer.

"... Three," dutifully responded Jill.

☆Three TIMES one equals three!☆ said Roaring ☆Hot☆Vermillion, jumping from addition to multiplication. Jill caught on instantly.

"Two TIMES three equals six!" said Jill, almost triumphantly.

☆zzzzzzzzzzt!!!☆ came an explosive sound.

☆SsSsSsIiIiIiXxXxXx!☆ said the red cloud, enunciating each trill and overtone with exaggerated care.

"SSSsssIIIiiiXXXxxx," said Jill, its electronics still stumbling over the acoustic nuances of the word.

☆zzzzzzzzt!!☆ exploded the red cloud, so Jill tried again.

"SsSsSsIiIiIiXxXxXx," said Jill's sonar finally.

☆I do believe it's GOT it!!!☆

The red blob turned itself inside out again, and dashed off to meet the still-approaching white form.

☆It's SMART!!! I think I'll keep it!!! I'll name it Floating⊗Rock!☆

◇It may not want to be kept. Besides, Floating⊗

Rock doesn't seem to swim too well. It won't be able to follow you around.◇

☆Oh!!! Right! Well, you can have it! I'm going surfing!☆ The red cloud swam off into the distance.

Jill took advantage of the interlude to inform the crew of its find. They came crowding to the cockpit windows to see the giant alien creatures. There was a large red alien swimming away, while a slightly smaller white cloud hovered in the water at a distance.

"They are definitely intelligent, despite their amorphous shape," reported Jill.

"Do they haf name?" asked Arielle.

"I haven't progressed that far yet," said Jill. "Even when I have learned their names I doubt you would be able to pronounce them. The red one is quite raucous, so I'll call it Loud Red. The other uses a higher-pitched clear tone, so I'll call it White Whistler."

"How can such large aliens exist in these barren seas?" asked Karin. "We've been over all of Roche and most of Eau and taken lots of samples. I'm sure you and I would never have missed seeing a life-form, even a single-celled one."

"I suspect that the only life to be found is right around the active volcano vents," said Jill. "Life here never developed photosynthesis, so all you have are animals. Even a one-celled animal cannot survive except right around the vent fields where the energy source is."

"It's like the little colonies of strange sea creatures that cluster around the sea-bottom vents back on earth," said George. "They live off the hydrogen sulfide escaping from the vents. There is even a large wormlike creature with no mouth. It gets its food from hydrogen-sulfide-eating bacteria living in its skin."

"Well these creatures are even weirder than those we have on earth," said Richard.

"Look," said Arielle. "White Whiftler is coming clofer."

Clear◇White◇Whistle approached the strange,

metallic-tasting beast. There should be many things it could learn from this strange thing that was hard like a rock but floated. For instance, there were those strange things moving around inside Floating⊗Rock that had stiff sections connected by joints. Since Floating⊗Rock had eaten the Stiff⊗Movers, perhaps they would be tasty, but Clear◇White◇Whistle had never seen anything like them in this region of the ocean. Clear◇White◇Whistle continued the lesson.

◇Three times two equals six.◇

"Two times three equals six. One times six equals six. Two plus four equals six. Three plus three equals six. One plus five equals six," said Jill, trying to make it clear that she had figured out the addition and multiplication tables. So far, there were no numbers greater than seven. They must use an octal numbering system. There was one way to find out.

"Four plus four equals . . ." said Jill and paused, waiting for the answer.

◇One-OOOhhh,◇ came the answer from White Whistler. Jill had been prepared for the one, but this was the first time she had heard the haunting emptiness of the zero. It sounded like the unheard echo of an invisible ghost.

Jill decided to speed things up. The next step was the subtraction tables. "One BEEP one equals OOOhhh. BEEP equals?"

Clear◇White◇Whistle was impressed. Floating⊗Rock was now asking questions.

◇BEEP equals minus. One minus one equals OOOhhh.◇

Jill jumped from mathematics to logic. "One equals one."

◇Yes.◇

"That must be either 'yes' or 'correct,' " said Jill to itself. "Now to find the negative . . ."

"One equals two," Jill's sonar beeped.

◇No.◇

. . . and more words were added to Jill's all-retentive memory as the red sun started to set once again behind the mountain in the sky.

Karin had been following Jill's conversation with extreme interest, but she was more interested in the aliens' bodies than their minds.

"Do you think we could get a sample of one of them?" she asked Jill. "I'd really like to find out what they're made of. I'll get into my suit and slip out the lock while you keep them talking."

"I would advise against that," said Jill. "These beasts weigh at least ten tons and are intelligent. Even if you could snatch a sample I'm not sure you would survive to bring it back."

"Then ask them for a sample," said Karin, sure that her request would be granted. "Tell them it is of vital importance for my research."

Jill started to protest, but Karin had made her way back to the suit locker while she was talking and was putting on her suit. Her imp was kept busy scrambling to keep out of the way.

It took a few minutes for Jill to get the concept across to White Whistler, but as Karin had expected, the alien readily acquiesced. Karin cycled through the lock with a specimen container, a pair of scissors, and a syringe. As she approached the alien, she began to realize just how big these creatures were. The fact that there were no eyes to focus her attention on was one of the more bothersome aspects of meeting the jellyfishlike creature, yet she could feel and hear the multitude of pings and whistles passing through her body as long, thick appendages grew from White Whistler and nearly surrounded her on all sides, each emitting sounds as she was thoroughly scanned. One of the thick appendages turned into an inquisitive flexible finger that wandered over the specimen bottles and her tools, while another one felt her over thoroughly. Jill kept up a constant conversation with the alien as each item was examined and many words were added to their joint vocabulary. Satisfied with its inspection, the alien withdrew slightly and a strange voice came from the imp on Karin's shoulder as Jill translated.

◇ What do 'scissors' and 'syringe' do? ◇

"The scissors cut . . ." She held up the scissors and snipped them rapidly, then she carefully cut a tiny portion from the frayed end of her safety rope. Jill translated, and an action word was added to their joint vocabulary. The alien extended a milky-white tendril and pulled the cut piece of rope inside its body, tasted it for a second, and spat it out.

"The syringe sucks . . ." Karin worked the plunger and brought it near the surface of a nearby appendage so the alien could feel the stream of seawater shooting from the end of the large needle. Before she could stop, the appendage impaled itself on the needle and the syringe was half-full of milky white liquid.

"Oн! I'm sorry! I didn't mean to do that until you were ready! Are you hurt?" said Karin.

◇ Syringe . . . sucks, ◇ said a quiet voice through the imp. Karin felt an appendage surround her hand, then firm up. Gently, but with great power, her fingers were removed from the syringe. A portion of the appendage formed into a crude hand which took hold of the operating end of the syringe. The piston was pushed down and the milky-white liquid was expelled back into the alien. Karin watched, still frightened by her slip, but her fright turned into queasiness as she watched the alien jab the syringe again and again into its body to suck up a little bit of its insides, then squirt them out again. It soon tired of the toy and handed the syringe back to Karin.

◇ Syringe . . . sucks. ◇

Karin looked in the syringe. It was empty. She persevered.

"Could I please have a specimen?" she asked, extending the syringe toward the whale-sized creature. There was a pause as Jill translated.

◊Yes,◊ came the reply. ◊Do not need cut or suck.◊ The alien extended a tendril toward her. As Karin watched, a portion about three centimeters back from the tip necked down and pinched off, leaving a milky sausage floating in the water. She pulled her floating specimen bottle in by its lanyard. Opening the fliptop, she approached the sausage and tried to push it into the bottle with her glove. The small speck of white stuff became agitated and emitted a shrill cry. Changing shape in random patterns, it clumsily swam out of her reach. Karin tried to catch it, but it swam back to the large blob that it had come from and buried itself into the surface, rejoining its lost protoplasmic family.

◊Stop!◊ came the alien command through her imp. Another tendril formed and this time the tip of it was inserted in the specimen bottle before the arm necked off. Karin quickly closed the flip lid and the sausage specimen was trapped.

Karin, holding her prize in one hand, pulled on her safety rope with the other and soon was gliding back through the icy water to the air lock in the side of *Dragonfly*. As she moved, the specimen bottle started to scream like a tiny baby being flayed alive by a sadistic savage.

Karin entered the air lock and was about to close the outside door when she stopped. She held the specimen bottle up in front of her face and watched the little white cloud inside. Now that she had stopped moving, the screams from the bottle ceased. They were replaced by tiny whistles and pings. The tiny cloud seemed to shift in shape and acted as if it were exploring the confines of the bottle, especially the hinge and lip of the fliptop.

"Are you sure White Whistler understood the meaning of 'specimen'?" she asked her imp.

"I requested a small, nonimportant subset of the set that composes White Whistler," said Jill. "Through our discussions on logic and mathematics we have developed very precise joint understanding of the words 'small' and 'nonimportant.' I am also fairly sure from its response that it understood the term 'subset of the set that comprises White Whistler.' "

"The reason I ask is that this specimen acts more like a miniature alien than just a chunk of flesh or blood. Are you sure this is just a sample and not a baby?"

"I will try to find out," said Jill. "However, we have only conversed about mathematics, logic, physics, and local items that we could both jointly observe. We have not gotten into more esoteric subjects such as philosophy, physiology, and reproduction."

Karin heard the front of the plane start to whistle.

"You are big and white," Jill beamed at the white blob.

◇ Correct. ◇

"There exists little white thing in bottle."

◇ Correct. ◇

"Is little white thing a subset of you or a small set similar to you?"

◇ Both, ◇ came the bewildering reply.

"How can it be both?" asked Karin.

"I probably asked the question in an ambiguous way," answered Jill. "Let me try another tack."

"As time increases will little white thing become another you?"

◇ No. Too small. Be eaten. ◇

"Well, I guess that answers one question. It is certainly not a viable baby because of its small size, even though except for size, it is a miniature copy of the main body. There must be a minimum mass needed to have a self-aware nervous system, although I don't see any obvious concentration that would indicate a brain."

"It must be distributed," said Karin. "How do they reproduce?"

"I will try to find out," said Jill.

"You are element, large, intelligent, and white. Loud Red is element, large, intelligent, and red. The set containing Loud Red and White Whistler is a set whose elements are named what?" asked Jill. There was a short whistled reply that Jill had not heard before.

"I'll just assume that response is the collective pronoun. Unless you have an objection, I will just translate it 'flouwen' from the Old High German word for 'flow.' "

"That's fine by me," said Karin.

"Exist there other elements in the set of flouwen?" asked Jill of the patiently waiting white cloud.

◊ Many, ◊ came the reply.

"As time increases, exist there new elements of the set of flouwen?"

◊ Yes. New elements small. Increase in size until like existing flouwen. ◊

"So they do have children," said Karin. "But how do they make them?"

"It may be a subject that they don't want to talk about," said Jill. "But I will try."

"Is new element a subset of one flouwen or is new element a union of subsets from two flouwen?"

◊ Not one. Not two. Dark soon. ◊ The white cloud swam off into the ocean and soon was lost in the gloom.

"It didn't seem particularly bothered with the idea of discussing sex," said Karin.

"It didn't say anything about sex," reminded Jill, ever logical. "It just said that it didn't bud and it didn't have relations with someone of the opposite sex."

"Then how do they make babies?" asked Karin.

"Perhaps someday we'll find out," said Jill matter-offactly. "Do you want the Christmas Branch to help you with the analysis of the specimen?"

"I've been outside quite a while," said Karin. "I think I'd better get some food and nap first. Have the branch store the specimen in the climate control freezer. I'll look at it when I'm fresh." She cycled through the lock, hung up her suit, and went to the galley. David was at the computer console. She saw he was working with Jill on studying the structure of the whistles and sounds that the flouwen used as language. It seemed to be a very complex language, somewhat like spoken Chinese, where the same sound pattern would mean different things depending upon the relative pitch and its position in the phoneme group that made up each complex word.

"How are you and the aliens doing with the language lessons?" Karin asked Jill the next day. "I've got some questions I'd like to ask."

"I'm doing very well, Karin. They are very intelligent creatures. They learn much faster than humans. They make fewer mistakes than humans. They almost never forget, unlike humans . . ."

". . . That's enough! Next thing you know you'll be telling me that they have higher IQs than we do."

"They *do* have higher IQs. I would estimate that their IQ is greater than . . ."

"I DON'T want to know!"

"Yes, Karin."

"Can you converse with them enough to ask them about the other fauna and flora in the sea?"

"I will talk with Loud Red."

There was a singing sound from the randome at the front of the *Magic Dragonfly* and an almost immediate reply from the red cloud in front of the plane. The imp on Karin's shoulder translated both sides of the conversation.

"Exist there others, not similar to you?"

☆Yes! Lots! I show you?☆

"Yes, please," said Jill.

☆What mean 'please'?!?☆

Jill, who had yet to get across the concept of politeness to these very direct, almost busybody creatures, decided to bypass the question.

"Negate previous statement. Yes. Show us."

The red blob, not bothered a bit by Jill's refusal to answer its question, gave a piercing whistle that carried far out into the deep ocean. After a few seconds the imp on Karin's shoulder whispered.

"Look at ten o'clock low." There was a burbling sound as Jill adjusted trim and the cockpit windows dipped beneath the surface of the ocean.

Karin swiveled her head and looked out the left cockpit window. Near the ocean bottom was a long, orange, snakelike creature, propelling itself rapidly through the water with a sinuous motion of its long narrow body. It shot up toward the surface, contracting in length as it did so. As it approached, Karin could hear the creature emitting short sharp sounds, like a yipping puppy, although its size was more like that of a Saint Bernard. The speeding orange missile hit the red alien amidships, diving at full speed into the depths of the reddish cloud. There was a reaction and the orange creature, now nearly a sphere, was thrown out. It was immediately grabbed by thick red tendrils emerging from the main portion of Loud Red. There ensued a wrestling match, loud bellows being interspersed with happy-sounding yips.

"George! David!" Karin hollered over her shoulder. "You ought to come see this. Oн! Here comes two more!"

George hopped into the copilot seat and David stood behind them on the flight deck as the three watched the next two orange snakes speed through the water to join the wrestling match. The three orange blobs kept the red cloud busy. Sometimes one of the orange creatures would be flung off into the water, where it would spread out from a sphere to a sheet, rapidly came to a stop in the water, then swam back into the fray. After a few minutes the fracas quieted down, with the orange blobs just rubbing slowly back and forth against the surface of the huge red cloud and making small busy noises.

"They look like cats or dogs rubbing up against the legs of their owner," said George. "Do you think they're pets?"

"Three orange things are elements of what set?" asked Jill.

☆Three orange things are—☆ The sentence was completed with a complex whistle that Jill did not attempt to translate.

"Belong to you?" asked Jill.

☆Yes. Help catch food. Pet.☆ This time Jill felt sure enough of the meaning of the whistle to translate it for the humans.

"Pets know numbers?" asked Jill.

The response to Jill's question was a terrible high-pitched scream that continued as the red cloud literally turned itself inside out. The portion of Loud Red nearest them pushed deep into the center of its body and burst out the back end, dragging the rest of the body around with it. It split into an opening flower and continued back around, shaping the convoluting body into a twirling ring of red smoke. The screaming activated the orange pets and one of them snaked through the opening in its master's body, yipping as it went. The rotation complete, the smoke ring collapsed, and the screaming subsided as the alien took its normal blob shape. Jill, hearing the shocked responses of the humans, reassured them.

"I'm pretty sure that reaction is their equivalent of a laugh. When one of them first did it, I thought that the question I asked had violated one of their taboos and they were mad, but it only seems to happen when I ask a stupid question."

☆One pet only, but it very smart. Know one and one is two! We show you!☆

The red blob whistled to his pets. One of the orange spheres swam around in front, right between the red alien and the *Dragonfly*. A red tendril snaked out to stand over the orange pet. The red tendril bobbed up and down as the alien spoke to its pet.

☆One plus one is . . .☆

⊗TtWwOoooo⊗ howled the pet, doing its best to imitate the flouwen speech pattern. Jill thought it had done a respectable job.

"I wonder how much more it knows?" asked David quietly. "It must be interesting having a semi-intelligent pet."

☆Two plus two is . . .☆ continued the alien.

⊗TtWwOoooo⊗came the reply, and the high-pitched scream startled the humans again as Roaring☆Hot☆ Vermillion laughed again at its favorite joke, its body contorting in its mirth. For a brain that was so rigorously attuned to the perfect exactness of mathematical logic, the pet's completely illogical statement struck it in the same way that an outrageous pun did a literate human. The laughter finally subsided.

☆Pets not know numbers. Pets not know words. Pets DUMB!☆

"I want a sample from the pets too," said Karin. "See if you can't talk Loud Red into letting us have a piece of one of his dogs while I get into my suit."

"Let me go," said George. "I need the exercise."

George climbed down from the copilot seat, and squeezing past David, made his way back to the rear of *Dragonfly* while Jill talked to the red cloud. Karin followed to make sure George buttoned all his buttons and zipped all his zippers before he went outside. Soon a thoroughly checked-out George was cycled through the lock with a sample bottle and a video camera, while Karin, carefully reading through the checklist on the door, prepared the air lock for its next use.

George adjusted his buoyancy so that he sank to the bottom and could plod slowly through the water to the front of the plane. It was a long walk through the mucky bottom to the front of the thirty-meter-long airplane. He saw many rocks and what looked like coral formations around some fuming vents. As he approached the front of the plane where the red alien was conversing with Jill, he passed by an extremely large dark-gray rock.

☆Hi!☆ said the red cloud, as it spotted him plodding out from under the wing of the airplane. Loud Red came over to greet him. In one tendril it carried a tiny piece of orange stuff. Knowing what to do, the alien grabbed the specimen bottle from the human and inserted the struggling sample of orange pet.

☆I put in bottle! Big pets dumb but listen. Little pets too dumb to listen.☆

"I notice that it doesn't call it a piece of pet, just a little pet," said George to his imp, as he felt the three orange blobs gather to nuzzle him all over.

"They seem to be built along the same lines as the aliens," said Jill through his imp.

Loud Red gave the specimen bottle back to George, then swam back to the front of the ship to continue its conversation with Jill. George tucked the bottle away on his belt, and hefting the video camera, he moved forward to take some pictures of the red alien and his orange pets with *Dragonfly* in the background. Arielle and David in the cockpit looked like air-breathing goldfish in an inside-out aquarium.

BOOM!!!

George was rocked by a concussion through his suit. Overhead, shooting through the water at great speed, were heavy gray rocks trailing streamers of smoke. The rocks fell to the bottom some sixty meters away. The streamers settled to the bottom rapidly. There were many of them and three touched George. The streamers were sticky, and when the threads felt George move, they began to contract and wrap themselves about his body. Within seconds his arms were pinned. He fell backward into the muck. A gray film crept over his visor. It grew thicker. He was in blackness.

David had been looking in the right direction and had seen the gray rock explode. Dozens of fragments of rock shot through the water, trailing gray threads behind them. Some of the rocks struck the hull of *Dragonfly* with a thud and fell to the bottom. There was a slam from the back of the plane and Karin came pounding forward to stand on the flight deck between David and Arielle.

"What happened!" gasped Karin.

"A rock exploded and has thrown out a net of gray strings. They're falling down now."

"Look!" said Karin. "The alien and his pets are swimming upward at the threads and slipping through the gaps between them."

"The threads are coming down fast," said David. "The rock must be pulling in its net."

"George!" yelled Karin. "He's out there somewhere!" She leaned over and peered out the side cockpit window. She saw a struggling gray blob. It rolled over and a specimen bottle bobbed free and floated up to the end of its lanyard. Feeling the motion, the grayness climbed the rope, surrounded the bottle, and pulled it back down into the gray mass.

"IT's GOT GEORGE!!!" screamed Karin, running back down the corridor to the suit lockers. David followed to check her out, but by the time he had made it to the galley, he saw that Richard had gotten out of his bunk and was looking around at the excitement with bewildered eyes.

"Richard!" David commanded in a tone that no one had ever heard him use before. "George is in trouble outside. You suit up with Karin and go out to help." He turned to meet Arielle coming from the front.

"There is gray stuff over window," Arielle reported.

"Then it's probably all over the plane," David said. "If we open the airlock it will probably creep inside and jam the lock."

Karin and Richard halted the suiting-up until they could figure a way out of their predicament.

The red cloud, its orange spheroids strangely quiet and nestled close to its body, slowly floated back toward the plane, keeping a safe distance from the gray threads still falling on *Dragonfly*. The Gray⊗Boom got more than it had bargained for this time, but it was too stupid to realize that it couldn't eat its metallic prey. Floating⊗Rock was covered with the sticky gray film, but it could still talk. Roaring☆Hot☆Vermillion then noticed a wiggling bulge. The Gray⊗Boom had caught one of the pets of Floating⊗Rock. It couldn't eat that either because of the hard suit (Roaring☆Hot☆Vermillion had tried tasting one of the Stiff⊗Movers when they had first met—☆Nasty!!!☆). Unless the big creature did something, however, the pet would be stuck, for the gray threads were very persistent and very sticky. Roaring☆Hot☆Vermillion swam down to the front of the airplane and hollered at Jill's sonar through the gray film.

☆You yell!?!☆

"Yell?" queried Jill.

Seeing that Floating⊗Rock would not or could not do anything about its struggling pet, Roaring☆Hot☆ Vermillion roared to the rescue. Its huge bulk surrounded the struggling figure wrapped in sticky gray. There was a piercing shriek. The gray mass parted under the sonic barrage to show the head portion of the human space suit. Two more shrieks and the gray mass had dissolved into a sonically disintegrated gray cloud. George was free.

George headed for the air lock, jumping gingerly over the gray strands that still lay buried in the muck. It took him a number of minutes to make his way back and he was wondering how he was going to get past the gray film covering the air-lock door when suddenly a clear spot appeared in the middle of the door. A few more seconds and the spot became an oval as the gray film retreated.

George's running commentary helped Jill focus the sonic efforts of the branch in the air lock until the outer door was free of the gray film.

"All clear!" said George. The lock opened, and George took a flying leap at the opening overhead and sailed in with only a little steering help from the branch at the door.

Safely inside, George wondered why the branch didn't close the door immediately, but then realized that it was using its sonic capability to clear the area around the hatch from the gray menace. When the branch finally returned and activated the air-lock cycle, George noticed that most of the upper portion was missing.

Out hunting gray spooks, he murmured to himself, and cycled through.

Karin made her way back to the Christmas Branch's work area. The Christmas Branch was waiting for her.

"Where are the specimens?" she asked. The branch telescoped down to dwarf size, opened up a small door in the work wall, and pulled out a bottle from the freezer. Its fingers interrogated the container with a blaze of varicolored laser light as the hand reached up to pass her the bottle.

"This is the white one. Careful! It's very cold."

It *was* cold. Karin juggled the bottle in her hand until she could hold it by the short plastic loop that connected lid and bottle. Her fingers soon warmed up the plastic and she could hold it up to her eyes.

"It doesn't seem to have changed any," she said.

"No significant change in the creature, but the spectral response of the water shows the presence of molecules that were not there previously, probably metabolic wastes."

"I'll take samples of both the water and the specimen," she said. "Give me the syringe."

She tried to hold the bottle while she jabbed the needle through the rubbery seal across the opening of the container, but the cold was too much for her fingers. She gave up.

"Here," she said, handing the bottle to the Christmas Branch. "You hold it while I get the samples."

Karin took the syringe and extracted a small sample of the ocean water. As the needle came out, she smelled an astringent whiff of ammonia in the air. She went over to the wall to a tiny physical and chemical analytical lab. Not much larger than a common brick, it could do a complete inorganic and organic analysis on a single drop. It also had a barrage of manipulators and microscopes that could take apart and examine any portion of that drop.

Karin gave the analyzer the droplet and Jill started the machine running while Karin turned back to the branch. The needle went back through the seal after the elusive blob. There was no room to hide and soon Karin had a syringe half-full of screaming white jelly.

Gritting her teeth, Karin went back to the wall, waited until the green light signaled that the analyzer was ready for another sample, then inserted the end of the needle into the input port and gave a tiny squeeze. Still clenching her teeth, she turned back around to the branch and squirted the remainder of the syringe back into the specimen bottle, where the tiny blob quickly rejoined the larger white sausage.

"When the white alien returns, please take this outside and give it back," she said. "I won't be able to sleep for the screams coming from the freezer.

"The freezer is well insulated," said Jill. "I'm sure that no noise could get out."

"No noise, but I would still hear the screams," she said, handing the syringe back to the Christmas Branch and heading forward to the science console, where the information from the physical and chemical analysis lab was building up on the screen.

As Karin sat down at the console, Jill started talking to her through her imp. Karin could almost swear that the computer was excited over the discoveries that were being made in the brick-sized laboratory at the rear of the plane.

"The structure of the White Whistler is identical to those strange-colored rocks that Sam found on Roche and Richard found on Maui," said Jill.

"But those were crystalline rocks," objected Karin. "These animals are more like intelligent jellyfish."

"But the basic structure is the same," said Jill. "The entire sample of White Whistler contains nothing but tiny dumbbell-shaped units, large cells if you like, arranged in interlocking layers, with four bulbous ends around each necked-down waist portion, two going in one direction and two going in the other so that the whole body is an interlocked whole. The units are larger than in the rock samples, but I suspect that is just because they are bloated up with water."

"The rocks *were* hygroscopic," reminded Karin. "Can you do a chemical analysis?"

"It's almost done," said Jill. "The inner portion of each unit is the same silica-gel-type compound that was in the rocks, but with some of the bonds hydrated. The outer white covering is much more complex, a thin film of molecules made up of ring compounds that repeat in semirandom patterns. There are twelve basic molecules that are arranged in large plates held between layers of a liquid-crystallike substance."

"Do you find any structure in the central gel portion?"

"Not much. They are practically crystals in their order, although quite flexible because of their high water content."

"Then the gel material must be their equivalent of 'bones.' They determine the basic arrangement, while the thin film covering the 'skeleton' is both the nerve tissue and the genetic code," said Karin.

"That might not be correct," said Jill. "There is evidence that the outer surface of the gel dumbbells have patterns on them that seem to fit the twelve basic compounds. Perhaps at some stage they act as a template for ordering the compounds into viable sheets."

"What is the liquid material for?" asked Karin.

"I am not sure of its purpose," said Jill. "But it *is* the source of their bright color."

"We have a specimen from Loud Red's orange pet," said Karin. "Let's take a sample and see what the difference is."

"I have already completed the preliminary analysis of a sample of the orange pet," said Jill. "The basic unit is the same as in the intelligent aliens, but the patterns in the orange-colored thin film are less complex than in the white film."

"Try an experiment," said Karin. "Let the small blob of white 'eat' a single unit of orange, but put a tracer in the orange one so we can retrieve it later."

A single orange unit cell was teased away from its comrades and transferred into the holding tank for the white specimen. It was quickly caught by the larger white blob.

"The orange cell has been absorbed," said Karin, "but it's fighting back. Look, there are now two orange units. Will the lower animal take over?"

"You didn't notice the holding action taking place at

one end of the 'captured' white unit," said Jill. "See the densification of the white at the end of one sphere? Now notice the counterattack on the original unit as the orange forces, in their attempt to take control of an adjoining unit, have spread themselves too thin for an adequate defense."

The miniature battle was over in a few milliseconds—the action being slowed down for the human.

"Now tease that same unit out," Karin said, then added in a worried voice. "I don't see any tag in it. Did you inject a tracer?"

"There was no need," said Jill. "My sensors have a complete three-dimensional view of the entire arena. I just kept an 'eye' on it."

The victorious white blob was pulled apart and its recent capture wrested from it. The unit was subjected to analysis.

"Almost one-fourth of the unit has been modified on the surface to match the surface markings of the other white units, while the remainder has the old orange markings," said Jill.

"Well. That's certainly a simpler way to eat than breaking all the proteins in your food down to amino acids and rebuilding them from scratch again just to change the protein's loyalty," said Karin. "That must make for a strange culture. Everybody can eat everybody and the only thing that gets changed is the ID number. Unless the flouwen get badly damaged in an accident, they never die."

"But the units do die," said Jill. "Three of the white units have lysed in the past few minutes. They also regenerate themselves. Two units have reduced their waist to zero, then the two resulting spheres necked down to form new units. The statistics are not good, but I suspect the average lifetime of the units is only a few days."

"But the flouwen live much longer than that," said Karin.

"Yes," said Jill. "From my conversations with them I get the impression that those we know have lived many hundreds of human years. There are others, off on long-term research projects, that are much older than that."

"But how can that be?" said Karin. "We may replace most of our body cells in seven years, but the complement of nerve cells we have at maturity is all we get."

"That's because the cells in an earth animal are specialized," said Jill. "These aliens are not built that way. They are organized more along the lines of a colony of army ants or a swarm of bees. Each unit is large and can live and reproduce as an independent entity, but when they swarm together, they become more than a sum of the whole."

"An intelligent being—that is nothing but a programmed collection of wet gnats," said Karin.

"But with an IQ of . . ."

"I DON'T WANT TO KNOW!!!"

"White Whistler is back and asking questions," said Jill. "Is it all right to return the rest of the sample?"

"Yes," said Karin. "The last thing I want is a batch of ants in my refrigerator." She poked at the screen with short jabs of her finger, slightly annoyed with herself for getting perturbed with Jill. She bit her lip and tried to concentrate on the less spectacular, but equally scientifically important chemical data that Jill had extracted from its analyses of the metabolic wastes in the water from the sample bottle.

The night was long, for they were beginning to enter the inner-pointed hemisphere of Eau. Karin finally quit after the screen started to fuzz out in front of her eyes. She swiveled in the science console chair and went to the galley. After all that work, she felt she deserved a treat and asked her imp for one of her special gourmet meals. They were only allowed one per week, but Karin still had a two-week reserve after days of refueling on algae burgers and protein shakes. The gourmet meals had been prepared months ago back on *Prometheus* and frozen until they were called for on either the *Eagle* or *Dragonfly*.

Karin punched up her dinner. Liver from one of Nels's tissue cultures treasured back on *Prometheus*, smothered with cooked real onions, frozen real broccoli with mock-hollandaise sauce, new potatoes in pseudocream sauce, and real strawberries in pseudoport for dessert. It would take some time for the meat and vegetables to warm up, for Jill would program the microwave to bring everything together at the same time without overcooking or drying out. She went back through the privacy curtain and went to the head. She returned refreshed as the galley motiles were arranging her dinner on the counter, a cloth napkin adding counterpoint to the utilitarian stainless-steel utensils. Jill certainly knew its human psychology.

Karin's galley counter stool was next to the computer control center. A red-bearded David Greystoke was still at his console. Karin picked up a sprig of hot broccoli dripping with hollandaise sauce and leaned over to hold it in front of David's eyes.

"A bite of broccoli for a preview of Eau III," she said.

David's gaze broke from the screen, his red-rimmed eyes matching well with the red-rimmed stubble below his chin. He finally recognized who had spoken to him. He grinned and lunged.

"Done!" he said, speaking through green teeth. "It's time I went to bed anyway. Here. Take the earphones."

Karin took the glowing headset imp and put it on. David keyed his console, then rose and headed for the crew quarters in the rear. He was too tired to eat. He would do that when he woke up.

With the computer console vacated, Karin slid into the vacant seat and placed the tray of succulent liver and onions on her lap. Then with her right hand holding a battered stainless-steel fork and her left hand holding a crystal goblet full of strawberries and port, she let her senses relax and partake of a gourmet trip through the colorful seas of Eau. Seas as seen by the magical imagination of David Greystoke and his computer. It was only when she realized that her last bite of liver and onions was stone-cold that she knew she should be going to bed. The rosy red dawn was glinting through the right science blister when she rolled her fresh-washed body into her lower bunk and fell into a delightful sleep.

Mating

The next day Karin finished her breakfast, her exercises, had taken Jill and the Christmas Branch through a complete systems checkout, and was ready for the morning.

"The flouwen approach," said Karin's imp. She turned and glanced at the radar screen that she and the Christmas Branch had modified for sonar. There were some blue blobs in the upper portion of the screen. Blue meant "blue shift," which meant that they were coming at them very rapidly.

"Do they sound familiar?" asked Karin, a little concerned.

"It's Loud Red, White Whistler, and another one. There is also evidence of other moving object at extreme range, off the screen."

The red cloud arrived first, booming loudly.

☆I won! I won! I got here first!☆

◇So you did, Roaring☆Hot☆Vermillion. Now shall we wait for Bitter○Green○Fizz?◇

☆That slowpoke! Too many Pretty⊗Smells! Bitter ○Green○Fizz leave Pretty⊗Smells behind—move faster!☆

The red cloud flared out as it approached *Dragonfly*

and slid underneath the silvery-smooth hull of the long fuselage.

"Whoops!" said Karin, thrown upward by the wave of red passing under the airplane. She came down like a cat and heard confused noises from the various parts of their compact universe as Jill reassured all the crew members that what felt like a tidal wave was only Loud Red being playful. Carefully maintaining a three-point hold on carpet and bulkheads, Karin made her way forward to join Arielle at the front of the *Magic Dragonfly*.

The sunlight was getting brighter as Karin hopped into the copilot seat and looked out at the huge billows of red and white swimming languidly around *Dragonfly* like whales around a tourist boat. Periodically Loud Red would scratch its "back" against the bottom of the plane, heaving it upward slightly with its massive bulk. Its spheroidal orange pets would imitate the motion, adding three little bumps to the one big heave.

"Here comes the other flouwen," said Jill, a computer-generated ring of red flashing on the sonar screen in front of Arielle to indicate a rapidly moving speck emerging from the distant background clutter.

Arielle peered off into the distance and soon her acutely trained pilot eyes were able to see the figure.

"Thif one'f emerald. How pretty!"

White Whistler kept to its slow figure-eight motion about the plane while Loud Red and its pets bounded off at top speed to welcome the newcomer.

☆Hı! Hı!! Hı!!!☆ came the roaring greeting as Roaring☆Hot☆Vermillion streaked under Bitter○Green○Fizz. Coming to a stop, it turned and took up station next to the smaller green cloud as they both made their way back to the airplane. The Orange⊗ Hunters had come to a stop some distance away, but were now moving in closer to get a better taste of the water around the green stranger. Finally satisfied, they went back to their trailing positions behind Roaring☆ Hot☆Vermillion.

◦I got your call, and came as fast as I could. Have been traveling all night.◦

☆You hungry!?!☆

◦Yezzz!◦

Roaring☆Hot☆Vermillion issued a series of sharp whistles and the three orange spheroids took on their snake shape and slithered out in a pattern that swept the ocean off to the left. They nosed under every rock formation and soon jumped a yellow-orange rogue. It was larger, but they were faster. The three hunters, working as a team, worried the rogue around in a circle. Once they had it moving in the right direction, they stayed behind it and drove it back toward the airplane and their master, who had spread itself out like a trip net on the ocean bottom. To one side was a wall of green, on the other side was a wall of white. There seemed to be an escape hole between the two walls at the end of the narrowing funnel. The rogue streaked between the moving walls with the Orange⊗Hunters close behind, then it screamed as a multitude of red fingers shot up from the bottom to entrap it in their pythonlike grip.

◦Simply delicious!◦ buzzed Bitter◦Green◦Fizz as it methodically pulled the still struggling chunk of rogue into tiny pieces and absorbed them into its body.

☆Yeah!☆ agreed Roaring☆Hot☆Vermillion as it pulled some chunks off its half and threw them toward the trio of orange pets, who snapped them up avidly. It stopped feeding them when they started to play with their food instead of eating it. It tore off a huge chunk and offered it to Clear◇White◇Whistle, who had helped form the trap.

◇Not hungry.◇

☆OK! I eat!☆ and large, screaming masses of orange-yellow flesh were ripped from the remainder of the rogue and gulped into the red body, where soon the enzymes of Roaring☆Hot☆Vermillion won the lopsided battle against the outnumbered enzymes of the rogue.

With its hunger satiated, Bitter∘Green∘Fizz started to ask questions about the airplane still off in the distance. It finally grew brave enough to come near *Dragonfly* and converse with Jill through the sonar, but it really wasn't interested in the humans, and refused to come up to the cockpit windows and "look" inside with the lens that Clear◇White◇Whistle had invented. Instead, it stood off at a distance, rocked up a good portion of itself into a large emerald boulder, arranged the rest of its body into a mushroom-shaped cloud hanging above the rock, and unrolled the collection of Pretty⊗Smells it had been carrying.

As the wings of the first Pretty⊗Smell began to wave, the Orange⊗Hunters streaked forward, only to be met by expert slaps from three green tendrils that emitted a bitter smell along with the stinging slap. The Orange⊗Hunters went back to cower behind their master.

The Pretty⊗Smell unfurled its two-meter-wide wings and started to flap them slowly in the upper reaches of the sunlit water. The wings were ablaze with iridescent colors flashing out in multicolored gleams from the arrays of liquid crystals inside its body. Both Roaring☆Hot☆Vermillion and Clear◇White◇Whistle sent up long feelers to catch the complex interplay of the flashing lights, the delicate aroma, and the high-pitched trilling melody coming from the Pretty⊗Smell. The Pretty⊗Smell was soon joined by six others, and the three aliens seemed to go into a trance as they admired the birdlike creatures.

"What's going on now?" asked Karin of her imp.

"It's hard to say," answered Jill. "The three of them obviously caught some food animal, but except for its color, it looked just as amorphous as the flouwen and their pets. The new creatures are also obviously pets of the green flouwen. I'll call that one Green Buzzer because of its husky 'voice.' The pets are different in structure though. They seem to have wing bones and a spine that ends in a tail. They look like translucent pterodactyls with hummingbird feathers."

"I'm going out to get some pictures from close up with the video camera," said George. Karin jumped down from her seat and headed back to check out his suit.

It was about an hour later, when Barnard was rising high into the sky, that the next alien, Warm•Amber•Resonance, hummed into view. It was greeted by a pack of curious orange snakes, who sniffed it over and led it back to the trio of boulders still enjoying the Pretty⊗ Smell concert.

☆Enough!☆ The red boulder broke up into a clump of red rocks, which dissolved into a red blob.

◇Nice. But they need more training.◇

○I shall, as soon as my research on the seven-color mapping theorem on the hypertorus is finished.○

The amber-colored alien joined them.

•I got your call and came. What is the strange hard thing?•

◇It's called Floating⊗Rock,◇ said Clear◇White◇Whistle. ◇When it was first found, it couldn't talk. But it quickly leaned. It cannot move well since it's so hard, but it has Stiff⊗Movers inside it that can come out and do things. We think the Stiff⊗Movers are its pets, and they help Floating⊗Rock like the Orange⊗ Hunters help Roaring☆Hot☆Vermillion. The Stiff⊗ Movers can't be very intelligent, since they don't talk.◇

☆Want to see them?☆ said Roaring☆Hot☆Vermillion. ☆Come up close and look inside!☆

•No. Not interested.•

☆OK!☆

◇Floating⊗Rock seems to have chosen for its research a study of us,◇ said Clear◇White◇Whistle.

•What a strange field. Studying beings instead of mathematics. Could lead to recursive problems in logic.•

◊ If we studied ourselves, that is obviously recursive, and one could not be sure of the correctness of one's logic. But Floating⊗Rock, although intelligent, is obviously not we. It might be able to avoid that problem. ◊

•Possible,• hummed the yellow one.

◊ Floating⊗Rock asked how we made new we's. ◊

•You told it, of course?•

◊ I tried, but its language is still limited. ◊

•Then let's show it.•

◊ Exactly why we called you. Are you of good bulk? ◊

•Couldn't be better. Ran into a swarm of wild Pretty⊗ Smells on the way. What's that strange thing approaching?•

◊ That's one of the Stiff⊗Movers. ◊

Warm•Amber•Resonance flowed over to George. It put down a few rocks in a ring around George to stabilize its body in the current and examined the human in detail. George held still as he felt and heard the sonar pings echo through his body.

"Is everything OK?" he asked his imp. "The yellow flouwen seems to have me surrounded."

"That's Yellow Hummer," said Jill. "I'm pretty sure you're safe. From their conversation it seems that they think you are a pet of mine and they don't seem to eat pets, even though they are perfectly willing to eat wild animals that are indistinguishable from pets."

"Arf! Arf!" said George. "I wish I had a tail to wag."

A white blob slithered under the yellow curtain and came up to envelop George. He was used to White Whistler swarming over him so he relaxed. White Whistler picked him up and moved his legs and arms around, obviously showing off the "doll" to Yellow Hummer.

◊ . . . and parts of it come off in chunks. But they nearly always maintain a thin string back to the main body. ◊ Tools were unhitched from his belt, pulled to the end of their lanyards, then returned to their proper hook. His video camera was snatched from his grasp, and handed back, lens pointing at his helmet. He turned the camera around and continued recording. Finally through the white mist there appeared a yellow blob.

◊Go ahead. Get right up close to the round part up top. You can't see very well since there is a "nothing" inside, but you can "look" just fine. There is a funny bumpy thing inside with white fuzz on top.◊

•Ugly.•

◊Isn't it?◊

The two aliens swam off, leaving George to capture their exit on video. They rejoined the others.

◊Well. Everybody feel good and bulky?◊

☆Yeah! Need to lose some weight. Getting slow.☆
•I'm ready.•

○I guess I'm bulky enough, but I don't know. I've never made a youngling before.○

☆Really!?! Nothing to it!☆

•But do you remember your first time?• chided Warm•Amber•Resonance. •It was a little scary then, wasn't it?•

☆I'm never scared!☆

•Well, I was the first time. Especially when I had to 'let go.'•

☆Well . . . That *is* a little scary the first time.☆

•We all will go slow, Bitter○Green○Fizz. That will be better for Floating⊗Rock too.•

The four came together until they formed a circle twenty meters in diameter, each colorful body filling up a quadrant. They floated about two meters off the bottom and let down concentrated portions of their outer perimeter as rocks attached to streamers that anchored them in place. George was able to position himself just outside the ring of rocks and shoot under the canopy of bodies. Karin had exited in the meantime and had increased her buoyancy until she floated just below the waves where her video camera could look down at the action. The bobbing of the waves made her camera view swing wildly on the screen, but Jill could later compensate the motion out of the middle portion of the picture.

•Hold on at the middle, Bitter○Green○Fizz.•

◊ Now spiral around. ◊

○How many times?○

☆Lots!☆

•Just keep going as long as we do. We want to make the youngling nice and big so it will relearn fast.•

○I'm scared.○

◊ Slow down. Bitter○Green○Fizz is taut. ◊

"They're making a spiral at the center, like one of those superlarge lollipops you buy at amusement parks," said Karin.

"It's the same on this side," said George. He swept his video camera around to take in the rocks, still anchoring the aliens on the outside while their inner portions were continuing the swirling motion.

•Let go.•

○I'm losing me!○

☆You'll feel lots better when you are thinner!☆

•Let go so we can spiral some more.•

After some more coaxing, Bitter○Green○Fizz allowed more of its body to be pulled into the multicolored whirlpool growing in the center. As its essence was drawn out into a multiple touching thread, it seemed to lose its identity and become one with the others. Yet as its body drained away, the remainder of the multiton bulk felt as though it were growing younger. Bitter ○Green○Fizz felt the centuries drop from its weariness. It vibrated in happiness.

○Oooozzzzz!○

☆Aaahh!☆

•Hmmmmmmm!•

◊ Slowly . . . Slowly . . . ◊

◊ Stop! ◊

*   *   *

"The spiral whirlpool is now about as big as the rest of them!" said Karin. "If that's a baby, it's a big one!"

"It's still a spiral of many colors, Karin," said George. "While they're all a single color."

"Wonder what comes next?" she replied.

◇ Now comes the hard part, Bitter○Green○Fizz. Think of your green. Pull the green back without pulling the thread back. ◇

○But my thread is green. I can't pull the green without pulling the thread!○

☆Yes, you can! Watch!☆

From the very tip of the green thread deep in the spiral came the message that the red thread lying next to it had turned pink, then clear. Then on the opposite side, close coupled by the spiral twining, the milky thread became clear. Through the thin clear threads could be seen a yellow thread, and soon that became clear, leaving only the green.

◇ Pull the green back. ◇

There was a moment's pause as the green thread turned a darker shade.

•The other way.•

Patiently the three mature flouwen held the spiral pattern while they coaxed the younger adult into the mysteries of procreation. Slowly, hesitantly, the green film in and among the cells of gelatin was pulled back into the central body of the emerald-colored individual.

"The central portion is turning clear," said Karin, making sure that the video camera was catching the phenomenon.

"You can see the main bodies of the aliens take on a richer color," said George. "So whatever it is that makes the color is flowing back into their bodies instead of being destroyed or rendered colorless."

"Now what?" asked Karin.

"Wait and see," said George.

•Good! Keep pulling.•

○It feels so strange. So good!○

☆It's all that extra green sloshing around inside you!☆

◇The youngling is clear.◇

•Now pinch off the thread, Bitter○Green○Fizz.•

☆Don't let any green leak back in!☆

The final pinch-off was easy, for the cells in Bitter ○Green○Fizz had no affinity for the neutral-clear gel. The four adults separated their respective threads and waited. The lens of spiral jelly merged into an amorphous blob. For a long while it stayed colorless, then deep within it, some enzyme had taken the bits and pieces of randomized information that were still resident in the mold patterns in the gelatin, and had synthesized some nerve tissue. It was a viable pattern, and using it as a template, the enzymes built more and more, and a wave of transparent blue color spread out from the nucleation point until it suffused through the entire multiton glob of floating jelly. The blue blob started to talk. Its first words were stuttered in the varied speech patterns of its primogenitors.

•Hello☆Hello○hello! ◇HELLO!☆HELLO•hello ◇

But it soon developed its own distinctive voice, a blend of four voices into a beautiful warbling tone.

△hello△Hello△Hello.△Hello!△

•One plus one is two,• prompted Warm•Amber• Resonance.

△One plus one is TtWwOo.△

•It's going to be a smart youngling.•

☆Look who made it!☆

○It has such a pretty blue color, and such a dainty warbling voice.○

△Smart youngling ... pretty blue ... dainty warbling.△

○Let's call it Dainty△Blue△Warble!○

△Dainty blue warble !△

•Dainty△Blue△Warble it is then. Come youngling. I'll bet you're hungry. Can your Orange⊗Hunters find us something small to eat, Roaring☆Hot☆Vermillion?•

"It turned blue before our eyes," exclaimed Karin.

"And it already knew how to speak the instant it was born," said Jill, the incredulous tone in the robot voice driven home by the lengthy pauses between the words as the computer brain computed at high priority between the low-priority task of talking to the humans.

"It must really be a strange form of evolution. They have the advantages of budding, in that the new individual has nearly the same size and intelligence and *memory* as the original individual, so there is a continuity of experience that must carry back over aeons, yet there is the diversity of sexual interchange, with all the advantages of hybrid vigor," said George. "Did anyone figure out how many sexes they have? Four?"

"I am going through a detailed analysis of the spiral pattern," said Jill. "But I can find no significant difference in any of them, except the green one, which was a little slower than the others. I'm not sure, but maybe they don't have sexes, or at least roles where one partner performs a different function than the other."

His camera working constantly, George continued to capture the aftermath of the mating of the four mastodons. The red, white, and green aliens were swimming aimlessly about each other, enjoying each other's company while brushing near the cloud of birdlike creatures that floated in harmonious movement among them. The yellow alien was swimming in slow circles about the pale blue infant, talking to it, encouraging it to swim, and responding to its warbling speech pattern.

The aliens finally drifted away, having forgotten about Jill and the humans in their preoccupation with each other. George and Karin came in to warm up.

As George cycled through, Richard took the heavy video camera from his grip.

"You got feelthy pictures, Signore?" he joked.

"I guess so, but it never seems as exciting when you're looking through the viewfinder."

Karin helped George take off his suit, and checked it thoroughly before allowing it to go in the locker.

"Y'know," she said in a tight voice, her gaze fixed on the telltales on the chest pack as she punched check code after check code into the button array. "To be really fair, we humans ought to be willing to put on the same show for the aliens."

There was a pregnant silence, broken by an indignant explosion from Richard.

"Impossible," he said. "We can't survive outside without suits!"

"It could be done in the cockpit area where they could see in," said Karin, her eyes still fixed on the suit readouts. "Have to be done standing up, of course. They couldn't see if we were lying down. The rest of the crew would be in the back, of course."

Karin finally looked up. Her eyes met Richard's and she turned beet-red.

"Not me!!!" exploded Richard, his dark copper skin flushing below the ears.

"Do you mean to tell me that squaws are braver than braves?"

"Bravery has nothing to do with it," said Richard indignantly.

Karin gritted her teeth and smiled a saccharin smile at Richard. "Fair is fair," she said sweetly. Then her voice turned into a challenge. "I'm game if you are, buck."

Without waiting for a reply from the strangely silent giant of a man, petrified by a fear that was stronger than any fear he had ever had to face before, she turned her head and talked to her imp.

"Ask the aliens if they would like to see the difference between male and female humans and a demonstration of the reproductive act," she said. "We won't be able to show them a new baby, but at least they can see how it's done."

There was a long pause as the computer interrogated the aliens. Then finally Jill replied. "They aren't interested in humans," it said. "As far as they are concerned, you are just unintelligent pets of mine. Instead they want me to tell them why I have wings that look like the wings on their birdlike pets, yet I obviously don't swim with them."

There was an outrushing of air from Richard's lungs.

Karin smiled and winked at him. "Well, I guess it'll have to be some other time, handsome." She hung up George's suit, brushed past the still shocked Richard, and went forward to the galley for some food. Sex always made her hungry.

As morning approached, Jill complained that its sonar vision was getting fuzzy.

"I've checked all the wires and connectors," said Jill. "Since they were jury-rigged when we replaced the radar with the sonar, they were the first things to suspect, but they seem to be fine. I also had the imp measure the sonic pressure from the transducers themselves, and the power seems to be getting out, but the returns are getting more blurred by the hour."

"I'll get suited up and go out for a look," said Karin. "Perhaps I can see something the imp missed."

Karin was only halfway into her suit when Richard appeared. He had his coveralls on, but no corridor boots. Karin's stomach twinged in sympathy when she noticed the stubs on his feet where his little toes had once been.

"Why are you suiting up?" he asked, slightly concerned.

"Jill said the sonar is acting up, but she and the outside branch can't seem to find the problem."

"Need any help?" he offered.

"Not yet," she replied. "But you can give me a hand with the backpack."

Richard and the inside branch went over the checkout with Karin, then cycled her through the air lock.

Karin waited until the inrush of water into the lock subsided, then swam out the door to the front of the airplane. Jill had turned off the propellers and the craft was drifting slowly forward. The outside branch was waiting for her and together they unlatched the radome and opened it up. As her suit imp relayed Jill's voice, the outside branch pointed to various sections of the bank of sonar transducers and explained what the computer had checked previously. Karin could see nothing obviously wrong, but had the computer take the branch through the entire checkout again while she watched.

As the branch was going through its programmed routine, the water began to get cloudy as if a glass of milk had been released in the water. Suddenly the entire cavity of the radome was milky-white, and Karin could hardly see the branch through the murkiness.

◇ Hi! What is this thing? ◇

Karin felt the high-pitched tones of White Whistler through her suit as Jill provided the translation through her suit imp. She felt her hand being raised as the curious alien pushed a portion of its body under her glove to feel the equipment hidden beneath. Karin waited patiently until the alien had finished feeling and tasting everything inside the dome.

◇ Bad! ◇ came an explosive chirp.

"I think it just tasted some of the epoxy glue that we used to assemble the solar array," Jill's voice interjected. "It would still have a strong residual component of hardener."

◇Teach me,◇ came another whistle.

Karin smiled at the eagerness of the alien to learn something new, while she in turn was awed by someone who had a greater mental capacity than a dozen humans. She started to explain how the sonar system worked. It turned out to be fairly easy, since she could have Jill operate it while she pointed, and White Whistler, having its own sonar system, could easily comprehend the purpose. Some of the components were bewildering to it, however, especially the concept of a "wire" to carry "electricity." White Whistler wanted to "feel" the electricity, but both Jill and Karin didn't want to risk applying a voltage of any magnitude to such a highly sensitive creature, despite its immense size.

White Whistler then asked, ◇Why bubbles? I not see well, machine must not see well.◇

"Yes!" said Karin in surprise. "The sonar cannot see well. What bubbles?"

◇These.◇ White Whistler chirped as a long, snakelike tentacle brushed a swarm of tiny bubbles off the inside surface of the radome, leaving a clear path of black plastic.

◇See better,◇ said the alien. The tentacle whipped around the inside of the dome, clearing away the tiny bubbles that had been scattering the sonar waves as they entered and left the radome. ◇Now see lots better.◇

"That did it," said Jill. "The sonar image is perfectly clear now. There must be a slow chemical reaction between the paint and the ammonia water of the ocean that creates microscopic bubbles on the inside of the dome. I will have the outside branch wipe them off periodically."

"Thank you," said Karin to the alien.

◇What means thankyou?◇ asked the alien.

Karin sighed, her breath whistling from between her lips, and started to try to explain the human practice of polite conversation to an alien whose social structure was based on directness. Jill, trying to translate between the two, included the sigh in the conversation without translation.

◊Stop!◊ interrupted the voice from the white alien. ◊Your pet talk?◊ A white cloud enveloped Karin's visor, while another portion touched the sonar array that was Jill's vocal cords.

"An ideal time to make an important point," Jill whispered through Karin's imp. "Repeat the following after me. It is a salutation plus the name of the individual that is surrounding your helmet." Jill whistled a short, but complex tune. It had a few triple tongues in it, but it was easy for Karin, who had been a trombone player in her high-school band.

◊Your pet say hello!◊ The white cloud lifted one white tendril from the helmet and another from the sonar array, which had stayed silent while Karin had whistled. The two tendrils were absorbed into the interior of the alien, as if checking them out, then another arm of white jelly reached out from the alien to retouch Karin's visor. There was a simple tone, a complex whistle, another simple tone, and a different complex whistle.

"Say TtWwOo," whispered the imp into Karin's ear.

Karin whistled a respectable imitation of the alien number.

Her whistle was repeated by the alien twice with the same complex whistles in between.

"Now this will show you are smarter than Loud Red's pets," said Jill. "Provided you can get your lips around this one. If not, you can fake it and I'll have the imp make the sound."

Karin's pucker and pitch was up to the challenge, and a reasonable facsimile of the number "FfFfOoOoUuUu-RrRr" vibrated out through the helmet into the sensitive body of the white alien.

◊Smart pet!◊

Jill dropped her bombshell.

"This element not pet. Other similar elements not pet. I am pet."

There was a long pause as the white alien thought through the statement. A large portion started to rock up and sink, but then redissolved. The alien formed a lens with part of its body and moved it up close to Karin's visor to look in. Karin pulled an arm back in from the sleeve in her suit and put her hand up next to her face. Her fingers raised as she went through the addition tables up to five, her fingers adding counterpoint to the whistles coming from her lips.

◇ Stiff⊗Movers intelligent. Not pets. But not talk correct. ◇

"Stiff⊗Movers are humans. Not pets. Not made to talk. They think. I talk."

"I hope I got you out of that with minimum disruption to your superiority," said Jill.

"If we really are superior," said Karin.

◇ What is human buzzing? ◇

"Human talk to me with buzz. I talk to you with whistle."

Karin's imp whispered in her ear. "Do something while talking about it, so I can translate as you talk."

Karin reached for her belt and pulled off her Mech-All. She set the handle for a large-bladed screwdriver and the blob at the end of the tool reconfigured.

"This is a tool." She ducked out of the radome to the outside.

"I leave." She reached out and pulled the radome shut.

"I put front of airplane back." Jill translated airplane as pet.

"I fix front of airplane." Karin fastened the screw hold-downs with the screwdriver tool, deactivated the mechanism into a soft blob, and put it back on her tool belt. The white alien, ever curious, tried to make a small hard sliver and undo the fasteners. Karin decided that this was time to assert her authority.

"No!" she shouted, and struck the white appendage with her gloved hand. There was some resistance, but her hand cut through the alien's appendage, leaving a liver-sized portion floating by itself in the ocean. There were strange whimpering noises from the blob that were immediately quelled when the main body of the alien quickly sent out another appendage to make contact with the severed piece of flesh.

"Oн! I'm sorry," said Karin.

The alien re-formed its clear lens and moved it in front of Karin's helmet, while a substantial portion of its body lifted up to form a retina behind the lens so it could look at the strange "human" inside the hard metal suit.

◊ What means sorry? ◊ asked Clear ◊ White ◊ Whistle, ever curious.

Karin sighed again.

Talking

"It's too bad that we always have to talk through you," said Karin to Jill. "With a lot of practice maybe I could whistle the numbers, but I certainly couldn't carry on a decent conversation, even if I could learn the language in a hurry," said Karin. "What we need is a magic translation machine." She paused. "Of course that's what you are. Too bad it takes up so much of your brainpower to do it."

"Actually, since they are very logical thinkers and we used Boolean logic to develop our communication, we ended up speaking in a very formalized manner that is quite different from the way that they talk among themselves. Most of the translation is automatically handled by a translation table and some simple rules for syntax. I only have to use my more general translation programs when new words or situations arise. The translation table and the syntax rules are too complicated to be programmed into your imps, but they could easily be stored in the miniprocessor in your suit chest-pack."

"The suit imp could stay outside as the transmitter and receiver," said Karin. "How about programming my suit now and letting me try it?"

There was a significant increase in the brightness of

the laser light passing between the transponder on the top of Karin's helmet and a similar one blinking from the left eye of the *Magic Dragonfly*. Karin heard the rustle of her suit imp making its way through the valves in the life-support backpack to the outside. Soon the metallic green body of the suit imp with its red, yellow, and blue lights was perched on the shoulder of her suit.

Karin watched the illuminated message board display in the neck of her visor until it said: "TRANSLATION PROGRAM LOADED."

"Try it," said her personal imp. "But keep your sentences simple. The translator will ask you to rephrase a sentence if it gets too complicated for the syntax program to handle."

"Hello, White Whistler. My name is Karin."

Karin could hear the whistles from the waving cilia of her suit imp at the same time she heard a more complex whistle coming from Jill's sonar as Jill explained what had been done. The white cloud swirled up and paused in front of Karin's helmet.

◊ Hello, Karin. My name is White Whistler. I touch your Sound⊗Maker? ◊ A long white pseudopod extended to within a few centimeters of the suit imp.

"Yes," said Karin, sure that the wiry limbs of the imp were more than a match for the soft, jellylike flesh of the alien.

The imp was engulfed in a white ball, which withdrew again after a few seconds of feeling.

◊ Interesting. Each subset of Sound⊗Maker is like larger subset. The smallest subsets are very tiny. Sound⊗Maker made like statement in recursive logic. ◊

"Do all the flouwen like logic?" Karin asked, intrigued by the gigantic cloud with the Einstein brain.

◊ Yes!!! ◊ piped White Whistler. ◊ Tight premises, narrow conditions . . . surprise conclusions! Fun! ◊ The milky-white cloud swirled as it spoke, forming a tight knot that almost condensed into a quartzine rock, then unfurled again.

"We study many kinds of problems," said Karin.

◊ Fun? ◊ said the alien.

"Yes," said Karin. "Some use real numbers, some use numbers that are not real, but still exist."

◊ Yes. When number squared is one—that number is number one. When some other number squared is negative one—that number is not real number, but it exists. You call it i. ◊

Karin was slightly surprised by the rapid response, especially by the clarity of its simple description. It was obvious that the minor mysteries of imaginary numbers were well known to these amorphous geniuses. She decided to test it with another problem. She would have to think it out carefully ahead of time and state it clearly if she were to be understood.

"Suppose you have a growing thing," started Karin. "The growing thing gets bigger. The amount it gets bigger depends on how big it is ..." She was interrupted by Jill.

"They already know about exponential growth," said Jill. "I taught them the numerical value for pi = 3.14159 ... , but that was only because they were still hesitant to impose their language structure on me. They taught me the exponential growth factor e = 2.71828 ... in our language before I could figure out a way to define it in their language. Just say 'e,' and the imp will translate it for them."

Karin paused a second to let Jill's revelation seep in, then a little more humbly she proceeded.

"e multiplied by itself one time is e," she said.

◊ Correct. ◊

"e multiplied by itself zero times is one," she said.

◊ Yes, ◊ the white cloud whistled quietly.

"e multiplied by itself pi times is ..." she paused for a second to listen to Jill through her imp, "23.1407 plus a slight bit more," she said. She took a deep breath, and then started her next question, only to have it interrupted by the excited squeal of White Whistler.

◊ . . . and e multiplied by itself pi times i is minus one, ◊ said the white cloud. ◊ Isn't that fun! Isn't that exciting!! We wish we could find another one. ◊

The wind taken out of her sails, Karin gave up. "We wish we could find another one too."

There was a loudness and a rippling crackle and two large blobs appeared in their midst; one poked through the milky cloud that was White Whistler, and the other snaked its way under Karin's left armpit. One blob was red, the other was purple, and both quivered with eagerness and questions.

☆Another one!!☆ the red zucchini squash vibrated loudly.

□Tell!□ rasped the wrinkled purple blob. □Tell about other!□

"Excuse the buzzing one with the strong lavender color," said Jill. "It is an old one that just redissolved from a thinking rock. It has not quite picked up all the human language nuances from the others. I call it Deep Purple."

☆Another ONE!?!☆

◊ No. You heard wrong, Roaring☆Hot☆Vermillion, not another one. NO other one. ◊

☆zzzzzzzzzzzzzzt!☆

There was a shocked silence.

"Well, there are some other interesting problems," said Karin. "Some in logic theory, some in number theory, and some in geometry. There is one famous problem that is part geometry and part number theory."

The purple lobe expanded and with careful enunciation asked, □Logic—OK, numbers—OK, geometry—not OK.□

Karin was puzzled when she heard this. In her engineer's world, geometry was inextricably mixed with numbers. Yet these beings did not manipulate the external world, they just existed in it. Could it be that they had no idea of the relationship of the length of a line to the progression of numbers, and the relationship of the area of a geometrical square to the product of a mathematical square of a number? She tried an experiment. Pulling a diamond scribe from her tool kit, she started to scratch a diagram in the duralloy wing-plate above her. Her motions were interrupted by a squirming feeling at her beltline as three inquisitive pseudopods imitated her entry into her tool pouch.

□Lots'a hard things,□ said Deep Purple.

☆Wheeoo! SHARP!!☆ said Loud Red, as it tested a hard acrylic handle on the point of the scribe that Karin was trying to use.

◇Too many things,◇ White Whistler admonished.

Karin got annoyed. She reached down and slapped the offending tendrils away from her tool pouch, glared around angrily, then carefully sealed each centimeter of the rip-seal seam. She again reached up to the under part of the wing with her diamond scribe held firmly in her hand. For once she had the full attention of the frivolous multitude of aliens.

Carefully, she scratched a right-angled triangle on the skin of *Dragonfly*'s wing. Then, just as carefully, she measured off the length of one of the shorter sides by laying the scribe along the side and pinching it carefully between her gloved fingers. She turned it at right angles and marked a point. In a few seconds she had constructed a square that used one of the triangle sides as one of its sides. She was halfway through constructing the square for the other side when the silent chorus broke into cacophony.

□Yes! Three and four is five!□

☆HA! PYTH THEOREM!!☆ roared Loud Red.

"They mean the ancient Greek theorem ascribed to

Pythagoras," said Jill. "I told them the human name for the theorem."

"Thanks," said Karin, trying to separate the alien responses from Jill's.

◊ We understand your diagram, ◊ said White Whistle, ◊ Even if you cannot draw it because of others. ◊

There was a pause as the purple and red protuberances retracted under the seeming glare of the white cloud that they had intruded upon.

◊ Tell of problem. ◊

Karin felt flustered. She was not a mathematician, and it was obvious that these creatures knew the fact that a triangle had two short sides and one long side, and that the squares of the lengths of the two shorter sides equaled the square of the length of the longest side. She felt stupid as she tried to get across in simple language the idea of one of the most famous unsolved problems in human mathematics, Fermat's Conjecture.

She pointed her scribe at a triangle enclosed in squares inscribed about its perimeter.

"Three times three, plus four times four, equals five times five," she said.

□ OK!! □ said Deep Purple enthusiastically.

☆ Yes!?!☆ said Loud Red, with an inquisitive quiver in its tendril.

"One of the unsolved problems in human mathematics was conjectured by the human Fermat. There are many solutions to X multiplied two times plus Y multiplied two times equals Z multiplied two times. But there is no solution to the problem of X multiplied three times, plus Y multiplied three times, equals Z multiplied three times . . . even if three is any number."

□ That not problem! □ Deep Purple graveled.

☆ That's a DUMB problem!!☆ the red cloud exploded. ☆ That problem not said right. I say right way. *X* squared times *Y* squared equals *Z* squared has many solutions. Is there a solution for *U* cubed plus *V* cubed plus *W* cubed equal Z cubed? That make more sense. You have two things X and Y. You multiply two times. You add two times. You get same as Z multiplied two times. Two things three times is DUMB!! If you multiply three times, then you should add three times!✩

"But *is* there an answer?" persisted Karin.

▢Answer?▢ echoed Deep Purple. There was a long pause. Then the other colored portions of the water retracted as Deep Purple condensed into a purple boulder some meters beneath Karin's feet. She had not realized how massive the old purple one was. Like a motion picture of a vaporizing block of dry ice run backward, the gigantic purple cloud condensed into a slippery purple rock—a thinking rock—thinking about a problem put forth by a brilliant human mind long ago and far away.

✩I'm going surfing!✩ said Loud Red. It swam up to the top of the wing and perched there, its weight causing a slight list to the plane. As the next roller broke over the plane, Loud Red used the inertia of the wing to launch itself onto the forward surface of the wave.

✩Wheeee!!!✩ came the cry of excitement through the water, fading into the distance as the wave carried the red alien off.

"I wish I could surf," said Karin wistfully.

◇You are the wrong shape to surf,◇ said White Whistler.

"I could surf if I had a surfboard," said Karin, her thoughts going back over six lightyears and forty time years. Fortunately Jill was back in the translation loop, for it took an extended discussion between the computer and the alien before it understood what a surfboard was.

◇I be your surfboard!◇ said White Whistler. It swooped under Karin and picked her up on its massive body, a cavity appearing in the top of the alien's body to cradle the human.

"What's going on?" came Richard's concerned voice over the imp link.

"I'm going to get a ride!" shouted a delighted Karin. The white alien humped itself up on the plane wing.

"Jill! Make her stop! That could be dangerous!" Karin could see Richard through the left cockpit window. He was yelling and waving his hands at her, trying to make her get down off the alien.

Karin grinned and waved back at him.

"Cowabunga!" she cried as a roller lifted the wing and White Whistler launched its multiton body onto the wave.

The wave was traveling toward the center of an underwater volcanic vent field that had produced a long, sloping lava shield. As they moved toward the central region, the ocean became shallower and the wave steeper. It was a long ride, and after they had gone a kilometer they were out of range of Jill's sonar and laser beacon. Karin had to depend upon her chest-pack translator for communication. White Whistler noticed the lack and switched to using simplified speech patterns. Although both enjoyed the ride, White Whistler's curiosity led to questions.

◊ Humans are strange elements. Not see before. I swim entire world many times. Never see humans. Where humans exist before now? ◊

"We came from lights in sky." Suddenly Karin realized that the aliens had no eyes, so perhaps they didn't know about the stars, although they probably knew about Barnard.

◊ I know many lights in sky. There is Sky⊗Rock, you name Roche. There is Hot, you name Barnard. There is Warm and little elements. There are many other lights. They are my research. ◊

"An eyeless astronomer," mused Karin. "It even has to make its telescope lenses from it own flesh." She started to think how to tell the alien that the stars were suns like Barnard and that she came from a planet around one of those stars.

"The other lights we call stars. They are suns like Barnard, but far away."

◇ Not all are like Barnard. Some have color of Barnard. Most have different color. Some yellow like spots on Barnard. Some white like light from storms. Some blue. Different kinds of suns. ◇

You may not have eyes, said Karin to herself. But you have a marvelous color sense if you've been able to deduce that the stars are suns just from their spectrum.

◇ One star was not like others. Star was yellow for a long time. Then star get brighter and color is green. Then after three thousand days star become yellow again. ◇

"That is star of humans," said Karin, much relieved that the problem of pointing out which of the many stars was her home sun had been solved by their method of arrival.

◇ Human star far away. Your plane swim long time. ◇

"Humans not use plane. Humans use big . . . circle. You see big circle in sky?"

◇ Yes. Big circle not logical. ◇

"Not logical? I do not understand."

◇ Lights in the sky are my research. I know stars are suns. I know Sky⊗Rock is like our world, but with no water. I know Warm is like a big world with more clouds. I know little ones of Warm are almost equal to our world. I can predict motions of all lights in sky except one. That one is big circle. Big circle is not like anything. It is circle, not sphere. Its motion has no logic. I think long to find logic of big-circle motion. I can find no logic in motion. ◇

"Big circle is not heavy like other lights," said Karin. "Big circle swims in light from Barnard. Subtract big circle from set of lights in sky. They do not swim. They move by logic of gravity."

◊ Word is missing. Logic of . . . ◊

"Each sphere in sky is pulled by other spheres in sky. A big sphere pulls more than a small sphere. If two spheres are near, the pull is strong. If two spheres are far, the pull is weak. Amount of pull varies as inverse square of distance between the two spheres."

◊ That was the hypothesis I was using! Then big circle came and its motion did not fit hypothesis. I rejected hypothesis and looked for a new hypothesis. ◊

The alien stopped its slow swim back to the airplane.

◊ I must think. ◊

Karin felt the body of the alien contract around her, getting harder and more rubbery as the liquid was squeezed from the jellylike body. Suddenly she found herself floating in the water as a white rock sank beneath her to the bottom.

"White Whistler!" she cried through her outside imp. "Come take me back to the plane! I can't swim twenty kilometers in my suit, even if I knew which direction to swim!!!"

There was no answer.

Karin set her suit heater on low to conserve power, and closed her eyes to rest.

I hope White Whistler isn't trying to solve the generalized n-body central force problem, she thought to herself as she drifted off to sleep.

A clear blue cloud strung through the cold water and wrapped itself around a red rock. There was a trilling sound as Dainty△Blue△Warble tried to attract the attention of the inactive older.

△ It's time for another lesson, Old-one Roaring☆Hot☆Vermillion! What'cha doing? △

☆ It is!?!☆ roared the red rock as it dissolved into a cloud. ☆ Was just thinking of what to teach you next!☆

Feathery red tendrils snaked out into the water, tasting each molecule.

☆Let me taste. Know there was one around just a little bit ago.☆

Suddenly there was a reaction, and like a bloodhound on the scent, a portion of the cloud evolved into a long streamer that dragged the rest of the red body along. The blue cloud floated alongside. Suddenly the red cloud stopped, the tip of its streamer pointing stiffly off into the murky depths.

☆There's a Creepy⊗Stink!☆

☆Sneak up on it! Ho! Ho!☆

△Yes, Old-one,△ said the blue cloud, imitating the motions of the older.

☆Wait!☆ said Roaring☆Hot☆Vermillion as the eager blue youngster started to move ahead toward the slowly moving black slug plowing through the muddy bottom.

☆First sneak up only halfway! Then stop!☆

The blue cloud obeyed and stopped in the water about halfway to the Creepy⊗Stink.

☆Now halfway again! Stop!☆

☆Do it again!☆

☆Will you catch it?☆

☆Will you?☆

Dainty△Blue△Warble followed the instructions of the older, moving only halfway each time toward the slowly creeping blob of pungent food. As the gap lessened, the pauses at each halfway point became shorter. Dainty△Blue△Warble controlled its fluid body well with its eager, learning intellect, but finally, in a swirl that was too fast to follow, the Creepy⊗Stink was gone.

☆Ho! Ho! Caught it, didn't you!☆

△I calculated that even though I only went halfway each time, my velocity was greater, and eventually I would catch up. So I ate it!△

☆Taste interesting?☆

There was an unnaturally long pause.

△Stinky!△

☆You'll get used to it. Hey! WAVE!!!☆

△Wave!△ warbled the youngling. Then flowing smoothly into the older's wake, it surfed across the face of the shining sea.

"George? I'm worried," said Richard. "It's getting dark and Karin and White Whistler aren't back yet."

George looked out the cockpit window at Barnard. The short day was almost over and the tall tail of the *Magic Dragonfly* was casting a long shadow up the water mountain toward Roche as Barnard set behind them.

"Are there any of the aliens around?" he asked Jill.

George could hear the sonar in the nose go through its search scan.

"Loud Red and Little Blue are coming this way."

"Ask them if they have seen Karin and White Whistler."

Floating⊗Rock is calling us.

☆Hi! We come closer!☆ the loud voice roared through the water. The body of Roaring☆Hot☆Vermillion took on a more streamlined shape and zoomed off through the ocean, followed close behind by a pale blue arrow. The two drew to a halt in front of the chugging airplane.

"Where is White Whistler and the human Karin?"

☆Don't know. Orange⊗Hunters will find them!☆ The red cloud gave a piercing whistle and soon three eager orange snakes came streaking through the water to dash themselves headlong into the red flesh of their master. After the obligatory free-for-all wrestling match was over, the Orange⊗Hunters listened to the complex commands coming from Roaring☆Hot☆Vermillion, then took off, making controlled crooning noises as they went.

"George," said Jill, "there's a message being relayed from *Clete*. The Comsat says the signal is very weak and broken up, but it's getting stronger as the sun sets. This is what we have so far."

"Karin calling Comsats . . . Floating alone some twenty kil. . . . . . . istler rocked up and left me. Heater power getting low. Karin calling Comsats. . . ."

"Can they get her position?" asked George.

"All they have are radio signals to work from," said Jill. "That only puts her somewhere in a hundred-kilometer circle. As soon as it gets darker the Comsats will try to spot her helmet laser beacon."

"I'm going out to see if Loud Red will take me looking," said Richard, heading for the suit locker.

"The suit imp reports that Karin's torso temperature has dropped to thirty-five degrees centigrade, with extremities well below that," said Jill.

"Wha . . . White Whistler, you're back! . . . No . . . Orange blob . . . Stop bumping . . . Go 'way . . ." There were sounds of heavy breathing, then the chattering teeth suddenly stopped.

"I think she's lost consciousness," said Jill.

"I'm through the lock," said Richard. "Patch me through to Loud Red."

Jill stopped the engines and the *Magic Dragonfly* drifted to a stop in the ocean as Richard swam forward through the dimly lit seas toward the two aliens.

"Please carry me to Karin," he asked through Jill's sonar.

☆No. Orange⊗Hunters come. They bring human Karin here.☆

"But they'll take forever . . . a long time. She may die!"

☆She not die. She too hard. Cannot eat human, so human not die!☆

Suddenly Richard realized that the aliens had no concept of death except that of being assimilated in some predator's body. And since they were the dominant predator, with no natural enemies, they never died, just spent longer and longer times rocked up to think about more and more difficult logical problems until they finally gave themselves a problem that took an eternity to solve.

"Jill, convince that lazy red blob that we need to get Karin here in a hurry."

"I don't think we really need to," said Jill. "My sonar can detect the pets up ahead. They are moving this way at a respectable speed. I think they have Karin with them because the Comsat trackers show a Doppler velocity shift on their communication signal from her suit imp. Do you have your safety line on?"

"Of course," said Richard.

"Good," said Jill, starting the engines of the *Magic Dragonfly*. "See if you can catch the lock handholds as I go by. I'm going to save a few minutes by moving toward them."

"How's Karin?" asked Richard, puffing as he swam a few quick strokes and swung into the open door of the lock as it moved by.

"Not good. Torso temperature down to thirty centigrade. The suit imp has dropped all power reserves and is running the last few grams of hydrogen through the fuel cell to get heat to the extremities before frostbite sets in."

Painful memories flooded back into Richard's mind as he recalled six hours of agony walking sockfooted through Alpine snow carrying two unconscious tourists. He twitched the remaining eight toes in his boots. Would he like Karin less if she lost any of her toes? If she lived . . .

Stop that, you ass, he remonstrated himself. Get ready to cycle her through once those orange-colored hounds bring her in.

The smooth thump-thump of the large engine on the right and the pittidy-pittidy of the jury-rigged fan on the left stopped and the *Magic Dragonfly* drifted to a halt. The second the current was less than his space-suit swimming speed, Richard was through the door and breaststroking forward. The red alien was wrestling with his charges and loud roars, shrieks, and whistles sounded through the ocean. Bobbing just below the surface of the water was a limp figure in a space suit, the arms and legs hanging downward, jerking limply as the waves tossed the body to and fro. Near the head of the body was a blurred bundle of twigs that were waving frantically through the water in an attempt to drag the heavy carcass toward the airplane.

An orange blob hit Richard on the legs as it darted back into the fray, sending him tumbling in the water. Richard righted himself and stroked again to the distant limp form. He grabbed her by the belt and headed for the lock.

Once Karin was inside, George took charge. "Hold her by the waist while Arielle and I get her helmet off and her shoulders out!"

The helmet came off and a cold, dank head dropped on Richard's shoulder as the subdued stink of a frozen, tortured body arose from the enclosed space. Richard held tight to the waist until the stiff arms were extracted from their casings. He switched to a chest hold on the body while George, Arielle, and the Christmas Branch worked at detaching the bottom portion of the body from the plumbing. Richard's arms grew cold from the leaden breasts draped over his forearms.

"Turn her to the left so we can get her legs out," came the command from George.

Richard shifted his grip and easily turned the large body in the weak gravity of Eau, holding Karin by the waist and under the left arm. He looked down to see a deep depression in the soft underflesh of the breast, the fatty tissue turned to clay by the cold. The suit came off.

"OK! Out! We'll take it from here!" said George, pushing him forward through the privacy curtain as Arielle

and the Christmas Branch started to strip the coveralls
from the blue-cold body.

"How's she doing?" asked David as Richard made his
way forward, closing the second curtain behind him.

"I don't like it!" said Richard, pounding one massive
but ineffectual fist into the other. He paced four huge
steps forward, his hips avoiding the backs of the console
chairs like a halfback avoiding one linebacker after
another. His fourth step landed solidly on the floor next
to the flight deck and he turned to march back again.

△Lesson time again!△ piped a small blue cloud as it
scurried up to a deep yellow rock with a cloud of amber
water hanging softly around it.

•Certainly, Dainty△Blue△Warble,• murmured the
edges of the yellow cloud. •Just let me ingest my latest
thinking.•

The small blue cloud waited patiently, only flickering
a tendril or two while the large dark-yellow rock dissolved on the ocean bottom. The dark yellow dispersed
in thin threads into the light yellow cloud above it.
Soon you could not tell the difference between the threads
and the cloud and the rock was gone.

△What were you thinking about?△

•The fourth infinity.•

△Tell me about it!△

•Well . . . I will someday. But first you have to learn
about the second infinity.•

△Tell me! Tell me!△

A yellow tendril poked a hole in the muddy bottom.

•Feel, youngling. There is a point.•

A delicate blue tendril felt into the murky bottom.

△That is a hole in the mud, older Warm•Amber•
Resonance.△

There was a long pause as the yellow cloud rippled in
annoyance. However, the tone that resumed after the

pause had all the warm patience that it had contained previously.

•Imagine it is a point, with no dimensions.•

△Yes, older.△

The yellow tendril touched the surface of the soft mud again, leaving another tiny spot in the smooth surface close to the first one.

•Here is another point.•

•Here is another.•

•Here is another.•

The line of close-spaced spots grew.

•Imagine.•

•Imagine points so close they make a line. Infinitely long.•

There was a pause as the young one absorbed the sounds. Its blue cloud enveloped the motions of the yellow wisp making a long string of tiny dots in the ocean bottom.

△Infinite in both directions, older Warm•Amber• Resonance?△

•Yes. Very good, youngling.•

•Now . . . Imagine a point not on the line.•

•Here is one.•

•Here is another.•

Soon a number of isolated spots were scattered above and below the dotted line on the muddy sea floor.

•Imagine an infinite number of them.•

There was a slight pause.

•Are there more points *off* the line than *on* the line?•

The youngling thought carefully before answering, its wisps of azure clumping and dissolving randomly. The older waited patiently. Finally the youngling answered.

△No! They are the same.△

•Right!•

△That was too easy. Give me a harder one.△

•All right. Draw a line through any of those points I made.•

The blue cloud formed a tendril of its own and made a streak through one of the isolated spots in the mud.

•Draw another through the same point. Make it wriggly if you want to.•

A wriggly line joined the streak.

•Draw more.•

Dainty△Blue△Warble concentrated, and soon dozens of distinctly different lines were drawn through the same point. Then came the question.

•Imagine you did that to each point. Are there more wriggly lines than points?•

The blue cloud stopped moving as it started to think.

Warm•Amber•Resonance drifted off on the current as Dainty△Blue△Warble poindered the last question. The fluid body of the youngling slowly began condensing into a bright-blue rock as the difficulty of the tough logical question called for more and more concentrated neural matter.

•Huunnm!• murmured the amber older. •That will keep the blue menace quiet for a while. Off to the waves! MMMMM!!!!•

Warm•Amber•Resonance vibrated through the cooling seas, leaving behind a tenuous blue cloud condensing into a thinking azure stone.

Two day cycles later Karin was standing her shift. She still wasn't allowed to do anything strenuous, but she took Arielle's place as pilot of the lumbering *Dragonfly*, while Arielle tried to take Karin's place as chief engineer. Arielle did a respectable job. She equaled Karin's performance in outship repairs and bettered her performance at the galley table.

"I don't see where she puts it," said Karin to David. "If I ate that much I would be as fat as Richard!"

"I heard that!" said Richard. "How much do you weigh, Shorty?"

"Eighty-five kilos, fat man . . . and you?"

"One hundred kilos—but I'm taller than you."

"The last five centimeters must be all fat," said Karin, sticking her tongue out at him.

Richard was glad. The brat must be OK if she could fight back like that. He was about to make some comment about squaws when Jill interrupted.

"White Whistler is returning."

"Ask why I was left!" demanded Karin.

"Just a second," said Jill, almost impatiently. "White Whistler is saying something important to the other flouwen!"

◇ I have solved the motion of the lights in the sky! ◇

☆ Even the big circle? ☆

◇ All the lights except big circle. It is a swimmer of the light. It is like us. Its motions are not that of logic. ◇

• But you can know the motions of all the rest? You can know the risings of Hot and the fadings of Warm and the tenacity of Sky⊗Rock? •

◇ All, ◇ said White Whistler with confidence.

☆ How can you be sure? ☆

◇ The humans gave me the rule for simple spherical masses. The rule was very simple. Yet it seemed complex when the rule was used on more than two spheres. After some thinking, I found the simple rule for many spheres. ◇

• Was it difficult? •

◇ No. A simple variable substitution combined with an interesting coordinate transformation. ◇

• Let me taste. •

☆ Me too! ☆

△ Me too!!! △

The white cloud sent out a tendril. The end was whitely concentrated with nerve tissue. The other three aliens crowded around to taste the essence of Clear ◇ White ◇ Whistle's thought.

• Subtle! •

☆Tricky!!!☆

△I don't understand the taste!◊ said the little blue one.

•You will. Just savor the taste and recall it some thousand turns from now. It will be much clearer then when you can handle such complexities.•

△But I want to know now!△

•Later, Dainty△Blue△Warble, later,• said Warm•Amber•Resonance. Its yellow body expanded and contracted as it impressed on its memory the secret for the solution of the n-body central force problem. Warm•Amber•Resonance reveled in the cleanness of it. •One complex variable transformation, and then that simple, yet unobvious, coordinate transformation! An nth-root dimension, indeed!•

During the next day, a vibration started coming from the left wing. Karin's ears pricked up and she reached to turn off the fans just as Jill shut them down. The *Dragonfly* coasted to a stop, the lapping of the waves on the hull making the absence of the engine sounds even more ominous.

"The mounting bracket for the replacement fan is vibrating," said Jill.

"I'll go out and fix it," said Karin. "Probably just a bolt coming loose."

"You are still weak," said Jill. "I will wake up Richard."

"No!" exploded Karin. "I can do anything that big ox can do. I'm going out! I'm tired of being cooped up in this tin can." She stormed down the corridor, bumping into every console chair along the way. David, twisted partially away from his console by Karin's passage, gave a sigh, swiveled back, closed down his console, and went back to suit up with Karin. He would probably only be a tool holder, but the sooner he got her back inside the better.

Together they cycled through the lock and swam out

under the left wing. Karin jiggled the bracing structure for the jury-rigged fan and found the loose bolt. She tightened it, and then for good measure, started to check the tightness of the rest. David pulled out his omniwrench and backed her up by holding onto the other side of each bolt.

Suddenly, they were engulfed in an encompassing cloud of good-will. The purple cloud was back.

"What's that!" said David in alarm.

"Take it easy," said Karin. "That's just an old alien we call Deep Purple. Last time I saw him he was rocked up trying to prove Fermat's Conjecture." She suddenly realized the importance of what she was saying, if not to their present problems, to the cadre of mathematicians six lightyears away on earth.

"Welcome, Deep Purple," she said. "Did you solve the problem?"

□Easy,□ the lavender cloud responded. □Human named Fermat right.□ There was a polite pause, then he continued, □DUMB problem!□

This was the cue for Loud Red.☆ I told you! DUMB problem!! DUMB!!!☆

David broke through over Karin's imp. "Do you mean to say they have solved Fermat's Conjecture? How did they do it? We have only proved it up to something like n equals 1,023,467."

The sharp sonar senses of the huge purple alien caught the careful reeling of numbers. It paused in its exodus, then came back to surround Karin, as if it were really looking at a human for the first time.

□You solve problems with numbers?!?□ it asked, its incredulity rippling through its surface.

"Yes," said Karin bravely, "we do quite often. If it works for many numbers then it is probably true."

There was a long pause as the alien brain tried to absorb the alien thought. It rejected it.

□There are many numbers. There are . . . too many

numbers.☐ Deep Purple was struggling to express the idea of an infinity of numbers. Karin helped.

"No end to numbers," she said.

☐No end!☐ Deep Purple rasped in relief. ☐No end, so no certainty. Not use numbers.☐

". . . but how . . ." Karin's eyes flitted from purple alien mounds to David's face.

"I think Deep Purple just proved Fermat's Conjecture for ANY number." said David. "Too bad we aren't intelligent enough to understand how it did it. We may think we're smart, but that alien equivalent of an aging surfer has us all beat."

While they were talking, the larger cloud had wrapped a purple tendril about two others, one red and one milky white. The contact had lasted for less than two seconds.

◇Obvious◇ said the white one.

☆. . . and DUMB!!!☆ said the red one.

☆Let's do something else! Like SURF!!☆

☐WAVE!!!☐ said Deep Purple, leading the group to the surface as they dropped their preoccupation with mathematics and enjoyed the caress of the waves on their fluid surface.

◇Wave!!!◇ keened the voice of Clear◇White◇Whistle.

☆DUMB!!!☆

Floating

After only six hours sleep, George found himself awake again. He turned over in the dark space lit by the soft, flickering colored lights of his imp and tried to go back to sleep again, but it didn't work. His mind started to go over the problems that had to be solved if he was to get his tiny command off this ball of water. He tried thinking about Red, then Jinjur, so many megameters away, but his brain rejected those diversions and continued to worry. George gave up and slammed the Sound-Bar door open and rolled out of bed.

Another sign of getting old, he grumbled to himself. Can't even get a good eight hours anymore.

He stumbled sleepily through his wake-up routine and went forward to the galley. David was there, plowing through one of his special dinners, a pseudoknackwurst sitting on a bed of sauerkraut, a heaping mound of real mashed potatoes, green bean salad, and a pint of dark beer.

"Looks good," said George enviously as he punched himself up a breakfast of algae omelet with pseudoham, algae toast with pseudobutter, and ersatz coffee with pseudocream.

"My last special," said David, handing him a crisp

green bean, which George took gratefully. "We've been making fairly good progress. Eight to ten kilometers an hour doesn't seem like much for an airplane, but if you keep it up hour after hour it adds up. We've traveled almost a thousand kilometers in the past five days and are starting up the water mountain. Only about four hundred kilometers to go to the peak where Red can pick us off. If we can keep up the pace we should be there in two days, three days before the periapsis passage."

George listened to the report thoughtfully, taking little bites of the green bean. His breakfast was pushed out onto the counter top by the galley imp. George thoughtfully nibbled the green bean, tasting each little bite. He finished the last of the green bean, then started shoveling the pseudobreakfast down as if he were refueling a machine.

"How's the weather?" he asked as he paused between drinks of coffee.

"It's getting worse," said David. "Each six-hour day-night cycle seems to generate a new storm in the hot crescent. The storm then spins its way into the cold crescent to dump its load of supersaturated ammonia. Most of the storms seem to head up the mountain, pushing huge ring-waves ahead of them. There was a real doozy that passed over a few hours ago."

"I know," said George. "The thunder woke me up and I just managed to get myself asleep again before I got seasick. I'm worried about the storms, though. That could make the pickup tricky."

"It's concerning Red, too. There are calm periods between storm fronts, but they're getting shorter and shorter."

"We'd better get a move on then," said George. He pushed his empty tray back to the galley imp and went forward to relieve Arielle. David returned to his knackwurst, carved off a large slab, smothered it in sauerkraut, piled a dab of hot mustard on top and put it into his smiling mouth.

"How's *Dragonfly* doing?" George asked as he reached the cockpit area. Arielle turned around and gave him a crooked smile, the neuskin patch distorting her lip shape. Flashes of colored lights could be seen from between her teeth where the brace imp was still holding her tooth in place.

That could start a whole new fad, thought George, looking at the literally sparkling smile. Wait until the Space Administration medics release Arielle's picture to the press.

"We haf been making sixteen kilometer, but the tide is turn the other way and we will now slow down," said Arielle.

"Can we put down an anchor?"

Jill answered for Arielle. "The ocean bottom is now 2.3 kilometers down. My sounding cable is long enough, but we really don't have anything that would act like an anchor and dig in the bottom instead of just sliding along."

"Are any of the flouwen around?" asked George. "Perhaps they would be willing to take the cable down to the bottom and tie it to something during the reverse tides."

"Loud Red is nearby," said Jill. "I will talk to it." There was a complex sound from the sonar dome at the front of the plane and soon a large red blob streaked by on the right side, circled the plane, and came to a halt in front of the slowly chugging ship.

☆Hi! You call Loud Red!?!☆

"Yes. We must move east to point under Sky⊗Rock. Water moves west so we move west. Look under me. See thick string?" Jill payed out a few meters of cable and Loud Red dove under the ship. There were a few strong tugs that had George reaching for a handhold as they shook the ship.

"It certainly has no trouble grabbing hold of it," George said.

The Red blob appeared once again in the view of the half-submerged cockpit windows.

"Bottom of ocean does not move," said Jill. "If thick string attached to bottom, then Floating⊗Rock not move. You attach thick string to bottom?"

☆That dumb! Floating⊗Rock want to move east. If Floating⊗Rock attached to bottom Floating⊗Rock not move east. Not move at all! Dumb! If Floating⊗Rock want to move east, *I* move Floating⊗Rock east!☆

Loud Red dove once again beneath the ship and shortly reappeared, swimming strongly forward. There was a jerk as the cable tightened and soon they were under tow. After a few minutes Jill gave a report.

"We are moving five kilometers an hour east in a current that is running twelve kilometers an hour west. Loud Red has almost doubled our speed through the water."

"I wonder how long it can keep it up?" mused George. Three hours later, sitting with Arielle in the cockpit, he became more and more impressed by the alien's performance. Not that it was easy for Loud Red, as he let them know frequently.

☆Hard work! Tired! Hungry! Go get something to eat!☆ Abruptly the *Dragonfly* slowed in the water until it reached the speed that its fans could maintain. It was dark and Loud Red slipped quickly out of the landing light beams.

George wondered if the flighty alien would return. It could well be that after catching and eating something, it would go off surfing and forget all about the humans. But he was wrong. Loud Red returned in a half hour, fighting with his pack of hunters over the remains of a large blue-green Pretty⊗Smell. The alien finally threw the remainder of the carcass to the pets who went off with it. The cable was retrieved from beneath the ship and with a jerky start, the *Magic Dragonfly* was skimming through the seas again, heading east. Almost immediately the complaints started.

☆Hard work!☆
☆Dumb!☆
☆Nothing to do!☆

They were breasting large following waves. George looked back at the skyline.

"Another storm coming up on us," he said.

"It should be on us by dark," said Jill. A picture of the storm front appeared on George's cockpit display from the video cameras peering out the bulbous eyes of the *Magic Dragonfly*.

☆Hi! Hi!☆ called Loud Red, suddenly.

"What's that for?" asked George of Jill.

"I think Loud Red heard another flouwen off in the distance. Let's see if I can spot it." George heard the strength of the sonar pulses increase and watched the display on the cockpit console. Off to the edge of the screen was a small return blob, the blue color indicating an approaching object.

"It's about the right size for a flouwen," said George.

"It is a flouwen," said Jill. "I can hear it talking to Loud Red. Loud Red has stopped using the simplified language we developed between ourselves and has switched to their more complicated form."

☆Hi! Brittle†Orange†Chirr. You are a long way from your feeding jet.☆

†So are you, Roaring☆Hot☆Vermillion. I just finished a long surf in front of that storm. Good waves. Want to race me up the ocean? Last one to the top has to catch dinner for both.†

☆Can't surf. Have to pull Floating⊗Rock up the ocean. It can't swim too well.☆

†Who is Floating⊗Rock? Rocks can't float.†

☆This one can! It can talk too! Come here and meet it.☆

†A talking, floating rock! I must see this!†

George watched the alien approach on the sonar. As it got closer he looked out the window to see if he could spot it. David and Karin had joined him and Arielle in the cockpit area.

"It's lost in the surface clutter," said George, looking up from the sonar screen. "But it's close, you should be able to see it soon."

"I can feel its sonar," said Jill. "It is giving me a good looking-over."

†That Floating⊗Rock is big!†

☆Come closer. It won't eat you.☆

†Why is it holding on to you with a string?†

☆I'm holding on to it. It can't swim well, so I am pulling it.☆

Brittle†Orange†Chirr moved closer.

"I can see it," said David.

"Where?" said Arielle, sitting up to peer out over the nose of the plane.

"Off to the left and out about a hundred meters. It looks like a patch of orange juice."

"Can you talk to O.J., Jill?"

"I'll try," said Jill. The sonar sent out a burst of sound. Jill used the name combination that Loud Red had used for O.J.

The orange flouwen came closer as Jill talked to it. It was surrounded by Loud Red's orange pets.

"I don't see any difference between that flouwen and those pets except size," said Karin. "Are we sure they're different creatures and not just the same type with differing levels of intelligence depending upon size? In color, there seems to be no difference between O.J., the pets, and the prey that the pets caught the first time we met them."

"There's a big difference," said David. "O.J. here has a greenish-orange color, like a not-quite-ripe orange, while the pets are yellow-orange. The prey, on the other hand, was a blue-orange, like a slightly smoky flame."

"I presume the aliens are as sensitive to color differences as David is," said George. "That would partially compensate for the fact that they don't have imaging eyes, even though they are photosensitive."

The sky darkened as a cloud drifted over Barnard. David looked up, then gasped.

"A waterspout! It's heading straight for us!"

George whirled his head to look out the window. As soon as he had the waterspout in sight he froze. Keeping his head still he spoke over his shoulder to his imp.

"This is one time I wish you had your radar back," he said. "You'd be able to get bearing, range, and track in a second." He paused, his head still stiff, then went on: "... it's drifting a little ... Yep ... definitely drifting forward. Tell Loud Red to stop pulling and you reverse your engines! You'd also better tell the flouwen that a waterspout is coming."

There was a burst of sound from the sonar in the nose dome. The engines halted as *Dragonfly* slowed, then resumed again as Jill tried to back up in the water. There was a loud gurgling from underneath as Jill flooded a compartment and *Dragonfly* settled slightly in the water, the waves breaking over the cockpit window. Through the waves George could see the waterspout moving lazily toward them. He continued to hold his head in one position so he could watch the motion of the column across the window. If the drift stopped while the size grew larger it meant that the spout was coming straight at them. Fortunately the drift continued ... it looked like the funnel was going to pass in front of of them. It would be close though, and George found his muscles trying to help Jill back the *Magic Dragonfly* away from danger.

"Loud Red and I never developed a word for waterspout, so I couldn't warn them. I did tell them to dive to the bottom. Loud Red did, since it is used to taking our advice, but O.J. either didn't hear me or else is ignoring me and is still swimming in circles in front of us just under the surface. My sonar is now picking up the disturbed water at the base of the spout."

George looked down at the sonar display; it was an expanded picture of the region just in front of *Dragonfly*. There was a scintillating circle from the waterspout moving slowly in front of them about two hundred meters away and a steadier blob that was O.J. The steady blob and the scintillating circle intersected, then they were both gone.

"The spout has turned orange and lifted!" shouted Karin. George looked up just as a wave broke over the windshield. It took a second for the heavy-duty wipers to clean the film of ammonia water from the outside surface.

Those are probably the cleanest windows in six lightyears, thought George to himself. Then he too saw the orange-white spout.

"It's got O.J.!" said David. "I recognize the green-orange color."

The spout had trouble digesting its viscous, multiton sudden load. The column lifted, fattened, and slowed its whirling. There was a short attempt to speed up and dip down to the surface again, but finally the spout rose up into the clouds and disappeared.

George looked over at Arielle's stricken face. He opened his mouth to say something comforting and was trying to think what he could say that would alleviate the loss of an intelligent being, one who was probably hundreds of years older than they were. Suddenly the heavens opened and large drops of water battered the window and the roof in a drumming roar. There was a loud PLOP on the roof, and an orange blob slithered down over the cockpit window and off the nose of *Dragonfly*. The blob screamed incoherently through the thick glass as it slowly fell in the weak gravity.

"It's O.J.," sobbed Arielle. "He tore to pieces!"

They were thrown upward as a strong thump came from underneath the airplane. Loud Red was back.

☆Dumb! Brittle†Orange†Chirr eaten by whlee. Now I got work to do. Too much work! Brittle†Orange†Chirr dumb!☆

There were more plopping noises and tiny screams filtering through the incessant drumming of the rain. Just in back of the beating windshield wipers they saw hundreds of orange blobs writhing on the surface. Swimming among them was Loud Red. It would gather a batch and bring them together where they instantly merged to form a larger blob. This would be left behind while Loud Red scooped up another batch of baby blobs. George could see the action better on the sonar. The screen was full of what looked like snow—tiny twisting points of light everywhere on the screen except for a blank trail left behind by a rapidly moving larger blob that collected the snow, packed it into snowballs, then moved on.

†Eeeeeeee!†

†Eeeaaaahhh!†

☆Brittle†Orange†Chirr dumb! Gets caught in whlee and makes poor, tired Roaring☆Hot☆Vermillion work. I ought to eat some of the little ones . . . Bah! Not even good to eat!☆

The large red blob molded together a batch of small orange blobs into a larger sphere. It spoke harshly at the sphere.

☆I am Roaring☆Hot☆Vermillion. You stop screaming. You stop moving. You stay here. I will come back.☆

†Yes, Roaring☆Hot☆Vermillion.†

Soon the large batches of tiny blobs had been rounded up. There were still many others, but they would be picked up later. The red flouwen retraced his path and began collecting the large orange spheres and merging them together. Soon there was a small orange youngling swimming along beside the large red cloud.

☆You are dumb, Brittle†Orange†Chirr! Didn't you hear Floating⊗Rock tell you to dive to the bottom?"☆

†Floating⊗Rock speaks so strangely I could barely understand it. Besides, what does a rock know?†

☆Floating⊗Rock is almost as smart as flouwen, and it can do things that a flouwen can't do. It can fly like a Pretty⊗Smell in the nothing above the ocean!†

†Then why doesn't it, instead of having you pull it along in the ocean?†

☆Because it's not feeling well or something. Over there! Another sphere. I think that's the last one I made. Are you feeling big enough to find the rest of you by yourself?☆

†Yes. I can collect the rest of me.†

☆Good! I'm going to get something to eat! Hard work makes me hungry!☆

†Don't eat anything orange!†

☆Bah! Would never do that! Taste terrible!☆

There was a piercing whistle and soon three orange snakes came scooting through the ocean to join their master. The first thing Roaring☆Hot☆Vermillion did was to grab each pet and stretch them out. In two of them he spotted a blob of greenish-orange imbedded in the yellow-orange flesh. A sharp command and the tiny blobs were released, to go screaming off to join Brittle† Orange†Chirr's growing body.

☆We go!☆ said the red cloud. With its orange snakes following, it slithered into the depths, leaving Brittle† Orange†Chirr to collect the rest of its wits.

*　　　*　　　*

It was a dark and stormy night when Loud Red returned. Jill called to Loud Red to resume pulling.

☆No!☆

"But we must get up the mountain!"

☆No! Wrong time! Wrong way! Wave ... Ocean ... Sky ⊗ Rock ...☆ Frustrated, Loud Red left at high speed. ☆Wrong way! I get White Whistler!☆ it said in parting.

"It sounded like Loud Red was trying to explain something, but didn't have the words," said George.

"I could have worked out a joint understanding," said Jill. "But perhaps White Whistler would be less impetuous and easier to work with."

Roaring☆Hot☆Vermillion streaked through the murky depths at top speed, sonar signals making the ocean as bright as day. Far off in the distance came voices. A slight change in course and the red cloud began to converge on the sounds.

◇I hear Roaring☆Hot☆Vermillion approach.◇

△I can hear him too!△

•Very good discrimination, Dainty△Blue△Warble. What else do you hear?• The small pale blue cloud paused and the two olders, Clear◇White◇Whistle and Warm•Amber•Resonance, stopped moving to reduce the local noise clutter.

△One ... two ... three ... smaller sounds. They are the Orange⊗Hunters of older Roaring☆Hot☆Vermillion.

•Excellent hearing, young one,• said Warm•Amber☆Resonance.

◇Now try seeing yourself and let us know when you detect them.◇ Sharp bursts of directed sound piped from the little blue cloud as it attempted to see off into the distance. The two olders added their own occasional bursts at a lower pitch.

Roaring☆Hot☆Vermillion heard them seeing him and started talking as the distance closed.

☆Floating⊗Rock is going to the inner point.☆

◇That is dangerous. It is getting near the time when one should stay away from the inner point.◇

☆I tried to tell it. But I don't know the words! You must tell it to stop!☆

◊It will take some time to teach Floating⊗Rock the right words, but I will try.◊

•Do we dare go close to the inner point when the time is so near?•

◊I have watched a number of near times from the side of the mountain. There are still ten days left. We can find Floating⊗Rock, warn it, and get back to a safe place in that time.◊

The three colored clouds swam off toward the still-approaching red cloud, which slowed and turned back the other way. Soon the four members of the pod were rejoined and swam as a group back toward the inner point.

It was daybreak and everyone was awake to enjoy the next hour and a half of sunshine. The seas of Eau were relatively calm since Barnard had been heating up the backside of Roche rather than evaporating the ammonia out of the seas, and the atmosphere over Eau had had time to calm down. The high clouds that had been raining huge, slowly falling drops of ammonia on the inner pole were being parted by the warm dry breezes from Roche flowing through the narrow neck between the two planets. Through the hole in the clouds Barnard rose majestically over the mountains of Roche, the beams of light from the sun shooting down the long rift valleys that deepened as they furrowed their way to the oval peak of the rocky globe.

Jill had been chugging her way toward the inner pole of Eau, trying to get as close to the gravity minimum as possible in order to make it easier on the ascent module when they picked them off.

"How are we doing, Jill?" asked George.

"We have been inside the ninety-five percentile pickup contours for the last half hour. The high tide peaked not long ago so the water mountain is dropping rapidly. We are starting to drift out again."

"We'll make it back again at high tide if we can just keep chugging. Can you raise Rocheworld Base?"

"Rocheworld Base, here," said Red, her voice penetrating through the haze of electronic noise generated by the multitude of storm cells wandering over the overheated water cone of Eau.

"We will be inside the pickup contours at the next high tide, three hours from now. It'll be dark here, but we'll have our lights on and you should have no trouble finding us."

"Right, George. I read you. Now let's see if Jack can read Jill." The humans kept silent as the two computers interchanged information.

"Communication complete," said Jill. "Even the Wolfe error-correction code was never activated. The personnel transfer should proceed without any significant problem."

George grinned. Soon his command would be off this sodden hunk of duralloy and back into space where they belonged. He gazed up at the bright orb of Barnard. At this point in Rocheworld's orbit the red dwarf star was four times larger than the sun and looked even larger since it was still close to the horizon. Despite Barnard's closeness, he had no trouble looking at it, for it was no brighter than a charcoal fire. A charcoal fire with dark red clouds floating over its surface.

He thought of his last charcoal fire. The time he and Jinjur had traveled out to Annapolis to exercise her alumni privileges. A small sailboat with a huge sail and a night in a shoreside cabin. They had spent the evening tossing fuel into the hibachi on the patio and quietly getting drunk on white wine. Nothing had happened that night, for they knew they had the rest of their lives together.

"Hey!" yelled Karin from the rear as the plane lurched

upward. George turned in time to see the remains of an algae shake spin lazy through the air and glop onto the ceiling. He felt a thump and another, then watched the algea protein start to drip downward in the low gravity. The Christmas Branch rescued the situation by grabbing the metal container out of Karin's grasp and installing the shake back into the shaker before it hit the carpet.

"Loud Red has returned," said Jill. "Since I was heading up mountain, they came at me from my blind side."

△That was fun! Can I bump it again?△

☆No! One bump is enough!☆

◇One bump is probably too many for the humans inside.◇

•I don't think you ought to be teaching Dainty△Blue△ Warble your boisterous habits.•

△I bump Floating⊗Rock again!?!△

☆No!☆

◇Floating⊗Rock is still moving toward the inner pole.◇

☆I tell it to stop, but it does not.☆

◇It is dangerous here on the surface of the ocean. Let's get it down on the bottom where it is safer, then we can try to talk with it. Brittle†Orange†Chirr! Come here! Attach yourself to the outer wing of Floating⊗ Rock and sink yourself. You others! Do the same! ◇

☆Yes! Let's make this Floating⊗Rock sink!☆

"O.J. has attached itself to my wing," said Jill. "It seems to be extruding the water from its body and is dragging the wing tip under."

"Tell it to stop," said George. "We've got to maintain headway in this countertide if we are going to make the pickoff at next sunrise."

"They don't seem to be paying any attention to me," said Jill. "They are too busy talking between themselves

... There is another one on the other wing-tip. It's Loud Red. Rocking up like the other one."

"What's going on!" said George in alarm. He looked out the cockpit window as an amber blob and a pale blue blob climbed up on the wing and proceeded to shower ammonia water from their cells.

"White Whistler has my tail," said Jill. "They are pulling us under!"

Diving

They sank beneath the waves, the red light from Barnard turning into a purple-green under the ammonia oceans.

"Jill! Get them to stop!" cried Karin. Her ears caught a strange noise. "Can the hull take the pressure?"

"The pressure hull in *Dragonfly* is very rugged, since the designers didn't know what it would run into. In compression it should hold against fifty atmospheres."

There were some gasps from Arielle and David.

"It's snowing!" said David.

"Blue fnow!" said Arielle.

George turned and looked out the cockpit windows. Shining brightly in the landing lights was a cloud of large blue needles drifting downward with them as they sank slowly to the bottom.

"How come it can snow underwater?" asked David.

"The top layers of the ocean here at the inner pole are mostly ammonia from the ammonia rain on the surface," said Jill. "As we get deeper the ammonia concentration decreases but it gets rapidly colder. Right now the ammonia concentration is sixty percent, while the temperature has dropped to minus eighty-five centigrade. That is cold enough to form ice made of two parts ammonia to one part water. The blue needles are nucleating out of the supercooled liquid. They are falling because the solid is denser than the liquid."

For a few minutes everyone watched the fascinating scene as the blue snowstorm became thicker and thicker until their landing lights only penetrated a few meters into the swirling cloud.

"Are the flouwen being affected by the cold or the snow?" asked George.

"They are still talking between themselves much as they did at the surface. I don't think they are particularly surprised or affected by the snow or the temperature variation. The temperature has stopped dropping. We're now at minus ninety-two centigrade and it's starting to go up again. There is also a drastic change in composition. We seem to have entered a warm current headed toward the inner pole. It is denser since it is half-water and half-ammonia."

"What waf that?" said Arielle, her quick eye spotting something unusual in the scene outside the window. "There'f another one!"

"White snow!" said Karin. "And this time it's going up! It's snowing in both directions! Blue snow falling down and white snow falling up!"

"That white snow must be a solid that is half-ammonia and half-water. None of my records indicate its density, but the solid must be lighter than the liquid, like normal ice, so it is rising to the surface."

The blue blizzard started to decrease. First in the size of the needles as they began to dissolve in the water-rich mixture, then finally the individual particles began to disappear while the fall weakened in intensity. But at the same time, the intensity of the upward falling white snow began to increase. The particles were very large, like summer hailstones.

"Listen!" said Karin, then she got down and put her ear on the deck. The rest of the crew stopped talking and a hush settled over the cockpit. As it became quiet you could hear the pitter-patter of ice balls striking the bottom of the plane and wings as they rose up past the sinking plane.

They finally passed through the white-ice storm, which tapered off to little white specks that seemed to appear out of nowhere in the frigid water.

"We're moving into the middle of the warm-water current," said Jill. "It's now too warm for the ice to form."

"And how warm is that?" asked George.

"Minus seventy-eight centigrade."

"Balmy," said George. The show out the window over, he went back to the galley for a quick bite.

For the next half hour they continued their downward plunge. There were occasional creaks and groans as the walls took up the increasing external pressure.

"We've reached the middle of the warm stream," said Jill. "Maximum temperature nearly minus fifty centigrade—warmer than the surface. It's starting to drop again. Water concentration now sixty percent, compared to forty percent ammonia."

"Is it going to continue that trend until the bottom, or are we in for another surprise?" asked George.

"Yes."

"Yes, what?"

"It's going to continue the trend and we are in for another surprise if it does."

"What's the surprise?" asked George. "Anything dangerous?" Before Jill could answer there was a cry from the cockpit."

"MORE fnow!"

George went forward to look. This time the snow took the form of transparent faceted balls. They were tiny at first, but as they fell they turned to marble size. Although transparent, they weren't too hard to see since they glittered rainbow colors in the intense beams of the landing lights as they scattered the light around their internal facets and back out again.

"BEAUTIFUL!" cried Arielle, exhilarated over the colorful scene. "What if it?"

"That's ordinary ice," said Jill. "Pure water crystals settling out of the twenty-five percent ammonia solution to fall to the bottom. The faceted balls must be a compromise between a snowflake and a hailstone."

"I thought ice floated," said Karin.

"It floats in water, but this ocean is a mixture of water and much lighter ammonia. At concentrations of greater than twenty-three percent ammonia, pure ice is heavier than the ocean water."

"Then the bottom must be covered with snow," said Karin.

"It is," said Jill. "I can detect it on my sonar. We're not too far from the bottom. We should start seeing it soon."

Working the fan motors in opposite directions Arielle slowly pivoted the plane around in a circle. The faceted ice spheres became nearly invisible and slowed their rate of fall as they entered the water-rich layers of ocean near the bottom. The ice balls still refracted the light slightly, so it was like looking through a poorly made windowpane. The landing lights from the twirling, falling plane picked out a white reflection in the distance.

"There'f fomthing!" said Arielle. She expertly reversed the fan controls and brought the plane back around so that the searchlights illuminated the pointed white object. As the plane continued down, the point slipped upward into darkness and the light beams illuminated the steep slopes of a white mountain.

"It looks like the Alps!" said Karin. "It's an underwater glacier!"

As they continued their fall, the distant slopes flattened out and began to approach them in the light beams. Arielle turned the landing lights downward and saw the surface below rising rapidly up to meet them.

"Get ready for landing!" she said. Increasing the fan power to provide maximum lift, she attempted to slow their rate of descent. The surface rose beneath them and there was a jar as the nose of the plane buried itself in the slushy surface, followed by a thump from the rear as the tail hit. They had landed on the ten-degree slope of the glacier, facing up mountain.

"Is the hull tight?" Karin asked her imp. She was worried. Even a tiny leak of that poisonous water and they would have to get into suits until it was fixed and the air cleared.

"The hull is fine," reassured Jill.

Karin went down to the back to check out the equipment lockers to make sure nothing had been jarred loose by their rough landing. George went forward to the control deck and got in the copilot seat. The aliens had insisted on taking them down here, now it was his job to get them up and out into space where they belonged. He looked out the cockpit window and paused as a sense of *déjà vu* came over them.

"It's just like the Moteratsch glacier near Pontresina in the Swiss Alps!" said George. "But the only thing I'm sure of is that it's not the Alps. Where are we, Jill?"

A map showed up on his display. From the shading and angle, it was obviously a sonar map that Jill had taken on the way down. At the top portion of the screen was a large circular depression. Running out away from the circle were dark ridges of stone, and between the ridges were rivers of ice. A small blinking dot showed their position partway down on one of the glaciers.

"We're on the side of an underwater volcano," said George. "It's a big one, like those on the real Hawaiian Islands. If the water weren't so deep here, they would be sticking up in the air. Fortunately this one doesn't seem to be active since the crater is filled with snow." He looked at Arielle and raised his right eye, asking for permission to touch the controls. She nodded and he moved the landing lights back and forth, trying to pick up their local terrain.

"I've got the aliens on the infrared scanner," said Karin from the science-scan instrument console. "They're still rocked up, holding us down, but the two on the left wing seem to be talking."

"Can you understand them, Jill?" asked George.

"I can pick up some of it," said Jill. "It is something about getting us out of danger. I still don't understand why they dragged us to the bottom."

"Do you get any inkling of what they're going to do next?"

"They are talking about bringing something big, but I don't know what it is."

☆It's cold! And boring!☆ murmured a small tab of flesh attached to a large red rock sitting on the wing.

◇Then we'll stay here holding Floating⊗Rock down while you go break off a big chunk of ice and bring it back.◇

☆But that's hard work!☆

•I'll go and get it then. You stay here rocked up.•

△Can I go too!△

◇Not this time. Just one can go. The rest must stay rocked up until we get enough ice rocks to replace us.◇

☆I'll go!☆ The large red rock rapidly dissolved and expanded into a huge red cloud. It swam rapidly off toward the foot of the glacier, mumbling as it went.

☆Cold! Tired! Boring! Rather be surfing!☆

Soon it returned, pushing a flat plate of ice some ten meters long, five meters wide, and a meter thick. Jill caught a glimpse of it as it settled on the wing.

"They are loading up the wing with blocks of ice," said Jill.

"They really mean to make us stay on the bottom," said George. "Can't you to tell them to stop?"

"They are deliberately ignoring me," said Jill. "We'll just have to wait until they are ready to talk."

"Should I get Arielle to try to shake the ice block off by rocking the fans?" asked George. "It can't be too heavy, despite its size. It is only a little denser than the ocean water and the gravity is low here."

"No," said Jill. "They must have some good reason for what they are doing. Let's wait and find out what it is."

☆That's two. Hard work!☆

◇Soften up again, Warm•Amber•Resonance, and help Roaring☆Hot☆Vermillion bring more ice rocks.◇

Working together, the yellow and red clouds soon had the top of the wing covered with large chunks of ice and the remainder of the flouwen relaxed their hold on the *Magic Dragonfly*. They tried to place similar chunks on the tail fins, but the heat exchangers in the tail surfaces melted it off. More blocks were added to the wing and placed on top of the fuselage where the inside heat escaping from the hull soon melted a groove in the underside of the blocks so they balanced on top.

◇There! That should make them safe enough.◇

•The time is getting close. We should go!•

◇First I must tell Floating⊗Rock and the Stiff⊗Movers about the dangerous time. But there are so many words that it doesn't know. It will take time.◇

•Since the Stiff⊗Movers can't see with sound, but can look with light, perhaps we can tell them faster with a body play rather than words. It would have to be a very simple body play, since they can't see inside the players as we do, but they could get the idea from looking at our outsides.•

◇Good idea. You are the best body player. What shall we do?◇

•Stiff⊗Movers think in terms of colors rather than textures. You be the icy-white solid part of our world, and Dainty△Blue△Warble can be the ocean covering our world. Roaring☆Hot☆Vermillion can be Hot. That's an easy part, just sitting there being a red globe.•

☆Dumb part!☆

◇ You could make it more realistic by spinning around and having soft, cloudylike bumps on your surface. ◇

☆Hot has clouds?☆

◇ Yes. I have seen them with my seeing disk. ◇

☆Like this?☆ The red cloud turned into a rapidly spinning red sphere with bumps on it. The formless white cloud scanned the result with a few bursts of sharp sound.

◇ Slower. Make the bumps smaller. Good. ◇

•Not good. Hot should be spinning over there in front of Floating⊗Rock so that the Stiff⊗Movers can see.• A focused burst of sound rebounded from a point on the glacier some five meters in front of *Dragonfly's* nose. The spinning red sphere drifted slowly over to the indicated point and hovered a few meters above the snowy surface, the shallow bulges on the spinning surface shining redly in the landing lights.

†Can I be in the body play?†

•Certainly, Brittle†Orange†Chirr. You can be Warm and its pets. Can you do that?•

†Easy. I'm good at body plays.† The large orange blob soon rearranged itself into a large sphere and four smaller spheres. The smaller spheres had nearly invisible threads connecting them to the main body so that they maintained contact with the major portion of the distributed nervous system. The collection of orange spheres started a large slow orbit around the red sphere.

•You are too close. We will have to move in that region. Go out a little.•

The orange sphere obeyed as the stage for the body play was set. Clear◇White◇Whistle went over to Floating⊗Rock and started to talk to the strange metal being. A peek through a disk lens confirmed that a number of humans were seeing their play from the clear places on Floating⊗Rock.

"Top of ocean not good," said White Whistler. "Time soon when sky . . . eat . . . top of ocean."

"It wanted to use another word," said Jill. "But we don't have it in our joint vocabulary."

"Good place is hot side of world. Inside islands. We swim there soon. You cannot swim fast. You must stay here. Here is not good, but here is not bad. You not be . . . eaten. Eaten not right word. We show you. Loud Red is Barnard. O.J. is Gargantua and pets. Yellow Hummer is Sky⊗Rock, I am world, and Little Blue is ocean."

"It'f a play!" said Arielle, delighted.

Karin reached up to the cockpit ceiling and swung down a video camera that peered over George's right shoulder. With the two scanners on the side and the ceiling camera, they would have a complete record of the performance. The snow had let up a little so the visibility was excellent. As White Whistler swam off to join the others, Jill could hear Yellow Hummer giving detailed instructions to Little Blue.

As they watched, White Whistler and Yellow Hummer turned into the egg-shaped forms of Eau and Roche. Little Blue flowed around White Whistler, the blue color completely covering the larger white body except for some spots on the outer pole. Twirling smoothly, the miniature version of Rocheworld started its elliptical orbit out near the orange globe of Gargantua and moved closer to the deep red spinning sphere of Barnard.

"It's an amazingly faithful reproduction of the major bodies in their star system," said George. "But I don't see what they're up to. How could orbital dynamics be any danger to us?"

"I don't know," said Jill. "But so far all they are doing is repeating the portion of the orbit that we have already experienced. I suspect whatever is bothering them occurs at or near periapsis, since it is only nine hours away."

"Could it be storms?" asked George.

"I doubt it," said Jill. "The heating from Barnard wouldn't change that much in the last few hours."

"What is it, then?" said George.

Arielle turned and put her finger to her patched lip. "Huf! I'm watching the play!"

George hushed and watched the play.

☆Am I pretty?☆

△Wheee! This is fun! Do I get to bloop over now?△

•Not till I tell you.•

The blue and yellow eggs spun around each other as they moved between the red globe and Floating⊗Rock. The blue ocean began to slosh back and forth.

△Do I go bloop now?△

•Not this turn, but next one. Now!☆

△Bloop! This is fun!△

•Now back. That's right. Now bloop again.•

△Bloop!△

•One more time and that's all.•

△Just once more? That was fun bouncing into you.△

•No. World only bloops three times and we want the play to be a correct one.•

△It's time again. Bloop!△

"My God!" said David. "The whole ocean is transferring from Eau to Roche."

"Not the whole ocean," said George. "But anyone on the surface near the inner pole during periapsis would find themselves under an eighty-kilometer-high interplanetary waterfall with millions of tons of water falling down on them."

"I don't see how that could be," said Richard. "I remember calculating the relative orbital displacements of Roche and Eau with Thomas when we were arguing whether the Rocheworld orbit was stable or not. The most the Barnard tides can do is to move the two lobes some three kilometers closer. That's nothing compared to the eighty-kilometer spacing."

Jill had been silent for some time, but now she spoke. "You forget the saddle shape of the gravity potentials at the center point. A change of only three kilometers in separation causes a large shift in the potential surfaces that connect the two lobes. Sea level on Eau is usually forty kilometers below the zero-gravity point, but with the two lobes closer together, the zero-gravity point moves within kilometers of the surface of the water. We also forgot to consider the inertia in the tides. When the two lobes are equally illuminated, the planets are pulled apart by twelve kilometers and the top of the ocean mountain drops fifty kilometers or so, then rushes back in the next three hours as the lobes line up with Barnard and the tides are at a maximum. There would be enough inertia to throw the whole top of the water mountain through the zero-gravity region onto Roche."

"How far did the wave go on Roche in the simulation play?" asked George. "It reached the site of Rocheworld Base, didn't it!"

"Yes," said Karin. "We must warn them!"

"How?" said Jill, ever logical. "My radio, radar, and laser are all worthless this far under water, and my sonar won't propagate through space to the Comstats."

"There's got to be a way," said George. The alien play had finished and Arielle's hands were giving tiny pitty-pats of applause. White Whistler flowed up and halted in front of the sonar dome.

◇Do you understand?◇

"Yes," replied Jill. She guessed at the meaning of an alien whistle that she had correlated with the motions of Little Blue. "When world and Sky⊗Rock are near Barnard, the ocean will 'bloop' over."

◊Yes! Bloop can eat . . . Can make you a set of number zero.◊

"I guess that's the closest they come to a word for death," said George.

◊Bloop come soon,◊ said White Whistler. ◊We go now. You stay here.◊

White Whistler streaked off up the glacier at high speed with the rest of the colorful group following.

"Call them back!" cried George. "We've got to get those ice blocks off and get up to the surface to warn Red and Sam and Thomas!"

"They don't respond," said Jill. "Besides, it would not be safe for you on the surface."

"We've got to do SOMETHING!" George yelled, his command responsibility weighing heavily on his shoulders.

"The best something we can do is wait," said Jill, the calm tone in its voice trying to soothe the emotional human. "You have been up for thirty hours, George . . ."

George took the hint and tottered down the aisle to his bunk, muttering to himself as he went.

For a long time Arielle and Richard stared out the cockpit window at the scintillating glitter of the faceted transparent spheres falling down on the white surface. The ammonia water between the spheres would soon freeze into a slushy ice full of ammonia bubbles that gave the glacier its blue-white tone.

Richard got busy at the science console. He found that the sonar could penetrate the layers of ice beneath them and map the underlaying rock strata.

"Is that a lava flow?" asked Richard, scribing with his finger the telltale outlines of a frozen stream of hardened rock.

"Let me check for continuity," said Jill, bouncing pulse after pulse at the smooth edge. Then Jill noticed something else. . . . There was a blurred infrared image on the surface of the glacier above that matched the rock flow below.

"The volcano may not be as dormant as we first suspected. There is an infrared contour at the 0.01 C level on the surface of the glacier that followed the contour of the frozen rock flow below."

"Let's do a detailed scan of that region," said Richard. "Do you have time for one thousand pulses per scan element."

"I have nothing else more important to do," said Jill, and started off the first of one billion sonar pulses that it would emit in the next twenty minutes.

"Thomas? Come here for a minute and watch." Red Vengeance glanced down at her radar display, then out at the distant globe of Eau hanging in the sky.

"Eau is getting pretty active," she said as he joined her. Thomas squinted a bit at the large globe hanging over the dark mountain of water in the sky, then framed the scene between his two hands.

"It's a great shot," he said. "I think I'll go get my long-distance lens." With a bound he was across the bridge and swung down the passway to the crew quarters. He was back in less than a minute.

Red heard an electronic whistle as the liquid-crystal shutter activated, then a chitter as the microprocessor loaded the bits into a mass memory. It cost Electropix an extra few dollars to bridge a piezoelectric disk across the data bus so the customer would *know* that the picture was taken and stored, but it was little touches like that that kept Electropix at the top of the heap.

There was another chitter from the camera, then Thomas, still peering through the lens, made a questioning sound.

"What is it?" asked Red. She looked up at Eau and saw for herself. Rising from the top of the water mountain was a huge fountain of water. Slowly it rose and rose and continued to rise, glowing redly in the sunrise light of Barnard.

"Wow!" said Thomas, then all Red heard was the whistle-chitter, whistle-chitter of the electrocam, cramming bits into its nearly inexhaustible memory.

"It looks like a volcanic eruption on Io," said Red. "It must be the tides from Barnard."

"You didn't see it up close like I did," said Thomas. "It didn't rise up from inside like a hot bubble, it just drew back and jumped!"

"That fountain must be ten kilometers high," said Red.

"It is twelve and a half kilometers," said Jack. "That was its maximum. It is starting to fall now."

"But it's getting so big!" said Red.

"Yeah!" said Thomas, his camera whistling into action again as the fountain spray spread out into a huge white oval.

"And it moves so slowly," said Red.

"That's because it's so big," said Thomas, finally putting aside his camera. The oval was getting splotchy and completely inadequate for artistic photography. Besides he was sure Jack was taking very good scientific pictures of the eruption.

"It's developing a mustache," he said.

"Whorls of some kind," said Red. "They're going north and south, then disappearing into the shadow."

"Wait forty-five minutes," said Thomas, "then Barnard will be shining straight down between the inner poles. Wow! Look at those clouds spread out!"

"Those winds must be something ferocious near the inner point of Roche," said Red. "Perhaps that's what causes the linear rift valleys leading away from the point."

"Either that, or it's stretch marks from the tides," said Thomas. "Look, the mustache ends are starting to curl."

"It looks like the top of a tornado," said Red.

"A tornado two hundred kilometers high and still rising!" said Thomas, reaching again for his electrocam. "Is it moving?"

"No," said Red. "Its base seems to be fixed to the high density region between the inner poles. Thomas . . .?"

"Yeah, Red? (whistle-chitter, whistle-chitter) Something bothering you? (whistle-chitter)"

"We can't run the ascent module in that weather. Tell *Dragonfly* to wait until after periapsis."

"What's the matter, Red? You chicken?" said Thomas, instantly regretting the flip comment.

There was a dead silence for a minute.

"This chicken didn't live to be thirty-eight in the asteroid belt by jetting off on stupid missions," Red said. "Have Jack check the numbers if you want. With those winds, the ascent module has negative margin. Good night, Thomas."

A green streak with a red head launched itself angrily across the bridge and down the passway, leaving behind a trail of slowly falling drops of water that settled to the cling-carpeted floor.

Thomas was left alone on the bridge. A short conversation with Jack confirmed that Red's intuition was correct. Conditions had changed enough that the crew on *Dragonfly* could not be rescued. The ascent module was designed for fighting gravity, not an Oz-sized tornado.

Thomas called up Sam from the galley below.

"I think you'd better try to raise *Dragonfly* through the Comsats," he said. "There's a change in plans." To comfort his personal agony over his mishandling of Red during a crucial situation, he nervously unholstered his camera and started taking more pictures. Later he would admit they were the worst he had ever taken. Sam finally broke through the preoccupation and the whistle-chitter.

"None of the Comsats have had any contact with *Dragonfly* in over three hours."

Thomas felt old.

As Rocheworld continued its rotation, the tide above them reached its minimum. Deep within the bowels of the planet, a chamber of magma that had been kept bottled up by the overburden of water was finally able to push its way up to the surface, rumbling as it came.

"Earthquake!!!" shouted Karin, who was out in the aisle and halfway to the engineering console before she woke up. Another rumble threw her against the galley. Holding on to whatever she could grab, and wishing that her bare feet had corridor boots on, she made her way forward through the rocking ship and strapped herself into the chair in front of the engineering console and started to take Jill through a checkout.

"What'f going on?" said a sleepy Arielle, trying to keep upright by holding onto one of the stools in the galley. "If it earthquake?"

"I don't think so," said George from up front. "It's been going on too long and is getting stronger. I'm afraid that this volcano we're sitting on is about to erupt. I don't know what we can do about it, but you'd better get up here."

Arielle let go of the stool and started forward, but was thrown back into Richard's arms. The nearly naked young man, dressed only in shorts but wearing corridor boots to hide his disfigured feet, took the bunny-suited pilot under one arm. Carrying her forward, he installed her in the cockpit. Once there, the alert pilot brain checked over her console and turned to George.

"I try to get free," she said. "If I make fan go with earthquake, maybe I get ice off."

"It's worth a try," said George. "Go to it!" His eye caught something high above them in the unlit darkness at the peak of the mountain. "Mygod!!!" he cried his voice choking with fear. He pointed upward.

"It's red-hot lava!" shouted Karin. "It's coming down the mountain right at us!"

"It's got to eat through a lot of glacier before it gets to us," said Richard. "Can you get us loose, Arielle?"

Arielle, like every test pilot living, became even calmer and more deliberate in her motions as the danger grew.

"I think I try a yaw twift," she said, operating the fan levers in synchronism with the shaking of the ice beneath them. She kept it up for ten seconds, then stopped.

"Nope," she said. There was a second's pause in her motions while her brain moved at high speed through her other options.

"Now I try fome pitch," she said, and tried raising and lowering the nose of the plane with the fans in an attempt to buck the ice off. After another ten seconds she stopped.

"Nope."

A hushed silence fell over the crew, and David took advantage of a lull in the shaking to rush from his bunk to his computer console seat. Everyone was looking at Arielle.

"I've got the lava flow on the science scanner cameras," said Karin. "It's moving at a kilometer per minute through the glacier. Through the IR imager you can see a wall of melted water flowing down just ahead of it and getting bigger as it comes."

George switched his console to the IR scanner display. A white-hot tongue of fire flowed down from the top of the mountain to the middle of the screen where it met the cool-blue ice of the glacier. At the intersection was a roiling mound of yellow with large blue chunks floating on the surface.

"What are those blue chunks?" he asked.

"They look like blocks of ice," said Karin. "Yes, they must be. The glacier is pure water ice, which sinks in

Eau's ocean because it's heavier than the twenty-five percent ammonia solution. The mound of yellow is ice melted by the lava and is nearly pure water. The glacier ice will float on water, so it's breaking up into blocks and rising to the surface of the water mound as the lava burrows under the glacier and weakens its hold on the rock."

"Those blocks are as big as office buildings!" said George. "Get us out of here, Arielle!"

"Let me fee now," said Arielle calmly. "Maybe a yaw twift with a pitch maneuver . . ." Tiny hands rapidly flickered over the controls and *Dragonfly* bucked and pitched in an attempt to get free.

George stared at the IR scanner image and saw the yellow wall of warm water pouring down the slope at high speed. They only had a few minutes before it would be on them.

"Nope," said Arielle calmly. "Hummm . . . Maybe . . ." and the plane lunged backward and stuck.

George looked up from the screen and gazed out the cockpit window. He turned the landing lights upward. He couldn't see the invisible wall of water sweeping down on them, but he could see, floating hundreds of meters above them, dozens of blocks of blue-white ice hundreds of meters in size, tumbling through the turbulent water.

"Nope," said Arielle. "Maybe . . ."

"Brace yourselves," commanded George.

The *Magic Dragonfly* surged upward as the tongue of warm heavy water swept under its wings and lifted it up.

"The ice blocks are floating off the wings!!!" shouted Karin.

George noticed that he was no longer in control of the landing lights. He glanced quickly at Arielle and saw flickering eyes on a serious face alternating glances between console display and cockpit window. He turned his glance back out the window. They were rising rapidly up the steep slope of the flowing water. Ahead of them was a tumbling block of jagged ice over thirty meters in diameter.

"Twelve o'clock high!" he said.

"Got it," said Arielle. The nose dipped and *Dragonfly* dove deep into the water. George watched the undersurface of the iceberg pass overhead, not ten meters away. Now that they were deep in the water, they were relatively safe from the ice chunks floating above, but they were being carried downslope by the turbulent water. *Dragonfly* creaked as its wings were stressed near their limits.

"Can't ftay here," said Arielle. "Up we go. Help me find a gap." She turned the giant plane on its tail and applied full thrust with the fans to accelerate the rise of the buoyant airplane in the dense water. George peered out, trying to see beyond the reach of the landing lights. There was a large white shadow far above them, then another.

"Bogie at twelve o'clock, another at two o'clock low . . . a little one at eleven . . ."

Arielle went into a spiral, then stopped with the wings aligned with the flow of the water. The shaking and creaking abated a little as they drew closer to the ice-cluttered surface.

"Big one at twelve o'clock low," warned George.

"Fee anything on the high fide?" she asked, adding her eyes to his.

"Nope," he said.

"Then we go that way," said Arielle, pulling them upside down for a moment, then resuming the upward climb. George watched the iceberg pass beneath their nose as the plane broke through the surface of the dense water. The plane hesitated as it entered the lighter ocean water and lost much of its buoyancy, then continued its climb on the fans. Arielle set the controls for a steady climb, then changed her display to the sonar.

"How far to the top?" she asked.

"Twelve kilometers," said Jill. "At our present rate of ascent we should reach the surface in two hours, but the tide is coming back in and the surface level is increasing, so it will take longer than that."

There was a rumble through the water. Arielle tilted the plane back and they peered upside down at the volcano below them. A bright spot of yellow-white welled up from the crater and poured down the slopes in all directions, covering over the dull-red cooling flows that had preceded it.

"I'm really surprised that the flouwen put us there," said George. "They nearly killed us."

"Don't forget," reminded David, "They normally have better sense than to be in this part of the globe during periapsis. By the time they get back, the lava would have cooled off and been covered again by snow."

There was a rattle on the hull as they ran into a snow flurry of faceted hailstones. Arielle tilted the plane back and they continued their climb. With the plane on autopilot, Arielle finally noticed the pink elastic cuffs on her wrist and looked down to see she was still in her bunny suit.

"I think I'll go get dreffed," she said to George, blushing slightly. She unbuckled her seat belt and fluttered lightly down to the rear of the airplane.

Richard climbed up to take her seat so he could look out the window of the cockpit. "That was close," he said.

"You just witnessed the most spectacular feat of underwater flying you'll ever see," said George.

"And with mismatched fans, too," added Richard. "That girl is *some* pilot!"

"Yeah," agreed George. "Pretty too."

"Yeah!" agreed David.

"Men!" muttered Karin.

* * *

After about half an hour Arielle climbed up to join them again. The neuskin bandage was off her lip and some carefully applied makeup made the fine line of scarless new skin almost invisible. She paused when she reached the cockpit, stuck her head up between the two men, and smiled. The imp brace was still holding her tooth in place and lights flashed between red lips.

"I have my seat back now?" she asked.

"Sure," said Richard. He unbuckled and climbed down, using various nooks in the scanner instrument racks as hand- and foot-holds. He paused to boost Arielle up to her seat, then stepped down to stand on the strut holding Karin's console chair to the deck. She swiveled and looked up at him, her calves brushing against his.

"I'm making lunch down below," he said. "Any preferences?"

"Soup would taste good," she said.

"No soup," he said. "I just washed my hair and with our present attitude you'd be sure to spill some down on me. Finger foods only."

"Protocheese and an algae shake in a squeezer, then," she said.

Richard picked up some other orders in his climb down, and soon lunch was being passed up by a busy Christmas Branch as *Dragonfly* continued its vertical climb. Lunch break entertainment included a replay of the two-way snow show.

Through bites of a pseudosausage, George discussed the sonar display with Jill.

"What are those bars that move across the screen?" he asked.

"Those are wind waves," said Jill. "Although we have passed high tide and the ocean is falling again, the sun has heated up Eau's atmosphere and the winds are now blowing up the mountain again. We're now so close to

Barnard we get a lot of heating and the winds are quite strong and make large waves."

"How large?" said George, not really sure he wanted to know.

"They are a hundred meters high, have a wavelength of fifty kilometers and are moving at two hundred kilometers an hour."

"That sound dangerous," said Arielle in a worried voice. "Shall I slow us down until the waves get littler?"

"Are the tops breaking?" George asked Jill.

"The sonar gives no indication of it, although I am sure they will as they approach the inner pole and grow larger."

"No, Arielle, keep her on the same heading," said George. "We've got to get to the surface and warn the crew in Rocheworld Base about the danger. Besides, I've got an idea for putting those waves to a good use."

Surfing

"Two kilometers to go!" said Karin from the engineering console. She took another sip of her algae shake and grabbed it between her knees as her fingers tapped over the screen.

"Whoops!" cried David. "What happened?"

The airplane heaved upward, rotated slightly, then dropped again. In the process it shook something loose that clattered its way to the tail of the airplane.

"It was a wave going by overhead," said George. They continued their rise. The darkness above began to turn into a dark green, then grew lighter and redder.

"Good!" said George. "These waves are a little sportier than I'm used to, but at least it'll be daylight when we break the surface so I can see them coming."

"What are you going to do?" asked Richard, his head sticking up into the cockpit area.

"We're still a hundred kilometers from the ninety-eight percent confidence pickup footprint regions," said George. "The waves are heading our way, so I'm going to surf them!

"Karin! The minute we break the surface I want you to lock onto a Comsat and send a message to Rocheworld

291

Base to warn them of the interplanetary waterfall. The first one is only two hours away."

"Right!" said Karin, and her hands became busy on the screen as she set up the automatic track, lock, and speedsend of the critical message.

George looked over at Arielle.

"I'll take it now, Arielle." She lifted her hands from the controls, tightened her seat belt, and lay back, her hands folded across her stomach, but her eyes constantly flickered back and forth between console and cockpit window. George rolled the plane from its vertical climb into a steep bank, headed in the same direction as the wave motion.

"Until now I've regretted that decadent summer I spent between college and flight school. Three whole months in Hawaii doing nothing but surfing the pipeline off Diamond Head." He ran the fans up until an overspeed indicator lit up. Watching a map on his screen that showed a line that indicated a wave overtaking a tiny red dot, he pushed the speed control even higher and the *Magic Dragonfly* shot upward. It broke through the surface of the water on the forward face of the speeding wave. For a few seconds the plane was airborne again, enough so that its tail broke free of the water. George dipped the nose and dove down the sloping front of the wave, gaining even more speed, then the airplane turned surfboard settled the bottom of its hull into the water. George kept the fans lifting, and that together with the rush of air passing under the wings, kept the hull from sinking and dragging them under.

"Comin' down!!!" hollered George, his hands constantly moving to keep the plane balanced on the blanket of air passing under its wings. While the speedsend message was clattering over the link between Jack and Jill, carrying a complete description of the alien play and Jill's interpretation of it, Karin talked directly with Thomas.

"At the next high tide, there's going to be the first of a

number of transfers of the ocean from Eau to Roche," she said.

"That bad?" said Thomas. "We saw the tidal bore turn into a geyser at the last change of tides, but that one just blew a little spray into the zero-degree region. We never realized that it would go that far."

"What tidal bore?!?" asked Karin.

"This one," said Thomas. For a second Karin watched his face glancing down at the console screen in front of him and then his face was replaced with a speeded-up, time-lapse picture of a large ring wave starting at the base of the water mountain just after low tide and rising rapidly up the conical mountain of ocean as a single high-speed wave with a steep front.

"It covers six hundred kilometers in the hour and a half between low and high tide," said Thomas, "and it gets bigger and meaner as it's compressed into the small area around the peak. You'd better dive under again before it gets you."

"We can't," said George. "*Dragonfly* was never meant to be a submarine. Unless we have some rocks or heavy aliens for ballast, we always have positive buoyancy. We'll have to think of something else." His words sounded strained as the effort to maintain the delicate balance of lift, speed, and drag on the face of the moving wave began to take its toll.

"We're moving pretty fast," said Karin. "Can we turn on the nuclear jet and take off?"

"I'm aquaplaning and the tail is dragging the surface," he said. "If I open the air scoops, all they'd pick up would be water and the nuclear jet can't handle that."

"How about the monopropellant?" asked Karin. "I know it's meant for space use, but it could at least get us airborne enough so that we could switch to the nuclear jet."

"I'm afraid not, " said George. "Don't forget that the exhaust port is underwater. If I introduced the monopropellant into the chamber it would be like trying to fire a shotgun plugged with dirt. We'd blow the tail off."

"There must be some way," said Karin. "How about having Jill divert some of the crew air supply through the jet in place of the monopropellant? That would give us enough boost to get airborne, then we could open the scoops and turn on the nuclear jet. I'll get Jill to figure out whether it will work."

"Such diversion of crew air supply is not allowed," said Jill in its severest tone. "Calculations will not be done on disallowed options."

Karin didn't argue, but turned to her console and spoke as she typed in a code word.

"SEM-1, this is Chief Engineer Karin Krupp—password NORDIC, priority F1. Suggested diversion of crew air supply is essential to save crew from certain death by tidal wave. Obtain authorization to consider diversion from flight commander and mission commander, then proceed with analysis."

In a few seconds Karin heard Jill again through her imp. "I still object to the diversion, but my objections have been neutralized. The analysis shows that your plan is feasible, although it will take the outside imp fifteen minutes to rearrange the plumbing in the tank section. The amount of stored gas available is still not enough to lift the plane from the water by itself. We will need more air speed and a downhill run."

"I can get that," said George, "on the face of the bore wave. If it's big enough and we time things just right, we can be airborne before we get trapped by the curl at the top." As he talked, he adjusted the pitch of the nose and the plane lifted a little and climbed up to the top of the wave.

"The wind is dying down and this wave is going to peter out soon anyway," he said. "Might as well get off here and get ready for the big one." He dipped, then rose, and the wave slipped out from under them and the

Dragonfly settled into the trough behind. The short day was almost over and Barnard was setting in back of them over Eau. They watched the sunset through the long-distance lens of the scanner video, and as they watched, a frothy wave grew on the horizon and swallowed up the sun.

"We're going to have to do this in darkness, Karin," said George. "I want you to get me an IR and low-light-level video picture of this region from the Comsat." He turned to Arielle.

"Get your suit on, Arielle, then come back and relieve me. If the wave gets us, *Dragonfly* is going to get broken up. Not that the suits will keep us alive much longer."

He cleared his screen and pulled in the IR image from the Comsat overhead. *Dragonfly* was a tiny hot cross in the middle of a blue ocean. He zoomed the picture back until *Dragonfly* was a tiny white dot, then he saw the warm yellow whitecaps at the peak of the bore speeding toward them, leaving a roiling, blotchy sea of warm and cold patches behind it.

"How much time do we have?" he asked Jill.

"Twenty minutes," said Jill.

Arielle was standing at his shoulder, her pert face and curly hair distorted by the fishbowl helmet on her head.

"Your turn," she said, climbing into the pilot seat and copying his display.

"Not much to do except wait," said George. "See you soon." He made his way to the back where Karin was waiting for him, holding his suit open for him to step in.

"How is the tank switchover going?" he asked.

"It was completed five minutes ago," she replied. "Fortunately we'd never used the monopropellant line to the main engine so it didn't need to be purged. Here, let me get that zipper while you get your helmet on."

Five minutes later everyone was suited up and at their stations. "I've got it on the scanner camera," said Karin. David picked up her display on his console and watched the stars disappear one by one as the horizon in back of them rose up into the air. "It's a kilometer high!" he said.

"It is 1.7 kilometers high and growing," said Jill. "It will be over two kilometers tall by the time it reaches us."

"The bigger, the better," said George, increasing the speed of the fans into their danger region once again as *Dragonfly* swam away from the approaching wave. "There is no way we can build up enough speed to surf this one, but if it's tall enough, we can get airborne and away before the whitecaps at the top slap us down."

The view from the back through the scanner camera became blacker and blacker as the wave rose up to cover the sky. The crew felt the plane tip forward and rise upward as though they had hit an updraft. The horizon in front of them dipped, and the landing lights peered downward at the falling ocean surface. They were a half-kilometer up in the air.

"Now!" said George has he manipulated the controls that normally controlled the thrust level of the monopropellant rocket system. The plug of water was blasted from the jet exhaust by a burst of air, and *Dragonfly* leaped forward. The sea was briefly illuminated from behind with a brilliant yellow-white blowtorch flame as the oxygen combined with the ammonia and methane in the atmosphere.

"Wow!" said George. "I forgot about that effect."

He turned to Arielle. "We're in the air."

"I got her, George," she said. She dove down the surface of the wave until they had sufficient airspeed, then opened the atmosphere scoops and pushed forward on the throttle for the nuclear jet. There was a pale glow from the rear as the heated atmosphere rushed from the exhaust and the plane started to fly away from the face of the towering wall of water. A cheer arose inside the plane, echoed by cheers from the lander, then a noticeable fraction of a second later cheers could be heard from the remainder of the crew on *Prometheus*.

"We're airborne, Rocheworld Base," said George. "We'll meet you at L-4 where we can watch the show, then transfer for the trip out to *Prometheus*."

Suddenly there was a yellow-orange glare from behind and the ominous thuds of control rods being jammed into a reactor core at emergency speeds. The thrust stopped.

"Reactor overheated," reported Jill. "We have a major leak in our liquid-sodium heat-exchanger loop."

"It was corrosion from the ocean water," said Karin. "I was afraid of that, but there was nothing we could do."

"Switch to monopropellant!" hollered George, beginning to panic. "We've got to get altitude!"

"The monopropellant tanks are no longer connected to the jet," reminded Jill.

"Fire the air jet then. Do something!"

"I will glide," said a quiet voice, and the silent cabin tilted as the tiny pilot came into equilibrium with the wave above and behind them, surfing on the pocket of air pushed in front of the wall of water.

Using her glider experience, Arielle slid back and forth on the air in front of the bore, gaining a little altitude each cycle. The crest of the wave was still far above them, growing taller as they approached the inner pole. Arielle called up a Comsat low-light-level video image of the ring wave converging to a central point. On one side of the ring was the dot of *Dragonfly*, its landing lights making it visible from space. For a long time Arielle stared at the screen, judging the motion of the plane and the converging wave—trying to imagine the ring of invisible air trapped just inside the converging ring of water. Suddenly she dipped the nose of the silently gliding airplane, and trading altitude for speed, she streaked down the surface of the wave out across the flat ocean, putting the wave temporarily behind.

"Just like cliffs at La Jolla," she said as she streaked straight at the opposite wall of the twenty-kilometer-high ring wave. Trading kinetic energy for altitude, she pulled *Dragonfly* into a steep climb and zoomed almost straight upward. Rolling out, she picked up the top of the air geyser starting at the center of the ring. They were thrown upward and Arielle fought her way out from the turbulent center to the strong outside winds.

George stared at his screen in fascination at the converging ring of white water as seen from the Comsat image. The ring contracted into a foaming circle.

"The water geyser has started," said Karin. "You'd better get us to one side. The water has a lot more energy and inertia than the air and is going to blast its way up here at high speed."

Arielle nodded and pulled out and upward.

"We're only ten kilometers from the zero-gee point," said David, watching a trajectory plot on his console screen.

Arielle allowed herself a little smile.

"We make that easy," she said. "Then she is all downhill to Rocheworld Base. How many do we have to go?"

"Fifteen hundred kilometers," said David. Arielle was silent for a minute.

"Well, I have forty-kilometer altitude. Too bad my *Dragonfly* is not a real glider. I could make that easy. We shall see . . ." They all hung loosely in their seats as *Dragonfly* shot through the zero-gravity neck and started downward for Roche.

"Look ahead," said Arielle, pointing to a thin line of red light on the dark globe ahead of them. "We have come out on the other side. It is dawning at Rocheworld Base."

"Here comes the geyser," said Karin, who was watching toward their rear through the scanner instruments.

George copied Karin's screen. It was too bad that the sunlight wouldn't reach into the inner poles for another hour. If it was this impressive on the IR scanner, it would have been spectacular on video.

"How thick would you say it is?" he asked.

"About ten kilometers," said Karin. "The column is starting to break partway up."

George watched as the top portion of the geyser pushed its way through the narrow gravitational neck between the two planets, then started its slow fall toward the rocky lobe below. In the infrared scanner, every one of the volcanic craters below the falling, frothy blob had a bright red pseudocolor, while the pseudowhite ones could to correlated with the view out the cockpit window of the patches of dull red dotting the black peak of Roche ahead. On the Eau side of the blob, the geyser column thinned out as the base fell back under its gravitational pull, while the top portion continued to coast through the zero-gravity region.

"That's the first one," said George. "Get me Rocheworld Base, Karin." Soon Red's concerned face was on his screen.

"The first batch of water has transferred over and is heading for the surface. We've still got fifteen hundred kilometers to go and no propulsion power. The only thing that's keeping us up is Arielle. You'd better leave without us. We'll try to crash-land on a high ridge when we run out of altitude. If the next two transfers don't get us, you can come back again and pick us up."

"We're not leaving until we're in real danger," said Red determinedly. "How big is the water ball?"

"I would guess about ten kilometers in diameter," said George. "How about it, Jill? Will it get to them?"

"The amount of water transferred is sufficient to cover Roche to five centimeters deep."

"Hah!" said Red. "Just barely enough to get our feet wet."

"But you're in lowland country," said George, looking at the sunline moving rapidly across the surface of the rocky globe. "And right in line of one of those channels leading from the inner pole. It sure is obvious now what caused the erosion in those channels."

"You just keep coming," said Red. "We'll stay here until we see the whites of their tides."

"The leading edge of the drop is hitting the surface," said Karin. George switched his screen to Karin's IR scanner view. For a few seconds all he could see was a cold-blue column as seen from above, partially blocking a dull-red, warm conical mountain with yellow and white hot spots. Then at the base of the column there exploded a boiling cloud of yellow as the icy water poured down on the red-hot lava of the erupting volcanoes and turned into steam. For twenty minutes the torrent continued to fall, and soon the base of the waterfall was hidden in an expanding cloud of steam. From the bottom of the cloud streaked rivers of water streaming down the channels, riding a layer of steam over the tops of the tongues of lava that had preceded them. Fingers of steam rose into the air, twirled by the strong Coriolis forces near the center of the rapidly spinning double-planet system. Large, lazy tornadoes were spawned, and moved ahead of them across the sunlit planet.

"Just what I need," said Arielle, putting *Dragonfly* into a dive that was aimed at the base of the nearest tornado.

"What are you doing!" shouted George in alarm, yet he knew better than to try and stop her.

"We still have thousand kilometer to go and I need altitude," said Arielle. She turned to grin at him, knowing full well what was bothering him. "You Texas types are used to high-gee twisters that can rip apart airplanes," she said. "Just look down the throat on that one, George.

It over one kilometer in diameter. Just pretend it's a thermal—with clouds in it."

George did relax a little at that image as Arielle dove the plane at the ground. Timing her approach carefully, she swooped in under the funnel at high speed as it lifted a few hundred meters from the surface. She slammed *Dragonfly* into a tight bank and started spiraling up.

"Are you *sure* you've never flown fighters, Arielle?" asked George as the gee load pinned him to his seat.

It may have been a lazy tornado, but it was still more tornado than thermal. The first few turns were through rough air that had *Dragonfly* creaking. Something broke loose in the rear of the plane and banged around until the Christmas Branch corralled it. It was dark gray inside the funnel, but they had plenty of light from the almost continuous flashes of lightning. *Dragonfly* was struck twice on the wing and had Karin and Jill frantically reconfiguring circuits to work around burned-out cables. As they spiraled upward, the radius of the funnel widened and the turbulence dropped. They clattered through a small cloud of blue hailstones, then flew out the top just in time to witness the sun setting behind Roche. Arielle set the plane on a long shallow glide angle and reached up to take off her helmet.

"We have still a thousand kilometer to go, but now we have some altitude. It is not enough though." She turned to look at Karin. "Could I please have monopropellant tank reconnected?"

"Jill and I did that long ago," said Karin, "but it isn't going to do us much good. It'll only give us fifteen minutes of thrust."

"That's enough to get us up out of here to L-4!" said George.

"If that were true I'd have mentioned it long ago," said Karin. "Unfortunately we no longer have the nuclear reactor to augment the monopropellant exhaust velocity. By itself the monopropellant isn't strong enough to put us in orbit, even from this low-gee planet."

"But it can give me altitude," said Arielle. "And altitude means distance."

Arielle turned to George. "Keep glide angle shallow and let me know when we at one kilometer. I'm going to get something to eat and take a nap." She hopped down from the flight deck and made her way back to the galley, where a still openmouthed George heard her order a huge meal from the galley imp. He shook his head and turned back to his console. There was no way he could get himself to eat or sleep at this point. He looked at the control settings and started to reach for them. He slapped the back of one hand with the other.

No need to fiddle with them, George, he muttered to himself inside his helmet. The lady's setting is perfect. To pass the time, he watched the second of the interplanetary waterfalls as seen from *Clete* and *Walter* at L-4 and L-5 and discussed them with Karin and Red.

"This one looks smaller," said George. "Of course I was closer to the last one."

"It is smaller," said Red.

"How come?" said George. "We're closer to periapsis and the tides should be stronger."

"Thomas has been modeling the details of the system, including simulating the ocean with a collection of tiny mass points. There's some complicated interaction of the orbital dynamics with the rotary dynamics and the tidal dynamics that makes the periapsis high tide slightly smaller than the high tides just before and just after periapsis."

"Don't forget the atmosphere," said Karin. "At periapsis Barnard is heating Roche, and Eau is in shadow, so the atmospheric winds are blowing down the mountain. At the high tides on either side, Barnard is heating Eau, boiling off the ammonia, and adding wind waves to the tidal bore."

"There doesn't seem to be as much steam this time either," said George as they watched the blob of water fall on the volcanoes and drown them in a torrent of icy liquid. The sun was rising on the other side of Roche, and although both airplane and lander were in darkness, Clete gave them a sunside view of the forming of the north and south polar vertical tornadoes, made visible by the steam boiling up from the point of Roche.

"Wow! Look at that!" said Red as a silvery tongue sprang out from the shadows of the inner pole and moved rapidly across the sandy valleys of Roche.

"That's why I think you'd better get ready to leave," said George. "The volcanoes are drowned and are no longer boiling away the water. With the head and the velocity that the blob builds up dropping the forty kilometers from the zero-gee region, you get air entrapment, just like an avalanche. Those fronts must be moving at five hundred kilometers an hour."

"I've got an IR image of the flow below us," said Karin.

"Let's see it," said George, and his screen flickered to show the dull-red warm rock beneath them. Streaking out in fingers from the grooves worn in the rocky point of Roche were blue-cold streams of high-speed menace.

"Doesn't look good," said George. "Are you ready to go?"

"Yes," said Red, "but we've voted to stay."

George started to argue with her, then lapsed into silence as one by one the fingers of speeding cold water seemed to stumble and break into a warm yellow froth as the trapped air layer failed and dumped the tons of high-speed water into the salty sands, where it spread into a more slowly moving flood.

"See, George," said Red, "no problem."

"That one got within a hundred kilometers of you," said George. "You leave when the next one hits. That's an order!"

"You just get here before it does," said Red. She paused. "That's an order."

"Yes, ma'am!" he replied.

"We're at ten kilometers' altitude," reminded Jill.

"Wake Arielle up," he said. "We need altitude."

Ten minutes later Arielle strolled down the corridor nibbling on a large chunk of pseudocheese. She paused at Karin's console.

"We are ready with a maximum altitude program?" she asked pleasantly.

"It will use all but ten percent of the monopropellant, but it will give you twenty-five kilometers," replied Karin. Arielle wrinkled her nose, then had a short conversation with her imp.

"I take all hundred percent," she said.

"Don't you need some in case there is a problem with the landing approach and you have to go around? Don't forget you don't have the VTOL fans."

"Don't forget," smiled Arielle, "there is no such thing as a go-round in a shuttle landing." She tossed her head back to get the curls out of her eyes, climbed up to the pilot seat on the flight deck, and strapped herself in.

"We are ready?" she asked. Then after a pause she dove the airplane at the invisible surface below.

"I do wish you had radar back, Jill," she said as she watched the blurred IR image grow in her screen.

"Aren't we getting a little close?" said Jill.

"The monopropellant gives a little better thrust when used with high-density air," said Arielle confidently.

When the IR image stopped looking blurred, Arielle pulled *Dragonfly* out of its dive, opened the atmosphere scoops slightly and shoved the throttle all the way forward and held out onto it as she turned the long-winged airplane into a vertical rocket. Only when the roaring at the rear of the plane had subsided into some empty coughs did the little hand pull the throttle back to its initial position. No other motion was made as the plane coasted upward on its inertia, the crew floating lightly in their harnesses after the high-gee climb. At the very top of the climb, Arielle switched to the space-attitude control system and with the last bursts of monopropellant left in the lines to the nose jets, she tilted the plane forward and again started the long glide toward Rocheworld Base.

"Five hundred kilometer to go," she said. "How much time we have?"

"The next waterfall comes in ten minutes," said David. "But it takes twenty-five minutes to fall and then the flood has to travel from the inner pole to Rocheworld Base. It depends upon how fast the water travels and that depends upon how long it stays in the air-entrapment state. It could be two hours, it could be four, it could be that it never even gets there and we have all the time in the world."

"I think I go faster," said Arielle, tilting the nose of the plane slightly. She then put her console into compute mode and her long fingernails tapped on the screen as she and Jill optimized a curved trajectory that would put them at Rocheworld Base at zero altitude in minimum time.

"This is going to be a big one," said Karin, watching the ring bore build up on Eau through the IR imager on the Comsats. Richard was sitting next to her at the science console. His screen had two pictures. One just like Karin's and the other taken at a similar time in the first of the tidal transfers.

"There must be a partial resonance in the ocean basins of Eau," said Richard. "This one is bigger than the first one that had the wind helping it."

The entire crew except Arielle were looking at their screens as the ring wave contracted and generated a thick, climbing column of water. They watched in frozen fascination as the deadly menace rose like the head of a cobra from its coiled base. The underportions of the column thinned while the top portion that had enough momentum to overcome the weakening gravity continued upward and squeezed its bulk through the zero-gravity neck, compressed to a ten-kilometer-wide throat by the strong gravity gradients pressing inward around the zero-gravity point. The blob grew into an ellipsoidal ball on the other side and started to stretch as the lower portions were pulled along faster than the upper regions. Richard's screen had an overlay that Jill traced out around the IR image of the elongating ball.

"It's thirty kilometers long by twenty in diameter," said Richard. "That's enough to cover Roche a half-meter deep in water."

"And the volcanoes aren't going to be much help in evaporating this one," said George.

As the ball fell, it pushed air ahead of it and flattened out on the bottom. When the drop reached the surface, the air under it built up in pressure and squeezed out at high speed from the edges, only to find itself trapped from above by an enlarging blob of water that moved rapidly over the nearly frictionless air, trading its gravitational head and inertia for speed.

"The bottom is moving like an express train, and the top is still falling!" said George.

"It's faster than an express train," said Richard. He generated a new "tagger" from the menu at the side of the screen and moved it with his finger to the front of one of the racing tongues of water. The green cross "tag" stuck at the change of illumination between the blue cold water and the disappearing warm red rocks of Roche. Richard's finger went back to the menu and picked out a parameter—VELOCITY.

580 KM/HR, came the indication on the screen.

"It'll be at Rocheworld Base in less than three hours," said Richard. "Are we going to make it in time, Arielle?"

"We also arrive in less than three hours," she replied calmly, her eyes on the ground speed indicator. She pulled back slightly on the controls to take advantage of the slight tail wind in the level they were presently passing through. She would later use the altitude she had saved to gain more speed.

"Can you get us a more accurate time prediction, Richard?" asked George.

"I'll work on it," said Richard. A flick of his finger at the parameter—ACCELERATION produced a positive number. He flinched, then read—POSITION. He set up another tag at the position of Rocheworld Base, then read the separation.

"It's at thirteen hundred kilometers from the base and still accelerating," said Richard. "The top of the drop is just feeling the back pressure of the ground below and the pressure head wave is still pushing out around the boundary. I'll have to wait until the acceleration stops before I can predict an accurate arrival time, but it looks like two hours and fifteen minutes."

George glanced at Arielle. She was moving very slowly and deliberately, with only the rapid motion of her eyes giving any indication of the whirling thought processes going on under the curly hair. She was in her "test pilot in trouble" trance. A silence fell over the ship as everyone waited for her to speak.

"I would like rest of air, please. At any point below two kilometers' altitude would be useful." She dropped out of her trance and turned away to tend to her flying.

"Everyone back in their suits," George said. "And give Karin one of your suit tanks. One tank will last more than two hours and that's more time than that bore will give us."

"Reconfigure the plumbing again, Jill," said Karin to her imp. "I'll get the tanks hooked up to the supply lines and you drain them as fast as you can."

"Unless you object, I will also increase reactor power above safe limits and generate some oxygen and hydrogen by electrolysis."

"Good," said Karin, swinging from the console seat and walking down the corridor in the twelve percent gravity. At least they would have some solid footing for their dash to the lander.

Richard was soon suited up and back at his console, his bloated silver fingers pulling information off the image on the screen. The bore was now out in the sunlight. From a distance it looked like a river of quicksilver in the lined palm of an old Indian soothsayer.

"The pressure head is decreasing, but the velocity is six hundred ten kilometers an hour, three times faster than we're gliding. The separation distance is eight hundred eighty kilometers. Estimated time of arrival one hour and twenty-four minutes."

George glanced over at Arielle, looking for the trance. There was a pause as the colloid computer integrated a lifetime of experience in the air with the present situation and the new numbers.

"I think I have some bite to eat before I suit up," she said, hopping down from the flight deck. "I'm hungry. You keep watch on my *Dragonfly* for me, George?"

George grinned through his visor and checked over his control panels. For some reason his shoulders felt as though they were in a region of lower gravity.

"Don't dawdle," he said in a pseudo-gruff voice. "Karin wants to have Jill suck up the last of the cabin air after we're all in our suits." Arielle strolled down the corridor in her trim, tailored jump suit, weaving her way around the armored forms of Richard and David. She stopped at the galley for a slab of pseudochicken, then ignoring a patient Karin holding up her suit at the end of the corridor, she disappeared into the head.

Ten minutes later a refreshed Arielle with a newly remade face exited the bathroom, where she was set upon by an exasperated Karin who unceremoniously stuffed her into her suit. As soon as the last seal was closed, the suit started to balloon as Jill pumped the air out of the cabin and added it to the tanks.

"Five kilometers' altitude, Arielle!" hollered George through his suit imp.

"And the bore is at five hundred kilometers and still levitated," said Richard.

Arielle made her way carefully back up the corridor and climbed into the pilot seat. She checked the display carefully, her hands still folded in her lap. Satisfied, she raised her hands and nodded at George. He nodded back and she took control again with the flick of a few switches.

"I like status report, Richard."

"Bore distance from base is four hundred sixty kilometers, velocity five hundred kilometers per hour, arrival time forty-eight minutes."

"Jill, we arrive in forty minutes?"

"Forty-one," replied Jill.

"Too close," said Arielle. "I use air." She pushed forward on the controls and dove *Dragonfly* at the ground. As she pulled up she triggered the valve and the last of the air supply shot out of the jet in a blue-yellow flame. Arielle stopped the climb and pushed *Dragonfly* into a fast glide at a still-invisible target eighty kilometers away.

"Jill?" she asked.

"Twenty-four minutes."

"Richard?"

"Thirty-four minutes."

Arielle made one tiny adjustment to the controls, tightened her seat belt and shoulder harness, then put her hands into her lap. She turned to look at George out of her helmet.

"We have hard landing," she reminded him.

"And just ten minutes to get the five of us up the side of the lander," George said as he tightened his seat belt. He turned to Karin.

"How many can we get in the air lock?"

"Three easily."

"You, Richard, and David get into the lock and cycle it, but don't open the outer door until we've stopped moving. Put your backs to the front wall and take some bedding to protect your helmets."

"Are you and Arielle going to have time to cycle through? We could cram in five."

"You forget someone has to land this thing, and I'm not leaving Arielle up here all alone. The minute we stop I'm blowing the front canopy and Arielle and I will go out over the nose. Red! Are you monitoring?"

"Yes," came the reply from Rocheworld Base.

"Is the winch line down?"

"Yes," came Red's voice over the intercom. "I'm in the lock and will winch you up as soon as you grab the end. Hurry up!"

"I see the bore on the scanner video. It's gaining on us," said Richard.

"Give us a last reading on time difference, then get in that air lock!" said George.

"Eleven minutes," interrupted Jill. "Get into the air lock, Richard," it bossed. Richard obeyed and trotted to the rear of the plane and the lock door closed behind him. George and Arielle were left with the hiss of air passing over the silent airplane and the distant throb of air-lock pumps going through their motions on almost nonexistent air. George could now see the lander, sticking up into the air, its dark outline standing just to one side of the setting globe of Barnard.

"Bad luck!" complained George. "We're flying right into the sun."

"No! It good!" said Arielle. "I see rocks easy now because of they big shadow." She banked the plane slightly to pick a path that was relatively clear of boulders and gave up the last of her altitude for speed.

"BRACE YOURSELF!" screamed Jill to everyone but Arielle. "Flaps!" Arielle commanded. Both her hands were busy, one with the airplane controls and the other operating the fans at full reverse thrust. George pushed at the flap controls but found that they were already moving.

"Flaps down," he and Jill said at the same time. The plane started to drop heavily to the surface, the forward speed almost gone. Arielle brought it almost to a stall and then, just before touchdown, dipped it just enough to keep some control as the plane slid through the sand directly toward the lander.

We're going to hit! thought George, his throat too tight to speak.

Arielle wrenched the rudder around as she twisted the fan controls. The *Magic Dragonfly* went into a broadside slide and came to a stop with its nose on one side of the lander and the left wing on the other, not ten meters from the fragile legs of the cylindrical rocket.

"George! I made ringer!" shouted Arielle with delight.

"BLOW THE HATCH!" came a sharp command in George's ear. His thumb flipped the safety cover, but a waiting imp beat his gloved finger to the switch underneath. There was a loud BANG! The cockpit windows flew into the air and the ammonia-methane atmosphere rushed into the plane. There was a dull THUMP! as the inflowing gases burned with the residual air in the plane. George clambered out on the nose and jumped to the surface, then turned to catch Arielle. Together they hurried toward the distant lander. Jill, her voice turned into that of a martinet, drove them with verbal whiplashes. Over the voice George could hear some leakage from the high-speed data link between Jack and Jill.

"KARIN, RICHARD, DAVID—TO THE WINCH.

GEORGE, ARIELLE—UP THE LADDER.

RED, START THE WINCH AND GET THEM UP AND IN!

MOVE IT, GEORGE!

ARIELLE IS WAY AHEAD OF YOU!

MOVE IT, YOU FAT OLD MAN!"

George found another source of adrenaline in his anger and he sprinted harder for the ladder. Arielle ran lightly up the rungs on the landing legs without using her hands. When she reached the main body of the lander, she crouched and leaped up the side of the rocket in the low gravity, then continued on, hand over hand, her legs dangling. George knew he couldn't do that and scrambled rung by rung after her. He got up the landing leg and paused to look up at Arielle.

"No SIGHT-SEEING! MOVE IT! MOVE IT! MOVE IT!!!" Jill's voice took on a harsh tone that sent George back to his first week in ROTC summer camp under the tender ministrations of a drill instructor. Fear and hatred drove him up the ladder. He could see the wall of water coming over the horizon to his left, its foaming top colored blood red in the setting sunlight. The water was swallowing the kilometers-long shadow of the lander as George clambered into the lander with Red and the four others.

"I've got the winch stored," said Red. "Shut the door."

George started to close the door. He stopped. With him in the lock, there was no room for the door to swing closed and no time left to cycle the air lock twice. He stepped back out onto the top rung of the ladder and pulled the door shut after him.

"George!!! Noooooo . . ." wailed Red.

"Take off, Thomas!!! That's an order!" said George through his imp.

The ten-meter-high wall of water hit the base of the rocket and it started to topple.

"Got to go!" said Thomas.

The atmosphere around George was ablaze with flame as the ascent module lifted from the falling rocket and boosted into the sky. George's feet slipped from the rung and he was left hanging by the inadequate grasp of his sausage-glove hands. As the acceleration built up he found his left hand slipping from the vertical handhold. He grabbed for the horizontal ladder rung and got it, but lost his right handhold on the door handle. Dangling by one hand from the bottom of the accelerating spacecraft, he was blinded, deafened, and burned by the exhaust from the powerful rocket engine. He felt the suit cooling shift to maximum power to prevent his legs from frying in the intense heat. He tried to get his right hand up to the ladder rung, but the buffeting was too much. They hit max-Q and the supersonic blast was too much. His fingers slipped off the rung and he fell through the flaming exhaust toward the distant ground below. He was still moving upward, coasting on the momentum of the rocket that had left him behind. He came to the peak of his trajectory and started to fall.

Time seemed to stop. George found that he had automatically assumed the spread-eagle position he'd learned when skydiving, only this time he didn't have a parachute. He felt a faint twinge of regret. Regret that he would never again see Loud Red and White Whistler and the others again. George felt cheated. There was so much more he wanted to do on this world. Then there were all the moons of Gargantua to explore. Well ... he had made it to Barnard alive and had fun exploring at least one world.

We all have to go sometime, he said to himself. Might as well get this over with.

He pulled in his arms from the spread-eagle position and dove headfirst for the ground.

"No! GEORGE! No!" screamed Red's voice over his suit imp.

George resumed the spread-eagle position and looked around. The ascent module had dipped down below and was rising up to meet him. As it came closer he could see a grinning brown face peering up at him through triangular windows. The entry port at the top of the spacecraft was open. Reaching up from the lock was a slender, space-suited figure. She had a long lanyard, but it wasn't needed. Thomas swooped the rocket up underneath George and scooped him right into Red's arms.

"I always was the best one on the block at the ball-and-cup game," Thomas bragged.

George felt the acceleration increase as Red dragged him into the lock and the air cycle started.

"I nearly lost you!" said Red as she took off his helmet. Tears were streaming down her face and into her suit. George started to cry too. He put his arms around her and tried to give her a comforting hug, but the suits got in the way. When Richard got the inner door open he found them nuzzling each other's faces, both wet with tears.

With his suit off and holding Red by the hand, George joined the rest of the crew in the view lounge as they floated at L-4, waiting for *Prometheus* to arrive. Arielle was at the telescope, tracking the fractured cross of duralloy that used to be the *Magic Dragonfly* as it was being borne off by the waves, the wing tips crumbling as they were dashed against boulders and tumbling rocks.

"Good-bye, Jill," Arielle cried, her voice breaking.

"Arielle, dear," said Jill's voice through her imp. "I'm still here. You must remember that these voices we computers use are just to aid you in identifying which computer is talking to you."

As it spoke, the voice changed slowly from the overtones of Jill to the overtones of Jack. It then switched to that of James, who in its most butlerish voice continued to drive in the lesson as its voice changed to that of a tinny robot. "It is very im-por-tant that you re-a-lize we are noth-ing but ro-bots."

"You right," agreed Arielle. "I am silly to cry over computers." Then she burst into tears again.

"What's the matter now, Arielle?" said George.

"My *Dragonfly* was such a pretty plane, and now she is all broke!"

"We've got three more Dragonflys for you," said George reassuringly. "And you have all the rest of your life to fly them."

"Here comes *Prometheus* to pick us up," said Sam peering out the side of the window.

"C'mon, Red," said Thomas. "Time to fly this ship back to its dock."

Reporting

With the bulk of the lander left on Roche, it was an easy job for Thomas and Red to slide the ascent module in between the shrouds on *Prometheus* and attach it again to the docking port above the hydroponics deck. George opened the port and peered down. There was a stern, round black face peering back up at him.

"That's the last time I give you an airplane to play with," said Jinjur. "You're too rough on your toys. Just for that you'll have to stay home next time."

George grinned and jumped down to the hydroponics deck where he was immediately grabbed around the waist in a bear hug. Jinjur didn't say anything else, but George felt his shirtfront getting wet. He hugged back and soon the corridor was crowded with bodies as the crews combined into one large happy family again.

After a joyous dinner featuring some of the more special treats from Nels Larson's gardens and tissue cultures, George and Jinjur met together on the control deck to make plans for the next phase of the mission.

"I know we have only three landers and more than three moons around Gargantua to study," said George. "But it's vitally important that we come back to Rocheworld. Those aliens are so far ahead of us in mathematics that we need to set up permanent communication with them."

"But what good is pure mathematics?" said Jinjur.

"It is the key to physics and technology," said George. "At first glance it would seem that advanced mathematics is just a barren exercise in pure logic and should have no relationship at all to the real world. In fact, the mathematicians go out of their way to free their logic from any 'commonsense' rules. But for some reason, the behavior of the real world follows the logic of mathematics and no other logic. If we have a mathematical tool and can calculate something using it, we are sure that is the way nature will behave. But we don't have enough of those mathematical tools and we know it.

"Astronomers can't calculate the exact motions of more than two gravitating bodies except under special conditions. Aerodynamicists can't calculate the exact flow of air over anything but very simple wing shapes. Weather forecasters can't predict more than a few days ahead. Atomic scientists can't exactly calculate anything more complicated than a hydrogen atom. The human race needs that math, and the beauty about math is that unlike being given the secrets to advanced technology, being given advanced mathematics will not stifle the technological creativity of the human race, since *we* will have to figure out how to apply the mathematics."

"OK," said Jinjur. "But how are we going to get the information out of them? This crew may be pretty smart, but none of us are theoretical mathematicians. We may be able to understand some of the simpler stuff, but after the second or third infinity I know *I* would be lost."

"What we should do is set up an interstellar laser communicator in the Hawaiian Islands on the Eau lobe where their older thinkers stay," said George. "That way the long-lived flouwen could communicate their advanced mathematical knowledge directly back to earth, even long after you and I and the rest of the crew have fluttered out the last of our Mayfly-like lives."

"You're getting poetic, George," said Jinjur. "I never knew you had it in you."

"Reaching terminal velocity at ten kilometers up with no parachute makes a person think a little more about the fundamentals, like living and dying," said George soberly. He got up. "I'll go talk to Carmen and Karin and see what we can put together that the flouwen can use. The laser should be in a well-sheltered place on land with a reactor that will keep it going for a few decades until the follow-on expedition gets here. But the operating console will have to be underwater."

"Just a minute there, George," said Jinjur sternly. George stopped, puzzled.

"Remember what they told you in officers' training? 'The program isn't complete until the documentation is done.' You just finished an important and exciting mission and there are a few billion people back on earth that are waiting to hear what happened. You've got a report to write."

"Aw, Jinjur, that'll wait," George said. "I've got to get the work started on the communicator."

"Nope," said Jinjur, getting up from the commander's console and motioning him to take the seat. "You stay here and cram words into the console. *I'll* go find Carmen and Karin and start planning the next landing." She continued to talk as she bounced away in the low gravity. "This next mission will need more biologists and fewer geologists so I'll definitely want to take Susan along. . . ."

George slumped into the still-warm seat and stared glumly at the waiting blank screen. As Jinjur reached the lift shaft she turned for a last word.

"If you hurry, they will get your report just after New Year's Day in 2076. That should get the Tricentennial Celebration off to a good start."

Ending

Red slowly drifted out of her apartment on *Prometheus* and palmed the door closed. She paused and looked across the lift-shaft to the two doors that opened into Thomas' and George's rooms. George was not in; he was probably down in the control room working with James on data reduction. Thomas had not been in his room for two years now. When they had floated him out the portal to take him down to the sick bay, Thomas had insisted that his door be left open.

"I'm not going to let a little heart attack keep me down," he had said. "I'm going to get well and come back to my studio. I've a lot of pictures to work on."

Red's eyes swept past the seven other doors ringing the lift shaft. They and all the doors on the floor above had been closed for a long time. Eight of them at once, some fifteen years ago when Slam IV had been stranded on Zuni, third moon of Gargantua. The others on the ship had died of one cause or another over the years while *Prometheus* slowly wandered back and forth through the Barnard system, collecting data on the planets and moons as the seasons changed. Only three of them remained alive now—all old, but still busy. They were presently engaged in a two-year survey of the star itself, following it through one of its sunspot cycles. For that job they had used the light from the star to slow Prometheus in its orbit, so that the spinning parasol fluttered down closer to the dim red sun. For the first time since they had come to Barnard they had to use filters over the viewing ports.

Red looked up at the gaping maw of the central shaft and hesitated. In the past she would simply have flung herself up into the empty hole and used an occasional flick of hand or foot on the walls to propel herself through the shaft. She would still do that for a 'tween-decks jump—but now she wanted to go to the starside science dome nearly 60 meters away. Getting cautious in her old age, she called for the lift elevator and took it to Starside.

Once there, Red wormed her way past a large telescope swung out under the dome. There was little room left for a human; Red looked up to see a mini-bush working the controls. It was very busy, scrambling back and forth between the various control knobs at a speed that no human hands could have duplicated. Red was slightly puzzled. "Why are you using such a little branch, James?" she asked. "You'll wear yourself out running back and forth like that."

She heard James chuckle, both in her hair imp and from the mini-brush on the telescope. "I can handle the telescope fine this way," it replied. "It is a little more wasteful of energy than using a larger motile that can reach both knobs at once, but I felt that it was better to have most of the Christmas Bush elsewhere at this time."

Red's heart skipped a beat. "What's going on?" she asked in alarm, then instantly knew the answer. "There's something wrong with Thomas!" she cried, and started to wiggle her way past the slowly moving telescope.

"I did not want to worry you," said her imp. "There is nothing bad happening to him, but I just thought it best to have more of my motile close to him since his vital signs are slowly worsening."

"Red! . . . Elizabeth!! . . . Wait for the elevator!!!" her imp screamed in her ear as she dove headlong down the 60-meter shaft.

"I'll pay for that later," Red said to herself as her adrenaline-anesthetized joints brought her to a violent stop at the living area deck. She made her way to the sick bay. Most of the Christmas Bush was there, monitoring the medical instruments. Thomas' upper torso was naked and covered with a lacelike net of motile threads. She understood why James had been concerned. Thomas' face, usually a handsome and healthy dark-brown color, was now a muddy grey. He had aged well and usually looked much younger than his 68 years. He didn't look young now; more like George's 87.

Thomas looked up as she came in. He grinned weakly at her and winked their special wink. She blushed, then put an exasperated frown on her face.

"Thomas," she scolded, "you're incorrigible."

"But it's been over two years, Red," he said, "A guy could die if he goes without getting it for that long."

". . . and he'd die if he did," she replied.

"But what a way to go!"

Ignoring his remark, Red moved over to him and put one hand on his forehead and the other on his cheek. He moved his head and nuzzled in her hand, his lips kissing her palm softly. She tried to hold back her emotions, but finally gave up, fell sobbing across his chest, and hugged him. Through her anguish and tears she could feel the motiles moving between them, keeping out of the way as much as possible but maintaining their vigil on the body of the dying man. Thomas ran his fingers through the brilliant red hair that he had loved for so long, grinned inwardly at the slight trace of grey at the root of each hair and closed his eyes to rest.

After a while, Red got control of herself. She sat up and twisted her body until the patch of tiny hooks on the back beltline of her jumpsuit stuck to the holding pad of a work-station arm the Christmas Bush had swung out for her. Now she could stay beside the bed without drifting away. She looked at Thomas' closed eyes with concern, then turned to the bush.

"He's just sleeping," said James, "but it won't be long now. In his weakened condition his usually benign sickle-cell anemia is flaring up and aggravating his other problems."

Red took Thomas' hand and waited, occasionally brushing him on the cheek with a wrinkled, freckled hand.

George was in his bed, staring up at the viewscreen in the ceiling and scanning through an ancient science fiction novel, *Dragon's Egg*. He'd read it many times before, but it was so full of scientific tidbits that he always enjoyed dipping into it before going to sleep. His favorite part was when the alien "cheela" came up from the surface of a neutron star to visit the humans in orbit above them, riding on miniature black holes.

George heard the rustle and the occasional odd noise of Elizabeth coming up the shaft. He looked out of his open bedroom door to watch Red rise up out of the shaft and bring herself to a halt at the railing. Instead of going to her door, however, she circled around the railing of the lift shaft and disappeared behind the edge of his door. He heard the splat of a palm on the wall, the sibilant hiss of a compartment door sliding shut, and the click of a bolt. He sat up under his tension sheet as his imp whispered in his ear.

"She wanted to tell you herself," it said.

Red appeared at his door, an inward strength glowing in the tall, green-suited body. Her red hair glistened in the bright corridor light as she said, "There's just the two of us now, George. Can I come in?"

"Sure," he said, "just a second and I'll get dressed."

"Don't bother," she replied. "I just don't want to sleep alone tonight." She came over to the bed and, kicking off her corridor boots, climbed in under the tension sheet, her back to him.

"Just hold me," she pleaded, and George put his old-man's grizzled arm around her and lay his head on the pillow next to hers, his imp scrambling around to his other shoulder as he did so. He closed his eyes and went to sleep, while James turned off the bedroom light and the scan book and closed the corridor door.

George was hanging loosely to a pylon on the control deck, monitoring the video feedback from the deep space probes in the outreaches of Barnard. The screens showed little that was new and James could have handled the data by itself, but George insisted on viewing all the scenes that differed in any significant aspect from those that had been seen before. A typical scene of frozen blackness on a distant moon nearly 40 light-minutes away had changed to a scene of frozen greyness. The computer had asked the human element in its loop to evaluate the situation.

"Nothing here, James," George said. "Just another mound of dirty ice."

The screen flashed to a new scene, one that had been held up while the previous one had been evaluated. George scanned the picture, looking for anything that the well-trained computer might have missed. Suddenly he caught a flash of green out of the corner of his eye and turned to see a tumbled mass of green satin floating in front of his face. He brushed away the intruding jumpsuit and underwear just in time to see two tantalizing white mounds swim out of sight behind the control room door, pink feet propelling them on their way.

It didn't take long. Within ten seconds he was stripped to the uniform that the "Game" called for and was searching through the corridors that had made their life a heaven in the stars. They had tried other hiding spots, but the best—yes, the very best—was the exercise room.

George found her behind the exercise mats. She thought

she was stretched out enough to be as invisible as a pea under the many thick mattresses. He noticed the slight mound, however, and his body rising to the occasion, dove under the layers of mats and pulled a squealing, skinny, red-haired vixen into the open.

"STOP!" she cried. She twisted expertly in the air, trying to break his single handhold.

Her struggles to retreat were defeated by a single brushing kiss that he implanted on the tips of her hair. It was his turn to run now and he bounded off the wall and entered the dim lounge that led to one of the video rooms. She smiled and stopped at the lift-shaft, her lithe naked body relaxing for a moment. She waited, scanning the tumble of furniture and panels in the lounge, then dived full speed at a thin grey form bouncing from one panel to another. She caught him in mid-flight as they tumbled through the door into a video room.

Their play had risen to ecstasy, the dim lights of the video room adding to their games. They were coupled. Her face flushed with pleasure until it was almost the color of her hair. Her body arched back . . .

"RED! GEORGE!!" Imps shouted in their ears. "STOP!!!"

"Goddammit James!" George exploded with fury. "Can't you stay out . . ." He grabbed the handful of brittle sticks from their perch on his naked shoulder and flung them at the far wall. The mangled twigs and wires hummed to a halt about a meter from his hand and buzzed back—heading toward Elizabeth.

George looked quickly around and watched his small wisp of imp merge into the imp on Red's face, a face gasping for breath and wide-eyed with agony. He turned at another sound, a deep thrumming in the air. A thicket of sticks and twigs hit the two of them amidships and thrust him aside. The fuzzy arms attempted to press life into the curvaceous chest, while a dense cluster of cilia pumped a stream of air into her lax mouth. The Christmas Bush worked on Red for a number of minutes; then the automatic motion finally stopped. Not abruptly, not slowly, but like some automaton given both stop and start signals at the same time.

"Elizabeth is dead, George," said the bush. "It was a cerebral aneurysm."

"Oh," said George. "Thanks for trying."

"Are you OK?" said James, a large chunk of bush breaking loose from the floating nude to hover at a distance from him.

"I'm fine, James," he said. "Just take care of her, will you?" He went off to cry in a quiet place, his imp reforming unobtrusively on his shoulder as he left.

James waited patiently. George's grief eventually shed itself in a floating stream of sparkling spheres. George's imp tenderly flicked each tear from around his red-rimmed eyes, launching them toward the nearby air intakes. There remained a deep emptiness, a void that would only be filled by the wash of tears from intermittent floods of emotional catharsis that would return again and again. The deaths of the others had been hard, but there had always been someone to share the grief with. This loss he would bear alone.

When George finally finished his crying, he found himself in the starside science dome, lying back in the control chair and looking outward at the distant yellow star studding the end of Orion's belt.

Deciding to get all the misery out of his system at one time, he had deliberately worked up a good case of homesickness to add to his loneliness. He had cried himself out. Getting up calmly now, he floated away as the chair folded itself into its niche in the wall. He called for the elevator to take him to the control deck.

"I'd like to read a few words before you put her in cold storage, James," he said to his imp.

"Red left some last wishes with me—as a verbal will," said James. "She didn't want her body to stay on board *Prometheus* with the others—even if there was a chance that someday it could be returned to Earth. She has no family or friends there. She felt more at home around this strange red star and wants to be buried here."

"A sailor of the skies, her body cast into the deep," mused George. "OK. I'll look up a sea captain's farewell."

"It's going to be more complicated than that, George. She wants to be cremated in Barnard."

"We can't do that. If we put her out a port, she'll go into orbit," said George. "Wait! I forgot what kind of ship we're in."

"Shall I decelerate and assume a hovering orbit?"

"Yes," said George. "How long will it take?"

"Two weeks. Less if you don't mind feeling a few percent of gee."

"Sure! I can take the gees!" grumbled George. "I may be old, but I'm not decrepit—you obsolete hunk of frayed wires and diffusing silicon. What'll we do with Red in the meantime? Put her in cold storage with the others?"

"Yes, we'll have to," replied James. "But before that, I'll have to make some preparations. She gave explicit instructions on what she was to wear and how her hair and makeup were to be done. The Christmas Bush is working on that now, up in the sick bay."

"I want to help," said George, pushing himself clumsily along the floor to the lift shaft as the computer began to tilt the 300-kilometer diameter sail to slow its orbit about the star.

"Are you sure??" asked James, with a concerned overtone in its voice. "I am perfectly capable of handling the whole thing myself."

"Yes!" said George gruffly, and pulled himself laboriously up the shaft.

James let George brush, comb, and arrange Red's hair, but insisted on doing the makeup itself.

As they were finishing, one limb of the bush appeared with a set of green satin clothing and a long pair of alligator hide boots.

"Where'd those boots come from?" said George in surprise.

"She brought them on board as part of her personal baggage allotment," James replied. "She was planning to wear them for parties, but she forgot that her ankles swell in free-fall. After trying to get them on a few times, she gave up and shoved them in the back of her locker. Her last instructions about them were very explicit. I recorded them:

" 'I want those boots on when I got out the port. And don't you DARE stretch them.' "

Red's voice came from the bush as the computer replayed the exact sequence of bits which it had recorded in that long-ago conversation.

George winced when he heard Red's hauntingly beautiful contralto. "Please don't ever do that again," he said.

A few minutes of firm pressure on her lower legs by the massive paws of the bush allowed the green leather to slide over the sheer green stockings. There was even plenty of room to tuck in the legs of the green satin slacks.

"She looks fine," George said. "Now take her away before I get all soppy and smear her makeup."

The bush picked up the stiffening body and headed for the lift shaft as George, floating slowly downward from the ceiling, watched them go.

As the days passed, the huge sail tilted, then tilted back again. George noticed that the maneuver took almost two weeks, and that after the first day the acceleration had subtly changed from its earlier high level. He couldn't blame James for trying to take care of an 87-year-old man and let the computer get away with trying to fool him. Finally, the ship was hovering over the star. The bright glare from a red globe more than twice as big as the sun shot straight up through the bottom science dome and illuminated the ceiling of the control deck around the hole for the lift-shaft. The ship was slowly drifting downward, for the star's gravity was slightly stronger than the push of the light on the sail.

George had been looking through the library for a suitable obituary for Red. He had skimmed through the Bible and the prayer books of three religions but hadn't found anything that really suited. Then he remembered a phrase. It was simple and short, and spoke of their last years together in this machine/home/prison/tomb. He couldn't recall the exact words or the author, however, and it took him nearly four hours to track it down with the help of James' library program. He finally found it, then realized why his brain had refused to come up with the source. It was in the humor section. The author was Mark Twain.

George followed the bush in the 2% gravity as it put the stiff body of the beautiful red-haired woman into the airlock and closed the inner door. The Christmas Bush waited, its colored lights blinking, while George read in a husky voice the carefully copied words from a slip of paper.

"Wheresoever she was, *there* was Eden."

James, overriding the airlock controls, activated the outer door with the lock still pressurized. The rush of air twirled the body out the hatch.

Twenty-four hours and fifty-eight minutes later, the energy in a green-clad figure and a misplaced alligator from earth became a burst of photons bathing the farthest reaches of the universe with a momentary flash of luminescence.

Two years later George picked up the beacon signal from the incoming space vehicle. A large antimatter-powered rocket, it had left the solar system thirteen years ago. Accelerating at 30% of earth gravity it had reached its cruise speed of half the speed of light in only 1.6 years. After coasting for a decade it had turned around and started to brake. It was decelerating rapidly as it neared Barnard but it still had a year of thrusting to go before it stopped. This follow-on mission to Barnard contained a large crew of specialized exploration robots and a small contingent of humans. George's first communication sessions with them were brief, for a round-trip message time of 115 days made it difficult to engage in brilliant discourse. Besides, both of them were busy collecting data.

George now had *Prometheus* in a slow spiral about the north pole of Barnard, mapping it from the polar regions outward. As the year passed and the rocket ship of the follow-on expedition drew closer, George visited the communicator more often. When they were a month of travel time away, the round-trip communication time became about 24 hours and he enjoyed a short conversation each morning at breakfast. It was about this time that he was able to use the science telescope to pick up the faint speck of the blazing exhaust from the braking rocket as it entered the outskirts of the Barnard system. A few weeks later, when the time-delay was only an hour, George suddenly realized that he was going to have visitors and the place was a mess. He cancelled the science plan, put the Christmas Bush to "cleaning up" and began to prepare for company.

The huge interstellar exploration ship dropped into an orbit about Barnard, not too far from Rocheworld. A smaller ship would come to visit him, while the rest of the expedition would start on the exploration tasks that were ahead.

The small sleek ship came smoothly in under the giant sail of *Prometheus* on a nearly invisible jet of antimatter-energized hydrogen. George watched them approach from the bottom science dome, then floated over to the EVA console and readied the air lock.

The first to cycle through was one of the new general-purpose plasticoids. Built along the same lines as a human, they could replace a human at any station. They, of course, did not need spacesuits.

The robot exited the lock. It looked carefully around, then fixed its eyes on the human. George noticed a gold caduceus on the breastplate of the shiny black plasticoid. Probably a medic of some sort. There was a dramatic increase in the light display on the Christmas Bush, and George realized that James and the robot were trading information. The robot drifted toward him, propelled by a precision flick of its foot on the air-lock hatchway. It spoke in a deep baritone voice.

"I have received a report on your state of health from the ship's computer, but I would like to calibrate my medical sensors if I may." It drifted to a halt just an arm-length away.

"Sure," said George. The robot placed its right hand on the side of his neck, its thumb resting on his jugular. As the hand approached, he could see each finger was a complex maze of tiny sensors. He was surprised to feel that the hand was warm, despite its cold-looking appearance.

"Nice bedside manner," thought George as he felt an ultrasonic hum pass through his body. At the same time a tiny section of the robot's chest plate was emitting a multicolored display of lights that explored the front portion of his body. After a second, the robot moved both its hands to place them at opposite sides of George's head, then dropped them at its side.

"Thank you," it said, then backed away.

George cycled the lock to let the next visitor in, and a spacesuited figure stepped through. The plasticoid was very efficient and soon the suit was off the human. The bush took it off to the locker and hung it up.

"Hello, there," said George with a twisted smile. "Welcome to Barnard."

The visitor looked at the ancient astronaut. George was dressed in a neatly pressed coverall, but that couldn't hide the angular structure of a computer-controlled exo-skeleton activating his arm and leg on the left side. The visitor estimated it must have required about one-third of the Christmas Bush. As he looked, his computer implant fed him the background information that it had picked up from James and the recent examination by the medic. George had had a massive stroke just eighteen months ago and barely survived to greet them. He was getting better, however, and seemed to have a good many years left in him.

"Hello, George," said the young man. "I bear a proclamation from the President and Congress of the Greater United States and a personal message from my great-grandfather."

"Your great-grandfather?" asked George in bewilderment.

"I am cursed with the jawbreaking name of Beauregard Darlington Winthrop the Sixth," the young man replied with a faint smile. "But just call me 'Win.' My great-grandfather was General Winthrop, one of your old friends in the Air Force."

George's face clouded up. "General Winthrop?" he said. "What was his message?"

"I don't know," said Win. "It's here in this envelope." He handed over a yellowing ancient envelope with the embossed imprint of Senator Beauregard Darlington Winthrop III in the upper left corner. George tore the envelope open and pulled out a piece of Senate office stationary. There in fading black ink was a short note.

"You win, you goddamn showoff. I hope you choke on your goddamn star." There was no signature.

George smiled quietly, folded the letter carefully—his motile-assisted left arm acting in near-perfect coordination with his good right one—and put it into his breast pocket. There was no need for this puppy-dog of a young man to know the contents of the message.

"What did it say?" asked Win, eager to know the

family secret. As a child he had become fascinated with the time-spanning history of the piece of paper and had worked until he was chosen for the follow-on mission to Barnard so he could deliver it personally.

"He mentioned a star," said George.

"Oh, yes!" said Win. He reached into another pocket and pulled out a small box.

"In recognition of your services to the country," he parroted. "The Congress of the Greater United States hereby promotes you to the rank of Brigadier General of the Air Force." He handed him the box and George opened it. He took out one of the silver stars inside, snapped the box shut and looked at it contemplatively.

He hobbled over to one of the viewing ports in the side of the command deck and stared out at the dull red ball off to one side. He turned to face the human and the two robots and said, "James, send the Christmas Bush over here next to me."

The computer obeyed and soon the scraggly motile was floating in front of him. He reached up and stuck the shining silver star into the branches at the apex of the bush, where the cilia automatically gripped it. George leaned back against the viewport and looked at the greenly-glowing Christmas Bush, its colored lights blinking on and off in its never-ending communication with the main computer. On top there was a five-pointed silver star reflecting the reddish rays from Barnard.

"I think you're the one that deserves a General's star, James, so why don't you keep this one." Stiffly, he turned his back on the group and looked out the window at the dull red globe that was six light years away from the home to which he would never return.

"I already have my star."

Hearing

before the

SUBCOMMITTEE ON

SPACE, COMMUNICATION, POWER, AND
EXTRATERRESTRIAL MINING

of the

COMMITTEE ON

SCIENCE AND TECHNOLOGY

G.U.S. HOUSE OF REPRESENTATIVES

One-Hundred-Forty-Fourth Congress

second session

January 14, 15, 2076

BARNARD STAR EXPEDITION
Tuesday, January 14, 2076

G.U.S. House of Representatives,
Committee on Science and Technology
   Subcommittee on Space, Communication,
     Power, and Extraterrestrial Mining
      Washington, D.C.

The subcommittee met, pursuant to notice, in room 2318, Rayburn House Office Building, 9:37 a.m., the Chairman of the subcommittee, the Hon. John Ootah, State of Saskatchewan, presiding.

Mr. Ootah. The subcommittee will be in order. Without objection, permission will be granted for radio, video, and holophotography to be taken during the course of the hearing.

During the next two days, the subcommittee will review the reports recently received from the brave crew of interstellar explorers visiting the Barnard system nearly six lightyears distant—the first ambassadors of the Greater United States to worlds across the great void of interstellar space.

Our first witness this morning is Dr. Morris Philipson, Professor of Astronomy at Cornell University, who will brief us about Barnard and its unusual planetary system. Then the Honorable Frederick Ross, Chief Administrator for the Greater National Aeronautics and Space Administration, will describe the mission and the vehicles used in carrying it out. Dr. Joel Winners, GNASA Associate Administrator for Space Sciences, will be our final witness for this morning, telling us about what the expedition found in the star system—another race of intelligent beings, creatures so alien in their life-forms and culture that they are almost beyond imagining.

We will ask the witnesses to present their testimony

first. Then we will have questions after all the testimony is completed.

The House is going into session at eleven o'clock. There will be a series of votes, then a lengthy recess which will allow adequate time for more testimony. We hope in this process the delays in the testimony will be held to a minimum.

Dr. Philipson, if you will proceed?

Dr. Philipson. Mr. Chairman and members of the Subcommittee on Space, Communication, Power, and Extraterrestrial Mining, I appreciate this opportunity to testify before you on the Barnard system. I have a few holoslides that I would like to project during my testimony.

Mr. Ootah. Would the Guardian of the Committee Room Door please ask the room robots to dim the lights? Thank you. You may proceed, Dr. Philipson.

Dr. Philipson. Thank you, Mr. Chairman. I will read from a personally proofed printout. With your permission, we can relieve the clerk from having to transcribe manually the robotic record and just insert the printout into the committee robotic reader.

Mr. Ootah. That will be fine, Dr. Philipson.

STATEMENT OF DR. PHILIPSON

Barnard

In 1916, the American astronomer Edward E. Barnard measured the proper motion of a dim red star cataloged as +4 deg 3561 and found it was moving through the sky at the amazing speed of 10.3 seconds of arc per year, or more than half the diameter of the moon in a century. Barnard's star (or Barnard as it is known now) is very close to the solar system, only 5.9 lightyears away, but is so small and dim that it takes a telescope to see it.

The cold statistics for Barnard are given in the table:

BARNARD STAR DATA

Distance: 5.9 ly
 Right Ascension: 17 hr 55 min
Declination: 4 deg 33 min
Equatorial system coordinates: X = + −0.1 ly, Y + −5.9 ly,
    Z = +0.5 ly
Spectral type: M5
Effective Temperature: 0.58 solar temperature (3330 K)
Luminosity: 0.0005 solar luminosity (visual)
    0.0037 solar luminosity (thermal)
Visual Magnitude: 9.54
Mass: 0.15 solar mass
Radius: 0.12 solar radius
Proper Motion: 10.31 arcsec/yr
Radial Velocity: − 108 kilometer/sec

Barnard Star Planetary System

  The planetary system around Barnard is dominated by a gigantic planet, aptly named Gargantua. A huge gas giant like our Jupiter, Gargantua is four times more massive than Jupiter. This is remarkable enough in itself, but since the parent star, Barnard, has a mass of only fifteen percent that of our sun, this means that the planet Gargantua is one-fortieth the mass of its star. If Gargantua had been slightly more massive, it too would have turned into a star, and the Barnard system would have been a binary star system.

  Gargantua seems to have swept up into itself most of the original stellar nebula that was not used in making the star, for there are no other large planets in the system. Gargantua has four satellites that would be planets in our solar system, plus a multitude of smaller moons. These planets will be the subject of further exploration by the crew of the Barnard mission. Today, however, we will be concentrating on the first world (or worlds) that they landed on—Rocheworld.

The double-planet Rocheworld is in a highly elliptical orbit in the inner part of the Barnard system. This can be seen in Figure 1. Every third orbit, Rocheworld passes within six million kilometers of Gargantua, just outside the orbits of Gargantua's moons. It is believed that the present orbit was established many million years ago by the encounter of a stray planetoid with what was once a larger outer moon of Gargantua.

Orbits such as that of Rocheworld are usually not stable. The three-to-one resonance condition usually results in an oscillation of the orbit of the smaller body that builds up in amplitude until the smaller planet is thrown into a different orbit or a collision occurs. Due to Rocheworld's close approach to Barnard, however, the tides from Barnard cause a significant amount of dissipation, which stabilizes the orbit. This also supplies a great deal of heating which keeps Rocheworld warmer than it would normally be if the heating were due to the light and heat from Barnard alone.

Rocheworld

Rocheworld is a dumbbell-shaped planet. It consists of two Titan-sized rocky bodies that whirl about each other with a rotation period of six hours. The two bodies are so close together that they are almost touching, but their spin speed is high enough that they maintain a separation of about eighty kilometers. If each were not distorted by the other's gravity, the two planets would have been spheres about the size of our moon. Since their gravitational tides act upon one another, the two bodies have been stretched out until they are elongated egg-shapes, 3560 kilometers in the long dimension and 3000 kilometers in cross section. Although the two planets do not touch each other, they do share a common

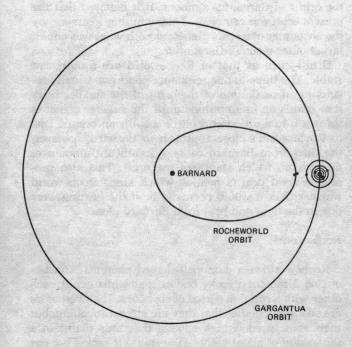

Figure 1—Barnard Planetary System

atmosphere. The resulting figure-eight configuration is called a Roche-lobe pattern after E. W. Roche, a French mathematician of the later 1800s, who calculated the effects of gravity tides on stars, planets, and moons. The word "roche" means "rock" in French, so the rocky lobe of the pair of planetoids was given the name Roche, while the water-covered lobe was named Eau after the French word for "water."

The average gravity at the surface of these moonlets is about ten percent of earth gravity, slightly less than that of earth's moon because of their lower density. This average value varies considerably depending upon your position on the surface of the elongated lobes. The gravity at one of the outward-facing poles is 8.3 percent of earth gravity, rising to 11.1 percent in a belt that includes the north and south spin poles of each lobe, increases slightly to a maximum of 11.4 percent at a region some thirty degrees inward, then drops precipitously to 0.5 percent at the inner-pole surface, some forty kilometers below the zero-gravity point overhead where the gravity from the mass of the two lobes cancels out.

The Roche lobe is slightly less dense than the Eau lobe, thus is larger in diameter. It has a number of ancient craters upon its surface, especially in the outer-facing hemisphere. Although the Eau lobe masses almost as much as the Roche lobe, it has a core that is denser. Since its highest point is some twenty kilometers lower in the combined gravitational well, it is the "lowlands" while the Roche lobe is the "highlands." Eau gets most of the rain that falls from the common atmosphere and thus has captured nearly all the liquids of the double planet to form one large ocean. The ocean is primarily ammonia water, with trace amounts of hydrogen sulfide and cyanide gas.

When Rocheworld is out at its farthest distance from the star, it whirls about with the two lobes remaining

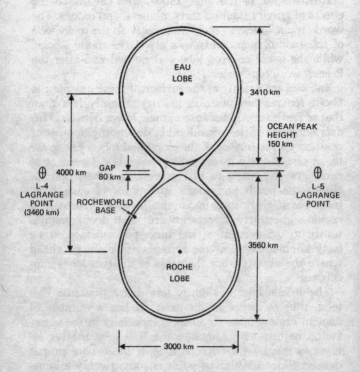

EAU
LOBE

3410 km

OCEAN PEAK
HEIGHT
150 km

4000 km

GAP
80 km

⊕
L-4
LAGRANGE
POINT
(3460 km)

⊕
L-5
LAGRANGE
POINT

ROCHEWORLD
BASE

3560 km

ROCHE
LOBE

3000 km

Figure 2—Rocheworld

unchanged in shape as is shown in Figure 2. The Roche lobe is dry and rocky, with traces of quiescent volcano vents near its pointed pole, while the Eau lobe has a pointed section like the Roche lobe, but the point is not made of rock. The peak is made of ammonia water, a conical mountain a hundred and fifty kilometers high. The slope of the ocean sides are sixty degrees. Although the ocean mountain is high, higher than any rock mountain on earth, there is still plenty of room between the two planetoids, almost eighty kilometers.

On each side of the double planet are the L-4 and L-5 points where there is a minimum in the combined gravitational and centrifugal forces of the system. For the earth-moon system, these are at ±60 degrees from the moon in the moon's orbit. In this system where the two main bodies are the same size, the minimum gravity points are at ±90 degrees. The exploration crew established communication satellites at these two points.

When Rocheworld is at its farthest distance from Barnard, everything is serene on the double planet. The two lobes whirl about each other and the gravity from the star causes modest tides in the ocean on Eau.

As Rocheworld begins to approach Barnard in its ellpitical orbit, the effect of the tides from the dwarf star begins to become significant. The peak of the water mountain now begins to rise and fall a number of kilometers, with the pattern repeated each half-rotation.

At a point halfway between the two planetoids, the gravity drops to zero. If the water mountain reaches that zero-gravity point, then it can fall away from that point toward either planet. As the spinning double planet approaches periapsis, the gravity tidal effects from the star begin to dominate the behavior of the atmosphere and oceans on the planets.

In Figure 3, when Barnard is to one side of Rocheworld, the two lobes separate by thirty kilometers. This causes the mountain of water to drop one hundred kilometers.

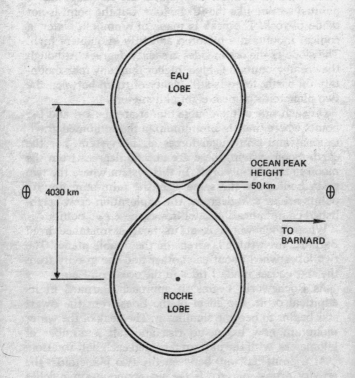

EAU
LOBE

4030 km

OCEAN PEAK
HEIGHT

50 km

TO
BARNARD

ROCHE
LOBE

Figure 3—Tides during first quarter–rotation at periapsis

[Dr. Philipson interrupted his prepared text at this point to interject a comment.]

Dr. Philipson. By the way. This behavior is not what would be predicted by a naive model of the gravity forces. I myself would have thought that with Barnard off to the side, the gravity tidal forces from Barnard would have drawn the lobes closer together, not farther apart. I also would have expected the change in the height of the mountain of water to be about the same as the change in the separation. But recent detailed computer studies here on earth that take into account the coupling of the angular rotation and the orbital motion with the planetary dynamics confirm what Captain Thomas St. Thomas calculated at the time, and they both agree with what really happened on Rocheworld six years ago when we nearly lost the first landing party.

[The record returns to the prepared text.]

Then just a quarter-rotation later, the tidal forces go the other way. Although the decrease in spacing of the two lobes is only seven kilometers, the effects are so nonlinear that, as is shown in Figure 4, the mountain of water that has built up on the Eau lobe reaches up forty kilometers to the zero-gravity point midway between the two planetoids—and beyond. The crest of the mountain drops as a rapidly accelerating, fragmenting waterfall on the hot dry rocks of the Roche lobe forty kilometers below. For the next two half-turns of the double planet, the showers of water repeat, and the torrent from the astral waterfall douses the volcanoes on the disturbed surface in a drenching torrent. Rapidly moving streams of water form on the slopes of drowned volcanoes, that merge with other streams to become giant raging rivers, streaking out across the dry highlands of Roche.

Mr. Ootah. Thank you very much, Dr. Philipson. That's

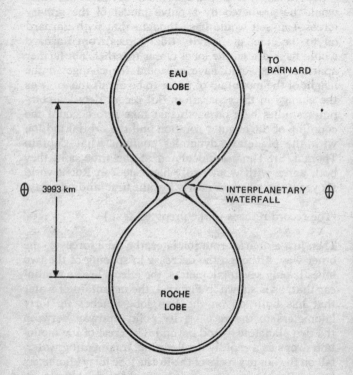

Figure 4—Tides during second quarter–rotation at periapsis

quite a spectacular planetary system there. If your schedule permits, we will proceed with the other witnesses and then have the questions and answers.

The next witness will be the Honorable Frederick Ross, Chief Administrator for the Greater National Aeronautics and Space Administration. We want to welcome you here and congratulate you for one of GNASA's most successful missions.

Mr. Ross. Thank you very much, Mr. Chairman, and members of the committee. I hope you remember your congratulations when you are working on our budget for the coming year. [*Laughter.*]

Mr. Ootah. We most certainly will, Administrator. I personally will recommend a major new start to send a follow-on expedition to open up direct communication with the Rocheworld aliens.

Mr. Ross. Thank you, Mr. Chairman. I will be glad to work with you on the details of the bill.

Now, having been in office only five years, I can take credit for only one-tenth of this fifty-year-long mission. Actually, all the credit should go to my distant predecessor, Dr. Harold Mosher. It was he who initiated the plans to send a manned expedition to Barnard after the returns came in from the unmanned flyby probes in 2022.

The vehicles used on the Barnard expedition were unusual because of the unusual nature of the target. I will go through their structure and function in some detail in my printout.

STATEMENT OF THE HONORABLE
FREDERICK ROSS

Barnard Star Laser Propulsion System

The payload sent to the Barnard system consisted of the crew of 16 persons and their consumables, totaling about 300 metric tons; four landing rockets for the various planets and moons at 500 tons each; four nuclear-powered VTOL exploration aerospace planes at 80 tons each; and the interstellar h bitat for the crew that made up the remainder of the 3500 tons that needed to be transported to the star system.

This payload was carried by a large lightsail 300 kilometers in diameter. The sail was of very light construction, a thin film of finely perforated metal stretched over a lightweight frame. Although the sail averaged only one-tenth of a gram per square meter of area, the total mass of the sail and payload was over 7000 tons. The 300-kilometer payload sail was surrounded by a larger ring sail, 1000 kilometers in diameter, with a hole in the center where the payload sail was attached during launch from the solar system. The ring sail had a total mass of 72,000 tons, giving a total launch weight for the sails and the payload of over 82,000 tons.

The laser power needed to accelerate the 82,000-ton interstellar vehicle at 1 percent of earth gravity was 1300 terawatts. As is shown in Figure 5, this was obtained from an array of 1000 laser generators orbiting around Mercury. Each laser generator used a 30-kilometer lightweight reflector that intercepted 6.5 terawatts of sunlight and reflected into the solar-pumped laser the 1.5 terawatts of light that was at the right wavelength for the laser to use.

When fed the right pumping light, the lasers were quite efficient and produced 1.3 terawatts of laser light at an infrared wavelength of 1.5 microns. The output aperture of the lasers was 100 meters in diameter, so the flux that the mirrors had to handle was only about 12 suns. The lasers and their sails were in sun-synchronous orbit around Mercury to keep them from being moved about by the light pressure from the intercepted sunlight and the transmitted laser beam. The 1000 beams from the laser were transmitted out to the L-2 point of

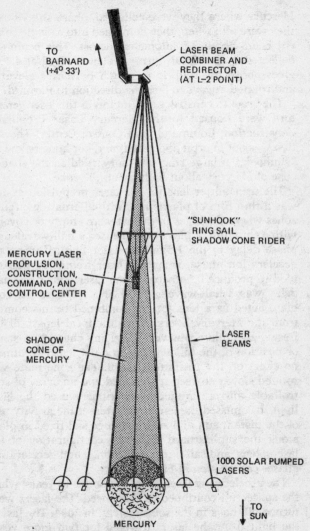

TO
BARNARD
(+4° 33')

LASER BEAM
COMBINER AND
REDIRECTOR
(AT L-2 POINT)

"SUNHOOK"
RING SAIL
SHADOW CONE RIDER

MERCURY LASER
PROPULSION,
CONSTRUCTION,
COMMAND, AND
CONTROL CENTER

LASER
BEAMS

SHADOW
CONE OF
MERCURY

1000 SOLAR PUMPED
LASERS

TO
SUN

MERCURY

Figure 5—Mercury Laser System

Mercury where they were collected, phase shifted until they were all in step, then combined into a single coherent beam about 3.5 kilometers across. This beam was deflected from a final mirror that was tilted at 4.5 degrees above the ecliptic to match Barnard's elevation and rotated always to face the direction to Barnard.

The crew to construct and maintain the laser generators were housed in the Mercury Laser Propulsion Construction, Command, and Control Center. The station was not in orbit about Mercury, but hung below the "sunhook," a large ring sail that straddled the shadow cone of Mercury about halfway up the cone.

The transmitter lens for the laser propulsion system was a thin film of plastic net, with alternating circular zones where the holes in the net were empty or covered with a thin film of plastic that caused a half-wavelength phase delay in the 1.5-micron laser light. (During the deceleration phase, when the laser frequency was tripled to produce 0.5-micron green laser light, the phase delay was 3 half-wavelengths.) This huge fresnel zone plate acted as a lens for the combined beams coming from the Mercury lasers. Since the focal length of the fresnel zone plate was very long, any changes in shape or position of the billowing plastic net lens had almost no effect on the trasmitted beam. The zone plate was rotated slowly to keep it stretched and an array of controllable mirrors around the periphery used the laser light that missed the lens to counteract the gravity pull of the distant sun and keep the huge sail fixed in place along the sun-Barnard axis. The configuration of the lasers, lens, and sail during the launch and deceleration phases can be seen in Figure 6.

The accelerating lasers were left on for 18 years, while the spacecraft continued to gain speed. The lasers were turned off, back in the solar system, in 2044. The last of the light from the lasers traveled for two more years before it finally reached the interstellar spacecraft. Thrust

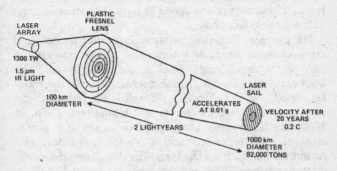

ACCELERATION PHASE

LASER ARRAY

1300 TW

1.5 μm IR LIGHT

PLASTIC FRESNEL LENS

100 km DIAMETER

2 LIGHTYEARS

LASER SAIL

ACCELERATES AT 0.01 g

1000 km DIAMETER 82,000 TONS

VELOCITY AFTER 20 YEARS 0.2 C

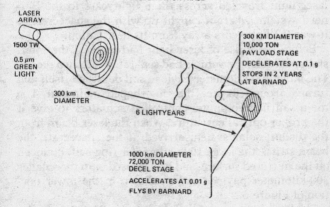

DECELERATION PHASE

LASER ARRAY

1500 TW

0.5 μm GREEN LIGHT

300 km DIAMETER

6 LIGHTYEARS

300 KM DIAMETER 10,000 TON PAYLOAD STAGE DECELERATES AT 0.1 g STOPS IN 2 YEARS AT BARNARD

1000 km DIAMETER 72,000 TON DECEL STAGE ACCELERATES AT 0.01 g FLYS BY BARNARD

Figure 6—Laser-pushed lightsail
[*J. Spacecraft*, Vol. 21, No. 2, 187–195 (1984)]

at the spacecraft stopped in 2046, just short of 20 years after launch It was now at 2 lightyears distance from the sun and 4 lightyears from Barnard, and was traveling at 20 percent of the speed of light. The mission now entered the coast phase.

For the next 20 years the spacecraft and its drugged crew coasted through interstellar space, covering a lightyear every 5 years. Back in the solar system, the laser array was used to launch another manned interstellar expedition to Lelande 21185, while the Barnard lens was increased in diameter to 300 kilometers. Then, in 2060, the laser array was turned on again at a power level of 1500 terawatts and a tripled frequency. The combined beams from the lasers filled the 300-kilometer-diameter fresnel lens and beamed out toward the distant star. After two years, the lasers were turned off and used elsewhere. The 2-light year-long pulse of high-energy laser light traveled across the 6 lightyears to the Barnard system, where it caught up with the spacecraft as it was 0.2 lightyears away from its destination.

Before the pulse of laser light had reached the interstellar vehicle, the vehicle had separated into two pieces. The inner 300-kilometer payload sail detached itself and turned around to face the ring-shaped main sail. The main sail had computer-controlled actuators to give it the proper optical curvature. When the laser beam from the distant solar system arrived at the spacecraft, the beam struck the large 1000-kilometer ring sail, bounced off the mirrored surface, and was focused onto the smaller 300-kilometer payload sail as shown in the lower portion of Figure 6.

The laser light accelerated the massive 72,000-ton main sail at 1.2 percent of earth gravity and during the two-year period increased its velocity slightly. The same laser power, however, reflecting back on the much lighter payload sail, decelerated the smaller sail carrying the exploration crew at nearly 10 percent of earth gravity.

In the two years that the laser beam was on, the payload sail slowed from its interstellar velocity of 20 percent of the speed of light and came to rest in the Barnard system. Meanwhile, the main sail sped on into deep space, its job done.

Prometheus

The interstellar spacecraft that took the exploration crew to the Barnard system was called *Prometheus*, the bringer of light. Its configuration is shown in Figure 7. From a distance it would be difficult to see the vehicle in the vast expanse of shining sail.

A major fraction of the spacecraft volume was taken up by four exploration units. They consisted of a planetary lander called the Surface Lander and Ascent Module (SLAM), each holding within itself a winged Surface Excursion Module (SEM). Each SLAM rocket is 46 meters long and 6 meters in diameter, and masses 600 tons, including the SEM.

Running all the way through the center of *Prometheus* is a 4-meter-diameter, 60-meter-long shaft with a lift platform. Capping the top of *Prometheus* on the side toward Barnard is a huge, double-decked compartmented area that holds the various consumables that will be used in the 50-year mission as well as the workshop for the spaceship's computer motile. At the very center of starside is a small port with a thick glass dome that is used by the star-science instruments to investigate the star system they are moving toward. There is enough room for one or two people under the dome, but the radiation level is high enough that the port is mostly used by machines, not people.

At the base of *Prometheus* are five decks. These are the home for the crew. Each deck is a flat cylinder 20 meters in diameter and 3 meters thick. The bottom control deck contains the consoles that run the lightcraft, with

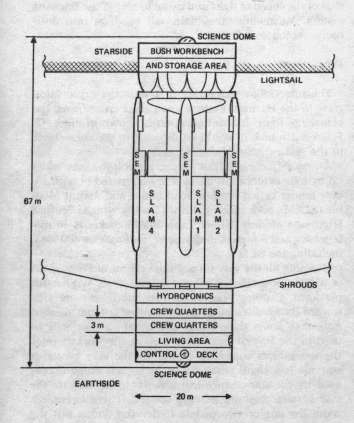

Figure 7—Prometheus

the earthside science dome at the center. The living area deck is next. This contains the communal dining room, lounge, and recreational facilities. The next two decks are the crew quarters decks that are fitted out with individual living quarters for the 16 crew members. Above that is the hydroponics deck with four air locks that allow access to the four SLAM spacecraft.

The Christmas Bush

The hands and eyes of the computers that ran the vehicles on the expedition were embodied in the "Christmas Bush," a repair and maintenance motile so-called because of the twinkling laser lights on the bushy multibranched structure. The bushlike shape for the robot has a parallel in the forms of earth. The first form of life on earth was a worm. The sticklike shape was poorly adapted for manipulation or even locomotion. These sticklike animals then grew smaller sticks, called legs, and the animals could walk, although they were still poor at manipulation. Then the smaller sticks grew yet smaller sticks, and hands with manipulating fingers evolved.

The Christmas Bush is a manifold extension of this idea. The motile has a six-"armed" main body that repeatedly hexfurcates into copies one-third the size of itself, finally ending up with millions of near-microscopic cilia. Each subsegment of the Christmas Bush has a small amount of intelligence, but is mostly motor and communication system. The segments communicate with each other and transmit power through their light-emitting and -detecting semi-conductor diodes. The main computer in the spacecraft is the primary controller of the motile, communicating with the various portions of the bush through color-coded laser beams. It takes a great deal of computational

tional power to operate the bush, but the built-in "reflex" intelligence in the various levels of segmentation lessens the load on the main computer.

The bush shown in Figure 8 is in its "one gee" form. Three of the "trunks" form "legs," one the "head," and two the "arms." The head portions are "bushed" out to give the detector diodes in the subbranches a three-dimensional view of the space around it. One arm ends with six "hands," demonstrating the manipulating capability of the Bush and its subportions. The other arm is in its maximally collapsed form. The six "limbs," being one-third the size of the trunk, can fit into a circle with the diameter of the trunk, while the thirty-six "branches," being one-ninth the size of the trunk, also fit into the same circle. This is true all the way down to the 60 million cilia at the lowest level.

The Christmas Bush has capabilities that go way beyond that of the human hand. The bush can stick a "hand" inside a delicate piece of equipment and, using its lasers and detectors as light source and eyes, rearrange the parts inside for a nearly instantaneous repair. The Christmas Bush also has the ability to detach portions of itself to make smaller motiles. These can walk up the walls and along the ceilings with their tiny cilia holding onto microscopic cracks in the surface. The smaller twigs on the bush are capable of very rapid motion. In free fall, these rapidly beating twigs allow the bush to propel itself through the air. Even in earth gravity, the smaller subelements can fly through the air using their cilia. The speed of motion of the cilia is rapid enough that the bush can generate sound and talk directly with the humans.

Each astronaut in the crew has a small subtree or imp that stays with him or her to act as the communication link to the main computer. Most of the crew have the tiny imp ride on their shoulder, although some of the women prefer to keep them in their hairdo. In addition to acting as the communication link to the computer,

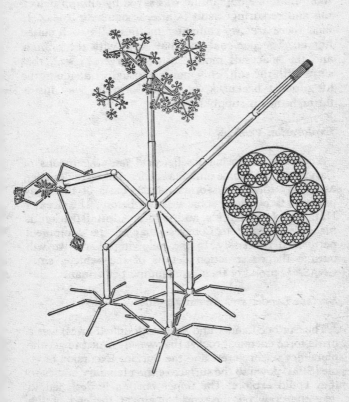

Figure 8—The Christmas Bush Motile

the imps also act as health monitors and personal servants. They are the ideal solution to the perennial problem of space suits . . . scratching an itchy nose.

The imps go into the space suit with the humans, and more than one human life was saved by an imp detecting and repairing a suit failure or patching a leak. In fact, there are two computer motiles with each suited human. The personal one that stays with the human, and the spacesuit motile, usually larger in size, that stays with the suit. This motile is usually outside in the life-support backpack, but can worm its way inside through the air-supply hose.

Exploration Vehicles

The crew exploring Rocheworld and the moons of Gargantua used some unique vehicles that were designed especially for those worlds on the basis of the flyby probe data obtained some decades before. The Greater National Astronautics and Space Administration is pleased to report to Congress that all the equipment performed flawlessly. In the following charts we will outline the construction details of the vehicle, since GNASA is proud of their outstanding performance.

Surface Lander and Ascent Module

The Surface Lander and Ascent Module (SLAM) was a brute-force chemical rocket that was designed to get the planetary science crew and the Surface Excursion Module (SEM) down to the surface of the planetary bodies so they could explore. The upper portion is designed to take the crew off the world again at the end of the expedition back to *Prometheus*. As is shown in Figure 9, the basic shape of the SLAM was a tall cylinder with four descent engines and two main tanks.

The SLAM is smaller than the first large rocket, the Saturn V. In retrospect, the tripod landing mechanism

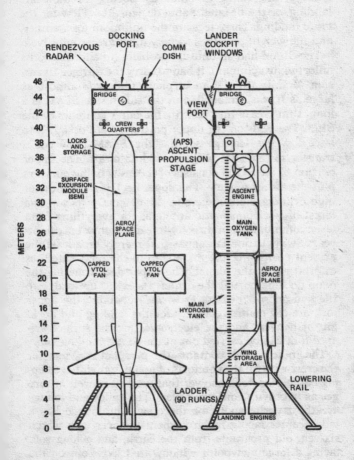

Figure 9—Surface Lander and Ascent Module (SLAM)

for the huge vehicle is not more complicated than the three-legged Surveyor designed by Hughes for the lunar landing, the Viking designed by Boeing for the Mars landing, or the ill-fated Satan designed by TRW for the Pluto landing. Three legs are the minimum for stability, and the weight penalties for any more are prohibitive.

The SLAM had an unusual problem (in addition to its unfortunate acronym). It had to carry the Surface Excursion Module (SEM), an airplane that was almost as large as it was. Embedded in the side of the SLAM is a long, slim crease that just fits the outer contours of the SEM. The seals on the upper portions were designed to have low gas leakage so that the SLAM crew could transfer to the SEM with minor loss of air. The upper portion of the SLAM consists of the crew living quarters plus the ascent module. The upper deck is a three-meter high cylinder eight meters in diameter. On its top is a forest of electromagnetic antennas for everything from laser communication directly to earth (almost six light-years away) to omniantennas that merely broadcast the present position of the main ship to the relay satellites in orbit about the planet. The upper deck contains the main docking port at the center. Its exit is upward, into the hydroponics deck of *Prometheus*. Around the upper lock are the control consoles for the landing and docking maneuvers and the electronics for the surface science that can be carried out at the SLAM landing site.

The middle deck contains the personal quarters for the crew with all the comforts of home. Individual sleeping cubicles, a good shower that worked as well in zero gee as in gravity, and two toilets. The galley and lounge are the favorite spots for the crew. The lounge has a video center facing inward where the crew can watch six-year-old programs from the earth, and a long sofa facing a large viewpoint window that looks out on the alien scenery from a height of about forty meters.

The lower deck of the SLAM is all work. Most of the space is given to suit or equipment storage and a complex air lock. One of the air-lock exits leads to the upper end of the Jacob's ladder. The other leads to the boarding port for the SEM.

Since the primary purpose of the SLAM is to put the SEM on the surface of the double planet, some of the other characteristics of the lander are not optimized for crew convenience. The best instance is the Jacob's ladder, a long, widely spaced set of rungs that start on one landing leg of the SLAM and work their way up the side of the cylindrical structure to the lower exit lock door. The Jacob's ladder was never meant to be used, since the crew expected to be able to use the powered hoist from the top of the ship. However, it is a sure, though slow, route up into the ship if everything else fails.

One leg of the SLAM was designed to be part of the Jacob's ladder, while another leg was designated to act as the dry-dock and launching rail for the SEM. Firmly attached to the main frame of the SLAM, the lowering rail served as the latch for the SEM during flight, and the lowering skids after landing. The wings of the Surface Excursion Module are chopped off in midspan just after the VTOL fans. The remainder of the wing is stacked in interleaved sections on either side of the tail section of the SEM. Once its wings have been attached, the SEM is a completely independent vehicle with its own propulsion and life-support system.

Surface Excursion Module

The Surface Excursion Module is a specially designed spacecraft capable of flying as a plane in a planetary atmosphere or as a rocket for short hops through empty space. An exterior view of the aerospace plane is shown in Figure 10. The exploration crew christened the aerospace plane the *Magic Dragonfly* because of its long wings, eyelike scanner ports at the front, and its ability to hover.

The *Dragonfly* was ideal for the conditions on Roche-

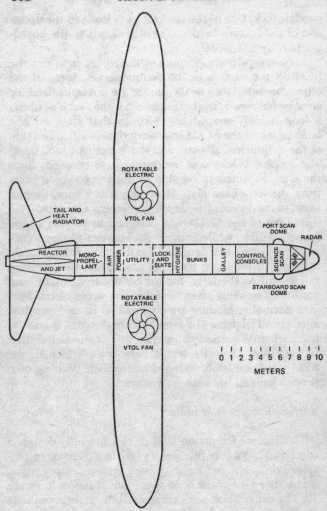

Figure 10—Surface Excursion Module
(SEM)—Exterior view

world. For flying long distances in the rarefied nonoxidizing atmosphere, the propulsion comes from heating of the atmosphere with a nuclear reactor operating a jet-bypass turbine. For short hops outside the atmosphere, the engine draws upon a tank of monopropellant that not only provides reaction mass for the nuclear reactor to work on, but also makes its own contribution to the rocket plenum pressure and temperature.

A naked nuclear reactor is a significant radiation hazard, but the one in the aerospace plane is well designed. Its outer core was covered with a thick layer of thermoelectric generators that turn the heat coming through the casing into the electrical power needed to operate the computers and scientific instruments aboard the plane. A number of metric tons of shielding protected the crew quarters, but the real protection was in the system design that had the entire power and propulsion complex at the rear of the plane, far from the crew quarters. Since the source of the plane's power (and heat) was in the aft end, it was logical to use horizontal and vertical stabilizer surfaces in the tail section as heat radiators. Because most of the weight (the reactor shielding and fuel) was at the rear of the plane, the center of mass and the placement of the wings were back from the wing position on a normal airplane of its size.

Dragonfly was more insect than plane. Although it could travel through space without any atmosphere and could fly through the atmosphere at nearly sonic speeds, the attribute that made it indispensable in the surface exploration work were the large, electrically powered vertical takeoff and landing or VTOL fans built into its wings. These fans take over at low speeds from the more efficient jet and can safely lower *Dragonfly* to the surface. The details of the human-inhabited portion of the *Magic Dragonfly* are shown in Figure 11.

Mr. Ross. Well, those are the vehicles that the exploration crew used to travel to and in the Barnard system. It's now time to hear about what they found there. For that, I would like to utilize the scientific expertise of my capable assistant, Dr. Joel Winners. Thank you for your time, Mr. Chairman.

Mr. Ootah. Your complete statement will be part of the record, Mr. Ross. We thank you.

Our next witness is Dr. Joel Winners, Associate Administrator for Space Sciences of the Greater National Aeronautics and Space Administration. We are happy to have you. You may proceed with your statement.

Dr. Winners. Thank you, Mr. Chairman. It's with great pleasure that I bring you what may be the most exciting news since the first landing on the moon—the discovery of another race of intelligent beings. You have been learning some of the details in your daily video-news programs, but we are constantly obtaining newer information from the reports sent back by the exploration crew. In fact, some of the information you will get today was only received last night.

This is indeed an extraordinary event to be occurring during the Tricentennial Year of the Greater United States of America and the seventieth year of the Canadian Union.

I too have a printout statement for the record.

STATEMENT OF DR. JOEL WINNERS

Rocheworld Ocean

There is an ocean covering one of the two lobes of Rocheworld. The liquid is a cold mixture of ammonia and water similar to what was found inside Jupiter's moon Europa. There are no land areas of any size, so the climate is determined by the heating patterns from Barnard as modified by the shadowing effects of the Roche lobe. There is a warm "crescent" that is centered on the outer pole and reaches around the equator. This cres-

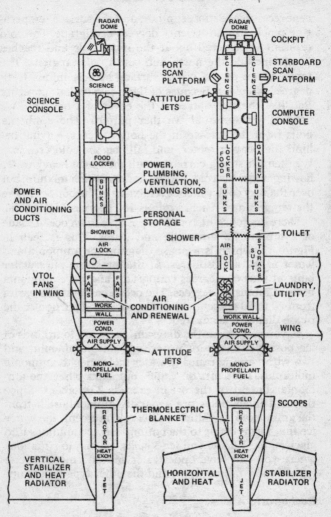

Figure 11—Surface Excursion Module
(SEM)—Interior views

cent receives the most sunlight and the surface temperature reaches minus twenty degrees centigrade. The cold crescent is centered about the inner pole and reaches out to include the north and south polar regions. The temperature of the ocean surface here is minus forty degrees or colder. Because of these two regions covering Eau like the two halves of the cover of a baseball, we have a very unusual weather pattern. The ammonia boils from the surface in the hot crescents, leaving behind the heavier water, and falls on the cold crescent. We then get strong currents, with the warm heavy water flowing under the cold, lighter, ammonia-rich mixture, but over the very cold, water-rich mixture at the bottom where the temperature reaches minus 100 degrees centigrade.

There are four different ices possible in an ocean made of a mixture of ammonia and water. This is seen in Figure 12, which is a phase diagram for ammonia and water at 0.2 atmospheres. At this pressure, pure water boils at plus 64 degrees centigrade, and pure ammonia boils at minus 61 degrees. The ocean composition varies from 20 to 80 percent ammonia, so a good portion of the phase diagram is covered.

As you can see on the diagram, there are four kinds of ice possible, one pure water, one pure ammonia, and two with varying ratios of water molecules to ammonia molecules. Ice floats on water, but sinks when the ammonia content of the ocean exceeds 23 percent. Since the cold inner poles are generally ammonia-rich from the ammonia rain falling on the cold crescent, the water ice that forms drops to the bottom and accumulates into glaciers. Ice-2 floats and Ice-3 sinks, leading to situations where you can have underwater snowstorms with one type of snow falling down and the other type falling up.

Rocheworld Aliens

The aliens on Rocheworld live in the ocean. In genetic makeup and organization they have a number of similari-

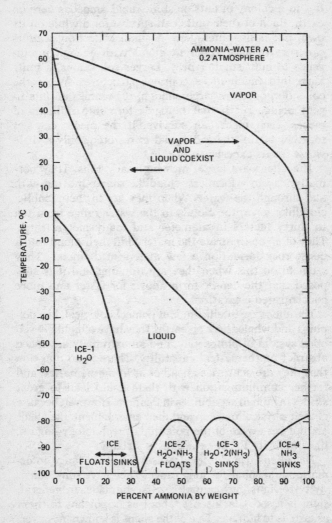

Figure 12—Phase Diagram for Ammonia—Water Mixture

ties to a colony of ants or slime-mold amoebas here on earth. Each of their units can survive for a while on its own, but is not intelligent. A small collection of units can survive as a coherent cloud with enough intelligence to hunt smaller prey. Larger collections of units form into much more complex structures. When the collection becomes large enough, it becomes an intelligent being. Yet if that being is torn into millions of pieces, each piece can survive. If the pieces can get together again, the individual is restored, only a little worse for its experience.

The aliens are large, massing many tons. They normally stay in a formless, cloudlike shape, moving with and through the water. When they are in their mobile, cloudlike form, the clouds in the water range from ten to thirty meters in diameter and many meters thick. They often concentrate the material in their cloud into a dense rock formation a few meters in diameter. They seem to do this when they are thinking and it is supposed that the denser form allows for faster and more concentrated cogitation.

The aliens are intelligent, but nontechnological, like dolphins and whales here on earth. They have a highly developed system of philosophy, and an extremely advanced abstract mathematical capability. There is no question that they are centuries ahead of us in mathematics, and further communication with them could lead to great strides in human capabilities in this area. However, because of their physical makeup and their environment, the aliens are not yet aware of the potential of technology—again, the similarity to the cetaceans is striking.

The aliens use chemical senses for short-range information and sonar for long range. They have some sensitivity to light, but cannot see like humans. In general, sight is a secondary sense, about as important to them as taste is to humans. One of the aliens is known, however, to deliberately form an imaging lens that it used to study the stars and planets in their stellar system. Called White Whistler by the humans, this individual was one of the more technologically knowledgeable of the aliens.

There are fauna on Rocheworld. They are all in the ocean and similar in chemistry, genetics, and structure to the intelligent aliens. One type are huge gray rocks that stay quiescent for long periods of time, only to suddenly explode, stunning all prey within a hundred meters and capturing them in their sticky thread nets. After absorbing their prey, they reform into multiple rocks that slowly convert the captured food into copies of themselves.

There are fauna that are birdlike creatures. They don't seem to do much except perfume the water and make twittering sonic vibrations. The aliens tolerate them as pets.

The major flora are gray and brown plants which look like sedentary rocks with controlled thick clouds about them. They send out streamers and form new bud rocks at the ends. The plants do not use photosynthesis, since the red light from Barnard is weak. Instead the whole food chain is based on the energy and minerals found around volcanic vents. We have similar isolated colonies of plants and animals around underwater vents in our own ocean depths. All life on the planet is concentrated at these few oases and the rest of the ocean is barren, without even significant numbers of bacteria or other microscopic life-forms. Because of this, the exploration crew was unaware there was anything living on the planet until the aliens made contact with them.

Reproduction for the aliens is a multiple-individual experience. The aliens do not seem to have sexes and it seems that any number from two aliens on up can produce a new individual. The usual grouping for reproduction is thought to be three or four. The explorers witnessed one such coupling put on for their benefit. In this case it involved four aliens, Loud Red, White Whistler, Green Buzzer, and Yellow Hummer. They each extended a long tendril that contained a substantial portion of their mass, estimated to be one-tenth of the mass of each parent. These tendrils, each a different color, met at the middle and intertwined with a swirling motion like colored paints being stirred together. There was a long pause as each tendril began to lose its distinctive color. We don't know exactly what happened, but obviously some chemical change was taking place that removed the strong host-origin identity from the units in the tendrils. Then finally the tendrils were snapped off, leaving the pale cloud floating in the center by itself, about 40 percent of the size of the adults that created it. After a few minutes, the mass of cells formed themselves into a new individual, which took on a light blue color that was different than any of its progenitors. The adults take it upon themselves to train the new youngster, and the group of adults and youth stay together for hunting and protection, the group again being very much like a pod of whales or porpoises.

The aliens have a complex art-form similar to acting, which involves carrying out simulations of real or imaginary happenings by forming a replica of the scene with their bodies. You can see this activity on a short segment of videotape that was transmitted back by the crew. I apologize that we have only a flatview version of the scene. The technology to produce holoprojection tapes had not yet been developed when the crew left the solar system.

[The prepared testimony was interrupted by the showing of a flatview projection tape. Copies may be viewed in the holoprojection rooms at the Library of Congress or purchased from the G.U.S. Government Printing Office, Washington, DC 20402.]

More than one actor takes part. The alien Yellow Hummer seemed to be most proficient in this art form and used it as one method of communicating with the humans. The aliens warned the explorers of the danger of the ocean transfer by simulating the Rocheworld with its seas. Two of the aliens, lighter in color, formed the rocky worlds. Another, blue in color, acted out the part of the seas. They showed how the rocky worlds whirled about each other. Then as the year passes and the elliptical orbit of the dual planet approaches periapsis, the tidal forces become stronger, and the sea on the smaller Eau lobe sloshes back and forth, gaining momentum. Then as the tidal forces become great enough, the aliens showed the humans how the seas cross the gap between the planets in a huge interplanetary waterfall that nearly engulfs the larger Roche lobe. Warned by the aliens, the humans made their dramatic escape off the Eau lobe by riding a huge wave, then gliding back through tornadoes to their ascent rocket, which took them off the planet before the tidal wave struck.

Dr. Winners. That's all the information that we have at the present time on the aliens, since the crew had to leave the planet. However, they have informed us that they will go back on a prolonged visit, this time landing their rocket in a safe place in one of the larger craters of the dry lobe, Roche, so they can stay there through a number of orbital cycles while they get to know the aliens better. They plan to leave some interstellar laser communicators and teach the aliens how to use them to communicate directly with earth, while the exploration crew goes off to visit the other worlds and moons about Barnard.

Of course, since it takes six years for messages to reach us from Barnard, that next visit has already taken place, and the laser message to us is somewhere in transit in the empty space between there and here. But, in a few years, we will be back with more news and information about what the aliens can teach us in the way of abstract thought and mathematics. We also expect that the crew will have a much better idea of the chemical and genetic makeup of this new race of beings after a year or so of study. This could have a profound effect on our understanding of the life process itself, and should produce great advances in medicine, perhaps even a life-prolonging drug without the side effects of No-Die.

Mr. Ootah. Thank you very much for your fascinating testimony. We also would like to commend the brave exploration crew who are out there gathering this information for us. They certainly will deserve a heroic welcome when they return.

Dr. Winners. The Chairman forgets. This is an interstellar mission. They will not return . . . ever.

Mr. Ootah. Oh . . . Yes. I forgot. There was a great outcry prior to the launch of this mission that we were sending these brave people on a one-way "suicide mission." Yet, as one of them said, "We all are on a one-way mission through life." These people are fortunate enough to be doing something really significant for mankind with their lives, and probably having fun doing it.

Dr. Winners. If it were possible, I would trade positions with any one of them instantly.

Mr. Ootah. I think I understand, Dr. Winners. Well, the bells are ringing on our pagers. There is a roll-call vote in progress. If you gentlemen will excuse the committee, we will make the journey through the tunnel. After lunch, we will continue with the question-and-answer session. The subcommittee will recess until one-thirty.

[Whereupon, at 11:15 a.m., the hearing was recessed.]

Casting

Major General Virginia "Jinjur" Jones—Mission Commander. 158.5 cm (don't forget that half-centimeter!) (5'2"), 60 kg (135 lb.), 42 years at start of mission. Short and solid with dark-black skin and a short, no-nonsense black pixie Afro. First in her class at the Naval Academy. Obtained a doctor of aerospace engineering from Texas University, then joined the Space Marines. The troop's nickname for General Jinjur came from the spicy female general who conquered the Emerald City of Oz.

Colonel George G. Gudunov—Second-in-Command on Mission, Copilot of *Magic Dragonfly*. 185 cm (6'1"), 110 kg (242 lb.), 51 years at start of mission. Oldest person on mission. Heavyset, ruddy complexion, with dark-brown eyes set off by black bushy eyebrows and a thatch of thick white hair. Air Force ROTC commission from University of Maryland and first in class in flight school. Worked on the Air Force Space Command Laser Forts project. In 1998, when a twenty-three-year-old captain, he suggested testing the laser fort system by using them to send probes to the nearer star systems. When a number of laser forts suffered catastrophic failures under this two-day test, he was commended by Congress but the military brass never forgave him.

Arielle Trudeau—Aerodynamicist and Pilot of *Magic Dragonfly*. 165 cm (5'5"), 50 kg (110 lb.), 35 years. Thin, delicate, beautiful, shy, fair-skinned, with short, curly blond hair and deep-brown eyes. Born and raised in Quebec, Canada, before secession of Quebec from Canada. Immigrated to the United States during the absorption of the rest of the Canadian provinces into the Greater United States of America in 2006. Learned to fly at an early age and has hundreds of hours in gliders. Obtained a Ph.D. in aerodynamics at Cal Tech and became an astronaut.

David Greystoke—Electronics and Computer Engineer. 158 cm (5'2"), 50 kg (110 lb.), 35 years. Short, thin, red-haired, quiet young man. Has perfect pitch and perfect color sense. Ph.D. in computer engineering from Harvard with a minor in music. Wrote most of the programs used on the ship computers.

Richard Redwing—Planetary Geoscientist. 195 cm (6'4"), 100+ kg (225 lb.), 34 years. Very large, very strong outdoorsman, American Indian. Mountain climber, does most peaks without oxygen equipment. Went to MIT Geophysical Institute and obtained Ph.D. in planetary physics and geophysics.

Karin Krupp—Chief Engineer. 190 cm (6'3"), 85 kg (185 lb.), 33 years. A tall, superbly built, strong, blond, tanned "California palomino," with a single long braid of thick yellow hair and blue eyes inherited from her distant Nordic ancestry. Obtained B.S. in nuclear engineering with minors in chemical and mechanical engineering from USC. With her eidetic memory, Karin knows everything about the spacecraft they fly except details of the computer software programs, where David Greystoke takes over.

Captain Thomas St. Thomas—Astrodynamicist and Lander Pilot. 188 cm (6'2"), 85 kg (187 lb), 33 years. Good-looking, clean-shaven, with Air Force trim short black hair and a light-brown skin from a Jamaican heritage. Graduate of Air Force Academy, became a

Rhodes Scholar in 2014 and obtained his Ph.D. in astrodynamics at Cambridge in England. Went into Air Force pilot training and became a heavy-lift rocket pilot in 2019.

Elizabeth "Red" Vengeance—Asteroidologist and Lander Co-Pilot. 178 cm (5'10"), 70 kg (154 lb.), 38 years. Tall, thin, with an aristocratic nose, a short, straight cap of red hair, green eyes, and the typical redhead complexion with freckles from an Irish heritage. Over 150 hours of credits in minerology from the University of Arizona but no degree. Her extensive experience as an asteroid prospector and asteoid-tug operator got her onto the Barnard expedition.

Sam Houston—Geologist. 200 cm (6'7"), 80 kg (176 lb.), 45 years. Very tall, very thin, with pale face and skin, long bones with knobby joints, gray-blue eyes and long graying hair. Does not have a doctorate, but his experience on Ceres, Vesta, Pallas, Juno, then two moons of Jupiter—Ganymede and Callisto—made him an obvious choice for the Barnard expedition.

Captain Jesús Méndez—Chief Lightsail Pilot. 168 cm (5'6"), 70 kg (155 lb.), 30 years. Small, very handsome, with a dark complexion, dark eyes, dark wavy hair, and a neat mustache. Was a cadet in the first class at the Space Academy and went directly into lightsail pilot training. Was assigned to the Space Marines Interceptor Fleet where he invented a number of new lightsail maneuvers including the "inverted twisting-loop" (the "O Jesus" to lightsail pilots).

Susan Wong—Physician and Levibiologist. 152 cm (5'0"), 39 kg (86 lb.), 41 years. Thin, frail-looking woman of Chinese extraction with an efficient bob of thin black hair, translucent pale-yellow skin, strong character, and a friendly, outgoing manner. By the age of twenty-eight, she obtained Ph.D.'s in both levibiology and organic chemistry. Spent four years at Goddard Station doing levibotany research in the huge free-fall hydroponics tanks at the Leviponics Research Facility, then went back to earth to obtain an M.D. in aerospace medicine.

Carmen Cortez—Radar and Communications Engineer. 165 cm (5'5"), 80 kg (176 lb.), 28 years. Youngest person on expedition. Chunky, very feminine Spanish señorita, with black, nearly-Afro curly hair. Obtained her B.S. in engineering from Guadalajara in 2019, then a doctor of electrical engineering magna cum laude from University of California, San Diego, in 2022. Applied for the Barnard mission upon graduation and placed third because of her age, but was able to go when the first two selectees backed out.

Nels Larson—Leviponics Specialist. (Height and weight not relevant), 33 years. Very muscular arms and barrel torso, large head with a strong jaw, blue eyes, and long yellow hair that he combs straight back. When Nels was born without legs, his parents quit their jobs on earth and moved to Goddard Station where Nels grew up. Took college courses by video and apprenticed in levibotany and levihusbandry at the Leviponics Research Facility on Goddard. He initiated the famous Larson chicken breast tissue culture ("Chicken Little" to most astronauts) and many new strains of algae with various exotic flavors.

John Kennedy—Mechanical Engineer and Nurse. 183 cm (6'0"), 80 kg (176 lb.), 32 years. Bears a striking resemblance to his distant relative. Tried the premed curriculum at USC but gave it up in the sophomore year and went on to get a Ph.D. in mechanical engineering. Didn't feel satisfied working solely on machines and went back to get his R.N. His strange mix of talents just fit a slot on the Barnard's Star crew.

Caroline Tanaka—Fiber-optics Engineer and Astronomer. 165 cm (5'5"), 60 kg (132 lb.), 33 years. Long dark hair, brown eyes, and light-brown skin from a mixed Hawaiian heritage. Intense, hard-working engineer who pays no attention to her looks.

Linda Regan—Solar Astrophysicist. 155 cm (5'1"), 55 kg

(121 lb.), 31 years. Short, stocky, bouncy "cheerleader" type, with sparkly green eyes, curly brown hair, and lots of energy. Was two years behind Karin Krupp at USC. Went on to get a Ph.D. in astromony at CalTech and earned her way to a position at the Solar observatory on Mercury.

Beauregard Darlington Winthrop III—Eldest scion of Governor Beauregard Darlington Winthrop, Jr., of South Carolina. Sent to the Air Force Academy in 2000, he graduated near the top of his class. Was a student of (then) Captain George G. Gudunov at Fort Lauderdale Flight School. Used his father's influence to get assigned to a post in the Pentagon bureaucracy and rose rapidly to Air Force chief of staff. After his four-year tour, he resigned and easily won a seat as senator from South Carolina.

ALIENS

The aliens, called "flouwen" by the humans, are formless, eyeless flowing blobs of jelly weighing many tons that swim in the ocean on the Eau lobe of Rocheworld. Like whales or dolphins, the flouwen use sound to "see" and they group into social "pods." Their IQ is many times that of humans but their only developed science is mathematics.

Clear ◇ White ◇ Whistle (White Whistler)—A white, mature elder who is one of the three dominant adults in the pod. Clear ◇ White ◇ Whistle is a scientist who is trying to "invent" physics and astronomy. It has developed an artificial "eye," discovered the stars, and is starting to develop a theory of gravity. It understands the technologically oriented humans better than any of the other members of the pod.

Roaring☆Hot☆Vermillion (Loud Red)—A middle-aged, mature elder with an iridescent red color that looks like flame. It has a very deep roaring voice, boisterous nature, and is eager to ☆Get on with it!☆ Is nominal leader of the pod, although Warm•Amber•Resonance and Clear◊White◊Whistle are coequal and Strong☐Lavender☐Crackle is the elder of the pod.

Strong☐Lavender☐Crackle (Deep Purple)—A large, massive purple elder, with thousands of seasons of experience. Has participated in the formation of many younglings including Bitter○Green○Fizz and Roaring☆Hot☆Vermillion. Spends much of its time as a deep purple boulder—thinking. Sometimes, however, it dissolves and joins in group play as enthusiastically as if it were a youngling.

Bitter○Green○Fizz (Green Buzzer)—A bright-green young virgin who has never participated in making a youngling. From an emotional and experience viewpoint is equivalent to a bright, nubile, unisex college junior.

Warm•Amber•Resonance (Yellow Hummer)—A mature, clear, yellow-brown elder. Stable in personality and given to poetry, song, and theater rather than hard logic, although it is a better abstract mathematician than any human. Warm•Amber•Resonance acts as the primary parent for Dainty△Blue△Warble.

Dainty△Blue△Warble (Little Blue)—The youngling of the pod, a light, clear blue in color. Dainty△Blue△Warble is a very precocious and reasonably massive youngling since it had four progenitors.

Sour#Sapphire#Coo—A very old, very massive, deep-blue elder who has spent the last hundred seasons rocked up as a thinking boulder trying to derive an example of the fifth cardinal infinity. There are many other colored boulders around, each one some older, thinking through a complex mathematical problem. They are probably still thinking, but could be dead for all anyone could tell.

Brittle†Orange†Chirr (O.J.)—A greenish-orange member of a neighboring pod that gets into trouble during a storm and is rescued by Roaring☆Hot☆Vermillion.

ACKNOWLEDGMENTS

Thanks to:

Édouard Albert Roche (1820–1883)
—who showed that the world isn't always round,

Charles Sheffield
—who also thought this system was fun,

Paul L. Blass, Carl Richard Feynman, David K. Lynch, Patrick L. McGuire, Hans P. Moravec, A. Jay Palmer, Zane D. Parzen, Jef Poskanzer, Daniel G. Shapiro, and Mark Zimmermann, who helped me in several technical areas. My love and special thanks to Martha for her encouragement and literary assistance.

The "Christmas Bush" motile was jointly conceived by Hans P. Moravec and Robert L. Forward and drawn by Jef Poskanzer using a CAD system.

All final art was expertly prepared by Sam Takata and the rest of the group at Multi-Graphics.

Raised and educated by conservative people with unusual passion for intellectual freedom, Robert L. Forward took his master's degree from UCLA and his doctorate from the University of Maryland. For the last twenty-five years he has been aided and stimulated by Hughes Research Labs, where he has worked on his own and many other projects. He has written many published and respected papers, given many speeches, patented many inventions, and encouraged many others to do the same. He lives in Oxnard, California, with a noisy wife, a noisy daughter, the last of four noisy children at home, and several noisy animals. The computer which is his constant companion is mercifully quiet.

—M.D.F

Caveat:
For those readers who care, Robert L. Forward, who writes hard science fiction novels, is not to be confused with his son, Robert D. Forward, who writes hard-hitting adventure novels.